THREADS OF SILK

THREADS OF SILK

AMANDA ROBERTS

RED EMPRESS
PUBLISHING

Red Empress Publishing
www.RedEmpressPublishing.com

Cover by Cherith Vaughan
www.CoversbyCherith.com

ALSO BY THE AUTHOR

For my daughter, Yaqian.

ONE
RURAL HUNAN, 1846

$\mathcal{I}$ giggled as the silkworm crawled across my feet. The fat little grub inched its way from my heel, along the tips of my toes, and down my ankle. I squealed with laughter as one of my cousins held me down to keep me from removing the worm. I could have kicked it off, but I didn't want to hurt it, and I enjoyed the sensation. Each little step of the silkworm sent tiny shivers up my legs to the small of my back. And it took hundreds of steps. It was delightful, but I knew it made my cousin happy to think he was torturing me, so I pretended to fight back.

One of my other cousins ran up and bashed his brother in the back of the head with a tree branch. My tormentor lost interest in me and let me go. The boys chased after each other. I could have followed, but I liked being alone with my silkworms. I picked up the little fellow who had been crawling across my toes and placed it on the largest mulberry leaf I could find and then went back to work collecting silkworm cocoons.

My family had a small piece of land near the Xiangjiang River in Hunan. Since my father was an only son and I was his only child, the capital granted us just one plot of land for cultivating silkworms and one for growing food. It was not enough to support a family of three, but we lived next to many members of my mother's family, who had many sons and, thus, more land. We all lived and farmed and shared together. I had three uncles and seven male cousins. I also had two female cousins, but they were grown and married. They had gone to live with their husbands' families, so I was the only girl at home from my generation. This was a good thing, though; too many girls would burden the family.

My parents were distressed that I was a girl. One daughter among a brood of boys would have been fine, but for an only child to be a girl was a source of despair. I know my parents tried to have more children. I often heard Father panting late at night as he tried to plant a seed in Mother, but sons never grew. My parents often fought – Father threatening to throw Mother out and get a new wife, Mother waving a knife in his face and threatening to cut off his planter. There was talk of adopting one of my cousins, buying a concubine, or arranging a marriage match for me just to secure a son-in-law. None of these things ever happened, and I learned to ignore my parents' threats. I spent little time at home and found solace tending to the silkworms.

In the summer, I took my basket out to the mulberry fields and collected cocoons. I had to pluck the soft, white cocoons very carefully off the leaves so I wouldn't damage the silk or hurt the little worm inside. Even on our single plot, I collected hundreds a day. I also tended the mulberry bushes and the live worms and moths. If a mulberry bush was sick or dying, I moved all the worms, one by one, to another plant and dug up the bad plant. If a plant had too many grubs and was growing bare, I relocated its residents so it could grow strong again. The worms ate so much. A bush could be lush and vibrant one day and completely bare the next.

In the middle of the day, when I was hot and hungry, I walked down to the muddy banks of the river and ate some baozi I kept from breakfast. I then stripped naked and swam in the shallow waters near the shore. Children from neighboring fields and those of fishermen and crab diggers joined me. We splashed and played until the hottest part of the day passed and then we returned to our chores. I stayed in the field until my basket was full and then walked home as slowly as possible.

Most days, I arrived home at the same time as Father, and he'd load my basket in the back of his small cart, along with the baskets my cousins had filled – if they managed to fill any at all – to prepare for the next day's journey to the nearest city of Changsha for selling and trading. My family was too poor to afford the equipment needed to extract the silk from the cocoons, so every day my father took the cocoons we harvested into town and sold them for cash or bartered them for rice or cheap cotton thread for sewing and embroidery work. I begged my father to take me to the city with him. From the shores of the Xiangjiang River where I swam, I could see the bridge that led into town and many buildings, some much taller than our little village houses. Dust rose from the passing of many people and carts on the city streets. But I had never been there myself. In fact, I had never been beyond my family's land.

"Your place is with your mother," Father would always say. I don't think he knew just how little time I spent with Mother. The house was stuffy and dark, and I had no desire to learn to clean or cook or sew. I loved being outside with my little silkworms. And since I was only a worthless daughter, I think Mother preferred seeing me as little as possible as well. She never asked me to stay inside with her to learn women's work. My family lived separate lives – Father in town, Mother in the house, and me in the field. And that suited me just fine.

TWO

RURAL HUNAN, 1847

I ran between the rows of mulberry bushes with tears streaming down my face. I knocked the silkworm cocoons I had so carefully tended that day before to the ground and felt them crush beneath my feet, but I didn't stop. Mother chased closely behind me, her large, unbound feet thumping against the packed earth. I crashed through a small opening in the line of bushes to the next row, sending scores of frightened moths fluttering in the air as they attempted to fly on useless wings.

"Yaqian!" Mother screamed my name, followed by curses I dare not repeat.

But I did not stop. Not for her, not for my precious silkworms. I had to protect my feet from what was coming. If my feet were bound and broken, never again would I be able to walk the field to tend to my gentle worms or return to the Xiangjiang River to swim in its cool waters with my friends. And I would never be able to convince Father to take me to the city to see what happened to the cocoons after they left my loving care.

I could not allow my feet, my only means of freedom, to

be bound like my grandmother's and aunties'. True, I did not want large, flat, ugly feet like Mother's. She was tall, broad, and built for hard labor. I was small, gentle, and dainty. Quick like a cat and quiet like a mouse. I had no doubt that my feet would remain small on their own forever.

There had been some debate about whether to bind my feet. As my parents' only child, the better my marriage, the better for them. But if I could not tend the silkworms, the responsibility would fall to my cousins, who were not known for being responsible and had their own chores to do. My family would surely lose much-needed income if I could not work. But if I made a good marriage later, the sacrifice could be worth it.

My parents decided to seek counsel from a fortune teller.

She arrived early one morning, before I had made my daily escape to the fields, tottering in on her tiny, bound feet with only a cane to hold her upright. Mother graciously accepted her into our home, offering her tea, nuts, and blackberries, all of which she declined as she pulled out her charts to look at my numbers. After a few minutes, she spoke.

"Three...six...nine..." she mumbled to herself. "Three...six...nine...How marvelous!"

"What do you mean, Laoma?" Mother asked.

"Are you sure these numbers are true? Born in the third month on the sixth day and the ninth hour?" the fortune teller asked. Mother nodded. "These numbers are all quite good. Not quite in line for a tiger, the year your daughter was born, but a goat, like your family name. I think the girl embodies the essence of the *yang*. Another good sign!"

"What does all this mean?" Mother prodded.

"She is lucky," the fortune teller said proudly. "Three, six, nine, all good numbers. The goat, the eighth animal, the eight is prosperity! And the goat is elegant, refined."

"Goats are ugly!" Mother declared, eyeing me.

I wrinkled my nose at her and laid my head on the table, sighing with boredom.

"Gray coat, big horns, offensive tongue. How can a goat be a good thing?" Mother asked.

"Have you ever seen a goat in the wild?" the fortune teller asked. "Have you not been to the great western mountains? The goats can climb a sheer rock face on stones too small for you to see. They step delicately and gracefully. They possess great skill at what they do. Many people who identify with the goat are very creative and clever. Believe me, the goat is a truly auspicious sign for a girl with such lucky birth numbers."

"But what am I to do with her?" Mother asked. "What good is a goat to me?"

"First, we will have to bind her feet."

I sat straight up at those words. "No!" I yelled. "You cannot touch my feet!"

"Silence, Yaqian!" Mother snapped. "Do not embarrass me so. You will do as you are told."

"It is a part of life, Yaqian," the fortune teller said, softly. "With lovely bound feet, good numbers, and elegant mannerism, you can make quite a good marriage."

"How will she become elegant?" Mother asked. "She is too spirited and not very beautiful."

The fortune teller shrugged. "When you bind her feet, everything about her will change."

My heart sank. I didn't want to change. I wanted to have more freedom as I got older, not less. I wanted to walk along the river and travel with my father to the city marketplaces.

But if my feet were bound, I would never leave my house again.

"I won't do it!" I shrieked and ran for the front door.

Mother jumped from her chair and ran after me, but she was too slow. I threw open the door and ran to the field as fast as my unbound feet could carry me.

That was why I was running from my mother. I didn't know what the future held for me. I was a child – I couldn't think that far ahead. I only knew that if my feet were bound, I would be confined to the house at my mother's side. I would be doomed to darkness, cleaning, cooking, stitching hideous embroidery day in and day out. I couldn't bear the thought.

As I ran, Mother fell farther behind. I thought I might escape, but where would I go? I had no money, not even shoes on my feet. But I was getting away. For now, that was all that mattered.

But I was betrayed. Like a pair of wild monkeys, two of my cousins fell upon me from behind a tree. They knocked me down and I lost my senses long enough for one to grab my ankles and the other my wrists so they could drag me back home. I screamed and kicked as much as I could, but they were too strong, and I quickly tired. They thought my impending mutilation and torture was hilarious fun as they triumphantly presented me to Mother. I was so exhausted, I barely even had the energy to cry when Mother beat me for good measure.

*T*he night after the fortune teller delivered her advice, Mother came to the upstairs room along with one of my aunts to begin the foot-binding process. Mother had seen it done, but had never done it herself. My aunt knew how the feet should feel as she had bound her own daughter's feet several years before.

Mother held my head and arms in her lap while my aunt began wrapping the bindings around my feet. At first, they were just tight and uncomfortable, but not painful. I thought maybe I had been wrong and the binding would not be so bad after all. But then they made me stand.

The moment I put my weight on my newly bound feet, blinding pain surged through my entire body. I screamed and tried to collapse to the floor, but Mother caught me and held me up by my arms, forcing me to stand. She stood in front of me, holding my arms and took a step backward, forcing me to take a step forward. It was as if I had been stabbed in the sole of my foot as pain shot clear through my head. I wanted to faint, but Mother would not let me.

"Do not fall, Yaqian!" she yelled. "You must walk. The more you walk, the faster your feet will find their new shape and this will all be over."

My aunt kindly rubbed my back to help calm me. She knew Mother was lying. The pain would never be over.

Every day, Mother forced me to walk on my bound feet in order to break the small bones. The only thing I looked forward to was evening time when Mother would unwrap my feet, wash them, clip my nails, and then rewrap them even tighter. For those few moments when my feet were free, sheer relief washed over me.

It took two weeks before the first bone broke. On hearing the crack, bright white light flashed across my eyes. I collapsed to the floor and vomited. Mother rushed to my side. I thought she would grab me and force me to stand, but instead she rubbed my back and whispered, "Good girl." Mother's sudden tenderness surprised me. In my six years of life, I did not remember her speaking gently, holding me close, or saying words of love. But perhaps seeing her child in such pain moved even her stone heart. Whatever the reason, it gave me the strength to keep going. My mere existence was such a disappointment to her. Surely I could endure this.

I panted with sickness and pain, but I knew there was no going back. I reached for her hand and slowly stood back up. I took another step and heard another crack. This time, I grabbed Mother's arm for support, but I did not fall. I took another step and then another. I lost track of how many bones I broke that day and in the days that followed.

*A*fter a couple of months, my feet had taken on an entirely new shape. I had not worn any shoes since the binding began and none of my old ones would fit now anyway. My aunt brought me a pair of her old slippers as a gift. They were blue with a black trim made of coarse cotton thread. But on the front they had the most beautiful embellishment I had ever seen. Mother told me they were peacock feathers. I had no idea what peacocks were, but from that day on, I loved them. The shape of the eye and the blue, green, and red colors in the feathers were the loveliest design I had ever seen. I didn't believe something so lovely could exist in nature.

Mother was terrible at embroidery. We did not have many embroidered things – we had no use for such frivolous decorations – but she had some small pieces of decorative cloths, shirts, and shoes she had made as a girl for her dowry, and I would be expected to spend my days creating embroidered items for my own dowry. I always thought Mother's embroidered items were the ugliest things I had ever seen. The thread was coarse and thick, the stitching was too far apart and uneven, the colors didn't complement each other, and the animals she attempted were unidentifiable. I always thought that if that was what embroidery was supposed to look like, I would rather not bother.

But the shoes my aunt gave me were the first piece of embroidery I had seen that had some semblance of beauty. True, they were crude and simple, but I could see how beautiful they could be.

I admired the shoes, turning them over and over in my hands. The black trim was quite boring, so I examined how I could remove the threads and re-stitch the design with angles and spacing, making it much more delicate and decorative. I ran my fingers over the peacock feathers and decided that if the thread had been thinner and stitched more closely together, they would appear more real from a distance. I took a needle from Mother's mending basket and retreated to my room to get to work.

I had planned to remove just a few threads and make some minor changes, but before I realized it, I had removed every thread. I used my fingernails to make the strings thinner and longer. Then I began to re-embroider them in the way I envisioned them in my mind. After a few hours, I finished the outline and my vision was coming to life. It took me two days to finish them, and they were the most beautiful things I had ever seen. I even had one long, red string left over, which I wrapped in a cloth and laid next to my bed to use on a future project.

The next day, my aunt came back and brought the fortune teller with her to examine my progress. When the fortune teller held out her hand to see my feet, I proudly sat in a chair in front of her, pulled up the leg of my pants, and placed my foot in her hand with the shoe still on. My aunt, the fortune teller, and Mother all looked at the shoe in surprise.

"Where did you get those shoes?" Mother asked.

"Those aren't the shoes I gave her," my aunt replied.

"These are lovely," the fortune teller said with a smile.

"I made them," I said with a wide smile.

Mother slapped my face. "Don't lie!" she snapped.

"I'm not lying," I said, rubbing my cheek. "I took the shoes Auntie gave me and redid the stitching to make them more beautiful."

The fortune teller held my foot with the shoe in her hand and turned it back and forth.

"This is truly beautiful," she said. "I have seen hundreds of embroidered slippers in my life, but this shoe is most unique. Imagine what she could do with good quality thread instead of this cheap stuff."

"What do you mean?" Mother asked.

"Let me take the shoes," she said. "I believe I can sell them in the city tomorrow."

"No!" I said. "These are my shoes. I love them. I made them myself."

"Give her the shoes, Yaqian!" Mother ordered. "If she can sell them, you can make another pair for yourself."

Hot tears filled my eyes. I didn't want another pair, but I had no choice. I took the shoes off and threw them across the room. Mother raised her hand to strike me again, but then thought better of it in the presence of the fortune teller. She stomped over to retrieve the shoes, dusted them off, and handed them gingerly to the fortune teller, who placed them in her bag.

"Now, then," the fortune teller said. "Let's have a look at your feet."

She said that my aunt had done a very good job of binding my feet and they would heal nicely. They were not the smallest feet she had ever seen, but they were satisfactory. I didn't speak to her for the rest of the evening and wanted to stomp away to my room after she left, but tiny bound feet don't stomp very well.

Two days later, she returned and handed Mother three silver coins. It was more money than my father usually got for selling two baskets of silkworm cocoons.

"All this for one pair of shoes?" Mother asked, shocked.

The fortune teller nodded and pulled out a piece of paper. "And orders for five more pairs."

Mother sank into a chair, unable to believe her good fortune. She looked across the room at my father who was sitting by the fireplace. "We're going to need lots of thread," she said.

He nodded.

*O*ver the next few months, I made dozens of pairs of shoes. To me, each one was more beautiful than the last. I experimented with different kinds of patterns and colors and techniques. The better the shoes got, the more money the fortune teller brought back, and the more orders as well. I started using better materials. My father purchased real silk thread, which made a big difference. The thread simply glided through the cheap silk that covered the shoes and within minutes an image would start to appear.

I loved making the shoes beautiful. With each finished pair I held in my hands, my heart soared. My fingers often cramped from working with such precision and my neck and shoulders ached from hunching over the shoes for hours at a time, but each shoe was worth it. To me, they were not simply shoes, but art.

The only thing I hated was that I never got to keep any of them. My feet had been bound for nearly a year, and though I had made countless pairs of shoes, I did not have a single pair of my own. Every few days, when the fortune teller or my father took my new basket of shoes away, I would fight back tears and sulk in my bed for a day or two until I felt like starting the process over again. So much work and beauty went into each and every one and I would never see them again.

I was grateful for my work, and my parents were grateful for the money I brought in, though as a six-year-old with newly bound feet, my only job should have been making my feet smaller. Binding a girl's feet was an investment. Her only goal was to have the tiniest feet possible to make a good marriage. It would benefit the family when they gained a wealthy son-in-law. For a girl to earn money on her own was an anomaly. Mother should have been wrapping my feet tighter and tighter every night and ensuring I walked every day. Mother or my aunt would still wrap my feet every night, the feet had to always be cleaned, oiled, and the nails clipped to prevent infection, but I was not made to walk on them to continue the breaking process. I was still in constant pain during that time, but at least the pain did not get worse. I focused on my embroidery to help me forget the pain.

*D*uring one of her visits, the fortune teller said she had good news for me.

"I will be bringing a very special guest to meet you next week, Yaqian," she said.

"Who is it?" I asked.

"Someone who will change your destiny," she explained with a twinkle in her eye.

"What is destiny?" I asked.

"Yaqian!" Mother squawked. "Stop asking stupid questions and get back to work."

I wandered over to the fireplace and picked up my embroidery work without getting an answer to my question, but I continued listening as they spoke.

"I told you she would be creative," the fortune teller said. "Her thread is long, straight, and strong. Her future is bright."

"You were right, Laoma," Mother said. "Her creativity has greatly benefitted us. For the first time, my husband and I will be able to give *hongbao* to our nephews for Spring Festival."

The fortune teller scoffed at that. "Why waste good money on worthless pigs?" She shook a wooden cup and a flat stick with numbers painted on it fell out. She picked up the stick and studied it closely. She glanced at me and then turned back to Mother. "This daughter will bring you great prosperity, far more than had she been a boy. I think there will still be boys in your future, and it is Yaqian will bring them into your life."

"She will marry well?" Mother inferred. "She will bring us a rich son-in-law and have many sons?"

"I cannot see clearly how this will come to pass, but

Yaqian will bring this family many blessings...with my help."

"The guest you are bringing?"

The fortune teller nodded.

*T*he fortune teller returned a few days later with her esteemed guest, Lady Tang. Lady Tang was the most beautiful woman I had ever seen. Tall with a long white neck, she wore a flowing, green silk robe embroidered with yellow flowers. Her hair was carefully arranged on top of her head and decorated with little jewels and her lips were painted dark red. I imagined that if fairies existed, they must look like her. When she walked into our sitting room with its dirt floors, I felt very small and filthy even though I always kept my hands clean for working on the shoes.

"Is this the little girl?" she asked, glancing at me. She smiled with a genuine warmth that I had never seen before, not even in my own mother.

"Yes," said the fortune teller. "Her name is Yaqian."

Lady Tang sat in a chair by the table and motioned for me to sit in the chair across from her. "Tell me, Yaqian," she began. "How did you learn to make such beautiful shoes?"

"I don't know," I said. "I see pictures in my mind and then I make the picture on the shoes."

"You have a natural talent," she said.

Mother used two hands to present Lady Tang with a cup

of hot tea. She accepted the cup and sipped it delicately before placing it on the table. She moved slowly and effortlessly, as if she had rehearsed every flick of her wrist and blink of her eyes a million times.

"Let me see your hands," she asked. I held them out. Her hands were warm from holding the teacup and very soft. She looked at my palms and examined each of my fingers, taking special notice of the calluses that had developed on the tips.

"Your hands are well-formed for this kind of work," she said to me. "Your fingers are thin and nimble and have developed calluses in just the right spots."

I blushed as she spoke. Her words were so kind, and they were directed at me. She spoke to me like I mattered. She made me feel important.

"I told you she was lucky," the fortune teller said to my mother.

"Indeed, some of it is luck," Lady Tang said as she let go of my hands and picked up her teacup. "But it takes far more than luck to become a master artisan, something that she could become in my care."

Confusion swept across my face. I looked at Mother, but her hard expression did not change.

"Yaqian," Lady Tang said, looking at my feet. "How old are you?"

"Six," I replied.

"Your feet are only in their first year of being bound, yes?"

I nodded.

She stood up and turned to my mother and the fortune teller. "The girl would do well at my school," she declared. "She has an amazing natural talent and fingers made for embroidery work, but she lacks training and the proper technique. If she becomes my apprentice, there is no limit to what could become of her."

If I didn't know Mother better, I would have thought I saw her eyes swell with pride in that moment.

"But...we..." Mother stammered. "We have no money to send with her. We have saved a little money since Yaqian started making shoes, but not enough to live with such an esteemed person like you."

"I cannot take her now," Lady Tang said. "She is too young and her feet are not finished. I cannot be bothered with the daily care she still requires. When she has reached seven years, I will take her. That will give you a year to raise money."

"Still, Lady Tang," Mother continued. "I do not think we could ever afford to send her away. If we saved money, you could take her for a few months, maybe a year, but what then? Without Yaqian to help us earn money, we would have no money to pay for her care with you."

Lady Tang shook her head. "No, my dear Yang Furen," she explained. "I have many clients in need of embroidery. The fortune teller and I have already found better quality buyers for your daughter's shoes. You only need to come up with the money for the first year of your daughter's training. After that, the embroidery she makes with me we will sell to cover her costs."

Mother fell to her knees. "Lady Tang, you honor us. To take this ugly, worthless daughter from our home and teach her to be useful is more kindness than my lowly family deserves."

Lady Tang bowed to my mother. "It is nothing, Yang Furen," she said. She stood tall once more and smiled to me. "I will see you soon, Yaqian." She walked out of the house where a red sedan chair was waiting for her.

"What is happening?" I asked Mother. "Am I going away?"

Mother collapsed into the chair Lady Tang had been sitting in and took several deep breaths. "Eventually," she finally said.

I tottered to the front door as two men carried Lady Tang away and I smiled wider than I had ever smiled before. Perhaps my tiny feet would carry me from this place after all.

THREE

RURAL HUNAN, 1849

I lost track of how many shoes I made over that next year; my numbers did not go that high. I did not walk as much as I should have to train my feet and keep making them smaller – my focus was on making shoes. From morning until it was too dark to see, I would embroider the tiny slippers. All through the winter, I sat huddled by the fireplace as close as possible to keep my hands from cramping in the cold so I could keep working.

When spring came back, it was still cold, but the sun was shining more often. As much as possible, I would pull back the tattered window covering so I could work in the sunshine. The colors of the threads were so much more vivid in the natural light. I tried to make each pair different from the last and to use different stitches and patterns. I was trying to train myself to be as good of an embroiderer as possible before going to stay with Lady Tang. I had no idea how much I still had to learn.

It was the first spring in my life that I did not go out into the field to tend to my silkworms, but I had something else to look forward to.

When my birthday arrived, Lady Tang did not send for me. Every day that passed was torture to me. It was over a month later before the sedan chair came back.

I took my few pieces of clothes in a small bag, some of my favorite needles, a brush for my teeth and one for my hair, a set of chopsticks, a teacup, a bowl, and the piece of red thread from my first pair of shoes. Mother, Father, Auntie, and the fortune teller were all there to bid me good-bye.

"Do not disappoint me, Yaqian," Mother said with the same stern face she always had. "Always do exactly as Lady Tang tells you."

I nodded and headed out to the sedan chair where one of the men helped me climb up. I opened the curtain and waved to everyone. The man closed the curtain and tied it shut. Then the whole thing rocked and I fell back into the seat as it began to move forward. I yelped in surprise and glee and then laughed at the sensation of being carried. I rocked back and forth in the chair. I sat up and pulled at the curtain to see out, but it was tied so tightly I could barely see the people on the street looking at me as I passed. I could not believe that I was forbidden from getting a better look at the world on my very first trip from home. I yanked on the curtain as hard as I could to try to get it to open, but it would not budge. I took a needle out of my bag and began to rip out the stitching on the ties holding the curtain shut. The thread began to come loose in one long piece. As I ran it through my fingers I realized I that it was the finest piece of silk I had ever seen. It was softer and smoother than any thread I had used before, but was strong enough to hold the heavy window ties shut. I coiled the thread around one of my fingers and placed it into my pocket with the other one.

I finally managed to completely remove one of the ties

and the curtain flew open just as we were crossing the Xiangjiang River! The bridge extended over the middle of Orange Island. The trees were bright green and little white flowers were beginning to bloom on them. The island was long and narrow and on either side the river flowed quickly. There were people on the river in small canoes and large steamers. People fishing and catching frogs and crabs were all along the sandy bank.

There were very few other sedan chairs on the road, but there were many people being pulled in rickshaws. I smiled and waved at people as we passed and most just looked back in confusion. Sedan chairs are usually reserved for weddings and the wealthy, and the women inside would never be seen by those outside. What must people have thought seeing this round-faced urchin looking at them from such a beautiful chair?

The main road heading through the city was crowded and noisy. There were so many shops and carts. There were people carrying all manner of birds and fish to market on long poles. A man clapping a piece of wood drew attention to the rat traps he was selling. An elderly couple wailed over the body of their son and begged for donations to bury him. I held my nose as we passed closely to a stall selling stinky tofu.

The sedan chair finally pulled in front of a large moon gate set in a long stone wall. Two men rushed from small guard stands to open the wooden doors. We entered the most beautiful courtyard. The grass and white stone walkways were laid out with precision and the flowers were planted in just the right places. It was clear that an artist had designed this place.

As we approached the main building, I fumbled with the curtain ties to try and make them look closed again. The sedan chair rocked forward unexpectedly as the men set it down. I still had not recovered my balance as the door was opened and I fell out onto the ground! I heard a tittering laughter. I looked up to see Lady Tang and several girls who had come out to greet me. I quickly stood to dust myself off and made a very low bow to try and hide my beet red face. But Lady Tang made no mention of my embarrassment and offered her hand as a greeting.

"Welcome, Yaqian," she said. "These girls are some of my other apprentices," she explained, motioning to the girls who each gave a small bow in turn. "They have been here for a few years and will help you get settled. Let me show you to your room."

The girls were each dressed far more finely than any young girl I had ever seen before. Their clothes were simple silk chaopaos, the high collared Manchu-style gowns that upper-class women wore, but very high quality. Each was a different color, from dark blue to pale red and heavily embroidered. I wore only a white cotton shirt and black cotton trousers. I did wear a pair of embroidered slippers I had finished the day before, but compared to the shoes they wore, I was beginning to doubt my talent. They also each had their hair properly done and delicately adorned while mine was simply tied back with a piece of fabric. I guessed the girls were about twelve to fourteen years old.

I followed closely behind Lady Tang as we walked through the building. "This is the main house," she said. "This is where the living and dining areas are and a few areas for small gatherings and places to read and study. The dining room is to the west and your rooms are to the east."

My family home had been quite small, a single open room with a small loft for storage and where I would sleep when the weather was mild. Lady Tang's home, no –

estate would be a better word, was sprawling, with dozens of buildings and courtyards connected by walkways and all surrounded by a tall wall. My feet began to ache at the mere thought of having to walk so far to get from my room to the dining and work areas every day. But Lady Tang and the girls all had bound feet, so I knew I would have to get used to it. I also noticed that they had a more elegant swaying gait than I did. I sort of hobbled in an attempt to put as little weight on each step as possible. I bit my lower lip to keep from crying out as I followed behind them and did my best to mimic their movements and keep up.

We walked down a long path and finally Lady Tang stopped. "This is your room," she said. I opened the door and was shocked at what I saw. There were four beds, one in each corner of the room. Each had silk blankets and embroidered pillows. Next to each bed was a small desk with embroidery tools, a candle, and a washbasin. There was a small chest at the foot of each bed. The room had a large latticed window facing the east that let in the morning sunlight. There was a stove in the middle of the room for warmth and boiling water. The room was beautiful, clean, and bright.

"You can enter the room, Yaqian," piped up one of the girls. "You won't get it dirty." All the girls giggled. Lady Tang simply held up one of her hands to quiet the girls and I took a step into the room.

"One of these beds is mine?" I finally asked.

"This one over here," one of the girls said pointing to a bed in the southwest. Even with my little knowledge, I knew that this was the least auspicious spot. But being the newest person, I didn't mind. I walked over to the bed and ran my fingers along the cover. A bed of my own. In my old home I slept on a bamboo pallet on the landing or on the floor by the fireplace when it was very cold.

"This is my bed," the girl said sitting on the bed in the northeast. "And those beds belong to Xiaxia and Mingzhu. But they are in the studio right now."

I nodded. "What's your name?" I asked.

"Su Wensong," she said with her head held high.

I smiled. I didn't have many friends back home. My female cousins were older than I was and my male cousins were spoiled and unpleasant. There were some local girls I liked to swim and play with, but I had not seen them since my feet were bound. It was exciting to be surrounded by so many young girls. I couldn't figure out if Wensong and the other girls liked me or not, but they seemed pleasant enough.

"Come, girls," Lady Tang said. "Time for lunch."

I left my small bag of meager possessions on my new bed and followed Lady Tang and the girls as they swayed to the dining hall. As excited as I was to be in this new place, all I wanted to do was sit down to rest my feet.

In the dining room were two long tables where five girls were already seated. Everyone was smiling and chatting happily. All the girls looked so lovely and proper. Each wore a brightly colored silk chaopao, some nicer than others, and all had their hair done up. A few girls had some nice jewelry pieces and some even wore paint on their lips and cheeks. Two kitchen maids came out and began to serve rice and soup to each girl. I looked down and realized I was dressed like a kitchen maid. My face got red-hot again. I was so out of place. I didn't really belong here with these nice girls. How did I get to be here?

Lady Tang directed me to sit next to her. The kitchen maids then began bringing out bowls of hot dishes. There were whole chickens cut up, bowls of potatoes, eggplant with green beans, tofu, dumplings, and egg and tomato soup. I had never seen so much food served for one meal. And it was all so good. I could have sat there and eaten all day. I tried to eat slowly, as if this meal was nothing special to me, but after a few minutes, I eagerly wolfed it down. I never realized just how hungry I was until I finally had enough food to eat.

After lunch was rest time, something else I was not familiar with. Many of the girls would return to their rooms to nap during this time, but some would visit with each other, read books, or continue working on their embroidery. With a heavy stomach and achy feet, I slowly returned to my room climbed into my own bed for the first time. The room was warm from the sunshine and the stove and Wensong, Mingzhu, and Xiaxia were already in their beds, so I quickly fell asleep.

*A*n hour or so later, everyone instinctively seemed to know it was time to get up and get back to work. I, however, continued to sleep soundly. It had been a long time since I had felt so warm and comfortable. I awoke sometime later to an empty room except for Lady Tang standing over me, frowning at me for the first time. I scrambled out of bed, bowed, and apologized profusely.

"Afternoon session begins promptly at the hour of the

goat!" she declared. I wasn't sure what to say. I had no idea how to know what time it was if I was sleeping, but I kept my head low and only repeated my apologies and promised it wouldn't happen again.

Lady Tang left the room and I followed her. We went out the back of the house.

"I heard that you tended your father's silkworms back home," she said.

"Yes, ma'am," I replied. "Until my feet were bound, I tended them every day."

"Good," she said. "Before you can properly embroider, you must get to know your tools. You must learn everything there is to know about silk. You must be able to determine where it comes from, its quality, and how it is made. You already know about growing silkworms and collecting the cocoons, but do you know what happens next? How we extract the silk from the cocoons?"

I shook my head no.

She nodded. "Then that is where we will start."

Behind the main compound were many small, ramshackle buildings. We entered one and there were many young women dressed in coarse cotton clothes sorting through thousands of cocoons on tables with raised edges. They would empty a large sack of cocoons onto a table, move the good cocoons into a basket on their right and put the bad cocoons in a basket on their left. Lady Tang picked up a good cocoon and a bad cocoon at random from the baskets and handed them to me.

"What do you see?" she asked.

I turned them over in my hands, feeling the little cater-pillar roll about inside, and tried to figure out which one was defective. I finally noticed that one had a slight yellow tinge to it. But if I had not been looking for such a slight impurity, I would never have noticed it. I took a few more bad cocoons out of a basket and looked them over. Some had dark spots, some had tears, some I simply could not see what was wrong with them. I was amazed at how quickly the women were able to sort the cocoons. It would have taken me much longer to examine each one.

"It takes practice and a keen eye to do what these women do," Lady Tang explained. "They have trained their eyes to know what to look for and their hands have learned to follow suit. You will soon learn the same thing, but in a different capacity. Your eye will learn what it takes to make a fine piece of embroidery and your hands will learn to bring them to life.

"A piece of embroidery is not just putting needle to cloth and making an image appear. Every part of the process is an art in and of itself."

As she spoke, I didn't realize that I had stopped breathing. Lady Tang's voice had a way of making the world slow down because you didn't want to miss a word. Even the women working within earshot of us noticeably slowed and quieted as they listened to her. Once she stopped, they picked up speed again.

"What happens to the bad cocoons?" I asked.

"I sell them to another silk house that has much lower standards than I do," she said. Her swan-like neck seemed to stretch a little longer when she said that. She then motioned for me to follow her to the next building.

When we entered, my eyes widened in horror. "What are they doing to the caterpillars?" I shrieked. I felt sick to my stomach as a basket of good cocoons was dumped into a vat of boiling water.

"We have to boil the cocoons to loosen and extract the

silk," Lady Tang said calmly as she nudged me deeper into the room of slaughter.

"But...the caterpillars! They are still alive inside!" I yelled.

"Yaqian, calm yourself," Lady Tang said. "If we waited until the moth chewed its way out of the cocoon, the silk would be ruined. Besides, so many silk moths would be far more than necessary. And boiled silkworms are very delicious. These marvelous creatures serve many purposes."

I put my hand to my mouth; I could almost feel my face turn green. "You...you eat silkworms?" I finally managed to choke out.

"Oh, yes," she replied. "We have so many we serve them nearly every night. I am surprised your family didn't eat them. Many poor people supplement their food supplies with them."

I felt weak. I bent over and put my hands on my knees. My poor little silkworms! I had no idea that by gathering the cocoons and giving them to my father every day I was sending them to their deaths. And my embroidery! Every thread of silk I used to make my beautiful shoes cause the deaths of countless silkworms. I had spent so many years with my silkworms as treasured friends. I tenderly cared for and reared each one, imagining that each one lived a beautiful life that led to beautiful embroidery work. To think they all ended up boiled, their safe, silken homes ripped from them, and they ended up in someone's dinner bowl was more horrible than I could bear.

I was suddenly so angry. I couldn't believe how heartless and cruel Lady Tang was. Why had no one ever told me this? I reached down, took off my embroidered slippers, and chucked them at Lady Tang. She easily batted them away, but her eyes and mouth were agape with surprise.

"You're a monster!" I yelled. I ran out of the boiling house as fast as my little broken feet could carry me. I ran through some of the other outbuildings, a dying house, a weaving house, trying to find my way back to the main house so I could leave. When I finally found it, I marched straight from the back of the house to the front and headed for the moon gate. It was locked.

"Let me out!" I demanded of the guards.

"We only open the gates on the order of Lady Tang," one of them said.

"I am not a prisoner," I said. "Let me out so I can go home right now." I did my best to stomp my foot in emphasis, but ended up wincing from the pain. The guards laughed at me.

"Yaqian," I heard Lady Tang call from behind me. I looked and saw her standing on the porch. I also saw the faces of the other embroidery girls peeking out the windows and doors at me. "Come back inside so we can finish your orientation."

I was surprised that Lady Tang was not seething in anger at me. She was just as calm as ever. I felt guilty for my outburst after the kindness she had extended to me, but I had already made a fool of myself. The only thing worse would be backing down and going back inside. I had to stand firm. I had said I wanted to go home so that is where I was determined to go. I turned my back on Lady Tang and the school and stared at the gate. They had to open it eventually.

The few hours I stood there in the sun felt like forever. The gate did not open and my feet and legs ached. The sun eventually went down, and it got chilly. I shivered as the guards were brought warm bowls of food. My stomach growled.

I finally sighed, dropped my head, and slunk back into the house. Candles and oil lamps were burning. Some girls were in the front room playing Go. Others were reading or working on their calligraphy. Some were playing music. They all immediately went silent as I entered. I tried to ignore their stares as I walked past them toward Lady Tang's rooms, but I could feel their eyes on me.

I knocked on her door so softly that I was shocked when she said, "Come in." I opened the door and stepped inside, keeping my head down.

Lady Tang was sitting at a desk, writing something with a horsehair brush. She did not acknowledge me, so I just stood there, saying nothing. She finally finished whatever she was writing, hung the brush on a small rack, and turned to me.

"One day, Yaqian," she began, "you will die."

I looked up at her sharply, wondering why she would speak to me of such evil.

"You will die and be buried under a mound of dirt. In that dirt, will live worms that will eat your decaying body. The rain will come. The ground will become so saturated that the worms will not be able to breathe underground. They will dig out for the chance to find the sun. But they will not find the sun. The birds will be waiting for them. The worms that ate your body will be eaten by the birds. But you know what will happen then? Up, up, up, the birds will spread their wings and fly to the heavens with you in their gullet. You, Yaqian, long after you are dead will soar through the sky like a bird."

She stood and walked over to me. She reached out and handed me the shoes I had thrown at her. "We are all connected, Yaqian. Your worms will live on in the beautiful works of art you make with their silk. They will fly like birds, swim like fish, and become beautiful women. Show them honor in death by becoming the best embroidery girl Hunan has ever known."

My chest swelled with emotion, as did my eyes. I was so embarrassed by my outburst and so thankful for Lady Tang's kind lesson. I took my shoes from her and kowtowed at her feet.

"I beg your forgiveness, Lady Tang," I said, doing my best not to cry. I was failing.

"Go to your room and rest," Lady Tang said, returning to her desk. "We will start fresh tomorrow."

"Yes, Lady Tang!" I said as I stood but stayed bent at the waist and backed out of her room. When I shut the door and turned around, all the other embroidery girls were there waiting for me. I wiped the tears from my cheeks, stood up straight, and cleared my throat.

"Excuse me," was all I said as I passed through the crowd and headed to my room.

I changed into a set of silk sleeping clothes that had been laid out on my bed for me. Sleeping clothes! I had never had separate clothes just for sleeping in my life. Lady Tang must have known that I would return and had them prepared for me in spite of the horrible way I had acted. I crawled into bed even though I was thirsty and starving. I did not deserve anything to eat or drink. I would sleep and start anew tomorrow.

*T*he next morning, Lady Tang and I started again. We never spoke about my first-day tantrum again and none of the other girls brought it up either. It felt strange living in a place where my past mistakes were not constantly held against me. It felt safe.

After a warm breakfast of hot corn juice and congee, of which I ate three bowls, we returned to the boiling room. Lady Tang showed me how the cocoons were boiled and stirred with a large wooden spoon to loosen the silk fibers. The silk was then slowly pulled in long strands from the water into a spinning wheel that spun the strands into thread. The threads were then taken to the dying room. The women who worked in that room looked barely human. Their skin and clothes were many different, unnatural colors from working so closely with the dye. Some of the women were blue from head to foot. Some of the women had green arms or purple hair. Some of them looked quite humorous, but the tired, worn looks on their faces told me it probably wasn't a particularly easy or enjoyable job.

I learned that in Xiang embroidery, embroidery from Hunan, silk threads of over 100 different colors are used! I couldn't even name that many colors. Indeed, many of the colors were extremely similar, only varying slightly in hue. Lady Tang was right; I would have to develop a keen eye for color to know when to use which threads. Not all of the colors were made in Lady Tang's workshop. She specialized in a few deep, rich – expensive – colors. Other colored threads she bought from other workshops.

After that was the weaving room, where the rolls of silk thread were fed into huge looms and woven into long bolts of silk cloth to be used for clothes, bedding, burial shrouds, banners, and many other things. The women moved so quickly, tossing the shuttle back and forth, whole sheets of cloth appeared in a matter of moments. The monotony was mind numbing, though. Left hand, close the loom, right hand, close the loom, repeating for hours on end. I felt drowsy after watching them for only a few minutes. I looked forward to working on my embroidery, when every day I would make a unique and beautiful piece of art.

After lunch and rest time, I finally got to go with the other embroidery girls to their workroom in the main house. Each girl had her own workstation with a small table where she kept piles of silk threads, needles of various sizes, small wooden frames, and drawings or paintings of flowers or animals she wanted to recreate in embroidery. Some of the girls had paints and paintbrushes so they could paint an image on the fabric before going over the image with thread.

Unlike the other rooms in the house that had small, latticed windows with wooden shutters that would shut out the cold and the light, the windows in the embroidery studio were very large, almost floor to ceiling, and glass-paned. For delicate embroidery work, the girls needed as much natural light as possible, but they also needed to keep their hands warm. Cold fingers cramp and shake, making it impossible to work. A large stove gave off plenty of warmth while the glass kept the heat in and let in the sunlight. The windows could also be opened in the summer to let the cool breezes through. Winters were especially nice for the embroidery girls, though, since there were so few hours of daylight. Some days, Lady Tang would dismiss the girls as early as the hour of the rooster, so they had the whole evening to read, play games, paint, or work on their music. Some of the girls would just get plenty of sleep since in the summer they might have to work ten-hour days. But my first day in the embroidery studio was a bright spring day, and I was eager to get started.

Lady Tang took me to an empty table in the back of the room and motioned for me to sit. She pulled a chair next to mine and handed me a bundle of ugly green thread, a small round frame with a thin piece of silk already in it, and a red pincushion with a few needles in it.

"We will start simply," she said. "Can you make a leaf for me? I want to observe your style."

I took a deep breath. I was a little apprehensive. I wanted to impress Lady Tang, but leaves were easy so I didn't need to be nervous. I had made many leaves before, and flowers, and even peacock feathers! I was sure I could impress her with a simple leaf. I picked a needle from the pincushion and reached for the thread.

"No," Lady Tang said.

I froze. What had I done wrong? Had I already messed up so badly? I looked at the needle in my hand. It looked fine to me – sharp on one end and an eye in the other. But I put it back in the cushion and reached for another one. I then reached for the thread again.

"No," she said again.

This time, I felt my face blush hotly. She did not sound angry or exasperated with me. Her "no" was calm and even, but I still felt myself growing nervous.

"I do not know what I am doing wrong, ma'am," I finally said.

Lady Tang took all of the needles out of the cushion and laid them in my hand. "Look closely. Each one is a little different. Some are longer, some are shorter, some are fatter, some are thinner. You have to learn which tool is best for each job, even if that job is as simple as embroidering a leaf." She handed me a longer, fatter needle.

I sat up straight, took a deep breath and reached for the thread again. I paused, waiting for the "no," but it didn't come. I started to use my fingernails to separate the thread into thinner strands.

"To make a leaf, you must start with the stem, which is very thick and dark. You can make fewer passes if your thread is thicker," she explained. "As the leaf fans out, you will want thinner strands."

By this point, my hands were shaking. "I thought you were only going to observe," I mumbled.

Lady Tang laughed. "I can observe and teach at the same time," she said. "Do not be so sensitive and take criticism so personally. If I did not think you had potential, you wouldn't be here. But you still have a very long way to go. Many of the things you taught yourself are wrong and you will have to unlearn them."

I had never even used a frame before, or such high-quality silk threads. I had only ever embroidered cheap shoes and even the silk threads my father had bought me felt coarse in comparison. My creations were nothing compared to the beautiful flowers of Lady Tang's flowing robe, undoubtedly embroidered by herself. I had no idea what I was doing.

I do not know how long I sat there ruminating, but Lady Tang never rushed me. I finally came out of my daze and looked at her.

"Whenever you are ready," she said.

"As long as you show me," I replied. "From the beginning."

Lady Tang nodded and showed me how to sit up straight so I wouldn't strain my shoulders and neck. She showed me how to hold the frame so my arm would not tire too quickly. She showed me the different needles and what each one was used for. She let me slide the thread through my fingers so I could feel how smooth and fine it was. I do not think I ever got around to making a leaf that day, but when her lesson was over, I took one of those ugly green threads and put it into my pocket alongside the red thread from my first pair of shoes and the thread I stole from the sedan chair. That evening, I tied them together in a bow and put them in the chest at the foot of my bed. I finally had a safe place of my own to store my memories.

FOUR

CHANGSHA, HUNAN, 1850

*M*y days at Lady Tang's were almost leisurely. I worked nearly every day, but the days were not too long; our embroidery work ended when the sun set so we would not strain our eyes. We were inside where the temperature was always comfortable. And we had plenty of food. My life was comfortable, and far more exciting than I could have imagined.

I didn't do nearly as much embroidery work that first year as I thought I would because there were just so many other things I had to learn first. I had to learn how to draw and paint because many embroidery images are first painted onto the cloth and then worked over with thread. I had to learn dozens of different stitches – satin stitches, fishbone stitches, shading stitches, shan tao stitches, ping tao stitches, souhe stitches, shunxian stitches, split stitches, back stitches, chain stitches, Peking knots, and so many more. I had to learn specific stitches for butterfly wings, fish scales, and crane feathers. I had to study colors and how the light can change the way an image looks. I had to learn to read and write! Embroidery work often includes characters, similar to how a painting may also contain calligraphy, so I had to know what the characters said. I studied Buddhism and Taoism and what their various symbols meant. Every color, every animal, and every plant has a meaning. Certain combinations of animals, plants, and symbols can have different meanings too. I even had to study the anatomy of humans and animals so that when I embroidered them, they would have lifelike movements. I thought my brain would explode from everything I was learning.

I couldn't believe how much was involved in being a good embroiderer. Embroidery work was something that almost all women did, but not all of it could be considered art or sell for much money. What we did at Lady Tang's school and studio was so far above anything I ever saw in the countryside. Embroidery was opening up a world for me I never thought possible. I wasn't sure what would happen to me, but I knew my life would be much better than if I had never gone to the school, or if I had insisted on leaving after that first day.

I dreaded the coming Spring Festival. After living for nearly a year in a warm home with clean clothes to wear and no chores, the idea of having to go back to the country-side filled me with dread. As Spring Festival drew closer and closer, though, my invitation home never came.

"Aren't you the least bit excited about seeing your family again?" I asked Wensong as she packed for her trip home.

"No," she said, shaking her head and slowly putting her clothes into a small trunk. "I doubt they care to see me either. One more mouth to feed. I can't help around the house because of my feet. They just think I'm spoiled now."

Even among us embroidery girls, Wensong *was* one of the spoiled ones. She came from a wealthy family that had lots of land and plenty of servants. She had big dreams and loved to tell wild, romantic stories. She was already promised to a local magistrate, but she never stopped thinking that a better offer might come along, one that included love.

"What will you do with your time?" I asked.

"Not much," she said. "They want me to do extra embroidery work to sell or give away as gifts, but I can't bring myself to do much. I would rather not even look at a piece of string for the whole month!"

"You are so lucky," I said, crawling up onto the bed. "Your family must value you very much."

"Oh, I don't know about that," she said.

"It's a good match," I said. "You aren't happy about it?"

"I've never met him!" she exclaimed. "And he's old! At least thirty! If it was up to me I'd run away and never come back!" she said with a laugh.

"No, you wouldn't," I teased. "You couldn't go a day without a roaring fire, your silk pillow, and your spent cocoons to wash your face."

"That's true," she said with a nod. "Oh well. Happiness isn't in the sticks for us. We just end up where we are told to go."

That was true enough. On this day, she was being told to go home; I was being told to stay where I was. It was such a strange feeling. I didn't want to go home, but as the New Year drew closer and most of the other girls left one by one, I was sad that my family didn't send for me. Didn't they miss me? Didn't they want to see what I was doing and how I had grown?

Eventually, only three of us remained at the school with Lady Tang. Sun-li was an orphan. After she had come to the school, her parents were killed in some rebellion down south. Lingling's family lived far away because her father was a court official. Even all of the women who worked in the silk houses out back were gone. Lady Tang paid a couple of maids and cooks double their wages to stay on so we wouldn't be completely on our own. I was angry and hurt that my family lived so close yet they did not invite me home. I wondered if I should just go, but Lady Tang advised against it.

"The best thing you can do is show them your worth, show them what you have become. Then they will send for you," she said.

So even though we were on holiday, I spent my days embroidering by the fire. I made several pairs of shoes, handkerchiefs, belts, fan cases, and baby clothes. Lady Tang bundled them up for me – along with a bit of money I had earned from selling a few pieces – and sent it all to my family. I never received a reply.

After that first year, I stopped embroidering special pieces for them. Every year, Lady Tang would select a few embroidery pieces I had completed and send them – and more money – to my family. After a couple of years without a single word from my family, even Lady Tang was worried that something had happened to them, so she sent a man to investigate. He returned and said that they were fine and had received her packages, but they didn't send any message to me. Lady Tang sighed and patted my shoulder. She and I spent every holiday together over the next few years. I suppose she had no family either, but she never told me what happened to them. I didn't like talking about my family either, so I just began to think of her as my family. I think she felt the same way about me, but she kept all of her thoughts and feelings rather close to herself. But I could tell from the way she treated me, that I was more than just a student to her.

Whenever she had good news to share, she always told me first. She and I shared all our meals together. She pushed me to be a better embroiderer. Anytime I started to feel sad or my mind would start to wander, I would focus on my embroidery or my studies.

I was soon the best embroidery girl at the school.

*a*fter I had been at the school for four years, Lady Tang called me to her office for a chat.

"Yaqian, you are immensely talented," she said. "I knew it from the first shoe I saw."

I blushed a little, but I knew it was true. There were no other students who came close to possessing my skill. My pieces were almost perfect copies of Lady Tang's. Only a master would be able to tell the difference.

"But you have stopped growing," she said. I could feel my face fall. "Your work is mere imitation. There is no originality, no soul, no...art in your pieces."

"I don't understand," I said. "My pieces look exactly like yours. If mine have no soul, then neither do yours."

"Mine have my soul," she said. "You can't copy that."

"But if they look the same," I said, "I don't see what difference it makes."

"That is why you are still the student and I am the teacher," she explained.

I snorted and crossed my arms. "So, teach me," I demanded. "Teach me how to fix it."

"Why did you start doing embroidery?" she asked.

"I thought all the embroidery I saw was ugly," I said. "My mother's embroidery, my auntie's. I thought I could do better."

"And now?" she asked. "Do you still think embroidery is ugly?"

I looked at the embroidered scene of a waterfall hanging behind Lady Tang's desk. The blue and white water cascaded down the side of a mountain and disappeared into a cloud of white mist. If you didn't know any better, you would swear the piece was a painting. You could even see the brushstrokes of the original artist.

"No," I said, "it is not ugly."

"Then why don't you enjoy your work?" she asked.

I wondered for a moment how she knew that I didn't enjoy embroidery work. I did enjoy my life. My bed was comfortable, the food was good, I was surrounded by smart and talented young ladies, my work days were easy, and I earned good money. I guess because I loved my life I didn't realize that I didn't enjoy my work. I might even go so far as to say that I hated it. It was so boring! Embroidery work, even on seemingly complicated pieces, was so easy I didn't even have to think about it anymore. I sat at my frame each morning, and by the time lunch rolled around, a tiger, a flower, or a butterfly appeared looking exactly the same as a hundred I had made before. I suddenly felt almost sick. My life felt like a waste. I couldn't imagine spending the next sixty years in such a horrid profession. But what was the alternative?

"I don't enjoy it," I finally admitted out loud. "I hate it."

"Do you remember the first pair of shoes you made?" she asked.

"Yes!" I answered quickly. "They were the most beautiful

shoes I ever saw when I was done with them. I think they might be the most beautiful shoes I ever made in my life even though I had no idea what I was doing. I still remember every stitch I made, every thread that passed through my fingers. They were peacock feathers, but I didn't even know what a peacock feather was back then. They faded from green to blue to black eyes. Around the top edge was a decorative trim as delicate as lace. After Mama and the fortune teller forced me to sell them, I made hundreds of pairs of shoes, but none were ever as magnificent as that first pair."

Lady Tang smiled and nodded. "Do you hear the passion in your own voice?" she asked. "That is what you have to do. You have to find the love, the beauty, the challenge in your work again."

"How?" I asked. "I'm already the best. How can I challenge myself and do better?"

"The fat pig gets slaughtered," she said.

"Bah!" I said. "Why shouldn't I give voice to the truth?"

"If you were the best," she said, "we wouldn't be having this conversation."

I sighed. "So, what do I do, teacher?"

"Forget it," she said. "Forget everything I have taught you, everything you have learned. Go to your embroidery table anew and find your own way. Do you think the fluffy hair stitch or the scale stitch have always existed? No! Some woman somewhere said, 'I want to make a lion, but none of the stitches I know can make a mane. I will make a new stitch and make a beautiful mane'. Find a new way to make your embroidery better. Make it more beautiful. Make it unique. Make it surprising. Give it your own soul."

I nodded and stood up to leave.

"Yaqian," she said, stopping me. "Water cannot stay stagnant. It must flow or it will dry up and all the fish die."

She didn't say it, but her meaning was clear: if my work didn't improve, my days at the school were numbered. This had not been merely an encouraging chat, but a warning.

I was given leave from my normal work for several days to focus on honing my skills and figuring out what I wanted to do. At first, I simply sat and stared at the white piece of silk in front of me. Is there anything worse than having a blank pallet and not knowing what to create upon it?

I looked around the room, but all I could see were the backs of the pieces being worked on by the other girls. Lady Tang and Wensong were standing on one side of the room, examining a piece Wensong was working on. I couldn't tell what it was because the back was such a disheveled mess. I thought about how marvelous it would be if a piece of embroidery could be beautiful on both sides. If that were possible, then a silk fan could weigh much less because it wouldn't need a wooden back to hide the mess on the opposite side. Silk panels could be used to separate rooms or cover doors instead of just hang on a wall to hide their backs. Clothes could be beautiful inside and out.

I started to get very excited about the possibilities if

embroidery pieces could be double-sided. Of course, I had no way of knowing how to go about it since I had never seen such a thing done before. But I remembered that every piece of embroidery work starts with the first stitch. I decided to start with something simple – a leaf. I started with a piece of dark green thread to make the stem. I pushed the thread through the gauze in a small round frame, but instead of bringing the thread back through where I normally would, I turned the frame over and did my first stitch on that side. When I flipped the frame back to the first side, though, the needle had not come out where it needed to be for me to continue where I had started the first stitch. I could tell this was going to be very difficult, if not impossible.

I experimented with various techniques for several hours. I tried just going back and forth between the two sides, doubling back where necessary. Sometimes it worked, but overall I made a mess of both sides and wasted too much thread. I tried working on one side for a while, then switching to the other and hiding the strings under each other. Again, this worked in some places, but much of the image appeared lumpy instead of smooth. I finally started working on making the stitches on the opposite side invisible. By using threads as thin as possible, only one or two strands thick, and trying to go back and forth through the fabric with the stitches close together, I was almost able to eliminate any visible stitches on one side of the gauze in some areas.

It was grueling work. My fingers and eyes were strained after only a couple of hours. But I did it. At the end of the day, a leaf was beginning to emerge. It wasn't the most beautiful leaf. It looked like something I would have made back when I was a beginner, but, in a way, I was a beginner again.

I was both learning and creating an entirely new way of embroidering.

I was both exhausted and exhilarated at the same time. I had to stop working with my hands, but my mind kept stitching. All during dinner and our evening free time, I barely spoke to anyone. I was too focused on my new project. I was imagining how my next stitches would look. If I used a directional stitch, how would it look on the other side? Even if I mastered eliminating the stitches on one side, how would I then create the image on the reverse? How could I stitch on the reverse side and not ruin the image I had created on the original side? I thought about how I could double back in some places, use invisible stitches in others, how I could use single layer shading instead of multiple layer shading and focus on different areas at a time.

My mind wandered so, planning my next stitches and working out problems before I sat back down to work again. When we went to bed, I laid with my eyes closed for hours but didn't sleep. I was embroidering in my mind, and every piece came out glorious.

*W*hen I woke up the next day, I was so excited to work I skipped breakfast and went straight into the studio. I had spent all night dreaming and planning and working out problems. I was confident today's work would go much smoother.

I was so wrong. Nothing worked out the way I imagined. Every stitch, every color, every needle was wrong. By noon, I had made no more progress on my masterpiece.

After everyone else had gone to lunch, I threw my frame against the wall and sulked. Lady Tang returned to the room just in time to see a flutter of cloth fly past her face. She walked over and picked up the frame.

"I know you have been diligently working on something," she said, looking at the piece. "Why is this little leaf giving you so much trouble?"

"Turn it over," I said, gloomily.

"*Aiya!*" she exclaimed, looking at me wide-eyed.

For the first time in all the years I had known her, it seemed that she did not have a perfect way to respond planned out. She looked from the leaf to me and back to the leaf. She started to speak, but she stammered. She sat down in the nearest chair, hard, not with the easy grace she normally possessed.

I sat up straight, at least pleased to have gotten such a reaction out of her, even if my experiment was a failure.

"Yaqian," she finally said. "Do you know what you have done?"

I shook my head. She looked at me and seemed to finally realize that I was not happy at all, but miserable. She straightened her back and pursed her lips as she composed herself.

"Yaqian, this is...extraordinary."

I got the feeling that "extraordinary" was not the word she wanted to use. She didn't want to stroke my ego or let on just how important my work was, but she could not find another word. I sat up straight, but I am sure my confusion was clear on my face.

"Embroidery on both sides of the cloth. I have never seen such a thing," she explained. "I didn't think it was possible. You are a very skilled embroiderer, but you have been working on this for two days and have only completed a very rudimentary leaf. It would take you forever to finish this piece. But you did it! That is the important thing. Do you think Confucius wrote the annals in a day? Or the emperor built the Forbidden City in a month? It does not matter how long it takes to accomplish something great, only that the accomplishment is made."

"So...you don't think I am a failure?" I asked.

"A failure?" She laughed. "Of course not! This might not look like much now, but if we work together to perfect the technique, and practice, practice, practice, you may have just discovered something that could change the way embroidery is done. You will certainly have changed your life and the future of this school."

"What do you mean?" I asked.

"If we perfect this double-sided embroidery, everyone will want it, but we will be the only ones who know how it is done. My school, and my students, could become famous for it."

"Your school? Your students? It's my idea," I said. "We should call it the Yaqian stitch."

Lady Tang waved her hand dismissively. "An arrogant army is bound to lose, Yaqian," she said as she stood. "Now, take a break, have lunch, have a rest. You and I have a lot of work to do."

I never finished that leaf, but I did take a string from that first attempt at double-sided embroidery and added it to my collection.

That Lady Tang and I had a lot of work to do ended up being an understatement. I could tell she wanted to take credit for my work to elevate herself and her school. Well, I wasn't going to let her beat me. I would perfect the technique long before her. I had the time and the willpower to do it. Lady Tang still had a school to run and a dozen other young ladies to teach.

For months, Lady Tang and I worked on perfecting the double-sided embroidery technique, both together and on our own. There was no one stitch that could be used to create a mirror image on the reverse side of a cloth. Instead, it meant finding the best way to make the stitches on the opposite side completely invisible for every thread. It was like learning to embroider all over again. Only this time I didn't have a teacher since Lady Tang and I were learning it together. But the work went quickly. It was exciting to be creating something completely new.

After many months of teaching ourselves new techniques, we then had to endlessly practice them. For years, I watched as my skills improved. I didn't make as much money during this time as I could have because many of my pieces were not suitable to sell, but the few I did sell sold for much more than I ever thought a piece of embroidery could sell for. Lady Tang's skill increased much faster than mine – she was a master after all – but I believed I was not far behind her. And if it hadn't been for me, she never would have imagined such a style was possible.

By the time I was fifteen, I was teaching the other girls in the school double-sided embroidery. It was long and tedious work, but Lady Tang wanted her school to become known for the technique. I grew from student to teacher, but was still far from being a master.

SIX

CHANGSHA, HUNAN, 1856

*I*n the sixth year of the Xianfeng Emperor, one of the emperor's concubines gave birth to a son, his first. The country rejoiced because a son meant that the dynasty was secure and that the emperor had Heaven's blessing. That was the official reaction anyway. In truth, unrest was boiling in the countryside. A long drought had left millions of people dead or hungry. Most people held the emperor responsible. Even though he was far away, it was the job of the emperor to please Heaven. If the gods were unhappy, the common man often suffered.

What was more worrisome was that south of us, in Guangxi Province, a group of rebels known as the Taiping had been amassing their own army against the emperor. Their leader had even set up his own capital in Nanjing. His men rode through the countryside attacking and killing anyone who supported the emperor. Much of southern Hunan had already fallen to the Taiping or joined them willingly. Their followers would cut off their long queues or let their hair flow freely. In Changsha, the city and most of the people in it were still loyal to the emperor, but there were often skirmishes in the streets and small battles in nearby areas. Sometimes, supply routes would be cut off or we would hear of friends or family members being murdered. No matter where a person's loyalties were, all blamed the emperor for our troubles.

Lady Tang's school was profiting. Some of her girls had gone on to placements with influential families, some of the girls were married to rich men, and Lady Tang's income and reputation were growing. She knew, though, that her position required her unwavering loyalty to the emperor. The most important families in China were still Manchu and Han mandarins in and near Peking. What the Taiping had in idealism they lacked in money and prestige, both of which mattered a great deal to Lady Tang and others.

Lady Tang saw the birth of the emperor's son as a chance to show her loyalty to the Son of Heaven. She decided to put together a gift package for the emperor, the concubine, and the new little prince. All of the girls thought it was a lovely idea and we all wanted to put something into the box as well. Lady Tang agreed.

Everyone put their best pieces into the box. Lady Tang put a large, double-sided piece that could be used as a window screen in the summer. But when I went to put in a double-sided fan for the concubine, Lady Tang told me I couldn't include it.

"Why not?" I asked.

"Because this is a gift for the imperial family! You cannot put in a piece that looks like it was made by an amateur! How insulted would they be? No, put in one of your lovely single-sided pieces. Maybe something with fish. Those are always beautiful and complex and bring good luck."

"How dare you call me an amateur?" I shrieked. "*I* have

been doing double-sided embroidery for as long as you have. Your pieces are not that much better than mine. I invented it! My pieces should be allowed to go."

"Yaqian," she said, firmly, trying to hold her temper, "you are not there yet..."

"Where?" I interrupted. "I invented it. I have perfected it. I teach it. You wouldn't have even tried it if it wasn't for me."

"You are not ready for what this could do to your future," she said. "You are still learning. You are still my student and..."

"Well maybe I don't want to be your student anymore!" I yelled. "I'm tired of you treating me like a little girl. You have learned a lot from me, too, you know!"

She held up her hand to get me to stop talking. "I am not having this conversation with you," she said. "I am your master. I say you are not ready, and that is all." She tied up the box, without letting me put *anything* into it, and turned and left the room.

I was angry and in shock. She decided I was not even worth talking to? She thought I was an amateur? Maybe I wasn't quite a "master" yet, but my work was good and I was proud of my pieces. I didn't even know what a master was anymore. She had spent the last few years learning as much as I had. If I hadn't started over again by learning the double-sided technique, I certainly would be a master of traditional embroidery by now. I decided I wouldn't let her hold me back. I would forge my own destiny.

That night, I snuck into her office and opened the box. I removed her double-sided window covering and put in the double-sided fan of a tiger for the concubine. I also included traditional baby shoes and clothes featuring tigers and an embroidered knife sheath with a tiger on it for the emperor. I kept one of the threads I had used to make the concubine's fan and placed it gingerly with the others. That thread could change my life.

But I went a step farther. I included a short letter to the concubine, explaining how I had created the double-sided technique and would happily devote all my work to her. I closed the box and tied it exactly as it was. I took Lady Tang's window covering with me to the main room and threw it into the fireplace. I couldn't help but smile as it quickly disintegrated into nothing.

The next day, Lady Tang sent out the package with a special courier who was to take the package directly to the palace. Undoubtedly, the royal family would receive hundreds, if not thousands, of gifts from loyal citizens throughout the country. The chance that the concubine or the emperor would ever see the box or what was inside it was infinitesimally small, but all of us felt a sense of pride as we thought about our gifts riding away toward Peking. It took all my willpower to not laugh out loud as I saw the look of satisfaction on Lady Tang's face.

I never let on that anything was the matter between Lady Tang and me. I suppose she thought I took her criticism to heart and learned from it or something silly like that. But in truth, I relished in my revenge. I felt no need to rebel against her further because she and I were already even, even if she didn't know it. I went about daily life as things were before: practicing my embroidery, teaching it to others, and finding ways to improve myself.

I had no way of knowing what would happen to that box, and I didn't really care. After a few weeks, I think we had all but forgotten about it and life went back to normal.

*W*e were all sitting, working as usual, when the door to the studio flew open. Lady Tang breezed into the room, her dress floating like a fairy's. Her face beamed, and her eyelids drooped as though she was dreaming.

"My darlings," she began as she glided around the room, throwing all the windows open wide. "You have all done such wonderful work, and you have all made me so proud." She walked over to several of the girls and patted their heads or rubbed their cheeks. "I have just received the most wonderful letter," she said, holding up a piece of paper. "The emperor himself was very grateful for our gift."

At this, all the girls jumped from their seats and squealed. They all began chatting excitedly, wondering what else the letter said.

Lady Tang motioned for everyone to quiet down. "The emperor is sending an emissary to meet me, visit the school, and discuss how the school can provide further services for His Majesty."

The girls could no longer contain their excitement at this and Lady Tang could not quiet them. This would most likely change all of our lives. If the emperor became a patron of the school, it would mean more money than we could ever fathom. The school's prestige would soar, making anyone who studied here an even more highly valued commodity. Forget the best families in the province – the best families in China would be after our work and our girls as personal artisans. We could wind up in the homes of princes and great ladies. Our work could be sent to dignitaries the world over. We could even work in the imperial studios in Suzhou. I couldn't begin to imagine what this could mean for Lady Tang. Her name might go down in history as an embroiderer for an emperor.

As for me, I was as excited as the rest of them, but I was nervous as well. What did the emperor think of my piece? Did it have any bearing on this great honor? What if Lady Tang found out what I had done?

But in that moment, and for several more weeks, it didn't matter. Changsha was a long way from Peking, and the capital was in the midst of celebrating the royal birth. Here in Hunan, the sound of gunfire was never far away. There were rumors that rebellions were springing up all over the country. Honoring an embroidery school thousands of li away would not be a priority for the court.

This was good for us, though. Lady Tang immediately set to work preparing everyone and everything for the emissary's arrival. Everything was cleaned from top to bottom – even the stepping stones leading to our front door were scrubbed. She set all of us to work on pieces as beautiful and complicated as our skills allowed so we would have plenty of gifts to bestow on our visitor. I wanted nothing more than to keep working on my double-sided embroidery technique, but Lady Tang forbade it. I still worked too slowly, she said. I wouldn't have anything substantial created by the time the emissary arrived. I was annoyed, but she was right. I focused on creating a large piece with nine red fish – fish because they represent good fortune and because delicate and wispy fish fins are among the most difficult thing to embroider. If I couldn't impress the emissary with my double-sided embroidery skills, I could at least impress him with my painting with the needle skills.

*T*he big day finally arrived. A single rider arrived at the school just after sunrise and told us that the emperor's emissary would be arriving before noon. He also informed us that the emissary was no mere messenger or even one of the hundreds of court officials, but was Prince Gong, the emperor's brother. This news seemed to worry Lady Tang more than honor her. The rider also said that the prince and his escort only required a single meal and a place to rest for a few hours. They would not be staying the night. The rider left to inform the prince that preparations had been made.

Lady Tang fretted. "After weeks of traveling, not even staying one night?" she asked to no one in particular.

We were all hovering around her office door, her anxiety running through each one of us. I was beginning to regret sending that fan and letter to the concubine behind Lady Tang's back. It was wrong of me to disobey her. It was her school and I was only a student. She had brought me out of my meager existence and given me a chance at an exquisite life, one filled with meaningful work, beauty, and plenty of money. Whatever happened in my life would be thanks to her. In my pride, I had scoffed at all she had given to me and betrayed her.

I was wracked with guilt. I was about to admit to what I had done when she came out of her worry enough to see us standing around.

"What are you doing?" she snapped. "Nothing has changed. Go ready yourselves and then get back to your work. Now!"

We scurried away in a mix of nerves and excitement. We went to our rooms and dressed in our best clothes. We all helped each other do our hair. Some of the girls added paint to their lips, cheeks, and eyes. We all slipped on our most elegant embroidered slippers. Then we gathered together in the studio to work, but we were too excited to concentrate. We were about to meet a prince.

*A*t almost exactly noon, we heard the thunder of horses. Nearly a dozen horses with riders stopped near our gate. Several carts pulled by horses and donkeys followed. A tall man climbed down from his very large horse and stood in front of our gate. He was dressed more finely than the other men and carried an air of command, his chin high. He didn't give any orders, yet men rushed to take his horse's reins, dusted him off, straightened his coat, and opened the gate. All of the other men fell in line behind him. We were shocked to see a few women climb down from some of the horses as well. I heard one of the older girls mumble something about a "chicken girl," but I didn't know what that meant. I did notice that they were not allowed to enter the compound and seemed very friendly with our guards.

We all lined up to greet our guest. Lady Tang gave one of her servants a nod to open the door before anyone could knock.

Prince Gong entered the room without a word. We didn't get a good look at him because we all immediately kowtowed with our foreheads to the floor. We heard the prince take a few steps into the room.

"Lady Tang," I heard him say. "You honor me with your hospitality." His voice was strong and clear, but I had problems understanding his accent and dialect.

I heard the rustle of Lady Tang's gown as she stood. "It is nothing, my lord," she replied. She assumed an almost foreign tongue to match the prince's, though she spoke a bit slower so she was easier to understand. "We are humbled by your presence and thank the emperor for bestowing us with his grace."

"Humph," he said softly with almost a chuckle. "Well, the emperor always gets what he wants." He took a few more steps. "And are these your students?" he asked.

"Yes," she replied. "Sit up now, girls."

We did so, but we stayed kneeling, and immediately our eyes went to the prince. He smiled, I suppose at the fact that we were all staring at him with beet red faces from bowing with our noses to the ground. He was even taller than he seemed when I saw him outside. I had heard that northern men and women were taller than us southerners, but I had never met a northerner before. His head was shaved in the front, but the rest of his hair was long and braided into a tight queue all the way down his back. All Chinese men, no matter their ethnicity, wore the Manchu queue to show submission to the emperor, but few non-Manchu went to the trouble of shaving the front of their heads. He was young, in his early twenties, and a bit on the thin side. He had a well-formed nose and a stern jaw, but his eyes...his eyes were incredibly expressive. His gaze could be firm enough to command an army one minute and playful the next. His face softened when he smiled. His teeth were white and straight, an uncommon sight in a place like Hunan. His clothes were simple for a prince, white with a gold embroidered dragon border and tall, black boots.

I don't deny it – he was handsome. He was the kind of man who women could easily love and men would trust to follow into battle. If he was only the emperor's brother, then the emperor must have been the most exquisite man in the world.

"You are all quite lovely," he said. Some of the girls blushed, giggled, and used their sleeves to hide their embarrassment. Lady Tang shot us all a stern look, but the prince only smiled. He seemed to absorb the attention.

"His Majesty was grateful for the beautiful gifts of embroidery work you sent for the birth of his son," he continued.

Lady Tang let out a sigh of relief. I think it was the first time I saw her breathe all day. She nodded to all of us in approval and we beamed with pride.

"Which one of you is Miss Yang?" he asked.

The room went silent. I blinked. I thought I must have dreamed that he said my name and didn't hear what he actually said.

"Yang Yaqian," he said, clarifying himself.

I couldn't move. I saw some of the other girls cast me quick glances, but I was frozen like a block of stone. I could feel my cheeks go hot and my blood pumping in my ears. I couldn't even move my eyes, I was so terrified of meeting Lady Tang's gaze. But then, she said my name.

"Yang Yaqian?" she asked. "Wh...why are you asking for her?"

"She is the whole reason I am here," he said.

I heard the girls gasp and few start to murmur.

"That can't be possible..." Lady Tang started.

"I only know my orders, Lady Tang," the prince interrupted. "Is the girl here or not?"

"She...she is," Lady Tang stammered. "Yaqian," she called.

The other girls looked at me. I wanted nothing more than to die in that moment, or to wake up. One of the girls behind me pushed my shoulder, hard, and I fell forward. Several of the girls laughed. I was embarrassed, but at least I had been knocked out of my stupor. I forced myself to look at the prince.

"Y...yes?" I managed to croak, causing another round of laughter from the girls. The prince smiled again.

"Come here," he said.

I slowly rose. I felt the blood from my lower legs rush past my knees and up to my head, making me nauseous, but I willed myself not to faint or throw up. I took a deep breath and stepped around the girl in front of me. I took a few small steps toward the prince and Lady Tang, but kept my distance.

"Hmm..." the prince sighed. "You have bound feet."

"Yes, Your Highness," I said.

"We are all Han people in this region," Lady Tang explained.

"Can it be undone?" he asked.

"Only with great care, my lord," Lady Tang said. "It is no small matter to force open a lotus's petals."

"It is no matter," he said.

"Yaqian is one of my most gifted students," Lady Tang said.

"So I have heard," the prince replied. "Tell me about this double-sided embroidery. The emperor said he had never seen the like before."

Lady Tang stared at me with daggers in her eyes. She finally understood what was happening, why the prince was here. She was both furious and heartbroken. "It is a new technique, discovered here at my school," Lady Tang said. "No other school can produce it. It is still in its experimental stage."

"The piece that was sent to the emperor was done by Yaqian?" the prince asked.

"Indeed it was," she said.

"You sent a representative piece of embroidery by a student? Surely a piece by you would have been more appropriate."

The sickening feeling of guilt returned to my stomach as Lady Tang searched for the words to right the situation. I had to repair the damage I had done.

"I would not be the embroiderer I am today if not for Lady Tang," I managed to squeak out.

"So Lady Tang taught you?" he asked. "Do you teach this method to all of your students?"

My heart sank and I looked to Lady Tang in desperation. My attempt to make things right was only making them worse.

"No," Lady Tang finally admitted. "The student has surpassed her teacher. No one else can make double-sided embroidery like Yaqian."

"That is amazing, Lady Tang, for a young girl to not only surpass her teacher, but to do so by practically reinventing the art. Your humility will take you far, Yaqian," the prince said. "Forgive me," he said to Lady Tang, "but my traveling companions are in need of a meal and a rest. Please send for the girl's parents so we can commence negotiations. I wish to be back on the road as soon as possible."

I was confused and a little bit scared. I had not seen my parents in nearly a decade. Why would he need to see them? What negotiations?

Lady Tang motioned for one of the servants to show the prince and his retinue to the dining hall. The other girls all finally rose to their feet. They followed after the prince and the others with giggles and chatter.

Eventually, only Lady Tang and I were left in the entry hall. I gathered up my courage to look at her. Her nostrils were flaring in and out as she took deep breaths. She didn't look as furious as I expected, but she was clearly displeased. She opened her mouth as if to say something, but then thought better of it and turned to leave.

"Wait," I managed to say. "Just tell me, what is happening."

"You don't know?" she asked. "The prince is here to take you away. You are going to serve the emperor."

*L*ady Tang sent a sedan chair to fetch my parents. While we waited, Prince Gong and his men ate lunch with us. The men ate their fill while the girls nervously picked at their food. We did not often have male guests in the house, especially not men so high rank-ing. We found out that Prince Gong had been in the area for several weeks, chasing down and suppressing the Taiping rebels. The emperor had apparently asked the prince to fetch me on his way back to the capital. I was so nervous about what was happening I was not able to eat a bite.

After lunch, Prince Gong and Lady Tang retired to her office and his men rested in the courtyard while the girls went to their rooms. I sat in the foyer to await my parents. I had not seen them in so long, I wasn't sure they would recognize me. What would I say to them? Why did the prince even want to see them? I also wondered what would happen to me. What did Lady Tang mean when she said I was going to serve the emperor? Would I be in Peking? Would I go to Suzhou? What about my studies? I was still far from being a master artisan; who would teach me? And my double-sided embroidery skills still needed years of practice. If I was working, when would I have the time to improve? I was a fool. My pride had put me on a path I was not ready for, just as Lady Tang had said.

Late in the afternoon, my parents arrived. They looked well – older, but not as worn. Their hair was well kempt and their faces more plump. Their clothes were clean and well arranged. I began to wonder just how much money my embroidery was selling for and how much was being sent to them every month. It had apparently been enough to make their lives much easier. I ran up and kowtowed before them.

"Mother, Father," I said. "It is an honor for you to be here."

"Stand up," Mother said in that annoyed tone I knew so well. I stood up but kept my head bowed.

"I am glad you are here," I said, trying to make small talk.

"Such a hassle!" Mother replied. "We had no warning, no time to eat or change. And riding in that...contraption! My back will ache for days."

"Perhaps Lady Tang will let you rest here. I am sure she would love to host you as her special guests."

Mother looked around the large room. "Yes, I am sure the great Lady Tang would love to show off to us."

I could feel my mouth drop. I didn't understand how Mother could be so insulting and ungrateful for all Lady Tang had done for us, and in her own home!

"Lady Tang has been a kind and generous teacher to me," I replied.

"I am sure Lady Tang has treated you well. After all, she wouldn't have such nice things without her slave girls to work for her."

"Is something wrong?" I finally asked. "Are you no longer happy with our arrangement?"

"Happy?" Mother asked. "I have never been happy with the loss of our only daughter!" Mother was nearly screeching now. I could hear her voice echo and saw some of the other girls peeking out of the rooms at us.

"I miss you too," I said, calmly, trying to get Mother to lower her voice. "But this is something we should discuss in private with Lady Tang."

"You miss us?" Mother spat. "All lies! You miss your dirt hovel and running naked in the streets? You miss having to collect worms to sell to eat? You miss nothing. You left us with nothing. Lady Tang stole you and left us to die..."

"She sends you money..." I tried to say.

"A pittance! And no money will replace the fact that we have no one to care for us in our old age."

At this point Prince Gong and Lady Tang entered the room. I do not know how long they had listened to Mother's ranting. I kneeled before the prince. I tugged at Mother's sleeve to get her to do the same, but she slapped my hand away.

"Yang Furen, Yang Laoye," the prince said with a nod. "I am Prince Gong, brother to Emperor Xianfeng. I am here to negotiate for your daughter's services. Please, join me in the study."

I do not know how he remained so calm in the face of such disrespect. I would have had Mother taken out and whipped in the streets, but the prince hardly reacted at all. He ignored her rudeness and walked into the study completely unfazed.

Prince Gong sat in a large chair in the middle of the room. Lady Tang stood to his right side. My parents entered the room and stood before him. I entered the room behind them and crouched on my knees to one side. Prince Gong reached into his boot and pulled out a long-handled pipe. Without being asked, an attendant stepped up and lit the pipe. The prince took a long, slow drag before addressing my parents.

"It is Emperor Xianfeng's pleasure to have your daughter in his service. I am here to negotiate an agreement. Do you understand?"

I am not sure how much of his accent they actually understood, but they both nodded in unison. Mother conceded a monosyllable, "Yes."

"Good," the prince went on. "The emperor is willing to pay you a large fee one time in exchange for your daughter. No more monies will be paid to you from the throne afterward. However, your daughter may send you money out of her own purse as she wishes. Is this fair?"

"Yes," Father quickly answered, cutting off Mother's objections. She pressed her lips together and narrowed her gaze.

"Yang Furen?" the prince asked. "Does the emperor's generosity offend you?"

"Of course not," Mother quickly replied. "But she is our only child. I am too old to have another. She may be a worthless daughter, but she could still marry, give us grandsons. If she is employed by the throne, she may never marry, never have children. Who will care for us in our old age? Perform funeral rites when we die? Burn money at our tombs to keep us from returning to this world hungry?"

Over the years, I had not given much thought to marriage. It was not something I had been prepared for, even though it would be expected of me. It was why my feet had been bound. Such a prospect always seemed far away and it was not something Lady Tang had discussed with me. I wondered why serving the emperor meant that I might not marry. But that was only one of many questions that were running through my head.

The prince strained to understand Mother's country accent, but he understood enough to get her meaning. He motioned to one of his men to his side, whispered something, and the man left. He quickly returned with one of the chicken girls who had been forbidden from eating with us.

"This is Fu Ting," the prince said, introducing her. "She is a lady of illustrious heritage. Consider her a gift from the throne. May she bare your husband many sons."

"What?" the chicken girl squeaked. "You can't just…"

"Silence," the prince commanded. He turned to my parents. "Will this do?" he asked.

"You mean to gift us with another mouth to feed?" Mother asked.

The prince sighed. "I will also increase the original monetary compensation so that feeding this woman will not be a burden to you. Do we have an agreement?"

"Yes," Mother said, finally happy, followed by a small bow. "The throne has been more than generous to us."

The prince stood and motioned to one of his men. "Pay them," he said. The chicken girl reached out and grabbed his arm. Everyone gasped that she would dare touch his royal person.

"You can't just sell me and leave me," she said. She was trying to whisper, but in her desperation, she was nearly screaming.

The prince remained calm and removed her hand from his arm. "The only reason I do not have you horsewhipped is because I would hate to spoil your face for your new master," he said, calm and cold.

He then turned to me. "Collect your things. Let's go."

I could not believe that my parents had just exchanged me for a concubine and a few pieces of coin. I wondered what Lady Tang had gotten for me. What was I going to get? No one had asked if I wanted to go. No one had said what my pay would be. I didn't even know where I was going. The worst part was that I believed it would be either impertinent or idiotic to ask.

I went to my room to pack, but I didn't know what to take with me. I had brought so little to the school with me all those years ago. Everything I had was given to me by Lady Tang. The only thing I knew for sure was mine was my small collection of errant threads, and they were nothing – just my memories. I didn't even have a bag to put anything in because I never traveled anywhere.

And who was this man, these people? It would take us

weeks to get to Peking. Could I really trust these strangers? What would happen to me when I got there?

It was all too much. I sat on the bed and started to cry. I was so scared and confused. There was a light knock on the door and Lady Tang entered. I didn't know why she was there, and I didn't care. I didn't look at her face to see if she was angry because I was so desperate for comfort. I ran to her, threw my arms around her waist, and cried on her chest. I must have surprised her because she didn't hug me back at first, she just stood there.

"Don't make me go," I begged through my tears. "I'm so sorry I disobeyed you. Don't send me away."

She put her arms around me but didn't speak. After a minute, I stopped crying. Once I started to calm down, she looked at me and said, "You have to."

"I don't want to," I said, trying to sound more defiant than whiny, but I am sure I failed. "This man just shows up and says I have to go, without asking me?"

"He asked me," she said. "And he asked your parents. That is all that matters."

"But what about *me*?" I asked, stomping away. "It's my life. Why wasn't I consulted?"

"You don't own yourself," Lady Tang said. "Your parents and I decide what happens to you. Now, the emperor will decide."

"Won't I ever get to make my own choices?" I asked.

Lady Tang blinked and then laughed. "You made your decision when you went behind my back and slipped that piece of double-sided embroidery into the emperor's package. The only reason any of this is happening is because you wanted it to."

She was right. I did make a choice and now I had to live with the consequences. For better or worse, whatever happened to me from this point on would be of my own doing. I couldn't blame anyone but myself.

"You are right," I finally admitted. "I was trying to blame my parents, the prince, you, but I did this. I only wish I had listened to you. I realize now that I am not ready for this."

Lady Tang sighed. "Ready or not, you are going, and you will have to make the best of it." She walked over to the foot of my bed and opened my trunk. "Which clothes are you taking with you?"

"None of them," I said. "I don't own anything. Everything I have you gave me."

"I haven't given you anything," she said. "I am a business woman, Yaqian. You think I was keeping you here and feeding you and giving you nice clothes out of the kindness of my heart? Don't you know me at all? Everything I've ever given to you I bought out of your earnings. You'll have a nice bag of coin to take with you as well."

I ran over to Lady Tang, hugged her, and began crying again. But this time out of...joy? Surprise? Gratitude? Probably all of those things and more.

"There, there, girl," she said, patting my back. "Get off me so I can find you a traveling case. Take these clothes out and fold them nice and small."

In the end, I took quite a few things with me. I had plenty of outfits, several skeins of thread, a dozen pairs of shoes, several small finished pieces of embroidery that had not been sold, a bag of silkworm cocoons to wash my face with, a blanket and pillow, and, as Lady Tang had said, a small bag of coins. It was far more money than I had ever seen at once before. I had no idea my embroidery was worth so much.

When I went downstairs, my parents – and their new concubine – had already left. They didn't even leave any sort of parting message. I decided it was probably for the best. Mother had not seemed happy to see me anyway.

Lady Tang and the other girls followed me out to the front yard as some of the prince's men loaded up my trunk on one of the wagons.

"Where am I supposed to ride?" I asked.

One of the men walked up and handed me the reins to a horse. My eyes widened as I stepped away from the large beast.

"What's wrong?" the prince asked.

"She can't ride, Your Majesty," Lady Tang replied. "She's never even been this close to a horse before."

The prince rolled his eyes and tossed his head back. He pulled his horse up next to me and held out his hand. "Fine, you can ride with me for now so we can get on the road. You can learn as we go."

Lady Tang hugged and kissed me one last time. "Remember us kindly," she whispered in my ear.

The prince took my hand and in one quick tug pulled me up as I scurried onto the horse behind him. I wondered why Lady Tang would ever worry that I would think of her in any other way. Lady Tang was like a mother to me, though I couldn't tell her that. I might be scared and anxious about what lay ahead, but thanks to her, I was no longer a peasant girl from the dirty streets of rural Hunan. I was going to serve the emperor.

SEVEN

I was in so much pain.

The horse was huge so my legs had to spread wide to sit astride him. Sitting up straight to try and keep my balance so I wouldn't fall off with every jostle was straining my back. Every step the horse took seemed to rattle my very bones. I held tightly to the prince, much too tightly than was proper and made me extremely uncomfortable, but I believed I would fall off and be crushed by the dozens of horses behind us if I loosened my grip. I could feel the muscles in his stomach as my fists clenched his shirt. My face was firmly planted in his back, so I could smell the salt of his sweat. We were both so hot from baking in the hot sun and our bodies being pressed close together. Finally, the prince slowed the horse to a gentle trot.

"You are killing me, Yaqian," he said. "Don't squeeze me so tight."

"I am afraid I will fall, Your Highness," I said, my reply muffled in the back of his shirt.

He twisted and shrugged his shoulders to force me to let

go. "You are not going to fall. Riding a horse is easy, especially from back there. Besides, I wouldn't let you fall."

I slowly opened my eyes and leaned back to put some space between us. I somewhat loosened my grip, but not by much.

The prince let out a sigh. "Finally I can breathe again," he said with a laugh.

I sighed as well, feeling a little relaxed. "How long will the trip take?" I asked.

"About a month if we are lucky; maybe six weeks if we aren't."

"Six weeks!" I exclaimed. "What am I supposed to do back here for six weeks?"

"Hopefully you won't be back there the whole time," he said. "You better be on your own horse soon."

"I am going to be so bored," I said. "I will forget how to even do embroidery in that time."

"You complain a lot," he said.

This shocked me. I had never thought of myself as a complainer. I admit that I had become accustomed to a rather comfortable life at Lady Tang's school, but I had suffered much as well.

"I think I complain just the right amount," I replied. "Maybe you are just not used to hearing complaints as a high and mighty prince."

"I think I'm just not used to hearing a woman whine so much," he said.

"Do you not spend much time around women?" I asked.

"I have a wife, but court business keeps me from her. My mother is in the inner court, so I don't see her much either anymore. But I never remember hearing them complain. They are very strong."

"So you think suffering in silence is a sign of strength?" I asked.

"What makes you think they suffer?" he asked.

"Because they are human," I replied. "All life is suffering."

"Perhaps," he replied. "But your life is about to get much better. If we ever get to Peking, anyway. If the Taiping don't stop us."

"Should we be worried?" I asked.

"Not for now," he said. "My force was able to push them back. We hurt them rather significantly. We were able to defeat several of their main brigades. But they have such numbers. I need more men."

"China is large," I said. "Surely the emperor has plenty of men he can call on."

"We can call on more, but that doesn't always mean they come. Many have flocked to the Taiping side. And sometimes farmers and peasants are worse than no men – they are untrained and unarmed. No, I need a real army. A strong army. A well-trained army." The prince got quiet as he pondered this problem.

It was strange to me that these rebels had been allowed to run rampant through the country for so long. Why didn't the emperor stop them? Maybe the emperor was not as strong as I thought.

"Where will you find this army?" I asked.

My question woke him from his trance as he shook his head and cleared his throat. "What? Oh, never mind. It is not for you to worry about."

By this time, the sun was setting. The group came to a large open area and the prince began barking orders. This was where we would camp for the night. The prince easily jumped down from his horse. He held a hand up to help me down, but I realized I couldn't move.

"I can't move my legs," I said.

"Oh, right," he said, laughing. "You must be quite sore." He reached up and grabbed me around my waist and pulled me down from the horse. He stood me on the ground, but as soon as he let go, I collapsed. The prince rolled his eyes. "Do you need me to carry you?" he asked.

I held a hand up to stop him. "No, I'm fine. I just need to rest. You just...you go on. I'll be fine."

He hesitated for a moment, but then went on. He had work to do. I managed to crawl over to a nearby tree and lean against it. Even though I was sitting in the dirt with nothing to do, nothing to eat, and no one to talk to, it felt good to be back on solid ground.

While I rested, the men started several fires and put up some tents. After it was dark, I hobbled over to my trunk and retrieved a bag of roasted silkworms, my pillow, and my blanket. I went over to a fire and laid out a pallet for me to sleep on and munched on my silkworms. Eventually, after all the work was done, a few of the men joined me, along with the prince.

"What did you find to eat?" he asked.

"A Hunan delicacy," I replied. I held one of the hard, round silkworms out to him. "Want to try one?"

"Sure," he replied.

As our fingers touched in the darkness, I noticed his hands were rough, as a soldier's should be, but for the first time I also noticed how calloused my own fingers were. Thousands of tiny needle pricks over the years had hardened to create protective layers over my fingertips. I placed the silkworm in his hand and he slowly pulled his hand back. I then heard a light crunching sound. I couldn't help but smile, as if I had gotten away with a very naughty joke. I had learned over time that there was nothing wrong with eating silkworms, but I doubted a royal diet consisted of many grubs.

"Are you feeling better?" he asked.

"Much," I said. "I am getting excited. I know I am in over my head. I have no idea what I am getting into, but I can't wait to find out. Maybe tomorrow I will even try to ride a horse by myself."

"Life in the palace will be nothing like your life was up to now," he said.

"What will it be like?" I asked.

"I don't want to ruin it for you," he said.

"Tell me about the emperor," I said. "Does he employ many embroidery girls?"

"I don't know," he said. "Well, all the ladies embroider, but I don't think there are any who only do that work. Honestly, I'm not sure why he sent me for you. I mean, I know he was impressed with your work, but is it that special?"

"It is," I declared. "It is something not even embroidery masters know how to do."

"I guess," he said. "I don't know a fig about sewing. But my brother does love art. Paintings, opera, all art forms. I guess if you are the best, then he has to own you. Has to add you to his inner court."

"I don't like the thought of being 'owned' by anyone, even if that someone is the emperor," I said.

"You have to belong to someone," he replied.

"So I've been told," I lamented. "Oh no!" I suddenly gasped. "I don't have anyone to help me with washing and binding my feet."

"You can't do it yourself?" he asked.

"Not very easily. It's quite painful. At the school, we all helped each other."

"You know, the Manchu, we don't do that to our women. Why don't you just stop?"

"I don't know if I can," I said. "Even my bones have been reformed. I don't think they could ever be normal again."

"They are sure to bring you lots of attention at the palace," he said.

"Really?" I asked.

He nodded. "Unwanted attention. There are not many women with bound feet in the palace, if any. In the past, Lan...I mean, Imperial Concubine Yi has forced women who come into her service with bound feet to undo them."

"I know you do not like my feet or understand our ways," I said, "but my feet are important to me. They may be tiny, broken, but they carried me out of the countryside and into the house of Lady Tang. And now, they will carry me all the way to the imperial city."

"I hear you, Yaqian," he said. "But when you get there, just be aware of the people around you. Be careful who you trust."

I glanced around at the other men near the fire. I saw a few men who were high ranking enough to have tents go into them with some of the chicken girls who were still following us.

"Am I safe here?" I asked.

The prince nodded. "I'll watch over you," he said.

*O*ver the next couple of weeks, I slowly learned to ride a horse on my own, and the prince would often ride beside me. It was fascinating watching the countryside change: wide-open plains, rocky hills, rushing rivers. The people changed too. Most places we went, I couldn't understand the local accents. Some of the people we talked to, no one in our group could understand them! The prince could only communicate with them through writing, if they could read. But I loved seeing how their clothes changed. The prince was even kind enough to help me buy and barter for pieces of embroidery by different ethnic groups we passed. I bought some beautiful head wraps, scarves, belts, and wrist cuffs.

The ride was very boring sometimes. Just sitting for hours with no one to talk to and nothing to do. We had to sleep on the ground and eat congee for breakfast, lunch, and dinner. But every few days we would come to a fort where we could get washed, a good meal, and a comfortable bed. We would rest for a day or two and then get new horses and set out again.

The prince and I got to know each other rather well during that time. I had a million questions and he enjoyed answering them. I think he found my naiveté amusing. I didn't care if he thought I was just a silly girl. He was handsome, educated, and even funny. I relished his attention.

He told me how the Taiping were ravaging the land in the south. Many people saw them as saviors, their heroes after years of neglect by the emperor. But thousands of people had been killed under their "protection." The leader of the Taiping, a man who called himself The Sun, forbade relationships between men and women, but he had eighty-eight concubines! The Sun was as corrupt as any man, and more bloodthirsty than most.

He also told me about wars with foreign powers. He told me about a war that happened long before I was born over opium. I was a little familiar with the dangers of this drug, but I was so sheltered at my school that I didn't really see its effects myself. The war cost China lots of money, far more than the emperor had, and also lots of land. The prince said his brother was old enough to remember the war and how much their father hated the Westerners because of it. Emperor Xianfeng still hated foreigners, far more than Prince Gong did.

"You don't hate them?" I asked.

"I hate how they treated us unfairly. I hate how they poison our country and our people with this drug. But you cannot ignore their success. 'The sun never sets on the British Empire', they say. I think that we could learn from them if we could work together."

But China and the foreigners were not working together, and tensions were mounting every day. Some of the foreign generals had offered to help the emperor fight the Taiping, but the emperor rejected them. He didn't want to owe the foreigners anything. So he was basically fighting a war on two fronts, and not winning either one.

This caused the prince great stress, but he did his best to support his brother and his policies. The prince was fluent in English and was one of the emperor's chief diplomats. He tried to teach me a little, so by the time we reached the outskirts of Peking I could say "hello," "good-bye," "thank you," and "big stupid egg." He got a real kick out of teaching me that last one.

He told me a little about his life. He talked about growing up in the palace and about his father, the Daoguang Emperor. He admitted that he was hurt when his father didn't name him as successor, but he respected his decision and understood it.

He told me about his own family. He had one son and two daughters by his wife and concubine. His son was only a little older than the emperor's son.

But who I loved hearing about most was Imperial Concubine Yi, the mother of the emperor's son. She had entered the palace along with twelve hundred other women the emperor could choose his consorts from. Somehow, Imperial Concubine Yi had managed to stand out from all the rest and catch the eye of the young emperor. She soon became his second favorite and bore him his only son. He also had a daughter, but she wasn't important. The empress was a woman named Zhen, and she was the little prince's official mother. The empress didn't have any children of her own.

The prince seemed to hover between respecting and despising Imperial Concubine Yi. In many ways he saw her as a spoiled child with ridiculous whims of fancy. On the other hand, her influence over the emperor was preferable to that of his other grandees. The grandees encouraged the emperor's closed-door policies and incited war. If the emperor would listen to Imperial Concubine Yi more than his ministers, then she would be more useful to Prince Gong as an ally than an enemy.

I didn't talk near as much on that journey as the prince did. How could my little life at an embroidery school ever compare to court intrigue? He was interested in my life before the school though, my life in the countryside. He wanted to know what life was like for average people.

"China is her people," the prince said. "The court must never forget that. But I feel they often do."

The trip was difficult, but I loved every minute of it. I never realized how beautiful my country was. We traveled through Zhengzhou, Shundefu, and Baoding. I saw majestic mountains, wide rivers, and forests that seemed to go on forever. I tried to remember all of it so I could turn them into embroidered scenes later.

I continued to struggle to understand the Prince's Peking accent, and sometimes he couldn't understand me. I made it my goal to become fluent in his foreign-sounding dialect by the time we arrived in Peking. I wanted to make sure the emperor and I would be able to understand each other when we met.

EIGHT

PEKING, 1856

e had been traveling for four or five weeks when we crested a hill and the prince pointed to the huge city.

"There it is," he said. "Your new home."

From the road, I could see the city of Peking spread out below me. Innumerable one-story buildings with red roofs that stretched far beyond what I could see. A layer of dust shrouded it in a fine fog from the millions of animals, people, and carts traversing its dirt roads.

As we made our way down the hill and entered Peking, I thought back to when I first arrived in Changsha and how awed I was by the sight. This place was infinitely more impressive. I felt as though I was on another planet. I had to hold tightly to the reins of my horse as it took small quick steps to avoid running over or into people, carts, and other animals. There were people dressed in funny clothes and animals I had never seen before, even in books. We passed by a long line of huge brown beasts with long necks and humps on their backs. People dressed in long sheets were riding some of them! I could never do that. I saw a woman with a white face wearing long black robes who was leading a long line of Chinese children. I saw a group of men in little hats kneeling on rugs and kowtowing to nothing in particular. I saw people in elaborate costumes singing in a way that sounded like an erhu. I saw a man with several monkeys for sale who was making them do flips. I saw white women in tight dresses with huge hats. There were people yelling, dogs barking, bells ringing, children laughing. Dung and garbage lined the streets. I wondered if the streets were ever swept or if they just waited for the rain to wash it away. After weeks of riding through China's idyllic countryside, the filth of Peking was shocking.

Finally, we turned onto a broad thoroughfare wide enough for several carriages to pass abreast of one another. Ahead of us was a large red wall with a brown gate and a red building behind it. The Forbidden City.

My heart began to race. I swallowed, but my mouth was dry. I needed to straighten my hair and get the dust off my face, but I couldn't look away as we got closer to the palace. The front gate began to open and a few of the riders ahead of us entered. I could feel myself grinning from ear to ear as my horse neared the gate. I couldn't blink even though the dust was burning my eyes. I didn't want to miss a moment of what felt like a triumph for me. A little peasant girl from the Hunan countryside was about to enter the Forbidden City and meet the emperor. If only Mother could see me.

But then, one of them men grabbed my horse by the reins and turned him to the side, walking away from the gate along the outer wall.

"Wait," I screamed as I tried to wrest the reins from him and go back to the front gate.

"Stop fighting me," the man said. "You enter this way!"

"No!" I screamed as I twisted around on my horse and

looked back at Prince Gong, who was heading through the front gate. "Wait! What about me?" I yelled at him.

"What?" he hollered back.

"Where am I going?" I asked.

"You enter the back!" he answered.

"Why?" I asked.

"You're a girl!" he said with a laugh.

I grunted and turned back in my saddle to face the front. The man ahead of me still held my horse's reins.

"No female is allowed to enter the Meridian Gate," he said, referencing the front gate of the palace.

"Why?" I asked.

He shrugged. "That's just how it is," he said.

I crossed my arms and sat in a huff as he led my horse on. It wasn't fair.

The man finally stopped by a side gate, which was little more than a big door, called the Gate of Divine Prowess. He motioned for me to get down off my horse. He let the guard at the gate know I had just arrived with Prince Gong's party. The guard nodded and opened the door. A wagon pulled up and two men removed my trunk from it. They deposited it inside the door and left. I entered the gate and the guard closed the door behind me. I stood there next to my trunk with no idea of what to do next. I had no idea where to go. I didn't expect to be separated from the prince and the rest of the party, so I hadn't asked what I needed to do when I arrived. I just stood there, waiting for...something. Finally, I saw a young man walk by, so I waved him over.

"Hello!" I called. "Can you help me?"

He walked over, but didn't say anything. I quickly explained who I was and that I had arrived with Prince Gong's party and asked him for help.

"Hmm..." was all he said at first as he pondered my

request. "I am not sure what to do with you. I could take you to your room…"

"I would appreciate that," I said, surprised I already had a room and that he would know where it was.

"…and not tell anyone you are here," he went on. Now I was confused. "Or I could present you to the emperor."

"That would be wonderful…" I said, even more confused as this seemed like the preferable option.

"Well, that might be difficult," he said, rubbing his hands together.

"I don't want to cause trouble," I said.

"It is no trouble," he said.

"Then can someone take my trunk to my room and take me to the emperor?" I asked, growing frustrated with the man.

"Well, I could, but that would take time. And my time is very valuable," he said with half a smile and a raise of his eyebrows.

I finally understood what he meant, but I had never paid anyone for anything before, much less a bribe for preferential treatment. Was it against the rules? Would I get in trouble? How much should I pay? Would I look stupid if I paid too little? Would I be setting myself up for a very expensive cost of living if I paid him too much the very first time I needed something? Honestly, I had no idea what money was even worth. Prince Gong had taught me a little when he helped me buy the embroidery from the villagers we had met, but that was a completely different situation. I decided it would be unwise for him to know how much money I had on me, so I turned my back to him before reaching into my bag and pulling out the same amount of money as I had paid for the least expensive piece of embroidery I had bought.

"I hope this will make the task easier for you," I said as I turned around and gave him two small coins and held my chin up as I spoke, trying to feign confidence.

He looked at the coins I handed him and then back at me. He stared at me for a good minute. I think he was trying to shake my confidence, but I didn't have any confidence to shake.

Finally, he turned around and called to another young man who was sitting nearby. "Take this trunk to the servant quarters at Imperial Concubine Yi's palace," he ordered. The young man was not able to lift the trunk on his own, so he gave a little bow to the other man and ran off to find help. "Follow me," the man the ordered me.

I didn't realize it at the time, but that was my first encounter with a eunuch. Like most people in the Forbidden City, one encounter was all it took to decide that eunuchs were not to be trusted.

The Forbidden City was huge. We went down so many hallways and took so many turns I thought I would never find my way back to the Gate of Divine Prowess. Not that I needed to go back to the gate, but I needed some point of reference to help me get my bearings. It was beautiful, though. Every wall, every pillar, every piece of wood was ornately carved with flowers or religious scenes and painted with lacquer of every color.

We finally arrived at a large, long room. There were several people standing around the edges of the room and several men on their knees in front of a man seated on a large chair on a raised dais. My heart nearly stopped in my chest at the realization that I was looking at Emperor Xianfeng, the Son of Heaven.

The eunuch put his finger to his lips and motioned for me to follow him. He kept his head down and shuffled his feet as he silently walked along one of the walls. I followed, stepping even more delicately than usual on my lotus feet.

When we were about halfway into the room, we could hear some of what was being said by the men kneeling in front of the emperor and I was able to get a better look at him. He was older than Prince Gong, but he looked younger, more delicate. His face was flawless and gentle looking. His eyes, nose, and lips were all small but well-defined. He wore an elaborate yellow robe, busily embroidered with dragons, clouds, bats, and random auspicious symbols. My mind immediately began imagining how I could make the robe more beautiful. His head was shaved in the front like Prince Gong's and he had a long queue down the back, but he also wore a black and red hat with what looked like a little tower rising from it. He leaned back in his chair, his chin in his hand, as if he was hardly interested in what the men in front of him were saying. It felt almost treasonous to say, but I didn't think he was handsome or impressive at all. Honestly, I was rather disappointed by my first impression of the Dragon.

I looked around the room and noticed Prince Gong on the other side, waiting for his turn to address his brother. He noticed me as well and smiled, apparently quite proud of me since I managed to find my way to the audience hall. I tossed my head, raised my chin, and turned my attention back to the emperor.

The emperor finally dismissed the men he had been half-heartedly listening to with a wave of his hand. They rose to their feet, but stayed bent at the waist as they backed away.

"Never turn your back on the emperor," the eunuch whispered to me. I nodded.

One of the court attendants announced Prince Gong. He

walked up to the front of the dais, bowed, and then kneeled before the emperor.

"I trust that your mission was a success, Prince Gong," the emperor said.

"Yes, Your Majesty," he said. "The Taiping are currently on the run. I have managed to cut off many of their supply lines and drive them out of several key cities in Hunan and Guangxi. However, they are still well-fortified in Nanjing and they are quite popular in the provinces around that area. We need more men to fight and take them down. They are like an infestation. If they are not completely burned out, they only come back stronger.

"The Taiping rebels have left nothing but slaughter in their wake. They have murdered anyone who claims to be loyal to the Son of Heaven. They have burned whole towns that still support you. The people need to be protected.

"The Americans and the British are greatly distressed by these rebels as well. They believe that Hong Xiuquan is not acting like a true Christian and is giving all Christians a bad face and wish to protect their converts. They have offered to send troops and ammunition and horses to help fight this evil menace."

For the first time since I arrived at the audience hall, the emperor sat up and gave his brother his attention. "Don't speak to me of help from those feckless foreigners!" he nearly yelled. "They can be trusted even less than the Taiping. Would you use tigers to rid your city of bears?"

"But the British are already here," Prince Gong tried to calmly explain. "They have ports in Shanghai and Guangdong with men and ships ready to fight. Let them die and suffer the losses instead of us. China has already lost enough..."

"I will not be indebted to them!" the emperor yelled. "I

can protect my own people! I don't need those white
barbarians running around with their weapons and their
gods and their armies in my country. If it were up to you,
you would let them walk right through the Gate of Supreme
Harmony and stand before me as equals!"

"I would never dishonor you, Your Majesty," Prince
Gong said, his voice low and eyes downcast. "Tell me what
to do and I will do it. Tell me how to rid your kingdom of
the Taiping plague."

"Now I have to tell you how to do your job?" the emperor
asked. "That is a matter for the generals. Talk to Sushun."

"Yes, Your Majesty," the prince replied with a bow.
"Thank you."

"Anything else?" the emperor asked.

"Yes, Your Majesty," the prince said. He motioned for me
to come to his side.

I felt my face go hot. I didn't have a chance to fix my hair
or get the dust off my face and clothes. But I straightened up
and walked as gingerly as possible to the prince's side. I
hoped that no one would notice how disheveled I was. I
kept my gaze low, but I could see the emperor watching me
from the corner of my eye. I bowed and then kneeled and
kowtowed before the emperor.

"This is the embroidery girl you had me fetch while on
my journey," he said. The prince sighed as he introduced
me, as if he was glad for a change of topic. "Yang Yaqian."

The emperor cleared his throat. "I am glad that you
arrived safely, Miss Yang." I did not reply. "I trust you had a
pleasant journey. Did Prince Gong treat you well?"

"Yes, Your Majesty," I replied. "The journey was wonderful. The country is so beautiful. And Prince Gong was
pleasant company." For some reason, my response elicited

light laughter from the crowd, but I did not know why. Even the emperor smiled at this.

The emperor raised his hand and motioned for someone to come to his side. From behind an embroidered screen that was set behind the emperor's throne, a woman emerged. Maybe it was her makeup, her elaborate hairstyle, or her ornate gown, but I thought this woman was the most beautiful I had ever seen. She would have put Lady Tang to shame. The woman bowed and then kneeled beside the emperor.

"Imperial Concubine Yi," the emperor said, addressing the beautiful woman. "I have brought a gift for you."

"Your Majesty is too kind to think of me," Concubine Yi replied. She raised her head to look at me.

This was the mother of the emperor's son. Her eyes were large, and she fixed them on me. I was at once honored by her attention, but fearful. Her face was porcelain white except for a bit of pink in her cheeks. Her lips were painted red and the edges curved up slightly. It gave her a pleasant, though not too friendly, demeanor. Her green chaopao was embroidered with pink and cream peonies and couched with small, gold-embroidered phoenixes. Her sleeves and the bottom of the chaopao were embroidered with blue waves in a variety of hues. On two fingers of each of her hands, she wore nail protectors that were several inches long made of gold and encrusted with jewels. Her hair was coiled and wrapped around a flat board in the traditional Manchu style and decorated with fresh flowers and jewel butterflies.

"This is the girl who sent you that beautiful fan in honor of my son," the emperor said. "Her embroidery is quite unique. I knew that you would enjoy her services."

"Oh," Concubine Yi replied. "How thoughtful. Though she seems rather young for a master needleworker."

The emperor nodded. "How old are you, Miss Yang?"

"I am sixteen," I replied. "But you are right. I am no master artist. I am shocked that my ugly embroidery work even caught your attention, Your Majesty."

"So humble," he said with a smile.

Concubine Yi stuck out her lower lip and pouted. "You call this a gift?" she asked. "She is just a child. My embroidery is probably more beautiful than hers."

"She is only being modest," the prince spoke up. "I spoke to her teacher, the talented Lady Tang. She assured me that Miss Yang invented the double-sided embroidery technique and that no one else can embroider as well as she can."

"Do you think I would give you anything less than the best?" the emperor asked Concubine Yi.

She looked at me for a long while, as if taking me all in. She sighed. "Her feet are bound. I don't like it."

"Oh, are they?" the emperor asked.

"She should unbind them," Concubine Yi declared. "It is a horrid practice."

The emperor nodded and looked at me. "How would you feel about unbinding your feet?" he asked me.

"I would do whatever is asked of me, Your Majesty," I replied. He nodded, but he didn't smile. I waited a short moment, and after no one replied, I continued. "However, if it was my choice I would leave them how they are. These tiny feet carried me from obscurity to your magnificent court. They are part of who I am."

The emperor laughed and clapped. "This girl speaks her mind and knows herself. If only my grandees were such honest men. Keep your bound feet, Miss Yang. They suit you."

I could hear murmurs ripple throughout the room. I glanced around and saw some men smiling, some scowling, some hid their mouths behind their large sleeves so no one could know what they were saying. The prince was trying hard not to smile, but I could see the edge of his mouth curling up. Concubine Yi did not look pleased. She did not look angry, but hurt.

The emperor sat up and stretched his arms. "Is that all, brother? It is nearing mid-day."

"Yes, Your Majesty," the prince said with a bow.

The emperor stood and everyone else in the room bowed as he stepped from the dais and out the front of the long building. I was shocked to see that he walked with a slight limp. How could the Son of Heaven, the Dragon, be lame?

Then Concubine Yi and some other women who had also been sitting behind the screen left from a side entrance. After they were gone, everyone else was able to stand up and either leave or stay and talk. As I stood, I could barely feel my legs. All this kowtowing and kneeling was so uncomfortable.

"Congratulations on finding your way here so quickly," the prince said to me.

I crossed my arms. "No thanks to you!" I said, angrily. "If you knew we were going to be separated, why didn't you tell me what to do once I got here. What would you have done if I hadn't found my way here?"

"Why worry about things that didn't happen?" He slapped my upper arm as he would one of his comrades. "Everything worked out."

"Yes, but..." I was about to explain how I had to give

money to a shady man and was worried about the repercussions when the eunuch himself stepped up to us.

"It was not your place to present her to the emperor!" he nearly shouted at the prince in his boyish voice.

"Go away, Shun," the prince said. "I don't answer to you."

"You have to follow court protocol like the rest of us," Shun snapped.

"Get lost before I have you taken out and beaten," the prince replied.

The eunuch's face turned red and his nostrils flared. He clearly wanted to yell at Prince Gong further, but he finally just turned and walked away.

"Wait," the prince said, stopping him. "Give it back."

Shun turned back to face the prince. "What do you mean?"

"Whatever you took from Miss Yang to agree to bring her here. Give it back."

"You know how things work here, Prince Gong," the eunuch grumbled.

"All too well," he replied, sticking out his hand.

"You won't be here to protect her all the time," Shun said, slapping the coins into the prince's hand. "She'll need important friends like me if she is to survive in here."

The prince scoffed. "You're nothing! You were hoping to introduce her to raise your own status. You cut off your own balls to be here, and she's more important just by showing up. Crawl back to your rat hole."

The eunuch mumbled something under his breath as he slinked away. The prince couldn't hide his smile. For some reason, he really enjoyed embarrassing that eunuch. When he looked at me, I made sure my displeasure showed on my face.

"What?" he asked.

"I don't think it is wise to make enemies on my first day," I said.

"Bah! Forget him. He's nothing."

"But what am I?" I asked. "I don't know what I'm doing here. What's my position? Where's my room? Where do I get food?"

"Oh, right," he said, as if he only realized that I was a total stranger to this world. "I don't know. You are the first *gōngnǔ* I've ever taken notice of."

"*Gōngnǔ*?" I asked.

"Yes," he said. "Just what we generally call women who are not maids but not ladies either. Just a palace girl."

I sighed and rubbed my temple. It had been a long trip and long day. I began to realize just how tired I was.

"Don't worry," he said. "I know who to ask."

I followed the prince through several buildings and down several walkways. The palace was exquisite and enormous. It was also very busy. It was like its own little city with men and women of various classes all coming and going. Coolies and cleaning ladies, eunuchs and grandees, concubines and princesses. Even palanquins bearing the most important of palace residents and visitors were being carried hither and thither. What a sight!

As we passed through the imperial gardens, I heard the strangest sound, something like *kaw-AWW kaw-AWW*. I looked up and saw a creature from my dreams fly over my head, the most exquisite bird who ever lived, a blue peacock. I completely forgot I was supposed to be following the prince and followed the bird. It landed in a grassy area nearby and fanned its magnificent plumage. It walked around and pecked at the ground. I wanted to touch it, but when I got too close, it started to walk away. I sat on the grass and watched it in total awe.

"What are you doing?" the prince asked, having come to my side.

"I had no idea they even really existed," I said. "I saw pictures, but I thought they had to be creatures of myth. Surely nothing so extraordinary could really exist in the world."

"It's just a peacock," he said.

"It is more than that to me," I said. "This bird is beauty itself. It has inhabited my imagination for as long as I can remember. It was the first thing I embroidered and became my obsession. I have stitched its feathers thousands of times, but that was all mere imitation now that I see one for myself. No piece of art could ever be as lovely."

"You know, that bird is a boy," he said.

"How do you know?" I asked.

"Because only male peacocks are beautiful. The females are very plain. There is one," he said pointing to a gray bird across the grass.

"Fascinating," I said, watching the two.

The prince crouched down beside me. He took my hand and held it out flat toward the male peacock. He pulled up a few blades of grass and sprinkled them into my hand.

Slowly and cautiously, the gorgeous blue peacock came toward me. He pecked at the ground and then tilted his head to look at me closely. He took a few more steps and then pecked at the grass in my hand! I gasped and instinctively pulled my hand back from the little pecks. The prince continued to hold my hand and encouraged me to reach my hand out again. The peacock pecked at my hand again, grabbing a few blades of grass. I felt like I was in a fairyland. I looked up at the prince with a wide smile.

"Thank you," I said.

He smiled back, delighted by my childish happiness.

We finally came to the gate of a palace called the Palace for Gathering Elegance.

"This is where Imperial Concubine Yi lives," the prince explained. "Wait here." The prince entered the gate and crossed the courtyard. He approached a well-dressed woman who was sitting on the porch. She ducked inside the palace. After a moment, a eunuch appeared and he and the prince joined me outside the gate.

"This is the only eunuch you ever need to worry about," the prince said. "His name is An Dehai, Imperial Concubine Yi's chief eunuch."

"You honor me, Your Highness," An Dehai replied. "But there are far more lofty servants of the emperor than me within these walls."

"But none with Concubine Yi's ear," the prince said. "This is Yang Yaqian, the new embroidery girl."

"Yes," An Dehai replied. "I know who she is. The inventor of the double-sided embroidery with the bound feet."

"He knows everything," the prince said, smiling.

"What do you want from me?" An Dehai asked.

"In the short term, get her situated. Find her room. Find her lunch. Explain basic court manners to her."

"And in the long term?" An Dehai asked.

"I'm sure you can figure that out," the prince said as he reached into his pocket and pulled out far more than the two coins I had given Eunuch Shun and gave them to An Dehai.

An Dehai put the coins into his pocket. He sighed as if he was annoyed with the burden of having one more thing to do.

"Very well, girl. Follow me," he said. He opened the gate and went inside. I followed after him. As he turned to close the gate, I looked back to say goodbye to the prince and thank him for his help, but he was already walking away without even a glance behind him.

An Dehai led me past Imperial Concubine Yi's palace, which was made up of several smaller buildings, and down a narrow walkway. The walkway was lined with windows and doors. Apparently, these were the servants' barracks, and as the newcomer, I was the lowest servant of them all. An Dehai finally stopped at the very last room and opened the door. The room was quite small. It had a bed about the size of my bed at Lady Tang's school. There was a fireplace in one wall and a chair by the window, which had a lattice screen. My trunk was already there next to the bed. The room was coated with dust and spider webs dangled from the ceiling. Because of the covering over the walkway, there was very little sunlight streaming into the room. It would be nearly impossible to do any embroidery work in such a dark and cramped space.

"What a fine room," I lied. I had imagined that palace quarters would be the best of the best, even for lowly servants. "I never had a room of my own before." At least that much was the truth. "And how convenient that my trunk has already arrived. How efficient the emperor's household is."

An Dehai rolled his eyes, as if annoyed by my praise.

"You must keep your room neat and attend your own fire," he said. "You are to report to Imperial Concubine Yi every morning at the hour of the rabbit to receive any orders for the day. Your meals will be whatever is left over from Concubine Yi's table after her ladies have eaten. Just follow the other servants to see how things are done."

"And where will I work?" I asked. "And how will I get supplies? Thread, needles, rolls of silk?"

"You will come to me for all your needs," he said. "And you will work in Concubine Yi's main hall. You will attend her as soon as she wakes and remain in her presence unless she gives you leave to do otherwise."

I nodded. I stepped out of the room and noticed a water pump. I remembered that I still must have looked quite a fright. And my room needed to be cleaned and aired out. "Do you think Imperial Concubine Yi will need me this afternoon? Or can I use the day to clean and get organized?"

An Dehai stepped out of the room as well. "I know you have had a long journey," he said. "Rest and make yourself ready. Your new life will start bright and early tomorrow."

NINE

The next morning, I was up before dawn. I hardly slept a wink the night before. I put on my best satin robe and embroidered slippers. I pinned up my hair and wore a little color on my lips and cheeks. By the time the front door to Imperial Concubine Yi's palace opened at exactly the hour of the rabbit, I was waiting to greet her.

I have no idea how early Concubine Yi woke up, but she already looked perfect. Her hair was magnificently piled on top of her head and her makeup was done in the Manchu style, with her eyes lined with black ink and her lips small and red. She was already seated at her dining table, which was covered with no less than one hundred dishes! No wonder all of her ladies and servants would be able to eat after she was done. There was enough food at this one meal for an army. Concubine Yi was seated at the head of the table and all her attending ladies lined each side, all standing. I stood at the far end of the table, but she saw me.

"Yang Yaqian!" she called. "Come down here!"

I shuffled down to her end of the table, sure to keep my

eyes downcast. The other ladies all moved down so I could stand in the first spot.

"How kind of you to finally join me," she said. "I expected you to present yourself to me last night."

I gasped and looked around. *Damn that An Dehai!* "Forgive me, Your Highness," I said. "I was told to attend you in the morning. I didn't want to interrupt your normal routine."

"I wish I had a normal routine," she said. "But something always comes up. Well, it is no matter. You are here now." Imperial Concubine Yi didn't address me for the rest of her meal, which took more than an hour. We stood there while she ate and read letters. Standing for such a long period of time was very painful on my little feet, but I didn't squirm or fidget.

Eventually, Concubine Yi finished eating. She turned to me and asked, "Isn't it painful for you to stand for so long?"

"Yes, My Lady," I replied.

"You should unbind your feet," she said bluntly. "It's a terrible and cruel practice. And I need you at your best. I can't have you distracted by such pain."

"They have never impeded my work before, My Lady," I said. "But if the emperor orders it, I will unbind them, if someone will tell me how."

"The emperor gave you to me," she said. "You should do as I tell you."

"Yes, My Lady," I said.

She stood to leave the room. The ladies then grabbed what they could and quickly ate as they followed her. After they left, several servants and eunuchs who had been standing to the sides or in other rooms emerged and picked at the food. I grabbed a few steamed buns since they would be easy to eat without a bowl and I could put some in my pockets for later. Then I also followed the other ladies.

I wasn't sure what I should do. Did she just order me to unbind my feet? The emperor had told me to keep them bound. What would happen if I defied him? What would happen if I disobeyed Concubine Yi?

Concubine Yi went to her main hall, where there was now plenty of light from the morning sun. She sat in a large chair in the middle of the room and motioned for her ladies to also sit. I remained standing. She eventually took notice of me and motioned for me to sit on a stool near her.

"Everyone can embroider," she said to me.

I nodded. "It is an important skill for a woman," I said.

"I embroider some of the emperor's clothes and I make little shoes for my darling baby prince. And my ladies embroider lovely scarves and handkerchiefs for me."

I looked around and nodded to the ladies. Indeed, some of them were already settling down with their needlework.

"I have never had a girl work for me whose only job was to embroider. What will you do for me?" she asked.

"I will do whatever you ask of me," I replied. "I can embroider whatever you need or want. I can teach your ladies how to improve their embroidery. And if you have no needs of me, I can improve my skills so one day I can be a great master."

"Usually if I need anything special I just send for it from Suzhou and it comes in a few days. Like this chaopao I am wearing now. Isn't it lovely? I especially requested the little white flowers. I asked for it special and it arrived within a week. Would you be able to make a new outfit for me in a week?"

I shook my head and looked closely at the chaopao she was wearing before responding. "My Lady, this garment is quite lovely. But my understanding of the embroidery work done in Suzhou is that it is a factory. They have hundreds of people working night and day for you. I am only one person. This piece you are wearing was not done by only one person, but probably four or five. And none of them spent much time on it."

"How can you tell?" she asked.

I pointed to one flower on her front panel. "See here, the person who did this one is highly skilled. But if you look at this panel on the side, under your arm where you cannot easily see, the flowers were done much more quickly. The thread is thicker and the flowers were done in haste. I would suspect the ones on the back panel are of even less quality."

"Less quality?" she asked, nearly gasping.

"I believe two master embroiderers worked on the front panels while apprentices of varying degrees worked on the side and back panels. This is how it was cobbled together so quickly."

"*Cobbled* together?" she nearly sputtered. "Well, this won't do! I simply must have the best. Can you make me one? A new one? A better one?"

"It will take time, My Lady," I said. "This chaopao is lovely, and I am sure most people would not think it was anything but the best. But I guarantee that after seeing a chaopao made by me, even following the same pattern, you would clearly see an improvement."

She nodded and called for An Dehai, who appeared almost instantly. "Make sure Yaqian has whatever she needs to make me a beautiful new outfit. I feel as though I am wearing rags now."

An Dehai nodded and left the room. Concubine Yi turned her attention from me and talked to her ladies about a new opera performance she was planning for the emperor. About an hour later, An Dehai returned with a whole basket of supplies for me: dark blue satin for the base, white silk threads of various shades, and needles of every size. I moved a chair over by the front door and began to work in the bright sunshine of the clear Peking sky.

That night, as I unbound my feet to wash them as usual, I pondered not wrapping them up again. I remembered the freedom I felt as I ran through the silkworm fields. When I was little, I was sure I could never live with bound feet. Now, I could not imagine them unbound. I soaked them in hot water for a long time. After, I did not bind them, but tried to stand on them without any wrappings. I could not put any weight on them. I could not stand, much less walk. It was as if without the bindings, my feet had nothing holding the bones together and my feet would shatter if any weight was put on them. I didn't know what to do. On our journey from Changsha, Prince Gong mentioned that Concubine Yi had in the past ordered women with bound feet to unbind them. It must be possible, but I had no idea how to go about it.

I sent for An Dehai and explained the situation to him, that Concubine Yi had ordered me to unbind my feet but I did not know how. I asked him if he could send someone to help me.

But no one came. I had no choice but to wrap my feet in the bindings the next morning so I could attend Concubine Yi. She did not remark on my feet and the subject was not broached again. My feet remained bound.

*a*fter a few days, I was settling into my new life. Imperial Concubine Yi was very excited about getting her first robe made by me, so while the other ladies had to attend her from before dawn until late at night – dressing her, entertaining her, following her around the palace grounds whenever she went somewhere – I was allowed to stay in her main audience chamber and work on her new gown. An Dehai eventually brought me a free-standing frame, so the work was much easier than having to work in a tiny handheld circular frame.

The other ladies warmed to me eventually. They would often hover over my shoulder to see what I was working on. Sometimes they would question me about my work or ask for tips to improve their own embroidery. They thought it was quite interesting that I grew up in a school instead of at home. Most of Imperial Concubine Yi's ladies were raised to attend to the court. They were princesses – daughters of other princes and royal cousins – and the daughters of high-ranking grandees. They were raised at home and were taught to clean, cook, sew, paint, play instruments, style their hair, organize a household, and raise children. Some of them were taught to read and write a little, but not much. Apparently, the emperor's chief wife, Empress Zhen, was the most well-educated woman they knew. She had been raised in a very wealthy family and had private tutors from a young age to teach her history and poetry.

Imperial Concubine Yi and Empress Zhen got on very

well. They would often visit each other and they both doted on the prince, Zaichun. The women seemed to love nothing more than to play with the little prince in the garden, together, every day. It was fascinating to me that two women who shared the same husband and the same child seemed to have no jealousy or strife between them.

But that is how Empress Zhen was. She was the most calm and cool woman I ever met. She was not as beautiful as Imperial Concubine Yi, but she carried herself with the most exquisite grace. She never raised her voice and never lost her temper. As the empress, her main task was to manage the inner court – the court of the ladies – and she had been the best choice for that. Her restraint and respect radiated throughout the community, so there was very little conflict among any of the women.

Sometimes Imperial Concubine Yi and Empress Zhen would be summoned to the emperor's audiences, usually when an important diplomat was visiting. Concubine Yi and Empress Zhen would have to dress up in their finest clothes and bring a large retinue of ladies and eunuchs with them – all for show, of course. Having so many beautiful women and servants at his command was one of the ways the emperor showed his power. On more than one occasion, Imperial Concubine Yi would include me among the ladies who were to attend her.

The audiences were mostly boring, but it did give us a chance to hear about what was going on around the country, and a chance to steal glances at some of the men. I always kept a look out for Prince Gong, but he was not always there.

At one particular audience, the prince was present, and my heart leaped. Even I was surprised by how excited I was to see him. At one point, he looked my way, and our eyes met. It was only for a moment, and I don't think anyone else noticed, but in that second we spoke without words. He wanted to see me.

After the audience was over, of which I hadn't heard a thing, I made sure I was the last of the ladies to leave, and I walked slowly so I would fall back. I couldn't linger in the outer court, I would surely be missed or caught, but I was hoping to at least catch a glimpse of the prince again. As I passed a large column, I felt a hand reach out and grab my arm. I looked up and saw Prince Gong, his finger to his lips. He pulled me aside.

"How is life in the inner court?" he asked me in hushed tones.

"It is wonderful!" I said. "Imperial Concubine Yi is a kind mistress, and I love my work. Thank you so much for bringing me here."

"No one has tried to bother you or cause you any trouble?"

"No. I don't think so. Everyone has been so kind. Oh, well, An Dehai tried to embarrass me the first day I think, by telling me I didn't have to appear before Concubine Yi when she expected me to. But she wasn't too mad. I'm sure she has forgotten all about it."

"I hope so," he said.

"Concubine Yi ordered me to unbind my feet," I said. "I tried, but I did not know how. I asked An Dehai to find someone to help me, but he never sent anyone. And Concubine Yi never mentioned it again. I hope I have not disappointed her."

The prince shook his head. "The emperor heard of Yi's order. He was displeased that she would contradict him. He told her to leave the matter of your feet alone."

"I hope I have not caused strife between the emperor and Concubine Yi," I said.

"Don't worry about her," he said. "But if anyone tries to hurt you or cause you problems, I want you to tell me."

My heart jumped again and I could feel my cheeks go hot. "Why do you care?" I asked.

The prince smiled and pinched my nose. "You are a little fool, you know that?"

I smiled and walked away, afraid Imperial Concubine Yi would miss me. After the initial excitement wore off, I realized that this was not the first time he had tried to warn me about something. He had also mentioned dangers at court while we were on the road from Hunan. What was he trying to tell me?

*E*ven though life was pleasant in the inner court, we knew a storm was brewing. It was not our place to comment on such things, but it was clear that China was on the edge of war. The generals and ministers were warning of it when we attended the audiences and hardly a day went by that someone did not hear gossip regarding the foreigners at our gates. Some people whispered that the emperor could not fight the Westerners because he was still also fighting the Taiping. He wasn't building a navy because his army was being drained in the south.

The emperor was under constant stress. He rarely sent for Imperial Concubine Yi, or any of his consorts, because he was always too busy or too tired. There were also concerns about his health, but it could be considered treasonous to speculate about the health of the emperor, so we refrained from talking about such things with Concubine Yi. It was clear that she was worried. She loved to laugh and joke and have fun, but there were moments when she would sit in her chair and her mind would wander. She would go very quiet, her brow would furrow, and her eyes would stare off into the distance.

Prince Gong and I still saw each other occasionally. Usually after audiences, but sometimes he would sneak into the inner court and catch my attention. He would tease me and touch my cheeks or my chin, but he never tried to kiss me or touch my body. I began to want him to, though. I had no idea how to initiate such a thing, but I began to fantasize about us being together, embracing, our lips touching, his hands all over me.

One day, one of Imperial Concubine Yi's ladies, Lady Yun, asked me about the prince, quite by surprise. "Yaqian," she started as she pulled a chair up next to me as I was working on my embroidery, "is it true that you rode through the countryside for many weeks with Prince Gong before you arrived here?"

I tried to keep my cheeks from going pink by keeping my face down, focused on my work, but I am sure I failed. "Yes. He escorted me from my school in Changsha to the palace. The trip took many weeks."

"Did you get to know him very well?" she asked.

"We chatted a bit, sometimes," I replied. "But it was hard to talk while riding on horses on those bumpy roads."

"What was he like?" she asked.

"He was always very polite. I didn't know how to ride a

horse at first, so he taught me. He always made sure I wasn't lagging too far behind and that the other men were respectful to me."

"He sounds very gallant," she said, beaming.

"I don't really know," I said. "I haven't known many men in my life to compare him to. Why do you ask?"

"Well, I heard that his mother is pressuring him to take another wife. He only has one son and two daughters. And the emperor only has one son as well. The dowager consort wants him to have more sons," she explained.

At this point, I glanced around and noticed that all the women were looking at us, listening to our conversation, including Imperial Concubine Yi.

"This may sound like a stupid question," I said to Lady Yun, "but are you allowed to marry? You don't have to stay here and serve Mistress Yi?"

The women all giggled.

"It's not a life sentence," Imperial Concubine Yi replied, followed by a round of laughter from all the ladies.

"Forgive me," I said. "I am still learning how things work here."

"These women are all princesses and the best courtiers in the land. I can't keep them to myself forever," Imperial Concubine Yi explained. "They serve me for a few years, and then I make marriage matches for them."

"What about me?" I asked. "You won't send me away, will you?"

She seemed to ponder this for a moment. "You don't want to marry?" she asked.

"It was never part of my plan," I explained. "I guess I always knew that I would have to marry someday, but I wanted to become a master needleworker. That requires all my focus, all my attention. I never planned to do anything else. I don't know anything about cooking or children. When I came into your service, I assumed it would be for the rest of my life."

Concubine Yi nodded. "Some artisans, my opera singers and the court painters for instance, are devoted fully to their art. That is a noble cause. But life is long, Yaqian. At least it should be. You never know what will happen."

I thought about this for a moment. As much as I enjoyed my little secret meetings with Prince Gong, and I could feel my desire for him growing, would I really want to give up my work to be with him? Would I want to become a wife, sheltered away in a little house in service to one man for the rest of my days? Would I prefer that to a life in a palace with the consort of the emperor improving my embroidery techniques? I knew I would not.

"Are you considering a match between Lady Yun and Prince Gong?" I asked Concubine Yi.

"Maybe," she replied. "But I am sure his mother already has her own candidates in mind."

"Where is the dowager consort?" I asked. "I don't think I have met her."

"Over on the other side of the inner court there is a special palace and temple just for the wives and concubines of former emperors."

"Then you should pay her a visit," I said to Lady Yun. "Why are you asking me about him? If you are thinking of marrying him, don't you already know him?"

"When would I have the chance?" she asked. "He rarely comes back here. He technically isn't allowed, though I have seen him a couple of times. When he brought you here, for example."

"Why are no men allowed back here?" I asked, rather stupidly. "I mean, why are the eunuchs allowed here but not someone like Prince Gong? Are they not all men? And Prince Gong is family..."

I was interrupted by an eruption of laughter from all the women. One of them even fell off her stool and I think Concubine Yi was crying from laughing so hard. My face went hot.

"The eunuchs are not 'men'," one of the other ladies said.

"At least not like Prince Gong," another one piped up.

"At least Lady Yun hopes not," another one quipped to another round of laughter.

"Yaqian," Lady Yun said when she composed herself. "Do you really not know?"

I shook my head, too embarrassed to speak. I was trying not to cry, I was so mortified.

"The eunuchs are not really men because they have been cut. Do you understand?"

I was moved by the fact that Lady Yun was trying to explain this to me instead of embarrassing me further. "No," I said. "I really don't. I wasn't raised around men. We had a couple of guards by the front gate of our school, but they were never allowed inside. They lived and ate elsewhere. I last saw my cousins when I was six years old. I wasn't taught anything about marriage or children. My life had a singular focus – to become the best embroidery girl in the country. That is really all I know."

At this, the girls stopped laughing and sat in awe. They were all raised to be wives and mothers. I think that until they met me, they never considered that there might be another path in life for a woman.

"Well, men and women are different," Lady Yun explained. "They are made for each other. In your...umm... secret area there are holes. And men, in their secret area, have something like a pole to fit into a woman's holes. Eunuchs don't have their pole anymore. They cut it off when they are children."

"They cut it off?" I asked, horrified. I then remembered Prince Gong remarking that Eunuch Shun had "cut off his balls." I didn't know what he meant at the time.

"Imagine cutting off your own leg, Yaqian," one of the other ladies spoke up. "It would be like that."

"For some men it would only be like cutting off a finger," one of the other ladies said, followed by a chorus of laughter.

I looked out into the yard at some of the eunuchs who were walking by or talking to each other. One was sweeping the walkway that led up to our porch.

"That sounds terrible," I said. "Do they cut it off themselves?"

"No," Lady Yun said. "Their fathers do it. Or sometimes an older eunuch."

"But there are thousands of eunuchs here in the Forbidden City," I said. "All of them have done this? It is so common?"

"More than that," Imperial Concubine Yi said. "Do you know how many castrated men apply to be palace eunuchs every year? Thousands. Do you know how many we take into service? Only a few, because once a palace eunuch is appointed, they usually serve for life. So countless families cut their little boys in the hope that they will one day serve in the imperial city, but many never do. So some become scholars, join temples, or work for other noble families that can afford their service."

"This sounds like a horrid practice," I said. "Why would they do that?"

"It is a protection for us and the emperor," Imperial

Concubine Yi explained. "The emperor must be the only man in his house. It is only he who can plant seeds among the flowers."

"But why cut men?" I asked. "If he doesn't want more men in the palace, then why not just hire more women? Women could do the jobs that eunuchs do."

"Oh no," one of the other girls explained. "The eunuchs have to be men. They are well educated in math and science and the military. They have to organize the palace and keep everything running smoothly."

"Maybe women could be trained in those jobs," I said.

"Don't be ridiculous," one of the ladies said. "Men and women all serve different functions, you know that. Men can't embroider. Women can't be soldiers."

"What about Hua Mulan?" I asked. The Flower Mulan was a story all young women knew, even if being a warrior wasn't something we were supposed to strive for. "Or... wasn't there a Manchu warrior woman? Mongyu...Mongey-isu! If women can learn to fight, I am sure a man with delicate fingers could learn to embroider."

"Surely they could not, Yaqian," Imperial Concubine Yi said. "Doing so would upset the natural order of the world." She stood. "I am tired of this conversation. I am going to lay down."

The other women all put down whatever they were working on and followed Concubine Yi into her bedroom. I sat by the door and looked out at the eunuchs working or passing by. I was so grateful to be a woman.

*I*t took me two months complete that first chaopao for Imperial Concubine Yi. She was very impatient for it, checking my progress every day. But when it was done, and she saw the two robes side by side, she was amazed at the difference. She said the flowers on my robe looked so real she wanted to reach out and pluck them. She honored me by giving me a larger, better-placed bedroom and increased my allowance. But she was dismayed at how long it took me to complete the robe.

"Art takes time, My Lady," I explained. "You watched me. I didn't slack. I worked every day."

She nodded but sighed with disappointment. "I suppose you cannot embroider all my clothes for me?"

I nearly laughed. "No, My Lady. Not if you want me to improve my skills and work on other projects. But if you know of a special event coming up and need an exquisite gown made for it, with enough notice I can make you the most splendid robes."

"That's true," she said. "Someday my son will marry. I would need the most beautiful gown in all the land for an event such as that."

"Of course, My Lady," I said with a bow.

She sat on her little throne in her sitting room and motioned for me to sit near her. "I truly admire the work you do, Yaqian. My husband knows me very well and knew I would appreciate your work. When I was a little girl..." She paused when we heard sighs from some of the girls across the room. Concubine Yi shot them a sharp look and they quickly hid their faces. I think they had heard this story Concubine Yi was about to tell me many times before.

"When I was a little girl," she began again, "my grandfather was an honorable Manchu bannerman. We were privileged children in a privileged home. I was the eldest. But one day, the Daoguang Emperor realized that some palace officials had been stealing from the palace coffers. The theft was so severe, the court was nearly bankrupt! He had no idea who had done it, and most likely many men had been stealing for years, so the emperor decided to punish *all* the nobles in the land. All of the heads of the Manchu families were ordered to pay a large amount of money to the Throne."

"That sounds quite harsh," I replied.

"It was," she said. "Many families were ruined and never recovered. My grandfather died from the stress and disgrace. But he only passed the debt on to my father. My father worked very hard to scrape together the money. We sold everything. Eventually, I was able to help by selling my embroidery work. I worked by the light of day and the fire of night to make as many pairs of embroidered and embellished Manchu pot-bottomed shoes as I could to sell. My work was highly sought after and I commanded a good price. Eventually, by pulling together, my family was able to pay off the debt. I no longer had to sell my shoes to survive, but I enjoyed the work. A few years later, I was ordered to appear before the Xianfeng Emperor for his selection of the royal consorts and I was chosen. Now I'll never have to worry about money again."

I was nearly in tears after she finished her story. "My Lady, I never imagined that someone so illustrious as you would understand the plight of the common people. I also made shoes for many years to support my family. And now I am so blessed to be here by your side."

Concubine Yi was quite pleased with my reaction, and after that day, I learned many things about her life both before and during her years at the palace. Likewise, she was very interested in what life was like for me in the interior of the country. I enjoyed our chats and I would like to say that Imperial Concubine Yi and I became good friends, but that would be quite presumptuous of me.

After that, Concubine Yi gave me almost total freedom. I was allowed to work on my art or create special pieces for her. I could sit with her in her main hall or outside in the gardens. I was quite spoiled, quite comfortable, and quite happy.

I exchanged letters with some of the girls from Lady Tang's school. Imperial Concubine Yi, Empress Zhen, and the emperor were all pleased with my work, and they showered honor on Lady Tang's school. Several of the girls were requested for the imperial embroidery studios in Suzhou.

To my surprise, Wensong was one of them. Apparently her betrothed had been killed in a battle and she begged to not be promised to another man. She wanted to do more with her life, so her family agreed to send her away. Some of the other girls had also come to Peking to serve in royal households. The value of works produced by Lady Tang and her girls grew exponentially. I was glad that so many people were able to benefit from my good fortune.

*M*y first spring in the Forbidden City was an especially memorable time for me. On the third day of the third month, which was only three days before my seventeenth birthday and the beginning of the silkworm-rearing season, Imperial Concubine Yi led all of her ladies in a ceremony to praise the Silkworm Goddess, Can-nü. She led us to a special shrine, hidden in a rear garden surrounded by a koi pond and shaded by trellised plants, dedicated to Can-nü where we burned incense and begged her to protect her precious silkworms. We then were all carried in a caravan of sedan chairs to the nearby imperial mulberry farm where we helped collect cocoons and fed the living worms. I showed Concubine Yi and the other ladies how to tell a high-quality cocoon from one that was poorly colored or damaged.

This ceremony was my favorite annual event and I knew I would look forward to it every year. The shrine to Can-nü became my favorite spot in all of the Forbidden City, and I would return to it as often as I could.

One day I was sitting in a pavilion in the imperial garden watching the peacocks and practicing my double-sided embroidery when who should approach me but the emperor himself! I was so surprised I dropped my work as I dropped to my knees. The emperor laughed at me.

"You don't have to do that," he said. "Just a bow at the waist is enough when we meet casually like this."

I stood up but remained bent at the waist. The emperor laughed again and bent over to pick up my embroidery hoop.

"Ah, peacocks," he said. He turned the piece over. "More peacocks! Wonderful!"

I smiled. "Thank you, Your Majesty."

He handed me the hoop. "Please stand upright. You are making me dizzy."

I stood and accepted the hoop from him, but I kept my eyes downcast.

"Will you walk with me?" he asked.

I nodded, but thought it was awfully strange that he

would want my company. We walked in silence for a moment around the garden. He appeared to be going nowhere in particular. He was being followed by no less than ten attendants.

"Are you happy here, Yaqian?" he finally asked.

"Oh, yes, Your Majesty!" I exclaimed. "Ever so much. Imperial Concubine Yi is such a kind mistress, and the palace is exquisite. And I have all the supplies I need to improve my embroidery."

"I am glad of that," he said. "Your skills bring honor to the court."

I blushed. "Your Majesty is much too kind to me."

"Not at all," he said. We followed a few more little paths. I noticed some of his attendants seemed to have slipped away. I wondered if they were using his distraction as a chance to escape for a while.

"Can you embroider anything?" he asked.

"Very nearly, but not quite," I explained. "I am still improving my technique. Running water, such as a water-fall, still gives me trouble, and humans, like a woman's face, always look like furry animals to me, but I am confident that one day anything you see will be able to come to life under my needle."

"That is exquisite," he said.

We came to a small grotto, an area covered by lattice that had ivy and wisteria dangling from them. A pond filled with koi flowed through the middle. There were stone benches to sit on and marble pillars holding up the lattice. None of the emperor's attendants had followed us inside, and I felt a heaviness in the pit of my stomach.

The emperor called me to his side as he stood at the edge of the pond and looked at the fish. I did so, but stood a couple of steps away from him. He then turned to me. I kept staring at the fish, which were swimming more frantically now, hoping I would toss them some treats.

"Yaqian," the emperor said softly. "Look at me."

I didn't want to. It was forbidden for a woman, any woman, even his consorts, to look directly at him. My heart beat fast and it was hard to breathe. He reached out and lifted my chin. He leaned in, and I quickly shook my head from his hand and stepped back.

"Please, Your Majesty," I said. "Forgive me. I should never have taken up so much of your time."

"What?" he asked, reaching out and lightly gripping my arm. "You have done nothing wrong. I invited you to walk with me, remember?"

"Yes, but I should have refused," I said. "I am a lowly servant and you are the emperor. I should not even be in your presence."

He laughed as he gripped both of my arms and pulled me close to him. He wrapped his arms around me, but I didn't hug him back.

"I can make you much more than a servant," he whispered in my ear. He ran his hands down my sides and around my buttocks.

I gasped. No man had ever touched me in such a way before. And what did he mean he could make me more than a servant? I pushed his arms away and stepped back.

"Please, Your Majesty," I said again. "I'm just an ignorant peasant, and I have no idea what you mean, but I am very happy in my position. I love Imperial Concubine Yi."

"I love her too," he said. "But you know how things are here. I have to spread my...my essence around."

"Yes," I said. "Among your wives and concubines. Among your Manchu women. I am a lowly Chinese. You should not speak to me, much less touch me."

"I am the emperor," he said, loudly, becoming annoyed with me. "I do what I want. And I want you."

"I cannot!" I said. "I serve Imperial Concubine Yi. I would be betraying my mistress if I were to lay with her husband."

"Where would you get an idea like that?" he asked.

"I...I don't know..." I stammered. I knew the emperor could lay with any woman he wished, but I didn't want one of those women to be me. I would never say it out loud, but the Limping Dragon was not the kind of man I wanted to give myself to, even if he was the emperor.

"It just seems wrong," I said. I started to cry. I felt like an idiot, blabbering like a child because the Emperor of China wanted to take me as a lover. I wasn't lying when I said I loved Concubine Yi. She was very good to me and I was happy in her service. I was more worried about hurting her than upsetting the emperor.

"How can you be so..." the emperor started, but he was interrupted by one of his attendants who had silently entered the grotto.

"Excuse me, Your Majesty, but we must head back. The council is waiting."

The emperor sighed. He looked at me as if he wanted to say something, but then he just stormed off. I leaned against one of the pillars and wiped the tears from my face. On one hand, I felt relieved, but on the other, did I just make an enemy of the emperor?

I ran back to my room and locked the door. I didn't want anyone to see me while I was upset, and I feared I would be upset for a while.

A little while later, there was a soft knock at my door. It was Lady Yun.

"Imperial Concubine Yi sent me to fetch you," she said.

"Why?" I asked. "I cannot see her like this."

"She already knows what happened," Lady Yun said.

"How?" I asked. "Who told her?"

"You are never alone here, Yaqian," she said. "Come, wipe your tears. You must go."

I washed my face, but there was nothing I could do about my red-rimmed eyes. When I entered Concubine Yi's audience hall, she dismissed all of the other attendants and motioned for me to sit near her. From one of the pockets in her sleeve, she pulled out the embroidery hoop I had been working on. I dropped it when His Majesty grabbed my arms and had forgotten it when I fled to my room.

"I heard what happened," she said, handing me the hoop.

"Forgive me," I said. "I never meant to hurt you. I am sorry I stole his attention."

Concubine Yi let out a small laugh. "Stole his attention? Dear, we both know you did no such thing. You haven't even seen him since you first arrived except at audiences. But he hasn't been able to stop thinking about you since that first meeting," she told me. "You see, us Manchu claim to hate the bound feet of you Han. We call it a barbaric, antiquated practice performed by uneducated people. But the truth is that Manchu men love it just as much as Han."

"I don't understand," I said. "What do our bound feet have to do with any man?" I asked. "I was just told it was what we had to do to have a better life. It was part of being a woman."

Imperial Concubine Yi gave me a confused look and shook her head. "Sometimes you really are stupid, Yaqian."

I nodded.

"The reason your feet are bound has nothing to do with you or women or growing up. Men believe that by binding your feet, it forces you to walk in a way that tightens your... the muscles in your..." she sighed, as though annoyed with her inability, even in this personal setting, to speak freely. "They think it makes you a better lover. They also think that you can use your tiny feet to pleasure them."

I couldn't believe what I was hearing, and I couldn't believe that the wife of the emperor was having to explain this to me.

"We Manchu don't do this," she went on. "But our men still desire it. That is why they make us walk on the flowerpot bottom shoes, to create the same effect. But they don't think it works as well, so they still take Chinese women to their beds."

"You mean...the emperor...?" I couldn't quite ask.

She nodded. "He loves the little feet of Chinese girls," she whispered. "I know he has Chinese prostitutes brought to the palace in secret."

"I am so sorry," I said.

"It was why he brought you here," she said.

"What?" I asked.

"Well, he did like your embroidery. He thought it was interesting and he does collect art, but it wasn't until he realized you were from Changsha that he considered bringing you here. He knew most women in Changsha were Han, so you would likely have bound feet."

"But you said he has women here already. Why go to such trouble?"

"The chicken girls are trouble. Sneaking them in and out. Riddled with diseases. Having to pay for their silence. But with you, having you here in the palace at his beck and call? Much easier."

"Couldn't he just bring any Han woman into the palace, make her a maid and have her near? I don't understand."

"It's not that easy," she said. "Have you ever seen another Han woman in the Forbidden City since you arrived?" I shook my head. "Exactly. You have to be Manchu to serve here. From the empress to the lowest *gōngnǚ*, you must be Manchu. You have to be quite exceptional to be a Han and be allowed to serve here."

"So, my embroidery was exceptional enough," I said.

"Exactly," Concubine Yi said. "He wanted you for your feet – your embroidery just gave him the excuse."

"So, what am I to do?" I asked. "I don't want to be with him. I don't want to betray you. I just want to be a master needleworker in your service."

"You won't betray me," she said. "That is how things are here. All of the women in the Forbidden City are at his service, no matter what he asks."

"But I don't want to..." I said.

"Why not?" she asked. "I was younger than you when I was selected to serve the emperor. When he approaches you again, just do it."

My heart sank. Is this what Prince Gong had been trying to warn me about? What would the prince think when he heard his brother had taken me for a lover?

It was only a few days later when I was approached again. Eunuch Shun, the first person who I had met when I arrived at the Forbidden City, the man who had tried to swindle me out of my coins, came to my rooms and announced, "His Imperial Highness requests your presence tonight. I will return this evening to collect you."

Shortly afterward, an elderly maid arrived and helped me bathe, wrap my feet in new bindings, and dress. The bath was exquisite. The water was scalding hot and she used the sweetest smelling salts. She scrubbed my skin until it was pink and then rubbed me with cool goat milk before rinsing me with jasmine scented water one last time. She then rubbed my whole body with jasmine scented oils. She wrapped me in a silk robe, bound my feet with new silk bindings, and helped me put on a new pair of embroidered slippers. She combed and oiled my hair, but let it stay down, flowing freely. Apparently, that was how the emperor liked it.

Just after dusk, a sedan chair arrived for me. I climbed into it and held my breath for almost the entire ride to the emperor's quarters. I remembered the chicken girls who accompanied Prince Gong's troops when he came to collect me in Changsha. Was I now any different from those girls? Going to the bed of a man I didn't care for in order to not lose my position? I knew that as my chair passed by the palaces of the wives and concubines, all the women of the inner court would know I was inside and where I was going. The thought made my stomach turn and made me feel ashamed. I wanted the floor of the chair to open up and swallow me.

The sedan chair came to a stop. Shun opened the curtains and helped me step out. He then led me up the stairs and into the emperor's palaces. I followed him through several rooms and down some hallways. It was like a maze. I was sure I would never be able to find my way out again on my own.

He finally took me to a bedroom and led me to the bed. He pulled back the gauze curtains and motioned for me to sit down. "Stay here," he commanded. Then he left.

I was examining a painting on the wall when I heard the door open again. The emperor entered with several attendants. The attendants helped him remove his headdress, his heavy outer robes, and his shoes. They brought him a bowl of water and a cloth so he could wash his hands and face. After he was done, they all bowed and backed out of the room.

The emperor walked over to the bed and smiled at me. "I am glad to see you again, Yaqian," he said kindly.

I slowly breathed out and said, "I am glad you are not angry with me, Your Majesty."

He laughed as he sat on the bed next to me. "No, silly girl. I know you are young, and I can be an imposing figure. Forgive me for startling you that day in the garden."

I only shook my head and averted my eyes.

He reached out and lifted my chin, as he had done in the garden. "Here, we need no such formalities," he said. "You are to look at me as a man, not an emperor."

"I don't think you could ever be less than you are," I said.

The emperor laughed again. "You are a clever girl." He placed his hand on my leg and I felt my cheeks go hot. "You are also a pleasing girl," he said.

"I don't think you will find much pleasure in me, Your Majesty," I barely whispered. I was so scared I could hardly talk. "I am just a stupid country girl."

The emperor ran his hand down my leg and lightly touched my foot. "Oh, I am sure you know enough," he said.

He stood up and waved me toward the head of the bed, where there were many pillows piled up. "Sit up against the headboard," he commanded.

I did so and he reclined long ways at my feet. He gently touched and petted my feet while still in their shoes.

"How old were you when they were bound?" he asked.

"I was only six," I said.

"I bet you were a sweet and delicate little girl," he said as he started to undo the ribbons around the top of one of my shoes.

I looked up at the bed's canopy. "Actually I was very naughty," I said. "My mother beat me regularly. When they wanted to bind my feet, I ran away and..."

"You dare contradict me?" he asked, slapping my foot.

I cried out in pain and instinctively pulled my feet away from him. Anger flashed in his eyes and he jumped up, lunged at me, and pulled one of my feet back toward him. "I am the emperor!" he yelled. "You will still respect me!"

I wanted to point out that he had told me to treat him like any other man, but I bit my tongue. He motioned for me to stretch my other leg back out and he lay at my feet again.

"I forget you have not been with a man before," he said. "You are still an innocent, though you have a feisty streak in you."

I sighed, relieved that he was not angry anymore.

He resumed undoing the ribbons around my shoes. He removed both of the shoes and sniffed them. Since I had just bathed and washed my feet, I suppose they smelled of jasmine and not of rotting flesh as they sometimes did if I went too long without washing my feet. He then looked at the images on the shoes.

"You embroidered these yourself?" he asked.

"Yes," I replied simply.

"Your skills have greatly improved," he said. "The pieces you sent to celebrate the birth of my son, they were not very good, you know."

"I know," I said.

"They were obviously the work of an amateur," he went on.

"Obviously," I agreed.

"Except for the double-sided piece. If it had been a one-sided piece, it also would not have been counted among the works of masters, but I could tell it was special when I saw the other side."

"Your Majesty has a keen eye for art," I said.

He laid the shoes aside and shrugged. "It is just womanly art," he said. "It will not stand the test of time like a painting or poetry, but it is aesthetically pleasing."

"I have embroidered poems by women," I said. "I could recite them for you."

He shook his head as he ran his fingers up and down my still bound feet. At one point, he bumped my big toe on my left foot and I flinched. "Does it hurt?" he asked.

I nodded. "They always hurt at least a little bit," I said.

He started to undo the silk bindings around one of my feet. "Do they hurt less when the bindings are removed?" he asked.

"Yes," I said.

He untied the ribbons and then quickly unfurled the silk bands from my feet. I was quite embarrassed. Bound feet were considered the most intimate part of a woman's body. We kept them hidden inside tiny shoes and behind long skirts and pants. Even in erotic paintings of naked men and women, the women still wore their shoes. Even though I was still wearing my robe, I felt completely bare before him. This was the sort of intimacy usually shared between a husband and wife. I wasn't sure why it was this way. I did not receive any pleasure from his enjoyment of my feet. Indeed, whenever I saw Prince Gong, I felt tingling and butterflies in a completely different part of my body. Feelings I didn't have for the emperor. Would Prince Gong want to enjoy my feet in this way as well? I hoped not. Not that I would ever have such an opportunity with the prince, but I could still dream.

I was so lost in my thoughts of Prince Gong I had almost forgotten that the emperor was still playing with my feet. It wasn't until I felt the cold wetness of his tongue on my toes that I was brought back to the moment. I wrinkled my nose as I watched him and tried not to flinch. He kissed the arches of my feet and caressed my ankles. He didn't look at me. He didn't ask how I was feeling or what I wanted. He had no interest in me aside from my feet. Did he make Concubine Yi feel this worthless?

The emperor then sat up and opened his robe. For the first time, I saw a naked man, and he was fully aroused. He was breathing heavily. "Do you know what to do?" he asked. I shook my head. He sighed, annoyed. "They should teach you what to do when they bind you. Otherwise, what is the point?" I couldn't argue with him. I had been wondering why we had our feet bound my whole life. If this was the reason why, it was truly disgusting.

The emperor took hold of my ankle and touched the big toe of my foot to his member. He groaned as he ran my toe up and down the shaft. "Keep doing that," he whispered as he let go of my foot. He leaned back a bit and moaned as I touched him. I couldn't believe he was getting pleasure from being touched with my feet, but I was a bit jealous. I wished Prince Gong would touch me in all kinds of ways.

The emperor then took hold of both of my ankles and bent my knees so that my feet came together at about the height of his waist and formed a small opening between the arches. My robe fell open and with my legs akimbo I could not cover myself. I tried not to think about the fact that he could see my private area on display. But the emperor did not seem interested in that part of my body. He ran his fingers around the arches of my feet. "Whoever bound your feet did a good job," he said. "They are a little big. I have had women with feet half your size, but your arches are very well formed and your toes have not fallen off."

"Thank you," I whispered, unsure of what else to say. I am sure that he would not appreciate talk of how Mother beat me to force me to let her bind them. Or of how the pain was so excruciating during those first few weeks I vomited on regular occasion. It seemed to me that the emperor lived in a fantasy. He licked the arches of my feet with no thought to what I endured in order for him to receive such perverse pleasure.

He then put his member into the hole formed by my arches. He moved himself in and out of the hole, slowly at first, and then faster. He griped my feet firmly, which hurt, but I did my best not to cry out. He went faster and grabbed my feet harder. He was forcing the hole my feet formed smaller and smaller, holding my feet tighter and squeezing them together. He groaned and grunted as he slammed my feet into his pelvis with each thrust. I leaned back and stared at the canopy while I gripped the bedding and tried not to scream out in pain. Tears began streaming down my face. I finally could no longer bite my lip hard enough to keep from begging him to stop. But my pain seemed to arouse him further and he yelled as he finally achieved satisfaction. I felt warm goo drip onto my feet.

The emperor then got off the bed and wrapped his robe around himself. He poured himself a cup of wine. I simply laid there on the bed in shock from what had just happened. My feet were throbbing and I was scared to move.

"Shun!" the emperor called out.

Shun emerged from a corner of the room. I didn't even realize he had been there the whole time. Shun approached the emperor and then kneeled.

"Take her back and then clean this up so I can retire," the emperor commanded.

Shun nodded. He brought a damp, warm cloth over and wiped my feet. He then took my hand and helped me from the bed. He collected my silk bindings but not my shoes. I reached for them, but he stopped me. "No," he said. "His Majesty will keep those."

The one time I had tried walking without shoes or bindings was painful enough. But trying to walk without the bindings and after the beating they had just taken was like walking on hot coals. I leaned on Shun as I tried to walk on my heels out of the room. Once we exited His Majesty's presence, however, I could no longer pretend to be strong. My legs collapsed under me and Shun picked me up. He was surprisingly strong. He carried me back through the emperor's palace to the waiting sedan chair. We were both silent as we rode back to my quarters.

When we arrived, he carried me inside. The maid who had helped me earlier was waiting for me. Shun put me in a chair and the maid rushed over with a small tub of hot water. As I felt the warmth of the water rush over my battered feet and surge through my body, I finally felt free enough to cry. I cried so hard I could not stop. The pain, the embarrassment, the shock of what I had learned about men that night was more than I could handle. I knew that Shun was waiting for a gift of coins from me. I motioned to a small table beside my bed. Shun opened it and brought me my coin purse. I reached in and pulled out several coins. I watched his face as I handed them to him.

"This is for your service tonight," I said. His eyes lit up, so I knew I had paid him enough. He turned to leave, but I grabbed his sleeve. I pulled out more coins and placed them into his hand. "And this is to make sure it never happens again," I said.

Shun nodded his understanding. While the emperor could demand my presence again, it was Shun who usually kept the emperor's conjugal calendar. If one of the emperor's women wanted a night with him, it was Shun who made the arrangements. Shun could encourage or discourage the emperor to sleep with certain women on certain nights, usually by lying about who was in her moon phase. Hopefully, Shun would do his best to dissuade the emperor from wanting to fondle my feet again.

a few days later, I saw Prince Gong walking through the inner court. I didn't want to see him. I was too ashamed. As I gathered my things to leave, though, he approached me. At first neither of us said anything. Eventually my emotions got the better of me and I began to cry. He pulled me to him and held me in his arms.

"Why didn't you warn me?" I asked.

"I wanted to," he said. "I didn't know how. I'm sorry I couldn't protect you."

."I feel so worthless," I said. "I thought I was being honored by being brought here. I was the greatest embroidery girl in China. But I am nothing, nothing but a chicken girl!"

"No," he said looking at me. "You are not worthless. You are wonderful. Smart and beautiful and so talented! This is...this situation is nothing. Life will go on and one day we can forget it ever happened."

"We?" I asked. "What are we? What are we doing? You have a wife, two wives! I am friends with Lady Yun."

"That is just my duty as a prince," he said. "I don't have any feelings for her, for them."

"You should," I said. "You should do right by them. Lady Yun loves you."

"I know," he said. "She is a good woman. Perhaps if I had never met you..."

I shook my head. "What now?" I asked. "What if the emperor sends for me again? I couldn't bear it."

"I don't think he will," he said. "The emperor has no time for women right now. The British attacked the Dagu Forts. We are at war with them and their allies, the Americans, the French. And we are still trying to hold the Taiping at bay. A revolt by the Miao people broke out in Guizhou, west of Hunan. The Hui minority in the southern province of Yunnan are inciting people there to revolt as well. The emperor's country is rotting from the inside."

ELEVEN

THE FORBIDDEN CITY, 1860

There was a knock at my door. It was still early, but the sun was just peeking over the tops of the trees. I wrapped myself in a blanket and cracked open the door. I was shocked awake when I saw Prince Gong standing there. I ran my fingers through my hair and rubbed my eyes. I quickly bowed.

"Dress, quickly," he said as he pushed his way into my tiny room. "Something dark and simple."

"Why?" I asked as I went to my trunk. "What is happening?"

"I need your help. My brother has imprisoned several diplomats underneath the Ministry of Punishments. They are being tortured. If they die..." he looked at me. "...The revenge of the English will be very great."

He turned away as I removed my sleeping robe and wrapped myself in a black garment. He handed me a metal file.

"Sheathe that close to your foot. The guards won't dare go near your feet."

I sat down on the bed and wrapped the file in gauze

around my ankle. "Guards? What do you mean? What am I to do?"

"Come on," he said opening the door. "We are going to rescue the prisoners."

Prince Gong had a palanquin waiting for us. We climbed inside it and closed the curtains so no one could see who was inside. On the way to the Ministry of Punishment, Prince Gong quickly explained what was happening. The emperor had been at constant war with the Western powers for years. After the English had seized the Dagu Forts outside of Peking, the emperor had signed a peace treaty with them. A year later, the emperor was supposed to allow a European delegation to come to Peking to formalize the treaty and allow more trade ports to open, but the emperor refused. The Westerners attacked, but the Chinese army, to the surprise of all, repelled the Western invasion. But in the year since, China had not built up its army enough. A combined force of British and French forces had returned, and the emperor could not fight them. The European forces did not invade the city, though. Instead, they sent an envoy of twenty men, headed by a man named Harry Parkes, under a flag of truce to negotiate. However, the emperor seized the men, threw them into the Ministry of Punishments, and had them beaten and tightly bound.

"Some of the emperor's advisors, including General Sushun, have advised my brother to kill the men. But if we do that, the British will attack and show no mercy. We didn't take the men in battle as rightful prizes, they were kidnapped from under a flag of truce! The British believe my brother can no longer be trusted. We have to save the men, make sure they don't die, as an act of good faith. I might still be able to undo the damage those wicked advisors have done."

"Your brother won't listen to you?" I asked.

Prince Gong looked pained. "My brother and I are not as close as we once were. We are at ideological odds. He thinks that my desire to work with the Westerners is a betrayal. But I am only trying to save his kingdom!"

"Betrayal?" I asked. "Is what we are doing treason?"

The prince looked at me with stern eyes. "I am asking you to risk your life, Yaqian, but it is the only way I know to save China."

My heart beat hard in my chest. I was terrified, but I knew that I would be willing to do whatever Prince Gong asked of me. I trusted him far more than I should. But I trusted him more than the emperor, so his decision had to be better than letting the men die if that is what the emperor wanted.

"Tell me what to do," I said.

he prince and I arrived first at the palace kitchens. The prince stayed hidden in the palanquin as I went in and asked a portly woman with a greasy face for a large kettle of beef broth and a small bowl. I told her it was for Imperial Concubine Yi. The woman seemed to doubt me, but when she saw the palanquin, she knew I must be there on important business. After only a few minutes, I climbed back into the palanquin with my ill-gotten broth.

The Ministry of Punishments was a small, dark building at the far southwest corner of the Forbidden City. When we arrived, the prince peeked out first to make sure no one was watching – even though someone was always watching. The prince had given me a piece of white linen to wrap my hair in. Between that and the black robe, I looked like a plain palace servant. The only thing that gave me away was my gait because of my bound feet. We entered a small side door carrying the kettle and bowl.

The emperor had ordered that the men only be given a small cup of weak tea every day. The prince feared that if the torture didn't kill the men, starvation and dehydration would.

We came to a dark stairwell, and I carefully descended the stairs, balancing on my tiny feet as I carried the large kettle, as the prince instructed me, and he waited above. At the bottom of the stairs was a long dark hallway leading to a door guarded by a single man. I felt a drop of water drip on my forehead. I could hear the squeaks of rats. There was no natural light down here, only torches. I would never have guessed that such a dark and frightening place existed within the walls of the Forbidden City.

The guard watched me as I carefully walked toward him.

"Never seen you here before," he grumbled.

I didn't reply. I kept my head down.

"Hold out your arms," he ordered.

"What?" I asked.

"I have to pat you down. Make sure you don't have any weapons."

I put down the kettle and held out my arms. He slid his huge hands from my wrists to my shoulders and touched my breasts on his way to my waist. He slowly ran his hands over my hips and buttocks and thighs. I stepped back before he could go any lower.

"That's enough of that," I said, picking up my kettle.

"I didn't check your lower legs," he said.

I looked at him with shock and disgust. "How dare you! My feet are sacred. No man save my future husband is allowed to go anywhere near them."

He scoffed. "Chinese..." he mumbled as he reached for his keys. He unlocked the door and let me in.

As I stepped into the room, the smell slapped me in the face. The room reeked of excrement, urine, decay, and death.

Prince Gong had told me there should have been close to forty men in the dungeon, but I only counted eighteen men lying on the floor, and they all started groaning as I entered. Some of the men were not moving, so they most likely were dead or very nearly were. Their bodies were so contorted, I would not have known they were men. They were all bound with their arms behind them as tightly as possible and their legs bent back, nearly tied to their hands. This kind of torture was known as *kao-niu* and was meant to prolong a victim's pain for as long as possible. Every day, water would be poured on the men's bonds so they would tighten a little bit each day.

I bent down beside one of the men to pour him some broth and got a better look at his hands. They were the most horrid things I have ever seen. They were crushed by the bonds and were green and black in color. Yellow pus was dripping from them. It reminded me of when my feet were crushed and reshaped during my binding years, only this was much worse. I had to hide my face in my sleeve for a moment to keep from gagging from the smell.

"Hurry up, girl!" the guard yelled, causing me to jump.

"Sorry," I said. "Forgive me." I poured some of the broth into the bowl and held it to the mouth of one of the men. He eagerly slurped the soup. I did my best to help hold his head up so he wouldn't waste any. The men started crying and calling to me. I looked around and began to worry I wouldn't have enough broth for all of them. Worse, the guard was watching me so I couldn't do anything about their bonds.

"You there," I heard Prince Gong call out. The guard turned around. "I'm here to check on your prisoners."

The guard turned to him and explained the situation. I didn't bother trying to hear what they were saying, how the prince was distracting the guard; I needed to focus on the men.

"Parkes?" I whispered. "Harry Parkes?" Prince Gong had taught me the name of the leader of the British envoy during our ride over. He said to make sure Parkes was a priority.

"Here," one of the men softly groaned.

I picked up my things and went to his side. "Parkes?" I asked again. He nodded. I poured him a bowl of soup and helped him drink it.

"Thank you," he said, one of the few English phrases I knew, but I could not reply in English. I only nodded.

I checked to make sure the prince was still distracting the guard. The door had swung shut slightly without the guard there to hold it open, so I pulled the file out of its sheath at my ankle and used it to loosen some of the ropes. I couldn't completely cut them, that would be too suspicious, but I did loosen them enough so that the blood would flow again. Then I loosened some of the ropes that were holding his legs taut.

When Parkes realized what I was doing, he tried to tell me something else, but I didn't understand him.

"I don't understand, I'm sorry," I said to him in Chinese.

"Who are you?" he asked me in Chinese.

I was so shocked I could only ask him, "You speak Chinese?"

He nodded. "Please, tell Prince Gong we must be released. If we don't return, the British will attack. I have lost track of time, but they will attack any day. Warn him."

"I will," I reassured him.

He nodded and lowered his head, too exhausted to continue. I patted his shoulder and he grunted in pain. I realized that his arm had dislocated from his shoulder, but there was nothing I could do about that. I rushed to help the other men while I could.

I went around the room, feeding them and loosening their bonds. At least three of the men were dead.

"I'll come back and check tomorrow," I heard Prince Gong say, louder than normal. I sheathed my file just as the door opened and the guard returned.

"What are you doing?" his voice boomed. "Cooking them a ten-course meal? Get the hell out of here already."

I gathered my things and headed for the door. As I exited the Ministry of Punishments, I saw Prince Gong berating a woman who had arrived with a kettle, undoubtedly the woman tasked with giving the men their weak tea. She dropped her kettle and ran away in tears. I have no idea what he said to her, and I didn't care. I only wanted to get back into the palanquin and tell him what happened.

"You didn't tell me Parkes spoke Chinese," I said as soon as the Prince was in the palanquin.

"I didn't think you would have enough time to talk to him," the prince said.

"He told me the British are going to attack if they aren't released," I said.

"I know," he said. "That is why I am trying to save their lives, so I can get them released alive."

"He said they are going to attack any day, any moment!" I said.

The prince groaned and banged his fist against one of the palanquin's support beams. "That is too soon. The emperor will never release them in time. Minister Jin and General Sushun are working against me every step of the way."

"Then what are we to do?" I asked.

"I don't know," he replied.

By then, we had arrived back at my room. The prince helped me out of the palanquin. In the sunlight of morning, I was able to see just how filthy I was. I had been so caught up in the moment, helping the men and then warning Prince Gong, that I had forgotten the horrors that I had just witnessed. In the calm daylight, it all began rushing back to me.

"The men..." I started. The prince nodded, as if he understood how I felt. "Some of them were dead. Their hands..." I held my hand to my mouth to keep from crying. "Why?" I asked.

"For some men, cruelty is the only way they know how to deal with any situation," he replied.

"No," I said. "Why me? Why did I have to see that? Why did you need me to help you?"

"Because," he explained, "I needed a woman's help and you are small and inconspicuous. You have bound feet the guard wouldn't dare touch...and..."

"And?" I prodded.

"And because you are the only woman in this cursed city I can trust."

At that, the prince took my face in his hands and kissed me. Even though I smelled of fecal matter and rotting corpses. Even though my clothes and my hands were smeared with filth. Even though our minds were riddled with the thought of torture and we knew the British were going to launch an attack on the Son of Heaven, he kissed me. And I kissed him back. I wrapped my arms around him and held him tight. He moved his hands from my face to my waist and lifted me from the ground. It was my first kiss, and I suddenly realized why some women would leave the glorious service of the empress herself for a man. I would have left with him right there if we would have had anywhere to go and nothing else to do, but too much was at stake. He slowly lowered me to the ground and let me go. I pulled my lips from his and backed away.

"Pack your things," he said. "You may have to be ready to leave at a moment's notice."

I nodded. "Should I warn Imperial Concubine Yi? Or Empress Zhen? Or the other ladies?" I asked.

"No," he said. "Tell no one. No one must ever know you were involved in this. Remember, it is treason."

TWELVE

The sound of gentle thunder rumbled. We all stood in the central courtyard and watched as white clouds billowed in the distance. We all knew it was cannon fire, but there was nothing we could do.

The courtyard was the busiest I had ever seen it. No one could bear to be indoors, just waiting for news. All the wives and concubines came out of their palaces to watch the clouds and try to get any information about what was happening. Some of the attending ladies had been summoned home by their families. Many of the servants had fled. The eunuchs were rushing about, trying to pick up the slack and keep everything running as it should, but we all knew that nothing was as it should be. It was not a question of if we would flee, but when. But we could do nothing until we received official orders. We were supposed to simply act as if nothing was wrong, as if nothing was about to change. I could tell that Imperial Concubine Yi was frustrated. She no longer laughed or enjoyed the daily distractions of a life of leisure. She was a smart woman who knew there had to be a way to avoid the coming disaster, but she was not informed about what was happening nor was she consulted about what to do. She, like all the women of the Forbidden City, suffered in silence.

Finally, Prince Chun, a younger half-brother of the emperor and husband of Imperial Concubine Yi's sister, arrived at our gate. He told us to pack Concubine Yi's necessary household goods and be ready to leave within hours. This was a monumental task. To an imperial consort, nearly everything she owned was considered necessary. She also owned priceless silks, jewels, and art, all of which would be ripe for looting if they were left behind.

One trunk was only large enough to fit two or three of Imperial Concubine Yi's gowns, and she had hundreds of gowns. She did limit herself to only taking a few dozen, but that still resulted in a great many trunks. She also had hundreds of boxes of jewels, perfumes, lotions, undergarments, trinkets, gifts, and her furniture. It would take a hundred wagons just to move her things from the Forbidden City to the Summer Palace, Yuan Ming Yuan.

It seemed crazy, that we were running for our lives yet worried so much about clothes and jewels. But that is what life at the Forbidden City was like. Life was opulent and exuded luxury. Everything the imperial family did had to reflect that same opulence. It was expected. It also helped to calm the people, or so they believed. If everything carried on as normal as possible, then nothing could really be wrong. The way the court fled to the Summer Palace was the same way they would have traveled there when we were on holiday, everyone just had much less time to pack.

The emperor had nearly two dozen wives, concubines, and consorts by this time, not to mention the hundreds of retired consorts of the previous emperors who still lived in the palace, the princesses, and the imperial court ladies. Then, of course, was the emperor himself, whose trunks numbered more than I could count.

All that I owned still fit into the little trunk I had brought to the Forbidden City four years before.

By the time the emperor, Empress Zhen, Imperial Consort Yi, and Prince Zaichun reached Yuan Ming Yuan fifty-four li away at the head of the caravan, the last of the wagons were still inside the Forbidden City!

Since my arrival in Peking, the imperial family had not journeyed to the Summer Palace because of all the troubles the emperor was facing, so this was my first visit to what had to be the most magnificent palace in the world.

The Summer Palace, like the Forbidden City, was actually hundreds of buildings and palaces within one large walled compound. The Summer Palace was five times as large as the Forbidden City. There was so much space, and it was all so green. There were buildings, halls, pavilions, temples, galleries, gardens, lakes and ponds, and bridges. Everything was of the highest quality. Every room was full of the most beautiful furniture, art, wall hangings, clocks, and other items from all over China and the world, dating back hundreds and even thousands of years. There were libraries that held thousands of books and scrolls containing the knowledge and wisdom of every culture and era. If only I could have read even one of them! If we had been there for a leisurely holiday, it would have been such a treat to explore every inch of this magnificent place. There were even buildings built in the European style, designed by an Italian architect, filled with white and gold French furniture. I felt like I had been transported to another world while I was there. But there was nothing leisurely about our flight.

Not long after we arrived at Yuan Ming Yuan, the British and French forces overwhelmed Peking and captured the Forbidden City. They found Harry Parkes and his men and were horrified at what happened to them. Of the thirty-eight men who had arrived under a flag of truce with Parkes, twenty-one had died in the most horrible manner. The British were furious and, just as Prince Gong had warned, they vowed revenge.

Prince Gong had stayed in the Forbidden City to try and work with the British generals. They actually preferred Prince Gong to the emperor because Prince Gong was known to be reasonable and practical in his dealings with foreign powers. The British saw these as positive traits, but the emperor began to loathe his brother for them. Every day, Prince Gong rode his horse back and forth from the Forbidden City to the Summer Palace to try and work out a solution, any solution, but the emperor would not yield. He was incensed.

His inner circle of advisors told him wild tales of China's size and strength, of how the foreigners would never be able to overthrow the Son of Heaven. The emperor believed them, but he had no army or navy to call on. This should have made him realize that his advisors, led by his top general Sushun, were lying to him, but instead, he prayed. He, Empress Zhen, Imperial Consort Yi, the little prince, and the other consorts would visit temples and kneel to silent gods. They prayed for help. They prayed for a storm. They prayed for an earthquake. They prayed for a pestilence. They prayed for any miracle that would destroy the foreign forces. But no help came. Only Prince Gong with his pleas to the emperor to honor the past treaties with the

British and come to a new understanding came. But the emperor would not budge.

We had only been in the Summer Palace for a couple of weeks when we had to flee again. It was late at night and I was about to retire to my room when Prince Gong stopped me. He grabbed my arm and dragged me to a secluded corner.

"You have to go," he whispered.

"What?" I asked.

"I have left a horse tied up outside your room. Take only what you can carry and go."

"Why?" I asked. "What is happening?"

"The British are coming. The emperor and his family are leaving for Jehol right now."

"What do you mean? I just saw Imperial Concubine Yi. Her attendants were putting her to bed."

"I guarantee she will be gone if you wait until morning," he said.

"They are fleeing? In the middle of the night? They are abandoning us?"

"Even many of court officials don't know," he said. "The emperor must move quickly. You know a caravan will slow them down. Tomorrow, when everyone realizes what is happening, they will want to flee as well, but it will be too late. The British forces will be here by then."

"What will they do?" I asked.

"I don't know," he said. "But they are still furious about Parkes and his men. They keep saying they want the emperor to fulfill his treaty agreements, that they want peace, but it isn't true. They want the emperor to fight them. They want their revenge. They only want a reason to overthrow him."

"What will you do?" I asked. "Are you coming with us?"

"No," he said. "I must stay here and do what I can to make peace and get them to leave."

I nodded. "Thank you for telling me. For helping me."

He reached up and stroked my face "Yaqian," he said. "Maybe...when this is over..."

I stopped him. "It is best not to think about the future right now."

He nodded and walked away into the darkness without another word.

I made my way to my room and, sure as he said, a horse was waiting for me. I gathered my things, mounted the horse, and went back to Imperial Consort Yi's palace. It was dark and everyone was gone. I went out the nearest exit, a side gate, which was suspiciously unguarded, and followed the trail. It didn't take long for me to catch up with the imperial family. They were still moving terribly slowly, but at a steady pace. Imperial Concubine Yi was surprised to see me, but she gave me a knowing nod, glad to have me by her side.

The next morning, we were only a few dozen li from the Summer Palace. We could still see it from the surrounding hills. We could also see streams of people fleeing the palace in the morning light as they realized that not only had the emperor fled, but that the British were coming.

We continued our slow pace until someone in the group yelled, "Fire!" We all turned around and saw smoke rising from the Summer Palace. Imperial Concubine Yi started screaming. The Summer Palace had been her favorite place to be in all of China. She loved the buildings, the gardens, but mostly the art. When she had first visited the Summer Palace as the emperor's favored woman, she explored every corner of the palace and collected the best paintings from all over Europe and Asia and used them to decorate her private quarters. We could see the fire spreading as thick black smoke filled the sky.

The emperor collapsed on the ground. He ripped his clothes and wept uncontrollably. To him, the Summer Palace represented everything the emperors of old had worked for. The Summer Palace had been transformed into a dwelling fit for an emperor under Qianlong the Magnificent, who had reigned over China for fifty years and was someone all emperors wished to emulate. Every emperor since Qianlong put their own mark on the Summer Palace, expanding it and filling it with the most exquisite items from around the world.

As the fire raged below, Emperor Xianfeng knew he was a failure – to himself, to his people, and to his ancestors. The loss of the Summer Palace was a loss too great to bear. The emperor continued to wail and beat his head on the ground. His attendants were finally able to pick him up and place him in a litter so they could carry him. We all felt the loss, not only of the palace itself, but what it represented. Slowly, one by one, we turned away from the blaze and continued our journey, all to the tune of the emperor's cries.

The progress from the Summer Palace to Jehol was slow and painful. Jehol lay over four hundred li northwest of the Summer Palace. While it took only a few hours to travel from the Forbidden City to the Summer Palace, it took over a week to arrive at Jehol. We had to constantly stop to take breaks, and we had to camp every night, which was an unprecedented ordeal. There were not enough tents, so most of us had to sleep outside on the ground. There was not enough food, so we were starving. It was October, so the temperature was dropping rapidly. By the time we arrived at Jehol, we were stiff, sore, exhausted, and hungry. But we did not find much relief.

The Mountain Palace at Jehol was not really a palace, but merely a hunting lodge that was occasionally used by past emperors. Emperor Xianfeng was not much of a hunter and had had no time for such frivolities in recent years, so the lodge had fallen into disuse. Some of the eunuchs had ridden ahead to try and prepare the lodge for the Emperor's arrival, but there had been too much to do in too little time. Most of the rooms had not yet been opened so they were dusty and moldy.

Eventually, though, everyone was settled in their rooms and the cooks fired up the kitchens to prepare a sumptuous feast. Most of the rest of the court stumbled in over the next few days. Apparently, there had been few deaths at the Summer Palace. The British allowed everyone to leave who wanted to before stealing whatever they could and then burning the palace to the ground. The fact that many of the items were stolen calmed Concubine Yi's heart.

"Imagine," she said. "Somewhere in the world, maybe on their way to England, or France, or America, your beautiful embroidered gowns and fans are on their way to a new life. They are not ashes, but will maybe find their way to the court of the British queen."

Imperial Concubine Yi found it endlessly fascinating that the British Empire was ruled by a woman. It was one of her deepest wishes that they would one day meet.

inally, after the burning of the Summer Palace, the emperor realized that he had to compromise. China was beaten. If he continued to defy the foreigners, they would eventually overrun the entire country. If the emperor agreed to a new treaty, he could at least keep the dynasty on the throne. But he would not do it himself. He appointed Prince Gong as Imperial Envoy with full imperial authority. The prince immediately set to work writing and rewriting treaties and making arrangements for the foreign forces to leave. The prince sent letters to his brother daily, keeping him informed and begging him to return to Peking. But the emperor refused. The emperor would not share the same city as the foreigners.

The emperor forced the court to remain in Jehol for the winter. Imperial Concubine Yi was inconsolable. She, like all of us, longed to return home, but she also feared for the emperor's health. After he collapsed on the trail in view of the burning Summer Palace, his health deteriorated and she feared he would not recover. In fact, his physicians warned him that the cold and the drafty palace would not be good for his health, but he would not listen. The snows moved in and we were trapped. We spent the winter in Jehol. Life did get more comfortable. The court officially moved to the Mountain Palace, bringing the luxuries of home with it, but it was not the same. We spent most of the winter indoors huddled by our fires and praying for the emperor's health to return.

By the time spring arrived, the snow had melted and the foreigners had either left or were confined to their limited concessions. But the emperor was too sick to be moved. We had no choice except to sit and wait for him to die. Imperial Concubine Yi requested that I sew the emperor's funerary robe. I told her that I feared I would not have time to sew all of the robe myself and asked if some of the girls from Lady Tang's school could come from Suzhou to help me. Concubine Yi agreed. By traveling up to Peking by the Grand Canal and then traveling by horse to Jehol, three of my former classmates, including Wensong, arrived within two weeks. I already had all the supplies ready and had drawn the embroidery patterns with input from Concubine Yi by the time the other girls arrived.

Even though we were supposed to be in a time of sadness, I was thrilled to have my sisters with me. I no longer felt so alone now that I had other women, other Han women, near me. The four of us sat huddled together in a circle in the bright North China sun and worked on the robe that the emperor would wear on his trip to Heaven. After the work was complete, the other girls were sent back to Suzhou except for Wensong. Apparently Empress Zhen had so admired my work she wanted an embroidery girl of her own. Wensong and I were so very glad to be together again.

THIRTEEN
JEHOL, 1861

*T*he emperor was only thirty years old when he died. All of Jehol, and the rest of the country, immediately went into mourning, but it was all an act. Honestly, a sense of relief swept over the land, as if every person in the world exhaled at once. Even though the emperor had only just died, he had been a dead weight for the country for years. He had been ill for so long, he used his illness as an excuse not to act. He knew his only choice for his dynasty's survival was to compromise with the foreigners, but he couldn't force himself to do it, so he, and the country, languished. With the emperor gone, someone else would be able to take the reins of the country and lead it forward, pull it out from the mire the foreigners had stuck it in. The only question was who that person would be.

As expected, the emperor named his son as his successor. Little Zaichun became the Tongzhi Emperor, or he would as soon as the mourning ceremonies were completed and he was officially entitled. Even after that, though, the boy was only five years old and was in no position to rule. In an unexpected twist, Emperor Xianfeng did not name any of his brothers as co-regent to rule until the boy came of age. Instead, he appointed eight members of his inner circle *all* as co-regents, including General Sushun.

As the mothers of the emperor, Imperial Concubine Yi was given the new title of Dowager Empress Cixi and Empress Zhen was given the title of Dowager Empress Ci'an. The women were now equals, but both were mere figureheads since women were not supposed to hold any real imperial powers.

Late one evening, Empress Cixi called me into her chambers. She dismissed everyone else except for An Dehai, who never left his mistress's side. She sat in her large chair silently for a long while before speaking. I kneeled before her, and I said nothing while I waited for her to decide what she wanted of me.

"You are one of Prince Gong's lovers, yes?" she finally asked me.

I gasped in shock at the bluntness of her question and also the crassness of it. "No, Your Majesty. I have never known any man in that way, much less the prince."

"But you are close?" she pushed. "You are familiar with each other and he has approached you for aid in the past."

I blushed. She was right, but how much did she really know? She was wrong about us being lovers, so maybe she was just guessing about this, or maybe she knew the truth. Did she know I had helped him save the lives of the British emissaries? It was impossible to keep secrets for very long among the court. Eyes were always watching. I realized that my silence only confirmed her suspicions. I kowtowed to her and begged her for forgiveness without acknowledging anything specific.

"Stop," she commanded of my blathering. "I simply

need to know if the prince trusts you, if he would listen to you."

"Yes, Your Majesty," I said.

She nodded and An Dehai silently walked over and handed me a letter. "I need you to get this to the prince," she said. "He must rewrite it in his own hand and return it to me. Like you, I am not much more than the daughter of a peasant and my writing is poor. I need a man of letters, a man with political experience to rewrite this for me. But more than that, if he rewrites it for me, I will know that I have his support."

An Dehai also handed me a seal of travel that would protect me on the road and provide me with lodging and fresh mounts at all the way stations between Jehol and Peking. Even so, I left under the cover of night to avoid as many of Sushun's spies as possible. It only took me three days to reach Peking.

Since the emperor and all of his consorts had long left the Forbidden City, Prince Gong was staying in a room adjacent to the emperor's quarters. He had been holding court in a library nearby. To the foreigners and officials in Peking, Prince Gong was the face of the empire.

I could not approach him formally. I didn't want anyone to know that I needed to talk to him and that I was there on the business of the empress. When I arrived, I walked past the open door of the rooms where the prince was holding court. I glanced inside and saw the prince. I slowed my pace and made sure he saw me. When our eyes met, there was an understanding. He knew that I would not be there without Empress Cixi's permission. He gave me the slightest of nods, one nearly invisible to anyone not watching for it, and I walked on past. I spent the day in Empress Cixi's rooms straightening it up. The room had been ransacked, as she feared it would be. I told anyone who asked that I was helping to prepare for the empress's return.

That evening, the prince slipped silently into Empress Cixi's quarters through a side door. It was exciting to be meeting in secret again. He looked older, as if the weight of running the country in his brother's absence had aged him, but he was still handsome.

"What are you doing here?" he asked me.

I pulled the letter out of a pocket in my sleeve. "Her Majesty requests your help. As a well-educated man, she needs you to rewrite this letter for her and then send it back to her. She requires your support at this difficult time."

The prince took the letter from me. He skimmed it quickly and then looked at me. "Have you read this?"

I shook my head.

"Do you know what it is about?" he asked.

Again, I shook my head. "She didn't tell me. She only told me to make sure it got to you."

"Why did she send you?" he asked.

I blushed. "She thinks you and I have a...relationship. She thought I could get it to you and convince you to do as she asked."

The prince nearly chuckled. "A 'relationship'? That woman is a child at heart. Girlish fantasies."

"I think she knows," I said. "About Parkes."

He shot me a look. "You didn't tell her, did you?"

"Of course not," I said. "But she hinted. You know how this palace has eyes."

"Well, she wasn't totally wrong in choosing you. You are probably the only woman I would give an audience to."

"Why couldn't she write you herself?" I asked.

"She has tried," he said. "But her letters are constantly

intercepted by Sushun's men. They don't want us collaborating."

"Will you help her?" I asked. I didn't even really know what she needed help with, but my loyalty was to My Lady. If she needed help, I would do whatever I could to secure it for her.

Prince Gong sighed and shook his head. "I don't know. This is a lot to ask. And it has never been done before."

He looked at me and could see my curiosity was killing me. He gave me a silly grin and finally continued. "She wants to get rid of Sushun and the rest of the council. She wants to be regent. Well, co-regent with Empress Ci'an."

"What do you think?" I asked.

"I think she is a better choice than Sushun. But he was selected by my brother for a reason. The Son of Heaven chose Sushun. I may not be able to see the reasons why, but if Heaven spoke through my brother, shouldn't I listen? Who am I to disregard his choice?"

"You've done it before," I said. "When the emperor demanded that Parkes and his men be tortured to death, you defied him. You saved those men."

"To what end?" he asked. "Do you know what we have lost? Do you know what is in those cursed treaties I have signed? Millions of taels of gold in indemnities, trade ports in Canton, Shanghai, Peking, Suzhou, Tientsin, Christian missionaries are to be allowed to run freely with the crown's protection, foreigners are not beholden to our laws, and the largest loss of land we have ever seen. Millions of li to the Russians and the island of Kowloon to the British. And all of this is on top of the money we still owe from the treaties our father signed decades ago! And the Summer Palace. You were there! Beauty and prestige collected by generations of emperors, my forefathers, all burned in a fortnight."

"But you saved the throne," I said. "If he had killed Parkes, if you had not signed the treaties, what would have happened? They would still be here in the Forbidden City. They would have chased us to Jehol. They wouldn't have allowed us to escape. They could have killed the emperor. They could have claimed China for Britain. They could have put someone else on the throne..."

The prince gave me a strange look at this point, as if I was reading his mind.

"They could have put *you* on the throne," I said. "That is what they really wanted, isn't it? They offered to put you on the throne."

"No one must ever know that," he said. "Even Empress Cixi would never trust me if she thought I could be a contender for the throne. But, yes, if I hadn't agreed, her son would not be emperor."

"You gave up the chance to be emperor of China for her son," I said. "Do not forget that. Do not forget what you did for her, for her son, for your brother. Do not be embarrassed about the treaty you agreed to if it saved your brother's kingdom. You can't let those eight men, who are really just all parrots of Sushun, destroy the empire you salvaged."

He held up the paper. "My name can't be on this," he said. "It will be too suspicious. And it can't be in my handwriting."

"What are we to do?"

"I will send for my younger brother, Prince Chun. He has the best education of all of us, classically trained. And he has no claim to the throne. Then, I will send the letter and her and Empress Ci'an's seal with you back to Jehol."

"Her seal?" I asked.

"Yes," he said. "That is partly what this is about. She needs the seals given to them by Emperor Xianfeng to give authority to imperial edicts since her son is too young to understand or sign them."

"What is Empress Ci'an's role in all this?" I asked.

"She is probably just following Cixi's lead. She has no mind or desire to rule. But she will want what is best for their son."

"I didn't know such seals existed," I said.

"They don't really," he said. "They are just gifts the emperor gives to all of his consorts. They don't mean anything. But the regents don't know that."

"Clever," I said.

The prince nodded. "Yes, she is. Believe me, Yaqian, she is a woman we never want to cross."

It took Prince Chun two days to rewrite the edict from Cixi. Then Prince Gong helped me hide the edict inside the lining of my garment and the two seals in one of my bags. It was dark and raining when I went to mount my horse to head back to Jehol. Prince Gong escorted me to the stables and held tightly to my hand.

"Don't stop for anyone you don't know," he said. "Who knows who has been watching you since you arrived."

I held his hand for as long as I could. "Thank you," I said, "for helping her."

"It's for all of us," he said.

"Can you not send some guards with me?" I asked.

He shook his head. "It would draw too much attention, and people would know I helped you."

"I think they will know no matter what," I said. "If the empress knows about us, other people must already be talking, spreading rumors."

"They can only ever be rumors," he said.

I nodded in agreement as he pulled me to him for a kiss. Thunder slowly rumbled as our bodies, now drenched by the rain, pressed together. The whole time we had been in the Forbidden City together, practically alone, he had not approached me in any improper way, but now that we were out of time and I had to leave, he couldn't let me go. There was almost a sadness to his touch. He stopped kissing me and hugged me as tightly as he could. I could see steam rising from him as we stood in the drizzle.

"Ride as fast as you can," he whispered. "I could not face what lies ahead without you."

"I will always be here for you, my prince," I whispered back.

He finally let me go and I mounted the horse. He held on to my hand for as long as he could, but eventually my fingers slipped from his grasp as I galloped into the night.

*I*t took me four days to reach Jehol. The rain was intermittent the whole way. The roads were muddy and I was constantly soaked. I was exhausted, coughing, and sneezing by the time I reached the gate of the Mountain Palace. As I rode through the gate, though, I was seized by a group of guards. They dragged me off the horse and I landed on my feet, hard. I screamed as I collapsed to the ground. They rummaged through my bags, pulling out everything and even tearing up my clothes.

"What are you doing?" I demanded as I wobbled to my feet.

"Making sure you aren't smuggling anything in or out of the palace," one of the guards sneered. "What were you doing?"

"I was on an errand for Her Majesty," I said. "I was making sure her rooms back at the Forbidden City were being prepared for her return. She will not be pleased with how I've been treated!"

The men glared at me and took a few menacing steps toward me.

"Stop!" a voice yelled. "Mistress Yang, where have you been?" An Dehai asked, pushing his way through the guards.

"I only just arrived and these men were helping me dismount my horse," I said.

An Dehai looked around at my things torn and tossed about, and at me, drenched and covered in mud. "I see," he replied. "Well, hurry up and come with me. Her Majesty is waiting to hear how the preparations of her rooms are progressing."

I nodded and picked up my things, stuffed them in my bag, and followed him toward the empress's rooms. We walked stiffly and at a normal pace. As soon as we were out of sight of the men, though, I leaned against a wall and nearly toppled over. An Dehai rushed to my side and helped me the rest of the way. When we arrived in the empress's main hall, she was waiting for me on her throne. I got down on my knees but she quickly rushed to my side.

"No need for that! Just tell me you were a success," she nearly begged.

I only nodded, fearful of who might be watching or listening to us. The empress smiled and ordered a hot bath to be run for me. She and An Dehai helped me hobble into her washroom. Once the door was shut and we were sure we were alone, I asked for a pair of scissors. I took off my robe and carefully cut the stitching on one of my long sleeves. I pulled out the decree, which had been carefully wrapped in several layers of cloth, and handed it to her.

The empress took the decree from me and held it close to her chest. "You did well," she said.

The empress and An Dehai helped me into the tub. The warmth wrapped around me like a blanket and I slowly warmed all the way to my bones. I unwrapped my feet and let the heat relax the pain away. I didn't want to ever get out, but eventually the water started to cool. I didn't want to catch a chill again, so I got out, wrapped myself in a new robe, wrapped my feet with new bindings, and made my way to my own room. An Dehai had taken the liberty of making sure I had a roaring fire going. He brought me a bowl of chicken broth steeped with medicinal herbs.

Thankfully I had a few days to rest and regain my health before we had to set out again. All of the funeral preparations had been made and it was time to return the emperor to the Forbidden City.

The emperor's casket would be carried by dozens of men, so it would take two weeks for the emperor to arrive back at the Forbidden City. His casket would be accompanied by Sushun, the seven other grandees, and a large military force. But for the Dowager Empresses, the Tongzhi Emperor, and their retinue, we would arrive five days ahead of Sushun.

Of course, as a servant, I was not privy to anything that happened next. I had to wait until most of it was over to find out what happened. Rumors were constantly flying, though. Apparently, the empress read the decree to the grandees and provincial governors who had arrived in the city for Emperor Xianfeng's funeral. She was met with overwhelming support. They didn't plan to kill Sushun at that time, though. Many of them still believed that the emperor's wish that Sushun be a court grandee had some purpose to it.

The day before Sushun was to arrive at the palace, however, Prince Gong went to meet him. Prince Gong claimed that he found Sushun drunk in a tavern and in bed with prostitutes and was outraged. As part of the mourning process, the emperor's men were to refrain from pleasures of the flesh. Prince Gong, that usually calm and calculating man, had Sushun dragged back to the Forbidden City in chains. Sushun denied the claims, said he was set up, but he was found guilty of betraying the emperor and was sentenced to death by a thousand cuts. Empress Dowager Cixi had his death commuted to public beheading. She couldn't stand torture. Two other grandees opposed the edict. They were allowed to hang themselves in private. The rest of the minsters submitted to the edict and were allowed to return to their homes, though they were stripped of their rank.

When the official funeral was finally held, the ceremonies were overseen by the new emperor, Tongzhi, his two mothers as co-regents, and Prince Gong as Prince-Regent. With only three lives lost, Empress Dowager Cixi was now the ruler of China.

*M*any months after Cixi's coup, I was called into the main audience hall where the young emperor was holding court. Prince Gong was there and smiled at the confusion on my face as I entered the hall and kneeled before the young emperor. Usually, if the empress wanted something, she asked me directly. I couldn't imagine any reason why I would be called before the Dragon Throne. The Dowager Empresses were sitting behind a screen behind the emperor.

"Mistress Yang," Empress Dowager Cixi began, "Prince Gong has requested your presence at this meeting. Proceed, Prince Gong."

"Majesties, I have a project in mind that I believe requires Mistress Yang's expertise. As you know, a British warship recently fired on one of our ships in our own waters."

This caused a few shocked gasps from around the room and angry outbursts. Things had been tense with the foreign powers since the coup, but peaceful. Empress

Dowager Cixi had been doing her best to meet the demands of the treaties, so there certainly was no cause for war.

"Thankfully, our ship did not sink and there were few casualties," Prince Gong continued. "I spoke with the British admiral. He told me that the captain fired on our ship because he thought they might have been Taiping rebels or marauders because the ship was not flying a flag showing its allegiance to China. I do not know if that is the real reason why they fired on our ships or not, but it did raise an interesting issue. I have also heard reports of our ships having trouble docking in certain ports or receiving aid at sea for similar reasons. We are one of the only countries in the world that does not have a national flag."

"This is an interesting issue, Prince Gong," Empress Cixi replied. "What do you think, Emperor Tongzhi?"

The Emperor had been reclining in his seat, playing with a toy when he heard his mother say his name. He may have been the emperor, but he was only a child and had no interest in sitting in an uncomfortable chair listening to adults talk.

"I don't know," the little emperor mumbled.

"I have an idea for a flag in mind, Your Majesties," the prince continued. "But I believe someone with artistic skills could create something more majestic and regal. Do I have your permission to work on this project with Mistress Yang?"

"I agree that this situation should be resolved quickly," Empress Cixi responded. "I expect to see some progress on this flag within a week."

The prince and I both kowtowed. Then we both rose to our feet but stayed bent at the waist as we backed away. After we exited the audience hall, the prince and I looked at each other, unsure of what to say but both happy to have a chance to talk. Men and women were supposed to remain separate within the Forbidden City. There were some exceptions and no one followed the rules all the time, but more than just gender kept us apart. I was still little more than a *gōngnǔ* while he was Prince-Regent, second only to the Empress Dowagers. There was no reason why we should be seen together, until now.

"Why did you do that?" I asked. "If the empress wanted a flag she could have just ordered one made in private."

"I know," he said. "But I wanted to see you. I want to spend time with you."

"Why?" I asked.

"Life is good, Yaqian," he said. He motioned toward the imperial gardens and we took a leisurely walk. "We have peace with the Westerners," he continued. "No one is happy about opening so many trade ports, but I have increased the customs taxes, so everything they take out or bring into China they have to pay for. Eventually, we will be able to pay back those foreign indemnities with their own money. Empress Dowager Cixi has also agreed to let me use British troops to fight the Taiping. We have peace abroad and soon we will have peace here. By the time Tongzhi is ready to rule alone, his country will be peaceful and prosperous and he will have an easy reign."

I nodded. "I have noticed that much of the tension that clouded my first few years here seems to have dissipated. I still don't know what that has to do with me."

"Oh, it has very little to do with you," he said. "But this feels like the summer of my life. I am still young and life is good. I intend to make the most of it."

"By working with a lowly embroidery girl on a flag?" I asked.

"No, by seducing a lowly embroidery girl," he said. He stopped walking and gently grabbed my elbow.

I couldn't believe what he had just said. I refused to look at him. How could he speak to me so improperly?

"Will you not look at me, Yaqian?" he asked.

"No," I said with a pout. "You know nothing can come of it."

"Why not?" he asked. "*Gōngnǚ* are often given as wives to court officials after several years of faithful service. And no one has been more faithful than you. I dare say the empress would not deny you anything you asked of her."

"We cannot marry, you fool," I said. "I am Chinese; you are Manchu. Marriage between races is forbidden. You know this."

He nodded. "I know. But maybe you could come to me under another title, be a servant in my house."

"A servant? In your house? For your wives and concubines to kick like a dog?"

"I am sure we could come to some arrangement," he said. "I could order them to treat you kindly."

"That would never work," I said. "You are rarely at home anyway. I would never see you and you wouldn't be there to protect me."

He seemed frustrated as he racked his brain for an answer.

"Besides," I said, cutting off any further rebuttals. "I am happy here. I love the empress and my work. I would not give it up to live in your home and birth your spoiled children. Did you ever consider what I wanted?" I asked.

"I considered the fact that you loved me too and would want to find a way to be together."

"I do love you," I said, almost shocking myself. "But the price of giving into that love is too high."

"You would rather live in a fantasy?" he asked. "Just loving in your mind but never really fulfilling what it means to love?"

"You should climb inside my head," I said. "It is a beautiful place."

The prince wasn't joking about his intention to seduce me. He came to see me at least once a week under the pretense of working on the design for the flag. He would take any opportunity to touch my hand, kiss my cheek, or say kind things. I didn't tell him to stop because I enjoyed the attention, but I simply couldn't imagine a future together.

The flag we created together was magnificent, just as he predicted it would be. He had imagined a red dragon on a yellow background, but I made a few artistic changes. I made the flag a triangle instead of a square. I knew the flags of other empires were square, but Manchu banners were triangular, so I thought a triangular flag would pay homage to the emperor's Manchu ancestors. I kept the yellow background because yellow was the color of the emperor. I changed the red dragon to a blue one because the azure dragon represented the east and the spring and was considered the king of the dragons. I could not imagine a better dragon to represent this new China under Emperor Tongzhi. I kept one of the blue threads from that first flag I made as a memory of this symbol of China I was creating, but also to remember those days with Prince Gong.

I also added another element, a red flaming pearl. It looked like the azure dragon was reaching for the pearl. The pearl symbolized perfection and enlightenment, the endless cycle of transformation, and was one of the Eight Treasures of Buddhism. Above the dragon throne in the emperor's formal audience hall there was a huge golden dragon with a pearl in its mouth. Legend said that if anyone who wasn't the emperor sat on the emperor's throne, the dragon would drop the pearl and the person would be crushed. Through the pearl, the dragon enacted justice. The pearl also represented wealth and good luck.

After the Dowager Empresses approved the flag, it was sent to Suzhou for mass production. Once the flag became standard, Prince Gong took me to the Dagu Forts where I could see hundreds of ships flying the flag of China. Dancing in the wind, it looked like a sea of dragons flying over the ocean. It was one of the proudest moments of my life.

One day, Empress Cixi called me to her. She sent everyone else away so we could speak privately.

"I have a task for you," she said. "We – the Emperor, Empress Ci'an, and I – are eternally grateful for what Prince Gong did in the service of us."

"I believe he is eternally devoted to you and your cause," I said.

"I agree," she said. "As thanks, I would like to commission a new robe for him. Something grand, the likes of which has never been seen before. I think the court needs a symbol. My little Emperor is too small to make a grand statement of power or prestige, but Prince Gong is the highest-ranking man in the country. He should look the part."

"I agree, Majesty. Do you have an idea for a design?"

"Yellow and dragons is all I know," she said. "But...amazing! Do you know what I mean?"

I smiled. "I have some ideas," I said. "Do you want to work on the pattern together and then have them sent to Suzhou?"

"No!" she said. "Well, I will help with the pattern, but I want you to do it, all of it. It must be the most beautiful dragon robe ever made! It cannot be entrusted to those idiot country girls. It must be made by your hand."

"But, Majesty, that could take a long time. Months or more if I am the only person working on it."

She nodded. "It is agreed then."

"Your Majesty," I carefully proceeded, "that will be a mighty gift. Do you not worry that people will talk?"

"No more than they already talk about you," she said.

I jumped out of my seat and kneeled before her. "Your Majesty, please forgive me and believe me when I say that I have done nothing that would bring you disgrace. I am loyal to you above all others."

"Are you?" she asked.

"Yes, Your Majesty," I said. "I want nothing more than to serve you for all of my days."

"How long have you been here, Yaqian?" she asked.

"Seven years, Your Majesty."

"How old are you?"

"I am twenty-three."

"If you are going to marry, it is time," she said. "I was only sixteen when I became the Emperor's consort. I dare say most men wouldn't accept a bride as old as you."

"I have no wish to be a bride, Your Majesty," I said. "I am happy here and would serve you all my days if you allowed it."

"As I said, if you are going to marry, it should be done now, otherwise it will not be done at all."

"I beg of Your Majesty," I said, knocking my forehead to the ground and nearly in tears, "do not speak of it again. I will seek no other life but one in your service."

"Sit up," she said. She looked at me and sighed. I am sure she believed me, but having a servant with such undying devotion was a rare thing. It was difficult for her to accept. "Very well, we will speak of it no more."

*F*or the next year, I worked on nothing but Prince Gong's dragon robe.

The robe was the most exquisite thing I had ever made. I started with the best yellow satin available for the shell and then lined it with perfectly white rabbit fur. With thread of real gold, I embroidered a massive dragon head that I couched onto the center of the robe. The body of the dragon, his legs, and tail were partly couched and partly embroidered directly on the robe and snaked around the rest of it. Each of the dragon's feet had four claws because only the emperor would be allowed to wear a dragon with five claws. I embellished the robe with pearls from the South China Sea. I didn't want the pattern to be too busy, I wanted the dragon to be the most important part, but I did include a few smaller dragons, bats, and auspicious symbols for good luck.

After I completed the robe, I didn't tell the empress immediately. I wanted to gaze at it, remember it for the rest of my days. I kept some of the extra gold thread and put it with the rest of my memories. For days, I kept the robe on its rack in my room and I just looked at it, amazed by this thing of beauty I had created. How I wished Lady Tang was there to see it.

I was not present when the empress presented the yellow dragon robe to Prince Gong. She did so at a formal ceremony I was not allowed to attend, but afterward, he sought me out. I had been walking in one of the palace gardens when he found me. He was the most handsome man in the world. He stood tall, his chest broader than when we first met. His boots were tall and black, embroidered with golden symbols. His queue was long and tight, his forehead recently shaved, and his eyes bright. Neither of us could speak. We simply stared at each other for a long time – me, admiring the most handsome of princes in his dragon robe, and he, truly appreciating my skill for the first time. Finally, I managed a respectful curtsey and he replied with a solemn bow before walking away. My knees gave out and I sat in the shade by the pond for a long time.

*S*everal months later, I was sitting by a little pond in the imperial gardens that was situated around a statue of Guanyin. The sun was already setting, so it was cool and dark in the little grotto. The golden koi swam in circles below me, mistakenly thinking I was going to throw them some food. I could hear some frogs chirping, but could not see where they were hiding. I twisted a lock of my long, black hair in my fingers. I had such soft hair.

I turned when I heard some footsteps behind me. My eyes widened when I saw Prince Gong, wearing the yellow and golden robe I had embroidered for him, standing there. I had not seen him since the day the Empress presented him with his dragon robe. Since the completion of the national flag, we had no pretense to see each other. My heart fluttered seeing him now before me, but I did my best to remain calm.

He smiled at me. "Evening, Yaqian."

I stood and gave a low curtsey before him. "My Prince," I said with my eyes to the floor.

"Yaqian!" he said, offering me his hand, "surely friends such as you and I are above such formalities."

I accepted his hand and stood. We left the little pool and walked down a long hallway decorated with teakwood carvings. "Are we ever above such formalities?" I asked. "Do not your wives and concubines still bow in your presence?"

He shrugged. "Some of the wives do; some do not. The

concubines all do, though. My wives would beat them if they refused."

I rolled my eyes, shook my head, and smiled. "I was raised too poor to understand the intrigue of such large families," I said.

"My brother the emperor paid for you with a very fine concubine to your father. How do you think your mother is handling her?" he asked.

My head instinctively dropped at the mention of my mother. "I don't know," I said. "I have had no contact with my family since I came here. I am sure the poor concubine is miserable. Unless she has had many sons like you promised. Maybe then my mother would be good to her."

He nodded. "Did you notice that I am wearing the robe you made for me, Yaqian?"

I looked at him, from his neck to his boots. The robe was every bit as exquisite as I remembered. My eyes wandered back up the robe and I looked at his face. On any other man, the robe might not have been as stunning, but on Prince Gong, with his broad build, strong jaw, long, black hair, and piercing gray eyes, he looked like an emperor.

He smiled at me as I surveyed him. He seemed to enjoy the fact that I was looking at him so intently. I finally managed to break my gaze away.

"You should stop praising me for that ugly robe," I said, turning from him and walking away. "It was a gift from the empress, your dear brother's wife, as thanks for helping her after his death. It pains her for you to give me credit for her gift."

"She did not make this robe," he said, catching up to me.

"She brought me from the dirt in faraway Hunan into her service. She provided the materials. She had the idea for the robe. Everything I am is because of her. Alone, I am nothing."

"Come into my household," he said, stepping in front of me causing me to stop and look up at him. "Some of my wives are skilled at embroidery but with a fraction of your skill. I would be very pleased to have you under my roof. I would praise you and your skills publicly every day."

I scoffed. "You think I am just some weaver girl you can buy into your house? I am in service to Empress Cixi, the most powerful woman in the country. Only she deserves the best. You are only a prince," I said waving my hand at him dismissively. "One of many." I started to walk away from him, but he grabbed my arm and turned me back to him.

"Do you truly despise me, Yaqian?" he asked.

"You are nothing," I said. "Just like me."

He pulled me close to him and kissed me. It was not the first time we had kissed, but this time was different. Before, the kisses had been sweet, flirtatious, and I could easily run away. This time, there was something more firm, more insistent about his kiss. I could not have run away if I wanted to. There was a hunger to his kiss. He needed me.

He held one hand around my shoulders and the other around my waist. I reached up and put one arm around his neck. I wanted to comfort him, let him know that this time I wasn't going to run away. He tasted like pomegranates and felt so hot against me. I could hear a small growl escape his throat as he moved from my mouth to my neck where he began to bite and suck. I felt a throbbing and wetness between my legs. I had not laid with a man before...not properly. I tried to push the unpleasant memories of the evening I spent with his brother out of my mind as I tasted Prince Gong. I knew what real desire was, and my body wanted him.

He stopped kissing me and looked deep into my eyes. He led me down a dark hallway, away from any prying eyes. He put my hand inside his robe. I gasped in surprised and tried to jerk my arm back, but he held my hand tightly, almost too tightly, as he kept staring into my eyes. He forced my hand to touch him. I did not shirk back this time and I let him show me what to do. He sighed, closed his eyes, and let go of my wrist. I kept moving my hand up and down.

He wrapped his arms around me, burying me in the long sleeves of his robe. He placed his cheek next to mine and sighed as I continued pleasuring him. "Yaqian," he whispered, "I want to come to your room tonight."

I let go of him and took a step away. I looked up into his eyes, which were rimmed red. "You think I am your whore to call when you want?" I asked.

"Never," he said. "I am the most decorated prince in all of China. I have wives and concubines for my pleasure. Any foolish maiden on the street would throw herself at my feet if I so desired."

I removed his arms from around my neck and stepped away. "I am no foolish maiden," I said.

He nodded. "Exactly. You are cold and utterly devoted to my dear sister-in-law. For you to choose to lay with me would be a great favor from you."

"It is more than a favor," I said. "Should we be caught, I could lose my life. I could be killed simply for daring to touch your great personage," I said glancing below his waist.

He stepped close again and kissed me gently. He squeezed one of my breasts with one hand and my backside with the other. "I am worth it," he whispered.

While I trembled and felt moist from his touch, his arrogance was appalling. I rolled my eyes and stepped away.

"Not even you are worth a moment of my time, Prince Gong," I said. "Much less my life."

I began to walk away, but he followed me. He grasped one of my arms and whispered in my ear, "Tonight, Yaqian. I will come to you tonight. I will pay the guards to let me in and out of the palace after dark. Wait for me."

I shrugged him off and kept walking. I did not look back at him. My heart was beating like a drum, my knees were weak, my stomach was dancing, but I managed to walk straight ahead until he was no longer behind me. I then ran to my quarters and looked at myself in the mirror. My face was flushed and my hands were shaking.

I poured water into my washbasin and rinsed my face. I could not believe what had just happened. Of course, I had felt a wanting for Prince Gong many times. He was so kind to me. He was the only person who openly acknowledged my embroidery skills. While my skills were known throughout the kingdom, Empress Cixi would only have the best in her service after all, humility was a cardinal virtue for a woman. I was never publically praised and when the empress thanked me in private, I kept my head low and denied the beauty of my work. But, secretly, I wanted to shout from the top of every temple in the empire that I was the greatest needleworker in China. I wanted to return to my hometown and show Mother the prince's robe so she could see how my talent had grown. A thousand years from now, I wanted people to sing laments about how no one ever created embroidery as beautiful as mine ever again. Prince Gong's public thanks for my work gave me a tiny glimpse into the glory I desired in my heart. And it made me desire him.

I knew I would never marry as long as I was in the empress's service. I would never have children. My life was utterly devoted the empress and I could not have such petty distractions in my life. Even taking a lover would mean less time working, more time worrying about my own wants or the wants of someone else. I could not afford such diversions from my work.

Furthermore, the very idea of laying with Prince Gong was absurd. The imperial family was above the rest of us, appointed and protected by Heaven. Only wives and concubines appointed by the Emperor or Empress had the right to touch a man of the royal family, and a Manchu could only ever marry a Manchu. If I was caught, even my great skill and the love the empress or the prince had for me could not protect me.

I paced as all these thoughts ran through my head. Allowing the prince into my room was an insane, deadly thought. All of my powers of reason told me not to do it. And yet, I wanted him to come to me. As much as I hated it, I loved the prince. It made me feel weak. Loving the prince put me in danger and could only lead to disaster.

Yet, here, in the darkness, I could give into my feelings, just this once. Being with him for just one night did not mean that I was his lover. One night of passion would not interfere with my duties to the empress. But not giving into my feelings would interfere. I could think of nothing else. Even right now, I should be working, but all I could think about was him. If I finally gave myself to him, it would be over and he would no longer occupy my thoughts. I could return to my work clear of mind.

I brushed perfumed oil through my hair, tied it up and decorated it with a string of jade beads. I put on my best purple robe and used a small amount of red color on my lips. Then I waited. Finally, long after darkness had fallen, I heard a tiny knock on my door. I had to calm my stomach before going to open it.

The prince was standing there, smiling brightly, almost as bright as the yellow dragon robe he was still wearing, and his eyes shined. He grabbed my hand as he entered and shut the door behind him. "Yaqian!" he exclaimed. "I cannot believe you are here. As soon as you left my sight earlier, I thought I had made a terrible mistake. I was sure that you would not be here, you would have hidden from me."

"It is my goal to make sure you never know what I will do," I said.

"But you are here," he said stroking my face gently. "That must mean you do love me."

"I never said that," I finally said. "I only wanted to know what it was like to sleep like a princess for one night."

He looked me up and down as he walked over to me slowly. "You will only know that," he said as he undid the sash of my robe, "if you spend the night with a prince."

He kissed me and took the pins and beads from my hair so it could fall freely. He kissed my cheek and my neck. He opened my robe and caressed my naked breasts. My nipples grew hard as he squeezed them. He was a head taller than I was, so it was a little awkward as he bent to try and kiss my chest. He made me feel beautiful and confident. I didn't want to shrink away from him; I wanted him to touch every part of me. He stood back up and reached through my robe to grab my backside with both hands and pulled me to him as he returned to kissing my mouth. I could feel his hardness poke me in the stomach as he did, which had the unfortunate effect of making me giggle like an idiot.

He stopped groping me and looked down at me confused. "My lovemaking humors you, my lady?" he asked.

I felt my face grow hot and I looked down to avoid his

gaze. I wasn't sure what to say, so I undid the sash on his robe and opened it to reveal his naked body. It was fantastic. His imperial raiment concealed the body of a warrior. His chest was hard and every muscle was clearly etched on his skin. He had a scar on the left side of his stomach from a battle he had almost lost. His legs showed immense power from years of riding horses. His member, which had been fully erect and stabbing me only a moment ago, was now drooping a bit, dejected at my cruel giggles. I realized at that moment that he was in my power. His pleasure or his pain was at my bidding.

"Tell me how to please you," I whispered.

He looked down and kissed me again before taking my hand and leading me over to the *kang*. He removed his robe and tossed it to one side. He slid his fingers over my shoulders and removed my robe as well. We stood naked before each other as equals. Both vulnerable, both full of desire. Just a man and a woman, not a prince and *gōngnǚ*. He sat on the edge of the *kang* and motioned for me to sit in front of him. I got down on my knees, between his, and my face directly across from his cock.

"Touch it," he said.

I gently ran my fingers down one side, causing him to gasp again. He wrapped my fingers around him and showed me how to move my hand up and down, with my thumb hitting below the tip, just the way he liked it. He moaned quietly at my touch. I could feel myself growing wet from the knowledge that I was pleasing him. Oh, how I wanted him to touch me in such intimate ways.

He reached down and ran his fingers through my hair then he pulled my face closer to his cock.

"Kiss," he said.

I was a bit surprised at first, and it seemed a little

strange. I wanted to laugh to cover the fact that I felt uncomfortable, but I didn't want to hurt his feelings again, so I leaned in and gave a small kiss near his snake eye. I looked up at him for approval. I wasn't sure how this little kiss could please him. He was smiling and ran his thumb over my lips.

"Open your mouth," he said. "And take me inside."

This seemed even stranger to me. I didn't know a lot about lovemaking, but I didn't think his member was supposed to go into my mouth. I was aching between my legs and wanted him to touch me there. He must have noticed the confusion and apprehension in my face. This time he chuckled.

"Don't be scared," he said. "Just try it for a minute."

I opened my mouth and he guided the head of his cock inside. He put his hand behind my head and moved me slightly forward and back so he went in and out of my mouth. He tasted salty, but he was certainly enjoying himself, moaning and panting, so I didn't stop. He gripped my hair as I tried to move my mouth and tongue all around his cock. He tried to force me to take him deeper, but I made a horrible gagging sound. He let go of my hair and stroked my cheeks.

"I'm sorry, Yaqian," he said. "We will have to work on that next time." He looked at me with gentle eyes and I didn't have the heart to tell him that there wouldn't be a next time. He pulled me up toward him and laid with me on the *kang*. He kissed me and stroked my hair and face. He massaged my breasts and once again made them pique with delight. He kissed down my throat and chest and then flicked one of my nipples with his tongue. His breath felt cool on the now wet nipple, which made my body feel prickly all over. He sucked, kissed, and bit all over my breasts as he slowly moved on top of me.

This was how it was supposed to be, I thought. This was nothing like the night I spent with the emperor. Prince Gong didn't seem to have a thought for my feet. He didn't touch them or caress them, which was how I preferred it. The way Prince Gong was loving me felt right. I wanted him on me, around me, inside me. I opened my legs when I felt his hand petting my soft hairs. I could feel him smile through his kisses as he touched my wetness.

"I'm glad you want me, Yaqian," he whispered.

"I would not be here if I didn't, my prince," I answered.

At that, he positioned himself between my legs and lay completely on top of me. I could feel his cock touching and prodding me, looking for its way in. His body was much bigger than mine, this battle-built stallion trying to mount a small, domesticated mare. I spread my legs as far as I could and arched my hips to welcome him into me. I could not help but moan as just the head of his cock entered my body. He pulled out and then entered me again. He repeated this motion several times over and I groaned every time he pulled out and gasped in pleasure every time he entered.

He then reached around with one arm behind my backside. He pulled out, and while I expected him to enter again gently, that is not what happened. He held me firmly and shoved the full length of his cock inside me. I gasped in horror as pain shot through my entire body. I am sure I screamed because he then placed a hand over my mouth, but my head was swimming in confusion, pleasure, and terror. I felt as though I had been run through with a sword.

Prince Gong kissed my cheek and shushed me. He rubbed my hips and said words to calm me. "My sweet

Yaqian. I'm sorry. I knew you were a virgin and it would hurt. I didn't want to scare you, so I did it quickly."

I was angry and sad at the same time. Part of me wanted to slap his face and stomp away. Another part of me wanted to curl up into a ball and cry. Was this it? Was this sex? This pain was something people killed, lived, and died for?

"Is...is that...it?" I finally managed to ask while choking back tears.

He kissed my face. "No, no, my dear. That was just the worst part since this is your first time. When you are ready, we can keep going."

I didn't know what he meant by "keep going," but I didn't want the one night I was going to spend with him to end like this, in pain and tears. I nodded and whispered, "Keep going."

He nodded and slowly began to pull his full girth in and out of me. I was sore, but as he continued to make love to me, with sweet kisses, soft caresses, and skillfully entering and exiting my body, I calmed down and returned to the state of ecstasy I was in before.

Once he got into a steady rhythm, he gripped my shoulders, placed his cheek against mine, and panted with each thrust. I loved feeling his hot breath on my skin, his body form sweat under my fingers, and the way his cock now so easily slid in and out of me. Our bodies moved as one and I took great pleasure in the fact that he was enjoying my body as much as I was enjoying his.

I don't know that I ever climaxed, the entire experience felt so good and was so exhilarating that every moment was euphoric, but I do know that he did. With one last hard thrust and groan, he spilled into me, filling me with warmth and satisfaction.

Afterward, I lay in his arms for a long time. I knew the sun would rise and he would have to escape the palace before dawn, but I didn't want my night with the prince to end too soon. One night of selfish pleasure had been too much to ask for and it couldn't happen again. So I savored him. I breathed his scent in deeply. I ran my fingers over every muscle and every scar on his body. I licked the salt from his cheek. This moment would have to last me a lifetime.

I awoke to a banging sound. I didn't remember falling asleep. I could still smell the prince and feel the soft silk of his robe under my fingers. The banging got louder.

"Mistress Yang! Mistress Yang!" a maid called. "Are you all right? The door is locked. You are late!"

I finally forced myself to open my eyes. The prince was gone. As the blur cleared from my eyes, a yellow blanket appeared before me. I sat up. It wasn't a yellow blanket, but Prince Gong's dragon robe!

"Mistress Yang! Is everything okay?"

Wide awake, I gripped the robe and jumped out of bed. I would never be able to explain why the robe was in my room. Why had the idiot left it? What was he wearing when he left? I tried to find somewhere to hide it, but my trunk was full. Besides, anywhere I put it, the maid who cleaned my room would find it eventually. Then I heard another voice calling for me.

"Yaqian!" called Wensong. "Are you in there? Are you sick? The empress is calling for you."

I would have to open the door. I was late. But what would I do with the robe? I panicked. In my fear and stupidity, I shoved the robe in the fireplace, which had a small fire still burning in it. The robe immediately caught on fire. It began to shrink and smelled like burning hair. I didn't have time to change my mind because in only a moment, the beautiful golden robe turned to black ash. All that was left were the little pearls I had used as embellishments. I reached in and made sure they were all buried in the ash. My fingers were black from the ruin of my most magnificent creation.

"Yaqian!" Wensong yelled. "Open this door or I'll bring someone to break it down."

A primal, guttural wail began to fill my ears. It took me a second to realize this intense sound of pain was coming from me. What had I done? The magnum opus of my life was gone in an instant. The cost of one night with the prince had been the most magnificent creation of my career. The empress would find out! The prince was supposed to wear the robe on official occasions. She would notice if he wasn't wearing it. She would demand to know where it was. I cried louder. I would die two deaths. One for sleeping with the prince, the other for destroying the great gift her majesty had bestowed upon the prince.

The banging on my door resumed, but much louder and more intense. An Dehai suddenly burst through the door, with the maid and Wensong right behind him. They found me kneeling on the ground in front of the fireplace, my hands black with soot and crying as if I had just been stabbed.

Wensong ran to me and took me in her arms. I mumbled something about being stupid and heartbroken because I dropped something into the fire. An Dehai quickly accepted this excuse and left the room, uninterested in caring for the needs of a hysterical female. Wensong helped me wash my hands and face and get dressed so I could attend the empress. I calmed myself as much as I could and went about my day as if the night before had not been the most wonderful and then the most terrible of my life.

*M*y guilt over the destruction of the robe consumed me. I could hardly eat but was constantly nauseous. Even two months after my night with the prince, I was vomiting nearly every day, often several times. I was once again late for reporting to the empress one morning when Wensong came up with her own diagnosis for the cause of my symptoms.

I was huddled over my chamber pot when Wensong entered my room without knocking.

"You're pregnant, aren't you?" she asked without any segue.

"What?" I screeched. "I don't even know what that means! Why would you say that?"

"It means you are going to have a baby," she said.

"I know that! I didn't mean literally! I just meant that it would be impossible to know what you are talking about because I've never been with anyone."

"Are you sure?" she asked. "What about that day a few months ago, when you were all hysterical over the fireplace?

Did something happen? Did someone...were you...did a man hurt you?"

I looked at the concern on her face. Is that what she thought had happened? Was she really worried I had been hurt? Now I felt even more guilt over causing my friend such stress.

"No," I said, getting up and moving to the chair by the window. "Well, no one hurt me. But...yes...there was a man. But it was only once! How can I be pregnant?"

"Have you bled since that night?" she asked.

I thought about it. I hadn't noticed since I had been so ill, but now that she asked, I realized she was on to something. "No," I said cautiously.

"That means you're pregnant!" she exclaimed.

"What?" I asked. "Is that really what that means? How do you know? Lady Tang didn't explain any of this."

"I have nine younger brothers and sisters," she said. "My mother and my father's other women were always pregnant."

"I can't believe this," I said, burying my head in my hands.

"I knew it!" she said, smiling. She shut the door and pulled up a stool to sit next to me. "Who was it? What was it like?"

"I can't talk about this!" I said, my face reddening.

"It was Prince Gong, wasn't it?" she said, her eyes sparkling. "Was he as wonderful as everyone imagines? He is so handsome! Was he gentle? Did it hurt?"

"You know I can't admit who it was," I said.

"*Aiya!*" she said, flopping over on my bed. "That is amazing. You are so lucky!"

"Lucky?" I said. "If anyone finds out, I'll be given a silk

rope! And now that I'm...you know...they are bound to find out!"

"Don't worry," she said. "Just tell the prince. He will know what to do."

a baby. I was going to have a baby? I couldn't do this. I didn't want to do this. It wasn't my life. The role of mother was meant for someone else.

I waited by the little koi pond for Prince Gong to meet me. I had caught his glance when he attended an audience with the empress earlier that day. I hadn't seen him since our night together and he seemed anxious to speak with me. I finally heard his familiar footsteps coming down the corridor.

"Yaqian!" he called out when he saw me. He ran up and embraced me. I gave him a cool embrace back. There was no tightness or warmth in my arms. He noticed, taking a step back and looking into my face with worried eyes.

"What is wrong?" he asked. "I heard you have been ill, but I had to pretend it didn't bother me, so it has been hard to get information."

"I haven't been ill," I said. "Not exactly." I turned away from him, unsure how to tell him. I felt his warm hands on my shoulders.

"What is it then?" he asked.

"I am with child, Prince Gong," I said.

He turned me toward him. His eyes were big and his mouth agape. "What? Is this true?"

"I would never lie to you," I said.

"But you are sure?"

I shrugged. "Apparently I have all the signs," I said.

"Are you sure it's mine?" he asked.

Anger flared up from my belly to my face and, without even thinking, I raised my hand to slap him across the face. I swung, but he jerked back and grabbed my wrist. I glared at him and he looked at me apologetically.

"I'm sorry," he said. "I should have let you hit me. It was a warrior's reflex to stop someone from striking me. I should not have questioned your honor."

I wrested my wrist from his hand and turned away. "What honor?" I asked as my eyes started welling with tears. "I have given into my most carnal desires. I betrayed the empress. I defiled a prince. I destroyed my most beloved creation. I have ruined my life. I have no honor left."

The prince stepped up and put his arms around me. "There, there. It will be all right. I won't let any harm come to you."

"What will we do?" I asked, turning to him.

"Can you get rid of it?" he asked.

"Get rid of it?" I asked, not clear about his meaning.

"I have heard that women know how to make sure that babies won't come if they don't want them."

I shook my head. "I have no idea what you are talking about."

"Well, maybe you can ask one of the other girls in the inner court. Someone must know how to make this go away."

"I can't tell any of those harpies what I've done! The only person who knows is Wensong and she said I should talk to you. Any of those other women will go straight to the empress if they find out."

"Then we will have to find another way. We will have to get you out of the Forbidden City."

"Wait," I said. "Do you mean get me out of the city so I can have the baby or kill it?"

He stared at me, clearly not wanting to speak the words out loud.

"But, this is your child."

"I have many," he said.

"And the blood of each one is sacred," I said. "The emperor is the Son of Heaven; you are the emperor's son; your sons, your grandsons, for every generation into infinity carry the blood of the Dragon."

"I don't know what else to do," he said. "Do you want to have the baby?"

"I don't know," I sighed. "Not really. I don't want to be a mother. I can't be. But...I don't know if I can kill it. Would that be right? Wouldn't that bring the wrath of Heaven down on us?"

"What is the alternative?" he asked. "Is there anyone who can help? What about your mother?"

I laughed. "My mother? Her heart is cold as stone. She would never help me."

"I don't know," he said. "Your mother struck me as someone who puts her own survival first. Think about it. She sent her only child to an embroidery school even though it meant sending you away because she knew a skill would reap more benefits in the long run than just marrying you to some farm boy."

"Maybe," I said.

"And she made a hard bargain for that concubine. She

knew the possibility of sons would be better for the family than just money."

I sighed and thought about what he said. He had a point. Mother was a survivor and worked hard every day of her life. Maybe the way she treated me didn't mean she didn't love me, but meant that she had to do whatever she could to ensure her own survival. It was funny to me how the prince seemed to know Mother and her motivations better than I did after only meeting her once over eight years ago.

"But how will this baby help her?" I asked. "She will call it one more mouth to feed."

"It is the child of a prince. Surely she will see the value in that. I can send money to make sure he is taken care of and I can make sure he rises in government and gets a good education. He can make a good marriage. He can elevate the whole family."

"What makes you think the baby is a boy?" I asked.

"You have to hope for something in order for it to come true," he said. "Every mother always prays for boys."

He wasn't wrong. I know my own mother prayed for boys. But I wasn't like other women. I wasn't married and didn't want to be a mother at all. I was in the unique position of not caring how the child turned out. I decided to hope for a girl instead, for no other reason than just to spite my mother, but I would never tell the prince that.

"Oh, I need my robe back," the prince said. "It was so dark when I left your room, I just grabbed whatever robe I could find. It ended up being one of your purple ones. My wife was not happy when she saw me try to sneak home in it."

"I...I burned it," I said, unable to look at him.

"What!" the prince nearly yelled. "How could you do that? What were you thinking?"

"I wasn't thinking!" I said. "I was terrified. I panicked. An Dehai was trying to break down my door and Wensong was yelling. I had nowhere to hide it."

"So you burned it?"

"I didn't know what else to do."

"The empress is going to be furious," he said. "She has already been asking why I haven't worn it. I told her I was saving it for very special occasions, but she is going to demand I wear it sooner or later. Can you make another one?"

"It took a year of my life to make that robe," I said. "It will take me forever to make another one in just my spare time. And I could never get the materials myself."

"It's a good thing we are already planning on getting you out of town then," the prince said. "If the empress finds out, she will have our heads."

$\mathcal{J}$ wrote to Mother and included some extra money and pieces of embroidery. I didn't tell her what was wrong, only that I missed my family and wanted to see her. As expected, I didn't receive a reply. I told the prince, and he forged a letter requesting my return home. We decided the only other person who could help me was Lady Tang. I would return to her school and beg her for aid.

A few days later, a letter arrived from my "mother" saying she was sick and dying and wanted me by her side. I went to the empress and begged her for leave. She was not happy about it, but since her own mother had recently died, she was feeling filial. She let me leave with the strict order that I also return to Lady Tang and prove to her that I was worthy of being appointed a master artisan. She said she would also appreciate it if I brought back an apprentice, but she knew that such a thing was a very personal decision.

In the spring of the second year of the reign of the Tongzhi Emperor, I once again mounted a horse to cross the country. I never thought I would return to Hunan. I had never hoped to. After so long in the imperial city, I could barely remember my life in the countryside. Would they even know me anymore?

SIXTEEN
CHANGSHA, 1864-1865

The trip was extremely difficult for me. I continued feeling nauseous, so I carried a bucket to vomit in with me at all times. Riding the horse was difficult as well. I felt unbalanced and uneasy, so I had to ride much slower than my escorts would have liked. I had to stop and pee every couple of hours. Once again, the trip took more than a month. Even though I was nervous about returning to Lady Tang, I was relieved when the city came into sight.

After living in Peking for so long, Changsha seemed like a country village to me. The city lacked the diversity I had become accustomed to. There were hardly any women on the streets; Han women were usually kept indoors. The men all dressed the same: white shirts, black pants, long queues. I did not see the colorful costumes or funny hats of the multitudes of ethnic groups I saw in Peking. There were no foreigners. The familiar, pungent scent of *chou doufu* – stinky tofu – filled my nose, calling me back to my childhood. No one ate *chou doufu* in Peking.

We finally arrived at the main gate of Lady Tang's

school. One of the guards helped me down from my horse. I didn't recognize him, but he opened the gate for me when I explained I was a former student. As I slowly walked up the path, I saw little faces looking out the windows at me. I gave them a small wave and they quickly ran away. A servant opened the front door as I approached. I asked for Lady Tang and was told she was in her office. Smiling, curious faces peeked out of the rooms at me. They seemed so small. Strangely, I realized that the only child I had seen in the last eight years was the emperor, and I didn't see him often.

I lightly knocked on Lady Tang's door. She was sitting at her desk, drawing an embroidery pattern. She looked the exact same as I remembered her. She didn't look even a day older.

"Lady Tang?" I called softly as I entered the room.

"Yes," she replied, not looking up. I was a bit hurt that she was not responding to me. Was she not proud of me? Surprised to see me? Did she not know who I was?

"It's me," I said. "Yaqian."

"I know," she said, still not responding.

"Are you not surprised to see me?" I asked.

"No," she said. "I knew you would come back someday."

"How could you know that?" I asked.

"Because you left me too soon."

I nodded to myself. She was right about that, but it hardly had anything to do with the reason I had returned. But since I needed her help, I decided humility was the best path to take.

"You are right," I said. "You were always right. I was a foolish child when I left and now I have returned. I am here to finish my training...and for your help."

She finally looked at me and her eyes widened. "Oh no!"

she said suddenly, jumping up from her desk. "Get out! I can't help you with that."

"With what?" I asked.

"I'll not help you with any baby! Get out of here before you ruin my school!"

"How can you tell?" I asked.

"I can tell!" she replied as she tried to push me back toward the door. "Now go, get out before the other girls figure it out and you give them bad thoughts."

I turned away from her and stepped further into the room. "No! I'm not leaving. I need your help. You can't turn me away."

"Yes, I can!" she said. "Go to your mother. That's what mothers are good for, helping when their daughters become mothers."

"Please, Lady Tang, you know I can't go to that woman," I pleaded. "She never gave another thought to me after I left her house except to sell me for a second time. She won't help me if I don't let her sell me again or sell the baby."

"I can't help you," she said. "What if people find out one of my girls is a whore? It will ruin me! It will ruin my girls!"

"I'm not a whore!" I said. "It was one night. And I won't tell anyone. Just keep me here. If you kick me out, then I will have to tell people what happened, which will ruin both of us. If I stay here, hidden from the world, everything will be fine."

"Will it?" she asked. "How will that be? What do I do after the baby comes? What if it is a boy?"

"I'll hire a nursemaid, or the prince will. He said he would take care of us."

"Prince? What prince?" she asked.

"Prince Gong, he is the baby's father."

"That man that took you away? You were just a little girl! How dare he..."

"No, it was nothing like that. Please, it's a long story, and I had a long journey. Please say I can stay. I beg of you."

In the end, Lady Tang allowed me to stay, though she never stopped letting me know what a burden it was to her. I never stopped feeling sick. Everything I ate, I vomited back up. I could only drink weak tea and eat some steamed – never fried – dumplings filled only with vegetables. Anything fried or with meat would make my sickness unbearable. I did gain some weight over the next few months, but not much. I worried about the health of my baby as she struggled to grow.

Lady Tang tried to limit my exposure to her girls as much as possible. She feared my presence would encourage dreams of love, romance, and babies. She made up a story about the empress giving me in marriage to a cruel general who sent me away to have my child. I didn't correct her, but I didn't embellish the story to give it credibility either.

When I was feeling up to it, though, I was grateful to have time to work on my embroidery. Lady Tang agreed to help me with a few issues I was still having. She listened to my detailed descriptions of the prince's dragon robe. She agreed to help me recreate it. She, a few of her best students, and I worked together to bring the dragon robe back to life. It was not as beautiful as the original since we worked quickly and I had students helping, but I doubted anyone who was not a master artisan would notice the difference. I would have to take the robe with me back to the Forbidden City when I returned, unless I found a way to get it to him sooner.

I asked Lady Tang to confer on me the title of master.

She said she would consider it, which was all I had the right to ask for.

The baby finally decided to be born on a cold, wintery morning late that year. I don't know how long the labor was exactly, at least a day and a night and into the next day. The pain was excruciating and I pushed all I could, but the baby would not come for a long time. I thought I was going to die. Lady Tang sent for a midwife to help me, but there was very little she could do. The midwife was discussing with Lady Tang the possibility of cutting me open when the baby finally ripped me asunder and clawed her way out. The midwife picked up the baby as Lady Tang tried to staunch the bleeding.

"It's a girl," I heard the midwife say.

"Thank Heaven," I whispered before collapsing on the pillow into darkness.

*W*hen I awoke, I wondered if I had dreamed the last eight years. I was in my bed in Lady Tang's school. The room was warm even though I could see frost on the outside of the windows. The smell of familiar Hunan spices wafted past my nose. I slowly opened my eyes and saw Lady Tang sitting in a chair across the room holding a little bundle in her arms.

"You have been sleeping for two days," Lady Tang said in a gentle voice. "We thought you would die."

"What would you have done if I had?" I asked as I tried to sit up. I felt a stabbing pain in my stomach and between my legs that sharply confirmed I had not been dreaming my life away.

"I would have kept her here and hoped that your embroidery skills had passed onto the next generation."

"It is a girl, then?" I asked.

"Yes, it's a girl," she said, unable to hide a smile as she looked at me.

"Good," I said. "That's what I prayed for."

"Why did you do that?" she asked.

"The prince told me that all wives pray for a son. I decided that since I was no man's wife, I would pray for a girl."

Lady Tang brought my baby to me and placed her in my arms. She was so tiny, it felt as if I was holding a blanket with nothing in it. Lady Tang said the baby weighed only a little more than four *jin*, which was very tiny, but she was healthy. She was eating well. Lady Tang had been purchasing goat milk and breast milk from a woman who also gave birth recently to feed her. I tried to nurse her myself, but because of my sickness and since I passed out instead of feeding her right after the birth, my milk did not come in. But holding her as she drank from a bottle was good enough for me. She was warm and smiled in her sleep. I couldn't ask for more from a baby I never wanted in the first place.

"What will you do now?" Lady Tang finally asked.

"I will stay here to recover, but I will have to return to the empress soon."

"And the baby?" she prodded.

I didn't respond because she knew the answer. She knew it all along. She knew as soon as she saw me standing in her doorway that I needed much more than a place to hide and give birth. I would need someone to raise the baby. I didn't want to say the words because it was too much to ask of anyone, but the request had been made as soon as I got on my horse and headed toward Lady Tang's school.

"I have a business to run," she said. "I can't raise her as a daughter."

"I know," I said. "But neither can I. This girl will have no mother. Just raise her as you would your students. You can start training her as soon as she can hold a needle. Just be a good teacher to her."

In the spring of the following year, while I was still recovering, Lady Tang received a notice that Prince Gong would be paying her school a visit. I had heard nothing from the prince since I left Peking the year before. I had received letters from the empress, but most of them were pleas for my return. The notice from the prince instructed her to have a meal ready for him and his men and rooms prepared for them to relax for a few days.

Lady Tang ordered me to stay in my room unless the prince sent for me, but I was able to see him arrive from my room's window. My heart jumped when I saw him, even though he didn't look my way. He was with a large battalion of men, all of whom looked well worn. The prince and his top men visited with Lady Tang for some time while I sat in my room alone with my baby.

Finally, I heard his familiar footsteps. I ran my fingers through my hair and straightened my robe for the hundredth time. He knocked on the door and I could barely whisper the word "enter." When he opened the door, his face must have matched my own. He looked both happy to see me and as though he could cry at once. I was supposed to turn my gaze down and bow, but I could hardly move. I noticed Lady Tang close the door behind him. I wondered what the students must have been thinking. What excuse did he give his men to stop at an embroidery school?

He took a small step toward me, which broke the silence enough for me to finally kneel to him and cast my eyes to the floor. He ran to me and grabbed my arms to pull me up to him. We hugged and did not stop the tears from flowing.

"When I didn't hear anything, I feared you were dead," he said.

"I very nearly was," I said. "Your daughter entered the world as vicious as a tiger."

He stood back. "A daughter?"

I nodded. "I am sure she means nothing to you."

He looked around the room and saw the baby sleeping on my bed. I had wrapped her in the new golden dragon robe. He walked over to her and kneeled down. He reached out and touched her hand.

"Yaqian," he said. "I have sons. It doesn't matter that she is a girl. Am I the first man in China that is not disappointed to see a girl in swaddling cloths?"

I didn't reply. I wasn't sure how happy to be. It didn't matter if she was his son because if she had been a boy, she would have no inheritance anyway. Boy or girl, my child was a bastard. I suppose being a girl was no more of a detriment to her. In this situation, it might even be a blessing. As a girl, she could be raised by Lady Tang and have a trade, like her mother. She could work and make her own way in life. If she had been a boy, I would have had nowhere to send him.

The prince picked up the baby and sat on the bed. My heart froze for a moment when he lifted her from the safety of her bed, but I forgot that he had much more experience with children than I did. I lost count of how many consorts and children he had by this time. I liked forgetting that he had a real family somewhere else in Peking.

"These are magnificent swaddling cloths," he said with a smile. "You created two beautiful things while hiding here." He held the baby to his face and breathed in her scent. "She smells good," he said.

"I bathed her before your arrival," I said.

"You are a good mother," he said.

"No, I know nothing," I said. "I have a nursemaid who tells me what to do."

"How old is she?" he asked.

"About two months," I replied.

"What is her name?"

"She doesn't have one yet," I said.

The prince chuckled. "Why? What do you call her?"

"Little Baby. I couldn't decide. I didn't know if she should have a Manchu name."

The prince shook his head. "If she is to live here, she should just be Chinese. Besides, most Manchu take Chinese names now."

"Well, most Chinese names are flowers, or 'fragrant' or 'kindness' or something. They are very boring."

"You said she came into the world like a tiger. Maybe something like that."

"Tiger names are usually boy names," I explained.

"I don't care. She can still be a tiger."

"What about 'Fragrant Tiger'?"

"Do tigers smell nice?" the prince asked with a laugh. "Maybe tiger and flower?"

"'Huhua' sounds strange," I said.

"What about "Hulan'?" he asked. "When Empress Cixi was first appointed as a concubine, the emperor gave her the name 'Orchid'."

"Lan?" I asked. "That is a pretty name."

"She hated it," he said. "Which is why she had it changed to 'Yi' as soon as her son was born and my brother made her second consort."

"So you want to give the baby a name the empress hated?"

"It might be a nice homage to her, even if she will never know about it."

"'Hulan'. Our little Tiger Orchid. I like it," I said.

"'Hulan," my prince repeated.

SEVENTEEN
THE FORBIDDEN CITY, 1865-1868

*B*y the summer of that year, Empress Cixi ordered me to return to court. I could no longer ignore her summons without consequences. Hulan was thriving. Smiling, playing, getting fat cheeks. I was surprised that I didn't want to leave her behind, but I had no choice. I had to return to the empress and could not take a baby with me. Lady Tang hired a nurse to live at the school and raise the child. She had made arrangements with Prince Gong to send him regular updates, which he would then inform me about. I knew that I would have very little say in the girl's upbringing, but I did have one request for Lady Tang.

"Don't bind her feet," I said as Lady Tang walked me to the gate to leave the school for the last time.

"But it is tradition. Everyone expects it from our girls. They must be the highest quality," she protested.

"I understand that. And I know my life would not have turned out this way if my feet had not been bound. But the world is changing. I fear we are facing a future where bound feet will be a burden and not a blessing. The

Manchu hate it. The foreigners hate it. As China moves forward, such traditions will be done away with."

"The Manchus are not Chinese," she replied indignantly. "The foreigners are not Chinese. Should we change all our ways just because outsiders don't understand them?"

"What is the purpose?" I asked. "If it wasn't for tradition, why do it? In what way does having bound feet improve a woman's life? Does it make her smarter? Make her embroidery better? Help her ride a horse?"

Lady Tang crossed her arms and her nostrils flared.

"I hope you will raise my daughter to respect all of our traditions," I continued, "except this one. She is half Manchu. She might never know it, but she is. In this one thing, she can follow the traditions of her father."

Lady Tang still refused to speak, but I knew she would comply. One of the guards helped me mount my horse.

"Thank you, Lady Tang. I can never show adequate appreciation for all you have done for me," I said.

She gave me a small nod as I turned out my horse and headed for Peking. As we crossed the bridge over Orange Island, though, I knew I had to make one more stop – I had to return home. I could not travel so far and not at least see if my parents were still alive. I told my escorts about the change of plans, and they agreed that we could make the short stop, but we would have to be back on the road soon.

As we left the city of Changsha and traveled deeper into the countryside, the more I felt dread grow in my stomach. The cobblestone street turned to mud, the tall buildings became one-story hovels. I had nearly forgotten just how far I had risen.

As our horses trotted down the lane where I grew up, though, things changed. The road was wider and the houses got bigger. The children who ran by were still dirty, as children will be, but they wore nice clothes and shoes. When we finally arrived at the place where my childhood home once sat, a mansion large enough to rival Lady Tang's school stood before me. I am sure my mouth was agape as I climbed down from my horse.

I walked up to the front door and knocked. A young woman I didn't recognize answered. "Is Yang Zhu here?" I asked. The girl nodded and went back inside.

"Mistress Yang," I heard her call.

Mistress Yang? I wondered. Did Mother have a maid of her own?

The door opened wide and Mother stood before me. She looked much older. She was still sturdy and stood up straight, but her face had more lines and her hair was nearly white. Her clothes were quite fine, high-quality silk, but hung off her thin frame and she still didn't wear shoes on her big, flat feet. The family had obviously done well in my absence, but Mother was little more than a peasant in a lady's gown. I tried to hide my surprise as I bowed to her.

"Ma," I said. "How I have missed you."

"Don't lie, Yaqian," she said. "It doesn't become you." She turned her back to me and went into the house. She left the door open, though, meaning she wanted me to follow.

The large room was sparsely decorated. A big table with a few chairs around it sat to one side. Three little boys and an older man were sitting and talking. Several books were spread out on the table. Mother walked over to them and ordered them all outside.

"Go catch some frogs for dinner," she said. The boys hooted and hollered as they jumped from their chairs and ran out the door.

The old man sighed as he followed them slowly. "I've

now lost them for the rest of the day, Mistress Yang," he said.

"Go home and rest," she said. "Start fresh tomorrow." He gave a slight bow before he picked up a few of the books and then left.

Mother stacked the rest of the books and then sat at the table. She motioned for me to sit. "Well, why are you here?" she asked. "Did the empress dismiss you? You can't come back here if she did."

"It certainly looks as though you have the room if I needed a place to stay," I said as I sat.

Mother waved her hand dismissively. "It's so crowded with so many boys and the servants and all the extended family always dropping by. I have no privacy."

"So the concubine was...productive?" I asked.

"Fertile as a dog!" Mother exclaimed. "Three boys in three years. Not a worthless girl among them. May have worn her out, though. No babies in the last five years. No matter, though. Three is plenty."

"Congratulations."

"They are so much work in my old age. And so expensive. Clothes and that tutor and they eat like pigs."

"At least you have the concubine here to help."

"That worthless bitch? She does nothing. Her and your father just eat opium all day. They did their job and now they have abandoned us. In the city for days on end lost in a fog."

"How can they afford it?" I asked. Opium habits were not cheap.

"We get by," she said. "Your father was smart at first. He invested the money the emperor gave us and bought more land and more mulberry trees. Then he bought a small building and equipment to extract the silk ourselves. So now, instead of selling the silkworm cocoons we sell the silk. Along with the money and embroidery pieces you send us, we are comfortable. The boys will help grow the business when they get older. Maybe one will get a government job if he takes the exams."

"I'm glad things have worked out for you."

"We all have our part to play, Yaqian. Your job was to leave to make way for your brothers. The fortune teller said boys would be in your future. She was right. I thought she was just saying what I wanted to hear, since I had to pay her for her services, but she was right."

"They aren't my brothers," I said. "They aren't my future."

"They are the only future you have," she said. "You are too old to marry and have children of your own. What else is there to live for? What is the point of having money or a job if there is nothing after you?"

"I am very successful," I said. "I am a master artisan in the employ of the empress. I created a new embroidery style. Foreigners from all over the world buy my artwork. Hopefully I will be remembered for that."

"None of that matters," she said. "Family is everything. The *only* thing. You should invest in your brothers. Help send them to better schools and get them employed in the Forbidden City."

"Why is it of value for them to work in the Forbidden City but not me?"

"Because they can still marry and have children, you dumb girl. They will build a name and earn titles that they can pass on for generations."

"I don't see any value in that," I said. "What good is that after they are dead?"

"Don't you know anything about tradition and the afterlife? Only sons can burn incense at your tomb when you are gone."

"I have money to buy incense and fingers to light matches," I said. "I can burn incense for you."

"The gods won't listen to you. They won't accept your offerings or hear your prayers."

"So I am nothing?" I asked. "I fulfilled my duty by making a way for you to have sons and now I am worthless?"

"You can support your brothers," she said. "That is how you can still be of use to your family."

I thought about little Hulan and how I imagined her future, so free and bright. Mother had lived her whole life for nothing but the men in her life – her father, her husband, and now her sons. She didn't know that a life could be fulfilling for a woman without a man. She wouldn't believe me if I tried to explain it to her. I wondered if her opinion would change if she knew I did have a daughter, but I decided that would only make things worse. I was a whore who had a child without marriage, a worthless daughter no less. I would be shamed and such knowledge would give her power over me. She could threaten to tell the empress what I had done.

I decided I no longer belonged in my mother's house. My duty to her was complete – I had given her sons. I wished her a long and happy life and took my leave. I thought about Mother often on my journey home, but I never wrote to her again. I also vowed to never send her more money or embroidery work to sell. My life in Hunan was at an end.

*S*omething was wrong. I had no idea what, but there was a tension in the air as I walked through the Forbidden City for the first time in what felt like ages.

I went straight to the empress's palaces. She was sitting in her main hall, a stack of papers on her desk waiting for her to deal with. This was not the lazy, pampered concubine I had served years before, but a busy woman of State with a never-ending list of demands for her attention. I entered the main hall, bent at the waist. One of the eunuchs announced me. I went forward, got down on my knees, and then kowtowed before her.

"You finally decide to grace me with your presence, Yaqian?" she asked.

I sat up so she could clearly hear me speak. "It was torture to be away from you for so long, Your Majesty," I replied. "But I return to you as a master embroiderer. I hope to only bring you honor and praise for the rest of my days."

"Well, at least your absence was not a total waste, then," she replied. She sat for a moment, wanting to say more, but not in the presence of so many others. She finally waved her hand to send them away and motioned for me to come to her side. I sat on a small stool near her.

"I have been without a friend or confidant for too long, Yaqian. There is no one I can trust," she said in a low voice.

I didn't reply, only looked concerned. I was surprised she still thought so highly of me.

"Prince Gong has nearly abandoned me," she said. "He loves the foreigners and that stupid school more than me."

"I don't know what you are talking about," I said.

"Tongwen College," she said. "He said he no longer wishes to serve as Prince-Regent, but wishes to be magistrate of the school. Can you believe such arrogance? To think he can just walk away from the throne? The emperor? Me? Being regent is not something you can just walk away from. No more than I can stop being empress. How can he be so selfish?"

"I do not know, Your Majesty," I said. "I have heard nothing of this. I have been so far away."

"The other grandees are furious at me. And it's all his fault! It was his idea to start teaching science and math and foreign books. It was his idea to start hiring foreigners as teachers! How could I have been so stupid as to agree with him? Foreigners as teachers? The highest position of respect and honor? *Foreigners*! But I've already done it. I can't back down now. I have to support him. But the other grandees, the lords, the literati, the students, they all hate me and think I am elevating Westerners and Western thought above Chinese and Manchu traditions."

I let her rant on and on while I listened. Of course, I knew that Prince Gong saw a value in adopting some Western ways. And the school had been established to educate the next generation as translators and emissaries to the West. As China faced the future, interaction with the West was inevitable. But it appeared that Prince Gong had overstepped his bounds. By wanting to adopt too many Western ways too fast, he had made many enemies, and was alienating the empress from the rest of the court.

"Did you know he doesn't even kowtow in my presence

anymore?" she asked. I shook my head. "If he was any other man, I would have him put to death for such impunity!"

"Your Majesty," I said, calmly, yet with a hint of warning. I had to chastise her against such words without actually speaking against her.

"I know, I know," she said. "I never would. He is far too important. But it makes me look weak. He treats me like a little girl!"

I couldn't help but laugh a little at that. The empress was around thirty years old at this time, which was young for an empress, but Prince Gong was only two years older.

"This entire court is young," I replied. "It does not have the benefit of gray hairs." As part of her coup, the empress executed, banished, or dismissed the majority of the established court. The court she appointed in its place was mainly young men.

The empress sighed. "And my son will take the dragon throne officially as emperor when he is even younger. Can you believe he is already nine years old?"

I shook my head. It did seem as though only yesterday I had heard the news of his birth and started sewing little tiger shoes for him.

"We will have to start preparing for his wedding soon," she lamented.

"Do not burden yourself with such faraway thoughts," I said.

She nodded. "You are right. I have too many burdens now. Chiefly, what to do about Prince Gong? He is ruining my reputation. Causing divisions in the court. I must get rid of him."

"Then send him away," I said. "Let him run the school if he so wishes."

"But then I will be here alone. How can I run a kingdom without his guidance?"

"You are more than capable, Your Majesty," I replied. "It was your idea to overthrow Sushun and his council in the first place. You only involved Prince Gong to give you more authority. Maybe you don't need his authority anymore. Take the reins yourself."

"Do you really think I can?"

I nodded. "And if you can't, it will only be for a little while. The emperor will take the throne in only a few years."

She narrowed her eyes at me. "Won't it make you sad if Prince Gong is not a regular here in the palace anymore?"

I did my best to ignore her implication. I did worry about how I would get letters from Lady Tang about my baby if I could not see the prince, but at this moment, I needed to worry about his safety.

"I am sure all the palace ladies will miss seeing the prince strutting around here. But that is a small price to pay if it means you can reassert your authority with the other grandees."

The empress nodded and then went on to ask me about my embroidery work and my new status as a master. She was quite proud to have me back in her household and asked me to work on making double-sided embroidery pieces she could have framed and sent as gifts to foreign grandees and dignitaries.

I did not see Prince Gong for a long time after I arrived back at the Forbidden City. I was not present when he was dismissed. A little while later, though, a new eunuch arrived, and he took a keen interest in me. He was only fourteen years old and had quite a lovely face and pleasant demeanor. He was called Liujian, which meant something like "the strength of a willow tree." It was a contradiction, since willow trees were known for bending their will to the wind, but it reminded me of Hulan, and how her name was unconventional as well. Living in the palace, it was easy to dislike and distrust eunuchs, but Liujian was like a sweet and innocent child. He was easy to adore. I would often see him watching me from a distance, as if building his courage to approach me. I would always smile or pretend I couldn't see him even though we both knew I did.

One day, he cautiously approached me. I looked up at him and he dropped a letter in my lap before running away again. I opened the letter, and it was from Lady Tang. Over time, Liujian snuck several letters to me, and he became more comfortable approaching me. I found out that Prince Gong had paid his debt to his family – all eunuchs started life in debt because of their operation and their schooling – in exchange for his loyalty. He smuggled in the letters to me and smuggled my replies back out. I have no idea how he managed it, and I didn't want to know, but I was grateful he could.

To be honest, I didn't miss my daughter as much as I thought I would. I was content in knowing that she was being raised in a happy, loving, safe home where she would always have nice clothes to wear and good food to eat. Her childhood would be much better than mine. What more could a mother hope for?

Over the next few years, life was relatively calm and quiet. Empress Cixi enjoyed a period of peace and prosperity. The rebellions were either squashed or died out on their own, there was always tension with the foreigners, but it was better to work together than to fight, and the customs taxes she charged for their exports brought the country great wealth. Most of the indemnities she was being forced to pay after the opium war that destroyed her husband she paid with money the foreigners paid her for the right to use the treaty ports they forced her to open. The empress was under constant stress trying to balance the world in her two dainty hands, but it was working, and she was in the process of leaving a prosperous future to the Tongzhi Emperor.

EIGHTEEN
THE FORBIDDEN CITY, 1869

*T*he year the Tongzhi Emperor turned thirteen was the year his glorious mother began to prepare for his wedding. He seemed awfully young to me, but the actual marriage would not take place for another three years. It would take that long to find the consorts, prepare for the rituals, and make all the wedding clothes. I was put in charge of designing all the wedding garments: the robes for the emperor, his future consorts, and his two mothers.

It was an exciting task, and I couldn't wait to get started. I would have to hand-draw unique embroidery patterns for each outfit to send to the royal embroidery studios in Suzhou, but inspect and complete the final embellishments myself in Peking. At least, that is how it was supposed to have been done. The empress called me before her one day for what I thought would be a discussion about how to best communicate with the embroiderers in Suzhou.

"I think you should go to Suzhou yourself," she announced.

"What?" I asked, not hiding my surprise.

"Yes, this is much too important of an event for you to manage from afar. You must go to Suzhou and oversee the embroiderers yourself."

"This is quite an honor, Your Majesty," I replied. "There is really no need. I could direct the embroiderers from here so you can better relay your wishes to me directly. But if this is your wish, I appreciate the opportunity to see the Suzhou embroidery workshops for myself. Thank you."

"We will arrange everything, all the designs and measurements and color pallets, before you go. And if I do need anything, An Dehai will be there to help you."

"What?" I asked, not hiding my shock. "An Dehai will be with me? Outside the Forbidden City?"

I stood there, my mouth agape along with everyone else's. The room went silent. An Dehai stood by her side with his head held high. No longer the sniveling, foot-shuffling whipping boy he once was, he *should* be, he stood tall and proud as any man. How had this happened? What had given him such confidence? Something must have happened between him and the empress that I had missed. But more importantly, why was she making such a dangerous decision. Palace eunuchs were not allowed to leave the Forbidden City. He could be executed just for stepping foot outside the gate. Even under the empress's orders, sending a palace eunuch outside of the court on court business simply wasn't heard of.

And An Dehai himself was not a popular figure. Since Prince Gong's dismissal, it seemed as though An Dehai was the most powerful, or at least influential, man in China. He had the ear of the empress and no one could get to her except through him. Many people suspected he was influencing her for his own gain and that he was the one making major decisions. It was ridiculous, mostly. I knew from my own observations that the empress ruled the country herself. But who knew what she and An Dehai spoke of in private, how he could have turned her one way or another. True or not, though, An Dehai had many enemies.

"An Dehai will be leading the trip," she explained. "He will take a small fleet to Suzhou, oversee the production of the wedding garments, and make sure they are safely returned to Peking early enough for me to inspect them and order any changes that need to be made."

"With all due respect, Your Majesty," I couched, carefully. "An Dehai is not an embroidery expert. If you want anyone to oversee this expedition, it should be me."

"Pride has always been your most egregious trait, Yang Yaqian," An Dehai piped up. I shot him a look so full of hate I think he nearly jumped back.

The empress raised her hand to silence both of us. "This is not meant as an injury to anyone's pride," she said. "Yaqian, of course I value your skills as an embroiderer, that is why I am sending you with him. But An Dehai knows me better than anyone. He knows my likes, my dislikes, my wishes for my son. And he has served me faithfully for many years." I bit my lip to keep from pointing out that the same things could be said of me. "He deserves this opportunity to stretch his wings."

"Then don't send me," I said. "An Dehai and I both love you and know you well. If you send him, I beg you not to send me along his side." This trip was a fool's errand that would only end in disaster. Anyone could see that. Why couldn't she? How could she be so blind? "I can work with you here and then convey your wishes to him in Suzhou."

"You will go where I bid you," she said firmly. "That is all. Start sketching some designs. We need to make sure everything is prepared before you go. You will leave in the fall."

I bowed and left the room. I went right to Liujian, who had already heard the news about An Dehai's Great Journey.

"He is looking for a group of eunuchs to accompany him. He is letting us pay him for his favor, for the right to go. How much do you think it would cost?" he asked me, excitedly.

"You are *not* going," I said.

"But when would another chance come? And you and the prince have paid me well. I have saved most of it, probably more than most other eunuchs have the chance to save..."

"Shut up!" I finally said, hurting his delicate feelings. "Another chance like this won't come because it shouldn't ever happen! You aren't supposed to leave. If you do, you are forfeiting your life."

"But the empress..."

"I know what the empress said," I said. "But I also know how much you all are hated. And An Dehai has many enemies in this world. Trust me. This is a bad and very dangerous idea."

"But you are going," he said.

"Not if I can help it," I said. "I need you to send a letter to Prince Gong."

*M*y letters to the prince begging for help went unanswered. Everyone was talking about the trip, and everyone was concerned. Nothing like this had ever been done before. All I could do was discourage everyone I could from tagging along. Strangely, even though everyone thought the trip was a bad idea, everyone wanted to go. The eunuchs and *gōngnǔ* of every station were virtual prisoners in the palace. The eunuchs were usually imprisoned for life. They couldn't have a life outside the palace walls. For years, the *gōngnǔ* would never venture outside the palace walls. Many of them would eventually be married off, but they would simply exchange one prison for another. For many of the *gōngnǔ* and the eunuchs, the chance to have an adventure outside of the palace walls was worth any consequences.

I worked with the empress every day on the designs for the wedding clothes. She didn't talk to me of anything else. It was clear she didn't want to discuss the trip with me any further. After a few weeks, though, she let her guard down and I took the last opportunity to try and convince her to change her mind.

"Your Majesty," I began. "There really is no need to send such a large retinue to have the clothes made. I am confident I can take just a few assistants and go to Suzhou and return with the most beautiful clothes in the world for you and the emperor so quickly you will not even realize we were gone."

"I can't cancel the trip now," she said. "Have you seen how happy An Dehai is? It would break his heart to tell him he couldn't go."

"But why do you care?" I asked. "He is just a eunuch."

"'Just a eunuch'?" she asked. "Are you just an embroidery girl?"

"Compared to an empress, yes," I said. "I wish I amounted to more, but I don't. We are all just servants."

"I thought you were my friend," she said.

"I am your friend," I said. "Which is why I have to speak about this."

"Well, An Dehai is my friend too," she said. "And he has served me faithfully for years. I would not be who I am today without him. It is time for me to repay his loyalty."

"There are many other ways to reward loyalty," I said.

"But this is his dream," she said. "To stand at the helm of a ship, not as a eunuch, but as a man. To have a taste of what his life might have been like had he not been cut."

"But it is dangerous," I said. "Are you not afraid something will happen to him?"

"What could happen?" she asked. "I am the empress! Oh yes, the men would like to diminish my power by calling me 'dowager empress', as if I am the wife of a dead man and nothing more. But they know the truth. Everyone knows that I run this country. I am the most powerful woman in China, and possibly the world, save Queen Victoria. She runs her country in her own right. She doesn't have to sit behind a screen. She can meet with foreign envoys. She doesn't have to sign her edicts in the name of a little boy. Well, if she can do it, so can I."

I couldn't respond, only express my distaste with my expression. I didn't try to hide the fact that I was angry and thought she was wrong. Three years before, she had dismissed Prince Gong for overstepping his bounds. She was overstepping her bounds now. She might envy Queen Victoria, but this was China, and in China women did not rule. I believed Empress Cixi had the ability. After all, I had encouraged her to send Prince Gong away so she could rule more freely, but even she could not fight thousands of years of tradition. She couldn't change the country overnight. She had only been able to make some reforms because she had the support of the grandees, but they were against her in this. Every man in China would be against her. From local magistrates and provincial governors to peasants, they would not want to see a palace eunuch at the head of a fleet of ships sailing down the Grand Canal in royal splendor. It was too ludicrous for words.

After my session with the empress, I realized that she could not be reasoned with. I decided to try and send letters to everyone I could think of who might be able to pressure her into stopping this folly. I would write to Prince Chun, Prince Gong's younger brother, the man who had helped Cixi write her decree against Sushun eight years before. Surely he would not want to see her undone by her silly infatuation with a castrated man.

I went to Liujian's room to ask him for help, but he was not the eunuch I found. An Dehai was there waiting for me.

"Where is Liujian?" I asked.

"Never mind that," he said. "We need to talk."

"I have nothing to say to you," I said, turning to leave.

He grabbed my arm. "Then listen," he said. "I know you have been working against me. Trying to keep me from going on this trip. I am ordering you to stop."

"You disgusting worm," I spat, ripping my arm from his grasp. "You don't order me. I could have you beaten just for touching me."

"You won't," he said. "You will stop speaking against me and this expedition. You will go along with it and support it as if your life depended on it, because it just might."

"What are you talking about," I asked.

"How do you think the empress would feel if she knew you had left her to have a baby in the countryside?"

I could never gamble – my face was too expressive. I didn't even have time to think about pretending I didn't know what he was talking about.

"Just as I thought," he said. "I am sure it would also go badly for your Lady Tang as well if it got out that one of her girls was a whore."

"I'm not a whore," I said.

"Yes, you are," he said. "And you are also a traitor."

"I have never betrayed the empress!" I yelled.

"No, but you did betray her husband. You and your faithless lover, Prince Gong. You disobeyed the emperor's orders. Helped the prince undermine his own brother's power. Was it to help the prince take the throne? Did he promise to make you a royal consort?"

"You have no idea what you are talking about."

"I know enough. If you don't stop fighting me, the empress will know. And if the death by a thousand cuts is not enough to frighten you, just realize that your dishonor will have far-reaching consequences. Lady Tang, your bastard, even your friend Wensong, I'll not spare anyone you care about from the death and ruin I could wreak upon them."

"You are a heartless monster," I mumbled.

"Maybe," he said. "But we are going to have such a glorious time sailing down the Grand Canal together."

He left me alone with the fact that I could do no more, and would soon be on my way to Suzhou with the most hated man in China.

I could do nothing to calm my nerves as I boarded one of the ships at the port of the Grand Canal. The ships and port were so crowded. As the ships started to sail, everyone ran to the side of the decks to wave to onlookers. Everyone except me. I went to my room and prayed the trip would be over soon and without incident.

At first, everything seemed to be going to plan. We had three ships with dozens of crewmen. There were eight eunuchs traveling with An Dehai in the first ship. He was so proud to be captain of the fleet that he brought his mother, sisters, and several aunts along. They sailed in the second ship. Myself, several other maids, and Wensong were on the last ship. In spite of An Dehai's warnings, I had tried to convince Wensong to not come along, but she wouldn't hear of it. Apparently, Empress Ci'an had wanted her to go along. When Ci'an had heard that Cixi was sending me, she decided to send her own embroidery maid to help out.

As we sailed down the Grand Canal, everyone was in good spirits. There was food and drink for all and several musicians on each ship. After a couple of days, my nerves started to relax, but I was still unable to join in the festivities. When the ship docked in Shandong, most of the revelers decided to disembark. Shandong was a large and lovely town with numerous taverns, restaurants, shops, and brothels along the canal. For most travelers, it was a must-stop place. I, however, was against making any stops, so I refused to leave the boat.

For a while, I sat on the deck in the cool evening and listened to the sounds of the city. Laughter and music drifted over the water and onto the ship. It wasn't enough to entice me onto dry land, but it was enjoyable to listen to. Eventually, I went to bed and let the rocking of the boat lull me to sleep.

At some point during the night, I heard heavy footsteps on the decks above me. At first, I thought it must be my shipmates returning from a night of drinking and singing, but then I realized the steps were rushed. I was still groggy with sleep when my door was kicked open and a burly guard burst into the room. I screamed as he grabbed me and dragged me above deck. The few other people who had stayed with me on the ship had also been rounded up. Then we were herded together down the gangplank and into town. Our questions about what was happening were totally ignored as we were pushed through town. An angry mob formed around us, screaming at us, but I couldn't understand what they were saying. Eventually we were taken to a large stone building that looked sort of like a fort. We were taken through the main gate and then through a small door. We went down a long, dimly lit hallway lined with heavy wood and metal doors. They opened one of the doors and threw the men from our group inside. We women were thrown into another room.

It was so dark, I couldn't see anything at first, but I could hear the crying of other women who were already in the cell. After a moment, my eyes were able to adjust to the very small amount of moonlight that was streaming in through a tiny window. I realized that all the women from our expedition were in the cell. I finally caught sight of Wensong and went to her.

"What happened?" I asked. "Why are we here?"

"I'm not sure," she said. "Everyone was drinking and laughing and having a wonderful time when a man, someone called him the governor, busted in and ordered us all under arrest. It was so chaotic after that. Some people ran away, others fought back, a crowd of people surrounded the tavern we were at and started screaming at us. We were all arrested and brought here. No one has explained why or what is going to happen to us."

I nodded and led her over against a wall. We sat down and held each other. There wasn't anything we could do until we were informed of what our crime was, though I had a feeling I already knew what it was.

$\mathscr{T}$he next morning, we were all given a bucket of congee and a few baozi to share. It wasn't enough to fill any of us up, but we shared as much as we could. There was no chamber pot, so we designated a pile of straw in one corner as the place to relieve ourselves. Of course, we had no paper or cloths to clean ourselves after. The nights were cold, but we all huddled together for warmth.

We sat in our miserable cell for days, with no informa-

tion about why we had been arrested or what might
become of us. After a few days, a guard finally entered the
room. He made us line up and clapped our hands in chains.
We were led outside, where a large platform had been built.
Then, we saw An Dehai, the other eunuchs, and the sailors
led to the stage. The guards made An Dehai get down on
his knees. A guard stood over him and unraveled a procla-
mation, which he read out loud.

"For insulting the governor, for daring to act on behalf
of the emperor, for leaving the imperial city without cause,
these men have been sentenced to death to serve as a
warning to all others."

At the mention of the word death, most of the women
started screaming. An Dehai's mother fainted. A guard
stepped in and started hitting us to get us to shut up, but the
rest of the crowd that had gathered started cheering as the
executioner stepped forward. An Dehai didn't try to fight
back. He calmly bent over at the waist and waited for the
death stroke to fall. I didn't want to see him die, I had never
seen someone die before, but I think I was in so much shock
I didn't think it would actually happen. The executioner
stepped forward and with one quick strike, An Dehai's head
fell from his body. Blood squirted everywhere and his body
slumped to one side. The women erupted in screams again
and more of them fainted. The crowd erupted in cheers
again. I was frozen solid. It was all too horrible to compre-
hend. Then, they brought the other eunuchs forward and
beheaded them one by one. I did my best to look away, but
my eyes were always drawn back to the gory sight. Then,
nearly twenty more men, the sailors of various ranks, were
also executed. In the end, every man who was on the
journey with us was killed.

When it was over, we were all led back to our cell.

a couple of days later, the guard returned. I could hardly respond when I heard him call my name.

"Yang Yaqian," he yelled.

My mouth went dry. Was he there to kill me?

"Yang Yaqian!" he yelled again.

I couldn't respond, but I stood and held up my hand.

"You are Yang Yaqian?" he asked. I nodded. He grunted as several other guards entered the room. "All of them but that one," he said.

The rest of the women were forced to line up and were once again chained together. Wensong and I held on to each other for as long as we could.

"Please, leave her too!" I begged.

"Get back, bitch," one the guards growled as he ripped Wensong from me and pushed me against the wall.

One by one, the women were led out of the cell, and I was left alone. The only comfort I had was that I didn't hear any screaming crowds outside, so hopefully they were not being executed. I huddled by myself in one little corner of my cell and waited.

Thankfully, I didn't have to wait long. A few hours later, the guard returned and ordered me to follow him. He wasn't as gruff or cruel as before. He didn't push me or clap me in chains. As we walked down the hallway, a familiar face came into view. When I realized it was Prince Gong, I wanted nothing more than to run to him, but his face was steely, as if in warning. I stayed calm and kept walking. He joined me at the foot of a stairwell and motioned for me to go up. He followed close behind, but didn't say anything. When we got outside, I paused to blink to adjust my eyes to the sunlight. The prince gripped my forearm and led me to a horse. Still without speaking, he climbed up on the horse and then pulled me up behind him. I breathed a sigh of relief as I wrapped my arms around him and we started to gallop away.

As we were leaving the city, I saw a bunch of wooden cages being pulled by heavy horses following another path. In the cages were all the women from the dungeon, including Wensong.

"Wait," I said, sitting up and tugging on the prince's shirt. "Wensong! The others! We can't leave them!"

"Keep quiet!" the prince barked. "We can do nothing."

The prince gave his horse a sharp kick and we rode away from the city as fast as we could. We didn't speak until we arrived at another town several hours away. The prince stopped the horse at an inn. He paid the blacksmith far too much to just board a horse for the night, and then he paid the innkeeper far more than was needed for a room for the night. But I said nothing. One of the barmaids took me to a room in the back of the inn that served as a bathhouse where she helped me undress and bathe. Afterward, she took me to the room the prince had rented for the night where some bowls of noodles and hot dumplings were waiting. After she left, and only the prince and I were in the room, I fell on the food like a rabid wolf. The prince stood by a window and smoked his pipe.

"Are we going to talk now?" I asked after I finished eating.

He shrugged. "What about?"

"What happened?"

"What did happen?" he asked.

"I don't know," I said. "We were traveling down the Grand Canal. We stopped in Shandong and almost everyone went into the city to eat and drink and shop. I stayed on the ship. That night, I was dragged away and thrown into the dungeon where the others already were. They only took us out once, so we could watch An Dehai and the others be executed. Then the other women were taken away. Then you came for me and now we are here."

"You probably don't need to know much more than that," he said. "I'm sure you can piece it together."

Obviously, whatever happened had to do with An Dehai. I don't know why the other men were executed, but the governor of Shandong must have been offended by An Dehai and had him killed.

"What I don't know," I said, "is what is happening to the other women."

"I'm not exactly sure. I wasn't able to ask. But they will probably be taken west, along the trading routes, and sold off."

"Sold off?" I asked. "You mean sold into slavery?"

He nodded.

"How is that possible? That free women can be sold like property?"

"They broke the law," he said. "They are no longer free."

"They didn't break any law. They were only following orders. The *empress's* orders."

"The empress is lucky that she is not being prosecuted for this," he said. "But the grandees just wanted to send a message. She is just a dowager empress, not a queen. Once her son comes of age, she will retire and have nothing more to do with governing."

"She knows that," I said.

"She does now."

"Why didn't you stop her?" I asked. "Why didn't you respond to my letters?"

"It needed to happen," he said. "An Dehai needed to die."

"But I could have died," I said. "Why am I here?"

"If I had stepped in, Cixi would have known something was going on and might have changed her mind."

"You mean, you knew about this? You knew this was going to happen? You could have stopped it?

The prince didn't respond.

"Did you plan this? Did you orchestrate the whole thing?"

Again, his silence confirmed my suspicions.

"Did he threaten you?" I asked. "Did he threaten to tell the empress what he knew?"

"Yes," the prince finally said. "He said he would tell the empress about Hulan. He would ruin you and Lady Tang. And who knows what would have happened to our daughter."

"You did this for us?" I asked.

"I did this for China," he said. "Protecting my family was just the catalyst."

"You consider us family?" I asked.

"The only family that matters right now," he said. He walked over to me and pulled me up to him. We kissed passionately as we made our way over to the bed. We quickly removed each other's clothes as we tumbled down on the mattress.

*O*utside of Peking, the prince stopped his horse and helped me down.

"Here is where I have to leave you," he said. "It can't be known that I rescued you, or else the empress will know I was involved."

"What will I tell her then?" I asked.

"Just make up something," he said. "Say you hid on the ship and then a kindly merchant let you ride back to the city in his cart."

He found a mule cart driver and paid him to carry me to the Forbidden City. Then he trotted off into the darkness of the cold, early morning.

It was daylight by the time I made it to the side gate of the Forbidden City. I was tired, cold, and hungry, but I went straight into the see the empress.

She looked terrible. Her head was in her hands, her hair was disheveled, and she looked as though she had been crying. As I walked toward her, she lifted her head and stared at me in disbelief. She probably thought the whole expedition had been lost. She quickly stood and descended the stairs, running toward me. As she approached, I fell to my knees and kowtowed to her. She grabbed my arms, pulling me to my feet and stared at me.

"You are alive?" she asked. "How can this be?"

"I hid," I said. "I was on the ship when the others were taken. I hid until I could flee."

"How...how is it you have returned?" she asked in confusion. I don't think she could quite process what I was saying.

"I asked for help on the road. A kindly merchant helped me return to the city…"

"No," she said, shaking me. "How is it *you* have returned?"

"I…I don't understand, Your Majesty," I said, unsure of how to respond.

"You! Worthless servant!" she said, nearly screaming as she shook my arms. "How is it you have returned when An Dehai is dead?"

"I…I don't know!" I yelled back. "There was nothing that could be done."

"Where is he?" she screamed. "They have refused to send him back to me! Is he still alive? Did they lie? Tell me he survived."

"He is dead, Your Majesty," I said. "They are all dead. The eunuchs, the seamen. The women were all sold as slaves."

The servants and ladies around us all gasped. I guess they didn't know that part. Perhaps they thought the women were still in captivity or had also been killed.

"But you survived," she sneered, pushing me away and causing me to fall to the floor. "You worthless little bitch. You always find your way out of trouble, don't you?"

I wasn't sure how to respond. She was obviously hurt and angry and lashing out, but I had tried to stop her. Everyone had tried to stop her. This was her own fault. I gritted my teeth and was about to lay the blame at her feet where it belonged, but another voice beat me to it.

"This is all your fault!" a young voice interrupted. "Don't blame Mistress Yang for your errors!"

Everyone looked and saw Liujian standing defiant. "An

Dehai and the rest are all dead because of you! Everyone told you not to send An Dehai as the head of the expedition. You can't blame anyone else. An Dehai's death is on your hands, and your hands alone."

Everyone sat or stood in total silence. Even though everyone was thinking the same thing, to point out an empress's failure was nearly an act of treason. And for a eunuch to speak against a member of the imperial family was a death sentence.

Empress Cixi was so shocked and angry she couldn't speak, but the whole room was trembling from her great rage. She finally raised her left hand and then gave a small wave with two of her fingers. Four or five other eunuchs appeared practically out of the shadows and seized Liujian.

"Forgive me, Your Majesty," he begged as he was dragged away.

I crawled back to my knees and kowtowed again. "Please, show mercy, Your Majesty," I begged. "He is just a boy..."

"Silence!" Cixi yelled. "Don't stick your neck out for him, Yaqian, if you want it to continue connecting your head to your body." She turned away from me and left the main hall, followed by her dozen attendants.

The sound of Liujian's screams floated into the hall as he was beaten to death by the other eunuchs. I sat down and put my head on my knees as I wept for him. He shouldn't have spoken out, but it was clear the empress killed him because he was my favorite. She had lost her favorite eunuch, and now I lost mine. The prince had killed someone close to her heart, and now the empress had killed one close to mine. I thought about how the two people I loved most in the world, the prince and the empress, were so capable of such passion and such cruelty. As much as the three of us loved each other, we could also hurt each other more deeply than most people could imagine possible.

The empress was so heartbroken by the death of An Dehai that she took to her bed for a month. I did my best to continue working on the wedding clothes, but I lacked the feelings of love and happiness such work required. I would sit, staring at my needle and thread for hours, unable to make a single stitch. All I could see in my mind was An Dehai's bloody, twitching body and all I could hear were Liujian's screams.

The day of the emperor's marriage was approaching. Eventually, the empress had returned to her duties and I returned to mine. We were hardly the friends we were before, but we at least were able to work together again. I had not seen Prince Gong in many, many months. Everyone was busy preparing for the marriage celebrations. The Forbidden City was draped in red silk and red lanterns hung from every beam. For the first time in two centuries, a woman had been chosen to be the emperor's empress, not just a consort. Her name was Alute, and she was a great beauty. I had the honor of being sent to her home to meet her and measure her body to make sure her wedding robe would fit her perfectly. She was lithe and white as a pearl. She had large dark eyes and pink lips, seemingly always plump and pursed, calling to be kissed. I could see why the emperor had chosen such a stunning young girl to be his number one wife.

I spent so many days and hours on her gown, making sure it would perfectly complement her splendid figure. Her red gown featured a golden dragon and a golden phoenix intertwining around her. She was smaller than I was originally told, so I had to adjust the panels so that the great beasts would perfectly coil around her breasts, her hips, and their tails would fan out on her train equally on each side. The gown was nearly as amazing as the one I had made for Prince Gong so many years before. I was heart-broken that I would not be able to see Alute ascend the main stairs into the Forbidden City in all her glory. Alute would be entering the front gate, a gate no woman had been permitted to enter in over two hundred years. I kept some red strings from that gown with my other mementos.

A few days before the wedding, I was sitting alone in my room, enjoying some tea by the fire and a moment of quiet when I heard something tapping on my roof. I thought maybe it was squirrels dropping acorns from the tree that hung over my room, but then I heard it again. Then I heard giggling and shushing sounds. I went outside and looked up and saw three young men scurrying around.

"What do you think you are doing?" I asked calmly.

The boys looked at me and I realized who they were. I dropped to my knees. "Your Majesty."

"Mistress Yang," the emperor said, jumping down from the roof. He held his hand out, inviting me to stand.

I had seen the young man more often lately since I was in charge of making his wedding clothes. The emperor had grown from a spoiled child into a handsome man. He was quite tall, taller than his father or his mother, with a clear complexion and charming smile. He was around sixteen years old now.

His two companions jumped down next to him, and I gave them polite curtseys. They were Wang Qingqi, a court scholar not much older than the emperor, and Zaicheng, Prince Gong's eldest son. The three had been inseparable for years, known for causing all sorts of mischief around the palace. There were also rumors that the two boys had been helping the emperor sneak out of the palace to visit Han prostitutes in the city, much like his father had before him, but not just female prostitutes. Of course, it was treason to speak of such things, and I really didn't believe it. The court was always a place for idle gossip by eternally bored young ladies. But now, I couldn't help but know the truth. They were clearly sneaking out via the oak tree that grew on the other side of the wall whose branches hung over my little room.

"That tree is rather dangerous," I finally said. "I am always hearing old branches break off when it rains," I said.

"You won't tell my mother, will you, Mistress Yang?" the emperor asked.

I must admit, seeing the emperor with his sheepish smile asking me for protection gave me a perverse sense of satisfaction. The other boys giggled. I crossed my arms.

"I don't know," I said. "What will you give me for my silence?" I asked.

"We could take you with us," Qingqi quipped.

"What could I possibly find out there that I can't find in here?" I asked.

"Maybe we could sneak in my father for you instead," Zaicheng suggested. At that, the three of them laughed so hard they nearly fell over.

"You cheeky monkey!" I gasped, feigning anger.

"We're sorry, Mistress Yang," the emperor said, offering me a mock bow. "Seriously, what do you want? Whatever you want, it is yours."

"I don't want anything from you, Your Majesty," I said. "Just so long as you are a good and just ruler when you come into your own."

"No wonder you and my mom are friends," he said, turning to climb back onto the roof. "You sound exactly the same."

The emperor married Alute and the two were officially titled as emperor and empress. Empress Dowager Cixi and Empress Dowager Ci'an retired from their administrative duties and no longer had any role in ruling the empire.

Only days after the emperor's wedding, I once again heard the little scamps sneaking across my roof and over the wall. I also began to hear them more frequently. I couldn't completely blame the emperor. He was a teenager and longed for freedom and adventure. Had I been so different? Of course, I didn't seek sexual adventures, but I knew their pleasures well enough. The emperor's life was completely regulated. From before dawn until midnight, grandees and eunuchs and magistrates led him from one side of the Forbidden City to the other making sure he fulfilled his never-ending duties. Of course he would want some time out of his prison and in the arms of waiting lovers.

But I couldn't condone his neglect of Empress Alute and his other consorts. It was something I would never understand. If he was fulfilling his husbandly duties and then seeking outside pleasures, there would be no qualms. But some of her attendants had whispered to the attendants of Empress Cixi that not only was Alute not pregnant, she was still a virgin. This caused great distress among Empress Cixi and Empress Ci'an. The only job of an empress was to produce sons. It should also always be the main concern for an emperor. The dynasty must continue. Of course, running the empire, making sure the country prospered, these were his most important daily jobs, but a successful empire meant nothing if there was not a son to leave it to.

Thankfully for the emperor, Empress Cixi had left him an empire that was running like a well-oiled machine. There were no rebellions, no wars abroad, and the economy was flourishing. If things continued in this manner, China could one day become a world power equal to those of Europe. Because of this, the emperor's life was mainly routine. Making appointments, approving agreements, settling minor disputes. With the empire running so smoothly, his main concern should have been having children. Yet, he could not be doing less to do so. Even if he sired a child on the outside, it could never be brought into the Forbidden City. Its parentage could never be verified. He had to sire children upon his official consorts.

Sitting in Empress Cixi's main hall, the silence was deafening. Now that she had officially retired, she had no daily administration to see to. She felt as though she had nothing to do. This left her all the time in the world to simply worry. And she worried about her son having children.

I probably felt her anxiety more than anyone else. Everyone else had only heard rumors, but I knew the truth. But if I told the empress what I knew, she would confront the emperor about it, and he would know the information came from me.

These were the sorts of thoughts that plagued my mind

when Empress Alute came to call on Empress Cixi. The young empress was brought to Empress Cixi's palace carried in a palanquin. Several eunuchs helped her step out of her grand carriage and half a dozen attendants followed her inside. All of us, including Empress Cixi, got down on our knees as she entered. For the first time in my life, Empress Cixi kneeled as low as I did, as though we were equals. I couldn't help but smile. Of course, Empress Alute then motioned for her mother-in-law to stand, a privilege she would never allow someone as lowly as me.

Empress Alute presented Empress Cixi with several exotic flowers for her to plant in her garden. Empress Cixi motioned for me to retrieve an embroidered fan to give to Empress Alute as a gift. Then the two empresses sat close together and shared their troubles. I was too far away to hear everything they said, but it was clear they were talking about the emperor and his lack of attention to his wife. At one point, the young empress burst into tears. Empress Cixi took her daughter-in-law in her arms. The lonely life of a consort was one she knew well.

After a couple of hours of shared commiseration and comfort, the young empress took her leave, but her troubles stayed behind. Empress Cixi seemed to have aged in the months since her son had taken the throne. Empress Cixi was still quite young, only in her late thirties. She was now a lady of leisure with decades of peace and freedom ahead of her. But the stress of knowing her son was not doing his duty by his wife weighed heavily on her. She paced the room in dark silence.

Finally, I could take it no longer. I approached the empress and asked for a private audience. She motioned for everyone else to leave the room and she returned to her throne and I sat on a stool nearby.

"Your Majesty," I said. "I have something to tell you that is very hard to say and very sensitive in nature."

She nodded.

"There is a tree over my house. It is very old and full of squirrels and bats. They climb and fly over my house every night. I fear they are causing all sorts of damage to the building and it is hurting my ability to sleep, which affects my ability to make lovely embroidery for you."

"You asked for a private audience to complain about squirrels?" she asked, hardly bemused.

"Yes," I said. "The squirrels are causing many, many problems. All *three* squirrels..."

She stared at me for a quite a while, as if she knew I was trying to tell her something, but she was having trouble putting it together.

"Tell me more about this tree," she said.

"It is a very old, very large tree. The trunk is outside of the palace wall, but its branches hang inside, allowing the squirrels free reign."

She nodded. "I see. Well, I will send someone to deal with this tree."

"Your Majesty," I said. "The squirrels will know I asked you for help. I am the only person the squirrels bother."

She nodded again. "I'll find a way to be discreet," she said.

I endured the pitter patter of feet across my roof for several more nights, but then there was a big storm. There was plenty of thunder and lightning and rain was on the way. I was lying in my bed, enjoying the rumbles from the night sky when I started to smell smoke. I quickly jumped out of bed and checked my fireplace, but the fire was contained. I went outside, and I noticed smoke rising from behind my house. The tree was on fire! I called for help and several maids and ladies came to see what the trouble was, but no one came to put out the fire. The fire grew and soon had engulfed much of the tree. Finally, palace guards and eunuchs arrived and worked to douse the flames. Thankfully, since most of the tree was on the other side of the wall, there was no damage to my building. After the fire had died down and everyone was returning to their rooms, one of the empress's eunuchs approached me.

"Excuse me, Mistress Yang," he began. "But the empress wanted me to tell you that lightning from the storm must have struck the tree, causing the fire."

I nodded to the eunuch and he left just as the storm's rains began to fall.

*a*fter the loss of the great tree, the emperor began rebuilding the Summer Palace. The empress dowagers were delighted. They had both so loved the palace and were heartbroken at its destruction. The emperor said the palace would be their retirement home so they could live in peace away from the busy court. But it never came to be. Several of the palace's buildings were restored, but the emperor chose to live there himself most of the year, leaving his mothers and his wives behind in the Forbidden City. Empress Cixi could not burn enough trees in the world to force her son to do his duty by his empress.

Two years after the emperor was married and took the throne, he contracted what everyone thought was smallpox. As a protected child, he never contracted the illness while he was little. The dowager empresses, who both had smallpox as children, stayed by their son's bedside constantly. The emperor's wives, though, were forbidden from going near him. The illness hit him very strongly and many feared he would die. Prince Gong returned to court to be near his nephew and to help with administration while the emperor was bed-ridden. Prince Gong and the other grandees asked the empress dowagers to resume their duties as co-regents as they had before the emperor came into his rule. The empresses agreed, but they were quite preoccupied with their son's well-being.

The emperor languished for several weeks. Finally, he showed signs of improvement. His pustules burst and his fever lowered. He was able to sit up and gave formal approval for his mothers to help with the country's governance while he was ill.

But the relief everyone felt at his improvement was short lived. Suddenly, the emperor took ill again and everyone realized he had been misdiagnosed. What everyone thought was smallpox was actually what we called big pox, a disease contracted from whores. Only days after the doctors thought the emperor was on the mend, the emperor died.

The dowager empresses were inconsolable. Cixi refused to leave her son's side while Ci'an was taken to her bed, which she did not leave for weeks. When the eunuchs went to remove the body of the emperor to prepare it for burial, Cixi would not let them take him. Eventually, Prince Gong sent for me, to see if I could help console her. When I entered the room, she was kneeling by his bed, holding his hand in hers as she continued to weep. I sat by her side and put my arms around her.

"My beautiful boy," she said. I didn't reply. How could I ever understand her pain? "I have no other," she lamented. "My husband had no other. He was everything. What am I to do?"

"Don't worry about that now," I said. "The empire is in good hands for now. You simply need to rest. You need to be strong to face the coming days."

"I am tired of being strong!" she cried. "I have been strong for everyone else for decades! This is not supposed to be my burden."

"Isn't it?" I asked. "If this is the burden Heaven has laid upon you, isn't it a burden you are meant to bear?"

"Why would Heaven take my boy? Why would Heaven leave China with no Son of Heaven to lead it?"

"I don't know," I said. "But I do know that no man on earth has a more capable mother than your son."

"You think too highly of me," she said. "How I wish I could be like any other mother. I want only to weep and cry and be locked away from the world in my grief."

"You can do that if you wish," I said. "But while you do that, you must allow the priests to take him away and prepare him to journey to his ancestors. He cannot stay here."

At this Cixi began to weep again, but she clung to me and let go of her son's hand. As I held her and rocked her, the priests and eunuchs quickly moved in to wrap up the body and take him away.

"Wait!" she called out. "Please, he can't go alone!"

"He will not be alone, Your Majesty," I said. "He will have plenty of attendants with him."

"No, that's not right. He needs a woman with him. Someone to care gently for him."

"You shouldn't go," I said. "You shouldn't see him that way."

"Will you go?" she asked. "Will you wash his hands and his face and his hair?"

I had not expected this, but nodded. It was out of the ordinary, but no one was going to deny a grieving mother any request, no matter how unorthodox. The prince called for the rest of the empress's ladies in waiting. They took the empress in their arms and led her out of the room. I started to follow the priests who were carrying the emperor's body. The prince walked beside me.

"You don't have to go," he said. "The empress won't know if you don't go."

"I'll know," I said. "I can do this thing she asks of me."

The prince nodded and I followed the priests. We went into a large room where they laid the body on a marble slab. They brought over buckets of soapy water and began to unwrap the body. I walked up and stood over the emperor's head. He was still so beautiful, just as his mother had said. And so young, only eighteen years old.

I held out the emperor's queue and undid the long braid. I ran my fingers through his hair and a few strands fell out. I wetted my hands in the water and then ran them over his long, sleek hair. I carefully but thoroughly washed his hair. I then oiled the hair and ran a wide tooth comb through it one hundred times. I braided the hair and securely fastened it with a red cord. I then took a silk cloth and washed the emperor's face, neck, and hands. I carefully gathered up all of the emperor's strands of hair that had fallen loose as I left.

I returned to my room and found a large piece of silk that had a wider weave than what was typically used for clothes or decorations. Usually, the weave of the cloth had to be very tight, almost seamless, because I would use the thinnest threads possible. But in this case, since I could not make strands of hair thinner, I used a larger weave cloth. For days, while the empresses rested and funeral preparations were made, I embroidered a piece of cloth with the hair of Cixi's son.

Even though the emperor had died a man, I knew a woman's child would always be little in her eyes. So I embroidered a scene of ten children playing, boys and girls, some with pigtails and some with queues, some in tiger clothes and some with flower dresses, some playing with kittens and some swinging from a tree. It was a precious sight, one that caused me to cry many times while making it.

When the piece was finished, it was not the most beautiful piece I had ever made, but it wasn't supposed to be. There was no shading or gradations, only the simple black and white images of children playing in a courtyard. I had one piece of hair left after I was finished. I suppose I could have used it to add some more flowers or to embellish a piece of clothing, but, for me, when a piece was done it was done. I could not make any changes to it, so I added the last strand of the emperor's hair to my collection of thread memories.

I presented the embroidered children to her majesty, and she held the piece and me in her arms for a long time. We didn't speak, but it was clear that any past animosity or hurt we had been hanging onto over the years was gone. She had the piece framed and hung in her sleeping chamber across from her bed so she could look at it every morning and every night. She said it was a way to keep her son close to her and remind her of the precious child he had been.

That night, I sought out Prince Gong. He was making plans to leave.

"What are you doing?" I asked him.

"I can't be here for now," he said.

"But the empress needs you," I said.

"Yes, she needs me to be gone, just as she did before," he said.

"She isn't staging a coup," I said.

"Isn't she?" he asked. "Empress Alute should be the dowager empress now, but that is not going to happen. She'll probably find arsenic in her tea if she doesn't look out."

"Don't say such things!" I snapped.

"Cixi will be the dowager empress again," the prince said. "But I can't be seen having a hand in it. She won't need my support anyway. The grandees, the magistrates, the governors, even the western diplomats all want her to take over again."

"Who will be emperor?" I asked.

"I have no idea. Hopefully none of my sons."

"Why?" I asked.

"Because then I would lose all of my positions and the child. I wouldn't be part of his life or the court. Plus, what sort of life would he lead? Look at how things ended for my brother, my nephew. No, being emperor is its own kind of death sentence."

"Where will you go?" I asked.

"I'm not sure. Maybe Jehol, to the hunting lodge. I could use a rest."

"Can you do something for me?" I asked.

The prince took my hand and kissed it and then he gently touched my cheek. "Anything."

"Would you return to Changsha and bring me my daughter?"

The prince hesitated. "That is a dangerous thing you ask," he said. "Do you want me to take her to my home? We could arrange for you to see her there."

"No," I said. "Bring her here. After what I saw the empress go though, I can't bear to be apart from our little girl any longer."

"But what will you say?" he asked. "People will surely realize..."

"The empress has been pressuring me to take an apprentice. I will tell her the girl is a cousin of mine or something who has been training with Lady Tang and comes highly recommended."

"Still, you are playing with fire, my love," he said.

"I know," I said. "But will you please do it?"

The prince nodded. We kissed and he mounted his horse and rode away.

The prince was right. Not only did every man in the country, foreign and Chinese, want Cixi and Ci'an to take the reins of power back, they handed them over willingly. They all agreed there was simply no one else in a position to do so. With Prince Gong out of the city and Empress Alute also ill – apparently starving herself to death so she could join her husband – the dowager empresses had no choice but to accept the heavy burden of rulership.

The prince was also right about another thing: the appointment of the new emperor. Cixi completely overlooked Prince Gong's sons and looked to Prince Chun's. Prince Chun had only one living son at the time, Zaitian, who was four years old. Prince Chun and Lady Rong's hearts were broken over the selection. Their three older boys had all died and Lady Rong was suffering from ill health. She most likely would not be able to have more children. The prince begged Cixi not to select Zaitian. He kowtowed to her, beating his forehead to the floor until he passed out. Cixi had the prince unceremoniously removed from the audience hall and sent some grandees to collect the child.

Empress Ci'an had no say in the selection of the new emperor. As always, she left administrative tasks to Cixi. Empress Dowager Cixi could have selected someone older so she would not have needed to rule as regent for so long. She also could have waited to name a successor until one of the other princes proved himself worthy of the title. But she opted for the youngest prince available so she could raise him, groom him, herself to be the emperor she needed him to be. She had her work cut out for her though. Zaitian was small, frail, and easily frightened. He had none of the demanding, commanding airs her son had already had at that age. He was a precious and darling boy, though, who loved toys and music and art. He probably had a far more delicate countenance than required for the task he had been selected.

A couple of months after Prince Gong had left court, he returned to pay his respects to the new emperor and to present my new apprentice to the empress as a gift. Finally, after the girl had been properly presented, Prince

Gong brought her to me. I had not seen her since I had left her with Lady Tang when she was only a few months old. She was even more beautiful than I had imagined she would be.

She wore a pink and white chaopao with matching pink and white pants, both embroidered with lovely pink butterflies and orchids. Her hair was braided and pinned up on each side, revealing adorable ears that stuck out a little too far. Her eyes were big and dark and her nose and lips were perfectly balanced. Her skin was a lovely fawn shade. She stood nervously chewing on one of her fingers. Her feet were, thankfully, not bound. I was so grateful to Lady Tang for honoring my request in this.

I walked up to her and bent down so we could see eye to eye. "You must be Hulan," I said. She nodded. "I am very happy to meet you. Do you know who I am?"

"Are you my new teacher?" she asked.

I looked up to Prince Gong, who nodded. Most likely he and Lady Tang had stuck to the story that Hulan was simply coming to the palace to train as an apprentice. She probably had no idea she had just spent two months traveling with her father.

"Yes," I said. "I am Mistress Yang, your new master. Did you embroider your outfit yourself?"

"Yes, ma'am," she said. Even though I had requested Hulan be brought to me because she was my daughter and not based on her embroidery skills, she did show great promise. I couldn't fight it anymore and pulled her to me in a hug. The girl was apprehensive at first, but she eventually relaxed and hugged me back. I mouthed "thank you" to the prince, who gave me a small nod as he left us alone.

TWENTY-ONE
THE FORBIDDEN CITY, 1875 – 1884

ith the death of the Tongzhi Emperor and the appointment of the Guangxu Emperor, life seemed to return to normal. Cixi, both out of grief and necessity, returned to running the empire while Empress Ci'an focused on raising the next emperor. I couldn't help but think that this arrangement had contributed to the fact that Tongzhi had been a very ineffectual ruler who could have completely undone all of his mother's work. The next emperor could greatly benefit from the firm hand of Cixi and learn much more about running an empire from someone who had done it as opposed to a disinterested empress and scholars who spent all their days reading ancient texts. But I was not in a position to comment on such matters. Instead, I used this time of peace and calm to focus on my daughter and my embroidery.

Hulan was my daughter by blood only, though, and not really by any action. At the age of ten, Hulan was a fully developed person who hardly needed to be raised. She could dress and feed herself. She already had her own likes and dislikes and opinions. She was smart and creative and obedient. She didn't need me to wake her up in the morning or tuck her into bed at night. She was a young lady who already had responsibilities and her own work to do, and she fulfilled her expectations dutifully. I did see her almost every day, but only in the capacity of master and student, and she was an excellent student.

The only thing we argued about was the fact that I would not teach her the double-sided embroidery techniques. She believed it was because I was selfish and wanted to keep the technique to myself, that I didn't want anyone else to have the honor of being able to bring this coveted work to life. But that wasn't it at all.

I had come to the Forbidden City nearly twenty years before as the brightest young embroidery girl in the country. With continued progress and training, I was certain to become the best in the land, maybe the world. My double-sided embroidery would become a new art form and everyone would shower me with gold just for the chance to own a piece. At least, that is what was supposed to have happened. In reality, I had spent so much time working as an embroiderer I'd had very little time to practice embroidery. In many ways, my embroidery skills were stunted, never improving beyond the skills possessed by that little girl from Hunan.

Perhaps I am being too hard on myself. After all, people loved my work. The empress, who considered herself somewhat of an embroidery expert, often praised my work and made sure I oversaw all her important pieces. My pieces sold for a lot of money, when I had the chance to make anything to sell. Cixi's new head eunuch, Li Lianying, would help me sell the few pieces I could part with to rich families in the city, even to foreigners. I had saved quite a bit of money, but I have no idea what for since I didn't have any expenses.

I had risen high enough among the court artisans to hire a small team of embroiderers to work under me in the Forbidden City, all from Lady Tang's school, and I had hundreds of embroiderers at my command in Suzhou. As such, I finally had the time and freedom to work on embroidery for myself. Hulan thought I was being selfish for not teaching her double-sided embroidery; the truth is that I was still teaching myself.

I think that I was never meant to be a mother. I grew to love Hulan, but it would have made no difference to my life if she had not been born. I really don't know why I felt the need to have her brought to me after the death of the Tongzhi Emperor. An emotional response, I suppose. And, of course, I didn't have to suffer through the growing pains of putting up with a child. The crying, the neediness, the restless nights. She wasn't a daughter to me, just a student, but that seemed to have worked out perfectly well.

*O*ne day I was summoned to see the little emperor, which was quite out of the ordinary. I was told to bring my embroidery supplies with me as well as several samples. I was taken, not to the audience hall, but to a large, informal room in the emperor's private residence. The emperor must have been around seven years old at this time. He sat on his throne, which was much too big for him, and watched me, without smiling, as I entered the room and kowtowed before him.

"Your Majesty," I said.

The emperor motioned for me to come and sit on a stool by his side.

"Your work is pretty," he said to me.

I smiled. "You are too kind, Your Majesty," I said.

He picked up a framed piece that had been sitting beside his immense chair. "I like this tiger," he said. "I like how it is growling and looks angry."

"Your Majesty has a good eye," I said. "This is a very well done piece. See here how I used a split stitch to create the wrinkles around his nose? And overall I used directional stitches to make the tiger look both furry and sleek. Doesn't he look soft enough to pet?"

The emperor nodded and ran his finger down the tiger's back.

"I am very pleased that you appreciate my work, Your Majesty," I said. "All artisans appreciate some recognition from time to time."

"You work for my Papa Dearest?" he asked. "Papa Dearest" was what Empress Cixi had instructed the little emperor to call her. From the moment he entered the palace, she had no intention of being a mother to him. She was the acting emperor and he was her heir, nothing more.

In truth, I suspect that Empress Cixi never liked children at all. Oh, she loved her son, but loving your own child is much different from putting up with the children of others. And, like me and Hulan, she didn't have to raise Tongzhi. Almost immediately after his birth, he had been given to a wet nurse and was moved to his own palace. Legally, he had been the child of Empress Ci'an, Emperor

Xianfeng's head wife, not Cixi, who was only a lowly concubine at the time. Empress Ci'an had been in charge of his upbringing while court tutors had been in charge of his education. Cixi had watched from a distance as her son was raised by other people. Perhaps she preferred this as I did.

But Tongzhi and Guangxu were not the only children in her life that she shunned. Emperor Xianfeng also had a daughter. After that girl's mother died, Princess Rong'an had been brought into the household of Empress Cixi. Cixi paid the girl hardly any mind, married her off as quickly as possible, and didn't mourn her when she died shortly after Tongzhi. Cixi also kept wet nurses in her employ so their milk could be used to flavor her tea. The women often had to bring their children with them into her presence. As soon as one of these children started to whine or fuss, Cixi would order them away and would be a sour mood for the rest of the day.

Now, little Emperor Guangxu was experiencing the same indifference as other children in her life. But as Cixi's adopted son, he felt the lack of a strong and attentive parent more than others. He had been ripped away from his own doting parents and Empress Ci'an's health was not good. When the boy asked me about his Papa Dearest, there was a glimmer of hope in his eyes. Hope for what, I didn't know.

"I do work for your Papa Dearest," I said. "But I call her 'Your Majesty', just like I call you."

"Can you take me to see her?" he asked.

"I'm sorry, Your Majesty," I said. "But I don't think I can take you out of your palace."

The boy sighed and looked down at the powerful tiger in his hands. "If I was a tiger, no one could tell me what to do."

"Really?" I asked.

"Yes. I would growl and bite them and do whatever I wanted."

"Well, violence is not always the answer," I said. "After all, no one keeps a tiger in their home. But a gentle house cat can sleep on even an empress's bed. Sometimes being gentle can get you closer to someone than being mean."

"So if I do something nice for Dearest Papa, maybe she will come to see me?"

I didn't want to get his hopes up. Not only was Empress Cixi indifferent to the boy's affections, she was very busy. She was once again rising with the sun to meet with the grandees by the gong at the hour of the rabbit. Even if she wanted to, she didn't possess much leisure time to spend with the child. But I couldn't completely dash his hopes away either.

"She might," I said. "But I cannot make any promises. She is very busy keeping your kingdom safe for you."

"I can't wait to be emperor," he said. "Then everyone will listen to me."

"They certainly will," I said.

"Will you help me make a pretty picture for my Papa Dearest?" he asked.

"I would be honored, Your Majesty," I said.

For several days, I visited the little emperor and helped him make his own embroidery. This took me away from my own work and my own pupil, so I started taking Hulan with me. She was quite good and she had a real knack for teaching the emperor. She seemed to take after Lady Tang that way. I was gifted at embroidery, but it was clear in watching Hulan with Guangxu that I was not a gifted teacher. She had a patience and a grace about her that captured Guangxu's attention. I let her take over his lesson while I sat to the side and did my own work. Our lessons eventually ended because embroidery work was simply not a suitable skill for a boy. After he completed a rudimentary piece of a pink peony, Hulan and I were asked by his head teacher, Tutor Weng, not to return. We acquiesced, but the emperor gave me the piece he had been working on and asked me to present it to his Papa Dearest on his behalf. One of the pink strings was loose, so I removed it and kept it for myself. I then made some minor changes to the piece to make it look like the boy was more skilled than he was. It ended up being a perfectly acceptable first piece of embroidery by any standard.

That evening, after the empress had finished her dinner and was reading some reports from the day, I approached her and offered her the little piece of embroidery.

"The young emperor has spent many days making this gift for you," I said. "He is a very sweet boy who loves you very much."

She took the piece from me, glanced at it, and then laid it to one side. "There is a reason boys don't do embroidery work," she said with a sigh.

I gave a small chuckle. "Yes, he certainly lacks any embroidery skills, but he very much wanted to make something pretty for Your Majesty, so he asked me for help. He wants so much to please you."

"He does please me," she said. "Tutor Weng says that he is already quite skilled at calligraphy and recites his lessons perfectly. He just might be the future emperor we need."

"You should tell him that," I said. "I am sure he would love to hear some kind words from you. He really thinks of you as his Papa Dearest. He doesn't call you that only out of duty, but affection."

"I might have to talk to Tutor Weng about the boy being too soft," she said.

"Well, he is only a boy," I said. "Still gentle and kind. Still craving motherly affection."

"He is not only a boy," she said. "He is already an emperor, and he better start acting like one. Lianying!" she called.

Li Lianying appeared. Lianying had come into her service while An Dehai was still her head eunuch and had filled many of his roles since his death.

"Tell Grand Tutor Weng that I wish to see him first thing tomorrow morning," she commanded.

"Yes, Your Majesty," he said with a bow.

I looked at my hands to keep from rolling my eyes and said nothing. Clearly my attempt at getting Cixi to spend some time with her adopted son had failed.

"What is it?" she asked, annoyed by my silence.

"Nothing, Your Majesty," I said. I was not in a position to criticize her parenting.

Not long after that, Empress Dowager Ci'an collapsed during audiences. She was rushed to her chambers and Empress Dowager Cixi and the little emperor did not leave her side until she died a few days later. The whole of the Forbidden City grieved her. Even though she was not the strong ruler that Cixi was, she was a good empress. Empress Dowager Cixi made sure that Ci'an was given all the funeral rites she was entitled to, and she mourned the loss of her friend, her co-ruler, and the woman who helped her take control of China twenty years before. The little emperor was inconsolable. After being ripped away from his own mother and ignored by Cixi, Ci'an was the closest thing he had to a mother inside the palace walls. Even long after Empress Ci'an was buried, the little emperor would weep for her and order incense burned in her name.

*W*hen Hulan was about sixteen, we were working on a piece of embroidery together, but it was clear her mind was not on her work. She was very slow and kept making mistakes and sighing.

"What is wrong?" I asked.

"I don't want to bother you with it," she said.

"You are bothering me with it when you keep making mistakes in your embroidery. Better to tell me and get it out so you can get back to work."

She hesitated for a moment. "I just…I am not sure where my life is going. I know I am your apprentice and I was supposed to follow you as a court artisan, but I am not sure that is my path anymore."

"Why?" I asked. "What has changed?"

"The emperor," she said.

"What do you mean?" I asked.

"He said he loves me," she said.

"What?" I asked, putting down my work. "When? How? How did this happen?"

"We have grown very close over the years," she said. "I often do my work in his presence and we talk and he has even kissed me."

"He is but a boy!" I said.

"I heard that when Tongzhi was his age his consorts had already been chosen."

She was right about that. The preparations for Tongzhi's wedding had begun when he was only thirteen, and his wives had been chosen by the time he was fourteen. He was married at sixteen. Guangxu was already fourteen, but there had been no mention of preparations being made for his wedding or for him to assume power. I began to wonder what was going on in Empress Cixi's court. Surely they wouldn't allow a woman to rule forever.

"But still, how did this happen? You have been going there without my knowledge?"

"You introduced us," she said. "Years ago."

"You have been going to see him this whole time?" I asked.

"Yes," she said, plainly.

I didn't know how this could happen. How I couldn't have known. Had I been so absorbed in my work and my art that I hadn't seen my daughter grow into a young woman who had caught the eye of the Son of Heaven?

"I can't believe this," I said. "Why didn't you tell me?"

"I don't know. It didn't seem important. His eunuchs know. I'm sure the council knows. They have often seen us together."

"And they haven't tried to stop you?"

"No. I think they see him the way you do, as a boy. As if we are mere childhood playmates. But he is a young man. He wants to be emperor. He wants to take his rightful place on the throne."

"Stop talking of such things," I said. "It is not your place to speak on such matters."

She sighed and looked back at her work.

"But you said that he loves you. That you are uncertain about your path. What did you mean? What does he want from you?"

"He said he wants me to be one of his consorts, when the time comes."

"You know that is impossible," I said. "You are Han. The emperor can only take Manchu consorts."

"But I am half Manchu," she said.

I stared at her and she stared back. I had heard what she said, but I was uncertain that she meant to say what I heard. We stared, as if daring the other to speak first. I realized then that my daughter was far more bold than I imagined.

"I know my father is Manchu," she finally said.

"How do you know?" I asked.

"I have always known," she said. "Ever since he first brought me here...to my mother."

I felt my face grow hot. I was...angry? Embarrassed? Ashamed? If she knew I was her mother, then she also knew I was the worst mother who ever existed. I abandoned her, only to call her back to me in a moment of weakness, and then continued to neglect her. I had never played the role of mother to her and I didn't give her a substitute in my place. I found myself unable to respond so I looked down and began fidgeting with my embroidery.

"I'm not angry," she said. "I know that you couldn't claim me without risking your own life."

"Did he tell you?" I asked.

"No," she said. "I just...I knew. The way he looked at me. The fact that we have the same nose. How gentle he was with me. I'm not sure. I just knew."

"And me?" I asked. "How did you know I was your mother and not just your teacher?"

"It is clear how much he loves you," she said.

My eyes welled up. I didn't want to know what she meant by that. Was it in the way he spoke of me? Looked at me? I didn't want to know because it didn't matter.

"I don't see what any of this matters," I said. "The prince can't claim you. As far as anyone knows, you are Chinese.

The council would never let the emperor take you as a consort. Besides, even if he did, then what? You will no longer be my apprentice? You would become a lady of the court?"

"I don't know," she said. "But why can't the prince claim me? He can just say I was the daughter of a whore and he was too shamed to take me home to his wives and gave me to the empress instead."

"'The daughter of a whore'?" I said, nearly choking on the words. "How dare you!"

"Forgive my careless words," she said quickly. "I didn't mean you were a whore. I was just speaking hypothetically about an imaginary woman who never existed."

"I know that!" I yelled. "But it is still stupid. You think the council would let the daughter of a whore be a consort? What would the empress say if she found out the daughter of a whore had been living in her household?"

"It was just an example!" she said. "You're missing the point! It could be any invisible lady. An aristocrat. Lady Tang!"

"It was a terrible example," I said. "It just proves that you haven't given this any reasonable thought."

"Mother, will you just listen?" she yelled, stomping her big, unbound foot.

"Don't ever call me that," I said firmly.

Her eyes welled with tears. She threw down her embroidery and ran off to her room.

*T*hat evening, the empress was clearly aggrieved. The ladies were all nervous to be in her presence and the eunuchs seemed to walk even more silently. I requested permission to approach her and she acquiesced. I asked if we could dismiss the other attendants and she nodded.

"You look as annoyed as I feel," I said to her after the others were gone.

"That bad?" she asked.

"Is there something you would like to talk about?" I asked.

"It is just that boy," she said. "He is testing me."

"In what way?" I asked.

"This kingdom is...it is unwell," she said. "I tried, after the death of my husband, to build it up, to make it strong. I thought that I had set things in motion that would keep us barreling toward the future. But then, my son, my dearly loved son, came into his own."

I nodded, not saying anything. She clearly needed to say some things that she couldn't say to anyone else.

"We came to a dead halt. He didn't keep moving forward. We froze. And worse, we fell back. China lost five years of progress while my son was the emperor. And we are still, a decade later, trying to catch up.

"I am afraid," she said. "I am afraid of letting go again. Do you see? I don't retain power for myself. I do it for everyone else. And not just the council or the foreign powers who want me here. I do it for every single person in China. My work will bring millions of people out of poverty. I will do so much for them."

"Everyone knows that you are a good empress," I said.

"Everyone except Guangxu," she said. "He wants to take over. He wants to be emperor."

"But you don't think he can do it?" I asked.

"I know he can't," she said.

I didn't tell her that it was her own fault. That if she wanted the boy to be a good emperor she should have taught him how to be one herself.

"Today he got angry," she said. "He demanded to know why preparations were not being made for his ascension. For his wedding. Can you believe it is time for that little boy to take wives already?"

"Time has traveled extraordinarily fast," I said.

"But the councilors don't want me to step down. They want to issue an edict and they want the emperor to sign it that says I am to retain the role of regent for a few more years."

"You don't think he will?" I asked.

"He declared that he would not sign it," he said. "He said it is against law and tradition to deny him his birthright."

Again, I didn't reply. Guangxu was right. As the emperor, no one had the right to deny him, even if it was in the best interest of the country.

"What will you do?" I asked.

"What can I do?" she asked. "If only there was some way to distract him, some way to placate him."

"Well, he is a young man," I said.

"What do you mean?" she asked.

"I think I might know a distraction that would work."

"How do you know anything about this?" she asked.

"Because Hulan told me."

"Hulan? Your embroidery girl?"

I nodded. "She told me that the emperor wants to take her as a lover."

"That would be impossible," she said.

"That is what I told her," I said. "But what if it wasn't? What if as part of the agreement to let you retain power for a few more years, he was allowed to take a consort before his official marriage?"

"I don't think we can do that," she said. "First of all, the girl is Chinese. Second, she couldn't have an official role as a consort. It would ruin the standing and wedding of his proper empress later on."

"There is no precedent for you to remain in control after your son comes of age," I said boldly, "yet the grandees are willing to do it. There might not be a precedent for him to take an early consort, but I am sure the grandees would find a way to make it happen if it meant everyone getting what they want and the country continue prospering."

The empress contemplated this for a while. It would be easy to retain power if Guangxu was distracted by a woman. Hadn't she used her own feminine ways to get into bed with her husband in the first place? No one knew the influence a woman could hold over a man better than she did. Finally, she leaned over and spoke in a low voice.

"You do realize that Guangxu and Hulan are cousins, right?"

My heart stopped beating and my mouth went dry. Did she know? Had she always known? "What?" I finally stammered out.

"She is Prince Gong's daughter," she said. "She has to be. She looks like him. Besides, why else would he go all the way to Hunan to get her?"

"I don't...who...who is her mother?" I asked. I am sure I sounded so stupid.

"I'm not sure, but I suspect it is Lady Tang. When he was in Hunan putting down another group of rebels he stopped to see Lady Tang before he returned. Why else would he stop there? They must have been having an affair. Probably started the first time he was there, when his brother sent him to get you."

I wasn't sure if I should be shocked that she would suspect Lady Tang of being Hulan's mother or relieved. Did she not remember that I was also in Hunan at that same time?

"I hope you won't hold this against Lady Tang," I said. "She has been nothing but loyal to the empire even when the Taiping were nearly at her door."

"I know," she said. "And who can argue with results? Her students are the best embroidery girls in the country. I only hope you won't hold it against her."

"Me?" I asked.

"Everyone knows you've had feelings for the prince ever since he brought you to me."

"It is nothing," I said. "I was a foolish girl."

"Weren't we all?" she asked rhetorically.

"But what does this mean for Hulan?" I asked.

"I don't know," she said. "I'll have to think about it. The fact that she is a Manchu of royal blood will strengthen her case, but I don't know if the council will accept her. And what if she gets pregnant? Would the baby be his heir? Then what about his empress?"

I didn't have any answers for her.

a few days later, Hulan was moved from her servant quarters to her own small palace. She was not given any official title or recognition, but it was simply accepted that she was the emperor's mistress. Not long afterward, the emperor approved an edict appointing Cixi as regent for a few more years.

I quickly began to miss my little apprentice. I didn't realize how much time we spent together until she was gone. As a court lady, I couldn't simply go visit her whenever I wanted. I would have to be summoned, which she didn't do for quite a while, but I am sure she was busy getting settled into her new life.

When she did summon me, I was shocked by the reason why. We sat down together and she dismissed her servants so we could talk privately.

"I need your advice, as a woman," she said.

I nodded, though I wasn't sure how I could help her since I didn't know anything about being in a relationship with a man.

"I had not been with any man before the emperor, so I can't compare our intimacy with anything else, but...I don't think it's right...what we do..." She started to tear up so I put my arm around her.

"Don't cry. I'm sure everything is fine. Just tell me what happens. He isn't hurting you, is he?"

"Oh, no, of course not. He is very kind to me. But...well. I know he is supposed to...go inside me. But many times he can't because he isn't hard enough. He says he wants to, and we kiss and touch and I will be ready for him, but he just... can't. Or if he can, it is over very quickly. He enters me and he spills and then he is soft again. Or he will spill before he can enter me."

I thought about my nights with the prince and how they were nothing like what Hulan was describing. The prince never had a problem becoming hard and he would last for a long time. I remembered how our lovemaking seemed to last for hours sometimes. Of course, I didn't want to tell my daughter this, but I was sad that she wasn't enjoying the pleasure I knew was possible from a man.

"I am sorry to hear about your troubles, my dear," I said. "I haven't experienced anything like you are describing."

"I was afraid of that," she said. "The other girls, the other *gōngnǚ*, I have heard them talk before about sleeping with some of the court grandees, so I knew something was wrong."

"There, there," I said. "I didn't say anything was wrong. I just said I hadn't experienced it. Some people, maybe they just experience pleasure differently. He is spilling his seed, so he must be enjoying you."

"Maybe," she said. "But it isn't very pleasurable for me for him to end so soon. I get so excited, but since he is done so quickly, I am not satisfied."

"Have you told him this?" I asked.

"Not exactly," she said. "He gets so embarrassed. I don't want to make it worse."

"You should try to talk to him," I said. "You can't be lovers if only he is feeling love."

"What do I say?" she asked.

"Well, just try other things," I said. "Don't let him run away afterward. Tell him to keep touching and kissing you.

He could pleasure you with his hands. You could also try taking him in your mouth. Some men like that."

She blushed, so of course she was imagining me with her father.

"Just try to figure out what each of you likes and try to meet each other's needs. Don't reject him just because he doesn't make love the way you imagined he would."

She nodded. "Okay, I'll try."

TWENTY-TWO
THE FORBIDDEN CITY, 1885

I don't think I aged the way most people do. It wasn't until I was forty-four years old that I felt old for the first time. My life didn't follow the trajectory of most women. Empress Cixi was married at sixteen and was a mother by twenty-one. She was a widow by twenty-seven and was raising a boy young enough to be her grandson by age forty. This was a timeline most women followed, married and with children by twenty and a grandmother by forty.

My life had taken a completely different course. I never married. I had a child at the late age of twenty-four, but I didn't raise her myself. I didn't see my life slipping away with each milestone my daughter crossed. Now, at forty-four, I was in no sight of a grandchild and would never be a widow. My life simply didn't have the age markers that most do. At least it didn't until I saw the effects of age in someone I loved.

I was sitting outside the empress's palace when I saw a familiar face walking by. I sauntered down the stairs and kneeled as I greeted him.

"My prince," I said.

"Yaqian!" he replied, happier than the moment required, and reached for my hand. "How are you? You are just the person I need to see."

"I am happy to see you too, Your Highness," I said. It had been a while since I had seen him. He was in the palace nearly every day, but our lives were completely separate.

"I think you can help me," he said. "The dowager empress's birthday is coming up and arrangements need to be made."

"As far as I know there will be no birthday celebrations," I said. "The country and the empress are busy with the war with France and she believes a birthday celebration would send the wrong message. You are the head of the council. Haven't you heard this?"

"Yes, of course. But it is her fiftieth birthday. Quite important. Such a milestone. We need to make arrangements for her birthday."

"What do you want me to do?" I asked.

"We need to make arrangements for her birthday," he said. "I am sure you can help me."

"That is not my area. Li Lianying would be in charge of celebrations. But, as I said, I don't think she wants any celebrations..."

"That little boy?" he asked. "Where is An Dehai? He is the only one who can turn her ear."

I could feel my face drop and my heart stop at this. Why would he be asking for An Dehai? He had been dead for years. The prince glanced around nervously, as if he was lost or looking for something. I studied his face and his manners. He fidgeted with his beard, which was now streaked with gray. His eyes were a little cloudy and he had lost weight.

"An Dehai is dead, my prince," I said. "Don't you remember?"

"Of course, of course," he said waving his hand. "But the arrangements for her birthday must be made. Will you speak to her?"

"Of course, I will," I said. "Is there anything else I can do for you? Should I send for your sedan chair to take you home?"

"No, there is simply too much to do. I must return to my office."

I kneeled as he left. He seemed to walk away more slowly than usual.

That evening, the empress was clearly agitated as she was reviewing papers from the day.

"Your Majesty?" I said as I kneeled before her.

"Yes, Mistress Yang?" she asked.

"I wish to speak to you about Prince Gong."

She took a deep breath before she moved her papers aside and motioned for me to sit near her.

"What is it?" she asked.

"He came by today, while you were at audiences."

"He was at audiences for a long time until I finally dismissed him. He must have come here afterward. You know we are fighting a war with France?"

I nodded.

"He just went on and on about my birthday! Can you believe it? For an hour and a half he talked of the importance of ranking gifts and how they should be delivered and who should be allowed to send them. And this was after I had already told the council that there would be no birthday celebrations this year."

"That was the crux of his visit here today as well. He wanted me to convince you to go ahead with the celebrations."

"What did you say?" she asked.

"Just as you said, Your Majesty. The war is the only thing the court is focused on right now." She rubbed her eyes as though they were weary. "Majesty, is there something wrong with him?" I asked. "He seemed...a bit confused when he was here. Almost like he was lost."

"He is...not himself," she said. "He has taken several long leaves. Some days, he simply doesn't come to the palace. He has been no help during this crisis with France. He hasn't offered any solutions. I don't know what is wrong with him."

"Perhaps he just needs to rest..." I tried to say.

"I need to rest!" she snapped. "Do you think running an empire is easy? I should have retired years ago and spent my whole days resting. We are all tired. Prince Gong is nothing special. If he is of no use to me, then he shouldn't be around."

"Have you asked for his resignation?" I asked.

"No, I can't. He is my brother-in-law, he is older than I am, and he has been the head of the Grand Council for over twenty years. And don't forget his reputation with the foreigners. I can't simply send him away. As much as he aggravates me, he is too important. He would have to do something egregious to warrant that."

The empress rubbed her chin and I could see her mind working. This was a woman who was exceedingly clever and always got what she wanted. If she wanted Prince Gong gone, I was sure she could manufacture a reason. But how far would she go? Would she be satisfied with his resignation, or would she require his total removal?

I took my leave and wrote a letter to Lady Yun, my old friend and one of Prince Gong's wives.

*T*he next day I received a letter of invitation to tea with Lady Yun at Prince Gong's mansion. I was nervous about being in his home, but I knew I needed to speak to someone regarding the prince's condition and what could be done to protect his future. Lady Yun was my only way to do that.

I hired a donkey cart outside the side gate of the Forbidden City to take me to Prince Gong's mansion. The mansion was located in the northwest corner of Peking, down a quiet green road. The mansion was like a little Forbidden City, with four great walls concealing dozens of four-walled courtyards. There were residence buildings and gardens. The estate had been home to grandees and princes for hundreds of years, each occupant adding onto the majesty of the previous.

The front gate opened as soon as my cart pulled up. I didn't have to knock or tell the guards who I was, they seemed to know innately. A maid was there to greet me and motioned for me to follow her. The palace was exquisite. We walked past several ponds and green areas to a court-yard in the north of the complex. I wondered if Lady Yun wanted to meet me here instead of closer to the front just so I could see how marvelous her home was. There were many people of all ages milling about. Children were playing by a koi pond. Elegantly dressed women were sitting and chatting. They hid their mouths behind fans when I walked by. Elderly women were scrubbing floors or shelling peas. An old man was tending to one of the gardens.

Finally, we arrived at a beautiful building. The two main doors were wide open to allow the breeze through and Lady Yun was reclining on a sofa with plush, silk cushions. She sat up as I approached, but she did not stand. I kneeled before her.

"Lady Yun," I said, my eyes downcast. "You were so kind to send for me. I am not worthy to be in your magnificent home."

"Please, Mistress Yang," she said, motioning for me to sit near her. "The honor is mine. I don't know why I didn't invite you to visit me years ago. You were one of my favorite people at court."

"You flatter me, my lady," I said, sitting.

"Well, I was intrigued by your note," she said. "You know, we don't know much of anything going on at court. We just sit here in our own little world as life on the outside passes us by. Life at court was so much more interesting than life in here."

"I am sure life in here has many more pleasures than life in service, though," I said.

"In some ways," she said. "I certainly don't want for

anything material, but the lack of mental stimulation can be frustrating."

"I can understand that," I said. "If I didn't have my embroidery work, I am not sure what I would do to occupy my mind."

Lady Yun nodded and a maid approached to pour us some tea. "So, tell me, Mistress Yang, why exactly have you come?"

"It is about Prince Gong," I said. "The empress is concerned about his health."

Lady Yun laughed. "I don't believe that for a minute. Did you forget I also served alongside that harpy?"

My face blushed. I had never heard anyone insult the empress in such a bold manner. She must have seen my reaction.

"Oh, don't worry," she said. "We can speak freely here. I just meant that I know Empress Cixi doesn't give one fig about the well-being of others. She is only concerned about the prince's health if she thinks it might impact her in some way."

I nodded and took a sip of my tea. "You are right about that," I said. "She is worried that the prince's health is hurting his ability to offer council."

Lady Yun stirred her tea and took a long sip before replying. "He has been sick for a while. He can't sleep but he is tired all the time. He is forgetful. He has even vomited blood."

I put down my teacup and reached for her hand. "I am very sorry to hear this," I said. "I had no idea."

"Didn't you?" she said, looking at me with tears in her eyes. "Don't you see him even more than we do? His own wives? His own children?"

"Lady Yun, I don't know what you think or what others

have told you, but I rarely see the prince. I am in the inner court, where the prince, where any man, rarely is allowed. I had not seen him in months before yesterday and realized something was wrong."

She shook her head. "You don't know what it's like, Yaqian," she said. "The loneliness is devastating. People talk of marriage, of love, as if it is some all-encompassing union between two people that will bring all manner of happiness, but it is torture. Do you know what it is like to devote yourself to one person you can never have all to yourself?"

I didn't respond because I knew I could never relate to the pain she felt.

"And don't fool yourself into thinking that children can fill the void. My sons are all gone, either at school or in military training. They will soon establish their own households. My daughters are all gone. Married young and at the homes of their husbands. I cannot embrace my husband or my children. All is lost to me."

"You are in a unique position to help him," I said. "The empress is not happy. If he doesn't step down or give her a reason to dismiss him, she could do far more than ask for his resignation."

Her eyes widened in fear. As sad and lonely as she was, if anything bad happened to the prince, she could end up without even a roof over her head.

"But they have been allies for thirty years!" she said. "It is only by his support she is even sitting on that throne."

"Yes, but her prerogative now is to stay on that throne. You know she shouldn't even be on it now."

"So I heard. Apparently your daughter has moved up in the world."

"I don't know what you are talking about," I said, though she knew I did.

"Don't worry. Your secret is safe with me, for as much of a secret as it is."

"What do you mean? I thought you were cut off from the court."

"This goes far beyond the court, Yaqian. Everyone knows you and prince are her parents."

I thought about how the empress accused Lady Tang of being Hulan's mother. Did she really think it was Lady Tang or was she just pretending?

"Lady Yun, please, I must apologize..."

"For what? That is just how life is. The prince has half a dozen wives and concubines, what is one more lover? The only difference is that you are the only one inside the palace. The only one with the ear of the empress. You wield a great amount of power in that little embroidery needle of yours."

I really didn't know what she was talking about, but I didn't want her to know that. And I needed to get her to listen to me about Prince Gong before I had to leave.

"Lady Yun," I said, setting down my teacup, "I am trying to help. The prince must take care. He must give the empress an excuse to dismiss him, but not something serious enough that she could take it further and seek to ruin him or worse. He must cause a small offense."

"I don't know. It seems risky."

"It is, but it is better than the alternative. If Empress Cixi is forced to come up with her own solution, it could have much more dire consequences. Besides, if he is dismissed, he can come home. He can be here with his family. He can get medical treatments."

"And what do you want, Mistress Yang," she asked me.

"What do you mean?"

"Why are you here? What are you hoping to get out of this?"

"Nothing," I said. "I don't need or want anything. I am only trying to help."

"Because you love him?" she asked.

"Because I love her," I said. "Prince Gong has been her friend and ally for decades. Sometimes, she can be impetuous and mourn her actions later. I don't want her to do something she will regret."

Lady Yun nodded. "I thank you for coming by," she said, motioning that it was time for me to leave. "I will consider what you have told me."

The next day, Prince Gong was absent from court, and he was gone for several weeks. He apparently took leave from work, the council, and the court without permission. This was considered an affront to Her Majesty and negligence in his duties. It was not a deadly offense, or even a greatly disgracing one, but enough for the empress to have cause to dismiss the prince from court.

When the prince returned, Cixi threw a red-inked decree at his feet and banished him from court. He easily accepted, but he still asked that she allow him to wish her well on her birthday. She refused to see him.

The day finally came when my daughter could no longer placate the emperor. According to her, he was fed up with being denied his rightful place on the throne. He even began throwing and breaking things in his palace out of frustration. He could not oust his Papa Dearest on his own, that would be unfilial, but his outbursts could no longer be contained. He was still quite young, but he was well-educated thanks to Tutor Weng and knew his rights. Empress Cixi could no longer hold the throne on his behalf and began making arrangements for his wedding and ascension to the Dragon Throne.

The empress knew this day would come eventually, so she already had the emperor's consorts chosen. My daughter was not one of them. She chose the younger daughter of her brother and named her Empress Longyu. Since Empress Longyu was the daughter of Empress Cixi's brother and Guangxu was the son of her sister, the new emperor and empress were even closer cousins than the emperor and Hulan. However, this fact did not seem to concern anyone.

By the time her wedding arrived, Longyu was already twenty-one years old, far older than most new consorts. She was also much older than the two women chosen to be Guangxu's concubines: Jade, who was fourteen, and Pearl, who was only twelve.

Empress Cixi's choices for consorts were shocking. Longyu was not only too old, she wasn't very pretty. When I was sent to her home to prepare her wedding gowns, I couldn't believe the difference between this plain creature and the astounding Alute I had made a gown for years before. Alute could seduce a man with a glance; this girl couldn't seduce a pig farmer. I am too cruel. She wasn't ugly, but she wasn't the type of girl any man would pick if he could choose any girl in the country. Longyu was kind, well trained in manners and etiquette, and utterly devoted to her aunt, but she wasn't very well educated. She could not read, write, sing, or play any instruments. Her personality was as dull as her face.

Pearl and Jade were not much better. Jade was pretty enough, though still forming. Her breasts were growing and her face was womanly and innocent at the same time. She would undoubtedly be a lovely woman. Pearl, though, was little more than a child. When she pinned her hair up, she looked so much like a boy one would only know she was a girl by the clothes she wore.

The emperor did not choose his consorts, which was a stark change from tradition. Even though the Empress Mother always had an influence on her son's choice of empress, the emperor typically made the final choices. Empress Cixi did not allow her adoptive son this luxury and he did not have the will to fight her. He wanted to be on the throne, and if giving into his Papa Dearest's choices for consorts was the price, so be it.

My daughter was ordered to leave the palace before the new empress and consorts arrived. But there was a complication.

"I am pregnant," my daughter told me the night before she was to leave.

"How is that possible?" I asked.

"I don't know exactly," she said. "But he must have spilled inside me just enough."

"Have you told the emperor?"

"No. I have told no one."

"Good," I said. "I think we should keep it that way."

"Why?" she asked. "This could be the emperor's first son. That has to mean something."

"I don't know that is does," I said. "You are not a consort."

"But the empress and the council had to know that this was a possibility when they allowed me to become his mistress. What was their plan?"

"I don't know that they had a plan," I said. "Maybe they just figured they would deal with that problem if it ever came up."

"Well, it has happened now. Shouldn't we tell them? Wouldn't it at least allow me to stay in the palace and my child to be raised like a prince?"

"My darling, I fear for your safety at this point. If the child had come months or years ago, I would allow you to take the risk and perhaps be appointed an official consort, but I think it is too late now. The empress has been chosen and you are a complication."

"What are you saying? You think they would kill me?"

"I think that killing you now would be easier than killing you later if you give birth to a son. They cannot allow you to supplant the new empress."

"So you would deny my child his birthright? Just as you denied me?"

"To save his life? Yes."

"Where will I go? What will I do?"

"Does the emperor know you are leaving? Has he given you any money?"

"He has never given me money. Any money for my household was given to my eunuch and he handled the accounts. But he has given me many gifts over the years, jewels and silks and such."

"That will do. Take whatever you can. If you think anything will be too suspicious to move now, give it to me and I will send it to you later. I also have money I can give you, and embroidery you can sell. I will send word to your father. He will take you into his home."

"That will be terrible," she said. "All those women who are not my mother and all those cousins? And me, pregnant with no husband?"

"Hopefully it will only be temporary. We can try to set up a household for you of your own. Or I can talk to the empress and ask her to make a marriage for you."

"I don't want a marriage," she said. "After what I have experienced with Guangxu, marriage is nothing to be envious of."

"I won't argue with that," I said.

"I'm probably too old to make a match anyway," she sighed. At twenty-four, she was probably right. How funny it was that my unmarried daughter was going to have a baby at the same age I did, also without a husband. I didn't raise the girl, but she certainly turned out like me anyway.

That night, I sent a letter to Prince Gong and Lady Yun and asked them to take Hulan into their home. Their reply accepting my request came quickly. The next morning,

Hulan left before the sun rose with as many jewels, clothes, and trinkets as she could carry.

*G*uangxu's wedding, for all its splendor, was a disaster. The emperor was furious with his Papa Dearest's choice of empress. He had not seen her before the wedding and was not told how old she was. He was cold to her and refused to kiss her or hold her hand. He feigned sickness and did not attend the marriage banquet. He thought little better of Jade, but he did seem to take a strange liking to little Pearl, the boyish child bride. I thought about his predecessor and cousin, Emperor Zaichun, and how it was rumored that he also preferred the company of boys in his bed to that of his wife. I wondered how long it would be before similar rumors swirled around Guangxu.

Empress Cixi was similarly unhappy. She retired to the Sea Palace, which was situated on a lake within the Forbidden City. She was so close to the seat of power but couldn't be further from it. The emperor refused to keep her informed about what was going on in the kingdom and did not solicit her advice. The grand councilors had no pretense to visit her and also could not communicate with her. She was bored and frustrated. Her only consolation was that now she could engage in her one true enjoyment – opera. The operas played day and night, the singing and clanging of symbols drowning out the misery that infected the palace.

I at least was able to feel some joy. Several months later, Prince Gong sent a messenger to me, since what she had to tell me was too sensitive to be written down.

"The Lady Hulan has given birth," he told me. "The child was a boy. They have given him a Manchu name in honor of his father. His name is Arsalan."

TWENTY-FOUR

THE SUMMER PALACE, 1889-1894

The years my empress spent in retirement were incredibly boring for all who waited on her. She did her best to make the most of it. We all retired to the Summer Palace and the empress was rarely invited back to court. She painted, she wrote operas, she bred little Pekingese dogs, but her mind was restless.

The rebuilt Summer Palace was exquisite. I have no idea how the throne paid for it, for it must have been expensive, but perhaps the magistrates of the court felt she had earned it. Most emperors would take long hunting trips, as many as three or four a year, to Jehol, and the whole court would have to be uprooted and moved for weeks at a time. Each trip would be paid for by the throne and were considered the emperor's right since he gave so much of himself to his people. Empress Cixi had never taken such a leisure holiday in her life. Her only trip to Jehol had been when the court had to flee when the British burned the previous Summer Palace, which led to her husband's death in exile. Even though Empress Cixi had only ruled on behalf of her sons and was not empress in her own right, everyone knew she was the ruler of the country, so she should have been entitled to such relaxing trips as her predecessors were, but she never took advantage of this right. I do know that she paid for much of the rebuilding work from her own savings and allowance because she became very stingy during those years. She was less free with gifts, had fewer attendants brought into her retinue, and told all of us to be as frugal as possible. I could not waste any thread. If any thread could be reused, I was to do so. But it was worth the sacrifice and difficulties because the new Summer Palace was splendid. It would never quite be as remarkable as the original, but mostly because the priceless gifts and artifacts from all over the world that had been collected there could never be replaced, but the quality of the artisanship and attention to detail of the new palace was just as exquisite and would forever be a source of pride for the Chinese people. In a way, the Summer Palace was a gift to the Chinese as a premiere example of Chinese architectural art.

Like she had for her son, Empress Cixi left the empire ready for new leadership. The empire was at peace, relations with the Westerners were good, the coffers were full, many modernization projects were underway, and the people were satisfied. The emperor had no need to fear uprisings or rebellions from inside his domain, but he also took no note of growing dangers outside.

Many of Cixi's modernizing projects, such as the railroad and the navy, the emperor saw as wasteful during such peacetimes. He didn't understand that times of peace were the best times to prepare for war. He also didn't fear other countries. He believed he and his country were superior to all others in every way. He didn't heed the warnings about a growing danger in the east.

Cixi knew danger was coming, but there was nothing

she could do. Earl Li, the general in charge of defending the coast, wrote to the dowager empress and told her the ships were not up to date and the training the men were receiving was not sufficient. They would never succeed at a sea battle. The emperor would not heed his warnings, though, and the empress could not advise the magistrates. Every day, all the empress could do was worry and wait. She would try to keep herself busy and her mind occupied through her various hobbies, but nothing could relieve her stress. Her hair began to fall out and she had to start wearing wigs to hide this change in her appearance.

That summer, Japan attacked Korea, a Chinese ally. This did not cause a panic in China since many knew a battle over Korea was coming, but it was the beginning of the end for Emperor Guangxu. The emperor sent many of China's troops and ships to fight Japan, leaving us with little defense back home. Warship after warship was sunk, along with thousands of men. It was a disaster.

Finally, the emperor had no choice but to ask Empress Cixi for help. He was only a boy, still in his early twenties, with no experience as a general. He allowed her to return to the Forbidden City and meet with the Grand Council. The situation was bleak. Ships and men had been lost and our foreign allies were refusing to help even though they had also lost men. Empress Cixi immediately donated millions of taels from her own private fortune to the army and canceled her birthday celebrations, her sixtieth, which was a monumental event in a person's life. Preparations for her birthday had started years before, but now all was canceled.

Cixi sent for Prince Gong. The years of rest had done him good. He was not as quick and clever as he used to be, but he was solid, reliable, and reasonable. He also still had good relations with the foreigners and could be of use to the empress.

But all was lost. One defeat followed another. The only chance China had of surviving the war was to broker peace. Prince Gong approached the British to negotiate the peace talks. As usual, his placating nature in the face of a foreign threat earned him condemnation from members of the court, including the emperor. The Japanese demanded millions of taels in indemnities and the cession of Formosa, several other islands, and land in Manchuria. The emperor was furious. Even though the worthless whelp had no one to blame but himself, he decided Empress Cixi and Prince Gong were to blame; thus, a power struggle ensued. Both Empress Cixi and the emperor agreed that the Japanese demands were too much, but they disagreed on what to do about it. Empress Cixi trusted Prince Gong and believed the West would not allow China to fall. The emperor wanted to agree to the terms offered.

Empress Cixi refused to move back to the Summer Palace. We all lived in the Sea Palace, safely ensconced in the Forbidden City where Empress Cixi could once again be informed and involved in day-to-day decision-making. Of course, she was no longer in charge – she couldn't make decisions on her own – but she carried much clout, and the emperor was forced to consult with her before making any decisions. It was clear the young emperor was not happy with the new situation, but there was very little he could do about it. We were all forced to live under the same roof, once again in an uneasy and unhappy situation. A henhouse cannot have two cocks, though, so the empress had to find a way to regain control.

While we lived at the Summer Palace, Empress Longyu had been in charge of the emperor's very tiny inner court. After we moved back to the Forbidden City, though, Pearl, Jade, and Empress Longyu once again came under Empress Cixi's purview. It was clear that the emperor gave little more than a thought to Empress Longyu or Jade, but Pearl was another matter. Even though the Emperor was not spreading his seed among any of his ladies – or any outside women or men, as his predecessors did – Pearl had a special place in his life. She who dressed as a man was constantly by his side and in his quarters. She had become quite well-educated, reading anything she could get her hands on, and quite influential – men seeking favors from the emperor flocked to her side. While many suspected Pearl was abusing her power as the emperor's special paramour, it was hardly uncommon for consorts to use what little power they possessed for the short time they had it. Empress Cixi did not begrudge Pearl her favored position, but she was aware of it, and she kept a close eye on the girl. She suspected that Pearl would be her key to regaining control of the emperor.

At one point, Empress Cixi learned that Imperial Concubine Pearl had taken an interest in my embroidery, so Cixi gave me leave to give the girl some private lessons. She also made sure I knew that I was to report back to her anything I learned that might be of interest. The job proved too easy. Pearl was confident in her place as imperial concubine and had no fear. She also regarded me as little more than a maid who seemed to be of little consequence to her while she was busy conducting her deals. I was privy to money exchanging hands between her and various palace eunuchs and whispered conversations about buying positions of importance. At one point, I was even able to steal a letter regarding a certain illiterate man who had paid a high price for the position of mayor. When I presented my evidence to Empress Cixi, she was delighted, and I was able to see just how ruthless the empress could be.

Empress Cixi called Pearl before her and asked her about her habit of accepting bribes in exchange for encouraging appointments by the emperor. Of course, she denied it. The empress had one of the eunuchs I had seen giving Pearl money brought in. The man was stripped naked and for the first time I saw what a eunuch looked like. I had seen two men naked in my life and several women, but this was unlike either. He had hair covering some of the mutilated area, but there was only a malformed stump where his penis should have been, and it was horribly scarred. The man was mortified and tried to cover himself with his hands, but the two other eunuchs who brought him in held his arms. Pearl tried to avert her eyes, but the empress slapped her on the back of her head and forced her to watch. The eunuch denied being involved in the bribery, at which the empress ordered he be subject to bastinado, beaten on his back with long, flat, bamboo bats by the other eunuchs. This sort of punishment was a matter of course for eunuchs. It was how my eunuch Liujian was killed. Eunuchs could be tortured or punished by a bamboo beating with no trial or permission from the Justice Department. The eunuch cried out in pain with every lashing. All of us winced with every snap of the bamboo on his flesh, but none more than Pearl. Even though Pearl was smart and cunning, she was still but a child, a teenager, and she could not bear the eunuch's suffering. As his flesh tore and blood pooled around him, she wept and begged the beating to stop. She got on her knees before the Empress and wept for mercy.

"Please, Dearest Empress," she cried. "Have mercy! This eunuch and I are innocent and would never betray His Majesty's trust!"

"Why must you continue to lie to me, Pearl?" the Empress demanded. She signaled for the beating to continue.

"I would never lie!" Pearl cried as the eunuch's cries went from loud to softer.

It was clear the eunuch was dying. Pearl was harder to break than the empress anticipated. The empress then grabbed Pearl by the ear, raised her to her feet, and struck her across the face. All of us, even the eunuchs punishing the other one, froze. While the empress was in her right to punish Pearl, we had never seen her strike another living person. The fact that she had everyone's attention seemed to give the empress more strength and she slapped Pearl again, this time so hard the girl fell to the floor. When Pearl raised her head, her nose was bleeding.

"So help me, Pearl," the empress said through clenched

teeth. "What you have done is punishable by death. And plenty of concubines who came before you have ended their lives on the executioner's scaffold. Tell me the truth or you will die today."

Pearl didn't speak. She only turned to the empress and nodded her head.

"You admit that you used your position as imperial concubine to purchase positions for men who paid you money?"

Pearl nodded.

The empress sighed. I do not think that the empress wanted to kill Pearl. In fact, I think she dreaded the possibility. But Cixi's first and only thought was of the empire. Guangxu was leading it to ruin. She didn't want to kill Pearl, she wanted to use the emperor's love for her.

The eunuch we all saw beaten was put to death. He was hit by the bamboo sticks until he was dead.

Empress Cixi took the information she had to the emperor. I do not know exactly how she threatened him, but if what Pearl had done was made public, she would have been executed and the emperor would have been seen as a weak mortal man in the thralls of a cunning and controlling woman. Even though he would still be emperor, his reputation would be ruined. Whatever Empress Cixi told him, she ended up back in some control. Pearl and Jade were demoted and publically censured. The emperor announced that he was grateful to the empress for bringing the misconduct of his concubines to light and ordered that all reports addressed to him would also be presented to the empress. She still was not in full control, but she did have access to information, and my empress knew that power lay in knowledge.

It was too late, though. In order to prevent the empress

from refusing the peace terms and prolonging the war, the emperor accepted Japan's demands. Everyone was horrified. Our empire could never afford the indemnitees Japan demanded.

Empress Cixi and Prince Gong did not give up. They continued to press the Western powers to support China. Finally, Russia, Germany, and France all expressed support and condemned the Japanese demands. Empress Cixi used this as evidence that should Japan press their advance, the West would support our defense. But the emperor refused to listen. He ratified the treaty and borrowed the money from foreign banks, an amount he would never be able to repay.

We lost our army, our navy, our money, our allies, and our hope. The empress, emotionally depleted, agreed to return to the Summer Palace. All of the magistrates came to kowtow before her as we departed the Forbidden City.

Prince Gong was especially worn weary by the war. He was thin, his long hair was gray, and he bent over a cane. "Dowager Empress," he said in a soft voice as she passed him. "I have failed you."

The empress shook her head. "No, we have all failed China."

His eyes watered as a eunuch helped him to his knees and he knocked his head to the ground as she was helped into her sedan chair. My heart broke for my poor prince. He had given his all to his brother and his brother's heirs and had nothing to show for it but failure. If only he had been emperor instead.

One day in May, I received a note from Hulan asking me to come to Prince Gong's mansion immediately. It was a note I had been dreading. The prince had completely withdrawn from palace life after the war with Japan and it was well known that his health was not good. I wanted to remember my prince as I had once known him – strong, brave, and smart. The man who should have been emperor. Seeing him wither over the last decades had been hard for both of us. It hurt his pride for me to see him weaken. It hurt my heart to watch from a distance as he had become a shell of the man he once was. But I went.

I took a donkey cart from the West Gate of the Forbidden City to Prince Gong's mansion. When I arrived, the servants were expecting me. They helped me from my cart and led me inside to a sitting room where my daughter and Lady Yun were waiting for me.

My daughter came up and took my hand and led me to sit beside her. "He has been asking for you," she explained.

"Is it soon?" I asked.

Lady Yun nodded. "Any day now. He has been getting his affairs in order. His mind is slow, but clear."

"What will happen to all of you?" I asked.

"The daughters who are old enough are to be married as soon as possible," Lady Yun said. "The women who have families willing to take them in are to return to them, but with some money so they are not a burden. His first wife, Lady Guwalgiya, and her oldest son will stay here. The other boys will set up their own households or go to school."

"And what of you two?" I asked. "And Arsalan?"

"Some of us women who have nowhere to go will set up our own household together," Lady Yun said. "We are looking for a suitable dwelling."

"I am hoping to open a shop," Hulan said. "I want to sell my embroidery. I could sell yours too, Mother."

I nodded. "That is a satisfactory situation," I said. And indeed it was. For the women to be free to live alone and as they wished for the rest of their days, not forced into the homes of someone else or into nunneries, would be a splendid retirement.

Hulan agreed. "Arsalan will be going to school in America," she said.

"But he is so young!" I said. He was only eight years old.

"I know, and it pains me to be separated from him, but the dowager empress is sponsoring his education. She is sending many young men to study abroad, but unlike the other boys, Arsalan didn't apply and I didn't request her aid. She sent one of her representatives to make the arrangements. She thinks all the boys will come back someday and be of great use to the empire, to help propel it into the modern age."

"I know what the empress thinks," I said. "But she

should also know the dangers of separating a boy from his mother. Just look at..."

"Shush! Mother," Hulan interrupted. "You shouldn't say such things. Even here." She glanced around. Just like in the Forbidden City, there were spies everywhere, even if you couldn't see them. Who knew to whom Prince Gong's wife was beholden to in the palace. Hulan lowered her voice. "I think she fears for Arsalan's safety without his grandfather here to protect him."

"Why?" I asked. "What does she fear?"

"I don't know exactly," Hulan said. "But who knows how many people know who he really is. I think she is sending him abroad both as a protection and for his education. I think she believes that he could be an important man in the Manchu court when he grows up."

"What does Prince Gong think about this?" I asked.

"He agrees it is for the best. Even if Arsalan never comes back to China, the boy is exceptionally bright. He will greatly benefit from a Western education."

"What do you mean, if he never comes back to China?" I asked.

Hulan shrugged. "The empress dowager is old and the emperor is impotent. Who knows what will happen."

With that, a servant appeared and announced that the prince was awake and was asking for me.

*H*ulan led me to Prince Gong's room, but didn't enter with me. The room was dark and smoky from incense. There was a servant present, helping Prince Gong drink some water, but she left when I entered. I went to the prince's side and sat on a stool by his bed. He smiled at me and motioned for me to take his hand. I held it with both of mine.

"I am glad to see you," he said.

"As am I," I said. "I have missed you at court."

"I am glad someone does."

"Everyone does."

"No, they miss the old me, the man I used to be. Not the useless one I have become."

"Hush," I said.

"Yaqian," he said. "I didn't want to die without seeing you one more time."

I didn't know how to respond to that, so I just held his hand tighter.

"I love you," he said.

"I know," I replied.

"You will not lie to me now, not on my deathbed?"

"I have never lied to you," I said. "I would not start now."

"Has there ever been anyone else for you?"

"What a thing to ask of me now," I said. "Why would you ask me that?"

"It would be comforting to know that I am the only man you have ever loved, have ever laid with."

"You have been with many women," I said. "You have more wives and concubines than I can count."

He coughed as he laughed. "Men are more fragile than women. They need exclusive devotion from a whole flock of women to feel powerful."

I smiled at that. "No, My Prince. I have never loved or laid with another."

"Not even my brother?" he asked.

I shook my head. "No, not as you and I had. He only wanted my feet."

"You gave me a beautiful daughter, Yaqian."

"I am glad that you find delight in her."

"I do, Yaqian. I told you many years ago that she was the one daughter I was happy to have. There were no expectations for her. And in my graying years, I didn't have to marry her away. She and her lovely boy have brought me great happiness."

Even though a part of me wished I could have lived with the prince and my daughter as a family all these years, it was my choice not to leave my empress, and I didn't regret it. I was happy in the palace. But if I couldn't be part of the prince's family, I was glad Hulan was. I wasn't part of their family, but I helped create it. That was enough for me.

"I have heard about the arrangements you have made for them."

"Do they please you?" he asked.

"They do," I said. "I am sad the boy is leaving, but it seems to be for the best."

"It is. The boy has a valuable heritage. Even if no one knows about him being the son of the emperor, he is my grandson, the great-grandson of The Daoguang Emperor. He has the blood of the Dragon. He must be protected." He was getting worked up and started to cough.

"Shush," I said, helping him drink some water. "He will be fine. Do not fear."

"I do fear," he said as he leaned back on his pillow. "And I fear for you. There, in the drawer." He pointed to a small table across the room. "Inside, there is paper with a name and address."

I went across the room and found the paper. It was written in characters I had never seen before. "I can't read it," I said. The prince motioned for me to return to his side.

"Marion Keswick," he said. "She is the daughter of Harry Parkes."

"The man from the dungeon?" I asked.

"Yes," he said. "He died here in Peking, but his daughter is still here. Well, sometimes. Her husband's family has business in Hong Kong. If anything happens, Yaqian, if you are ever in any danger, contact her and she will help you."

"Oh, my love," I said. "I am sure we will be fine. The empire will be fine. The empress is strong."

"Just in case," he said as he reached for my hand again.

I held his hand in mine for a long time.

*M*y prince left this world three days later.

TWENTY-SEVEN
THE SUMMER PALACE, 1898

*C*hina's position advanced from bad to worse. Since Japan had been given so much land, other countries, even our few supposed allies, demanded the same. Germany, Russia, Britain, and France all demanded treaty ports and independent concessions and Japan took more land on the Chinese mainland. The empress could do nothing but watch her country be chipped away by foreigners bit by bit. There were skirmishes throughout the country between Chinese and the foreigners. The missionaries went wherever they wanted, claiming land, even sacred spaces, for their odious religious edifices. The opium trade exploded. The throne needed the cash from sales and exports of the drug, but it was eating away at our people. China was still large and we still had our Dragon Throne, but we were weak and crumbling, and everyone knew it.

I also felt myself deteriorating. The death of my prince affected me greatly. Even though we often went years without seeing each other, the knowledge that my friend and lover was no longer in his home and could not protect me in dangerous times made my heart heavy. I think the empress felt the loss as well. We would often sit in silence for hours, not talking, not embroidering, not watching opera, just sitting, reminiscing about happier days when we dreamed of a prosperous empire and a peaceful retirement.

My hands began to ache. I could not embroider for hours on end anymore, but only for short stints. Every couple of hours, I would have to soak my hands in warm water infused with herbs to release the stiffness and pain. My feet ached more often and I tottered slowly and carefully wherever I went. Seeing me in pain would bring tears to the empress's eyes and she would beg me to unbind my feet.

"Please," she would implore me, "have some relief in your graying years. They can be of no benefit to you now."

But I could not forget how far my tiny feet had brought me. I wasn't ready to let go of them just yet.

Thankfully, my mind and my eyes were as keen as ever. I could easily recall my memories and reflect on brighter days. And my eyes were still clear enough to focus on the most delicate embroidery work. Because of my hands, my work slowed, but it was the best it had ever been. The empress still praised my work, I was able to help the young ladies-in-waiting who continued to join the empress's retinue improve their embroidery, and Hulan was able to sell the few pieces I could bear to part with for a high price in her shop. I was so proud of Hulan. She was a competent businesswoman, the only businesswoman I ever knew other than Lady Tang.

My grandson was ever a delight. He would write me often, telling me about all the fascinating things he was seeing and doing in America. He sent me drawings of strange animals and I was able to make embroidered versions of some of them. I once sent him an embroidery of a creature that looked like a fat, gray cat with a black mask. He wrote back and said all of his friends and teachers thought it was quite a good rendering, even though I had never seen one in person. He said he donated it to a museum in New York so that people from all over the world would be able to see it. I could hardly imagine it. He even sent me a photograph of himself once. He was so handsome. He looked just like his grandfather.

At one point, I realized that I had not received any letters from Lady Tang in quite a while. She never mentioned being sick. I never received any letters from her students or employees informing me of her death. Hulan never mentioned if she knew what happened to her. On one hand, I was curious. If my mentor and teacher, the woman I thought of as a mother, had died, I should mourn her. I should wear white and cry and even attempt to journey back to Hunan to burn incense and paper gifts at her grave. But I did none of these things. I had always believed that Lady Tang was not like other people. She had the air of a fairy. I consoled myself with the belief that she simply tired of this world and retreated back to her fairyland where she would live forever in youth and beauty. Maybe someday, when another girl needed her as much as I did, she would return.

*S*trangely, the emperor began calling regularly on his Papa Dearest. After the devastating defeat by Japan and the continual loss of territory, he began to appreciate her counsel. She had been the only one of his grandees and counselors to reject the Japanese demands, and he began to see that he should have heeded her warnings. The empress also began to appreciate her adopted son. As a woman, she could never command the court the way he could. The grandees needed a man to follow. They could not follow the laws and edicts of a woman. They began to see the need to work together.

"Can you believe it?" she asked me as we and some of her other ladies sat in her sitting room together one day. "The emperor actually asked me about reforms. He wants to make changes and make the empire strong again."

"That is wonderful, Your Majesty," I replied. "What will you tell him?"

"Well, we must start where I left off. The railroad must be completed. Russia has shown great interest in building a line that would connect our countries. The army needs new training methods. We could expand the prince's college into a full university!"

I couldn't help but smile at how excited the empress was. Her face practically glowed as she began to list all the modernizing efforts she could put in place with the emperor's support.

"I know someone you should speak to," Pearl broke in.

Since the relationship between the empress and the emperor had been improving, the empress had been making strides to improve her relationship with Pearl as well. She often invited Pearl to sit with her, she bought her presents, and she even restored some of her imperial titles to her.

"Who is this?" the empress asked.

"His name is Kang Youwei, and he is only a minor official now, but he has a brilliant mind that is not being used to its full potential."

"How are you so well-informed about this man?" the empress asked.

Pearl reached into one of her large sleeves and handed the empress a pamphlet. "He has been writing about his grand ideas for years. One of my friends sent me this pamphlet. It is quite enlightening!"

The empress quickly scanned the pamphlet and then handed it to me. "What do you think?"

"I know nothing of this Kang. If you think his ideas for reform align with yours, then invite him to present some of his ideas to you. There is nothing to lose. At worst we will get an afternoon of entertainment out of it."

The empress took the pamphlet back and began to read it in more detail. After several minutes she addressed Pearl, "What other writing by him do you have?" The girl happily ran off to her rooms to find more of his papers.

A few days later, we all traveled to the Forbidden City so the emperor and the empress could hold court to meet Kang Youwei. I was fortunate enough to be included among the ladies the empress took to the court.

Even though it was often difficult to see court petitioners from my position in the back of the room, Kang was easy to see and hear. Even on his knees, he sat up straight and tall. His voice was loud and clear, though not booming. There was a serenity in his voice that could lull you to sleep. He mentioned at one point that he practiced Buddhist meditation, which greatly appealed to the empress, herself a devout Buddhist who many people called Old Buddha, *Lǎo Fóyé*. Kang spoke with a great flourish of his hands. Indeed, I think that he would not have been able to speak if his hands were tied behind his back.

Kang broke with tradition by heaping great praise on the emperor. While the emperor was known as the Great Dragon who held the Mandate of Heaven and knew the best way to rule, unbridled flattery was discouraged. A good emperor does not need to hear such things and any man who praised the emperor so must want something in return. A good emperor embraces criticism so as to always improve. Kang cared nothing for such rules and precedents. He said Emperor Guangxu was the wisest in history and his abilities were sublime and unparalleled. The emperor sat on the edge of his throne, enthralled with Kang's words.

The empress displayed little emotion during the audience.

Afterward, in the privacy of her rooms, the empress was torn.

"Such arrogance!" she exclaimed. "Have you ever seen such a thing?" she asked.

"I certainly have not," I said.

"That man cannot be allowed to rise too high. He clearly is too ambitious."

"Clearly," I agreed.

"And yet, he does have some good ideas," she said. "Did you hear what he said about the advisory board? The emperor is so weak, and running the empire is too much for one person's shoulders to bear. An advisory board would be good for the emperor and for China."

"It certainly would, Your Majesty," I said. I wanted to say that ruling the empire had not been too much for Her Majesty's shoulders to bear, but I held my tongue.

"I'll have to give him a special appointment, but keep him out of the Forbidden City. Use him, learn from him, but not allow him to climb too high."

Empress Cixi offered to make Kang the head of a newspaper in Shanghai. A very good position for someone who started so low in life. But he refused. He would not leave Peking. He was determined to be close to the emperor. Somehow, Kang's writings were getting past the empress and directly into the emperor's hands. The emperor was drinking in his every word like a draught and began acting impulsively. He issued an edict dismissing all of the officials in the Forbidden City and appointing all new ones, all chosen based on the suggestions of Kang. Everyone, especially the empress, was horrified.

The empress refused to endorse the edict. "Hundreds of men suddenly out of work? And he plans to do this throughout the empire! Thousands of men and their families suddenly with no income? The whole country will revolt against us. We are Manchu. We already are despised by most of the country. We only rule because they allow us to. The people will not stand for this."

The emperor, furious that she refused to endorse the edict, began dismissing individual officials at will and making new appointments in their place, all without the approval of the empress. Men began flocking to her, begging for an audience so they could plead for their jobs, but there was little she could do.

"Who is this man that he thinks he can advise an emperor? He is a nothing from nowhere. He should be glad that he even saw the emperor. I should order his eyes cut out of his head!" Cixi raged.

"You said he had good ideas, Your Majesty," I said.

"Many people have good ideas," she said. "Does that

mean they should all rule in tandem with the Son of Heaven? We were already working on reforms together anyway. Me and Guangxu. I was starting to love the boy, really I was. But this Kang, this...wily...*Wild Fox* is trying to change everything overnight. It will not happen. It cannot happen."

While the emperor had the right to dismiss officials and appoint new ones, the new appointments could not be confirmed without Empress Cixi's approval. She refused to endorse any of the new appointments if she thought they had any connection to the Wild Fox, as he came to be known among those who did not trust him. The emperor was forced to reappoint some of the men he had dismissed since the empire could not function without the officials.

The emperor was angry, but his hands were tied. He had given the empress the authority to block his appointments after the incident with Pearl. He couldn't dismiss the officials and leave their position vacant. The empress tried to placate him and encourage him to continue with the reforms they had set in motion before the Wild Fox appeared, but he no longer wanted to work with her. The two were at a standstill.

*C*ixi refused to sit idle. She continued with the reforms she had put in motion before Guangxu took the throne. She focused first on the military, appointing a man named Ronglu as the commander of the army and Yuan Shikai as his general. Even though China was at peace, she knew it was the time to plan for war. Relations with the Westerners were worsening. Strangely, though, the emperor had begun, under the Wild Fox's advisement, courting friendship with Japan! Kang thought that China and Japan should band together against the West. While an Asian federation was not a bad idea, Empress Cixi refused to believe that the Japanese would help and support China. As always, Japan would only be looking for a way to advance their own nation.

When the empress found out that the emperor had agreed to meet with the Japanese Prime Minister, Cixi refused to stand aside and let the emperor hear what the man said and be endorsed by Kang without her there to critically examine the situation. She decided that she would also be present for the audience.

The day before the audience, as I was walking through one of the lovely gardens, I heard a whisper calling my name. I turned and saw General Yuan hiding behind a pillar. I approached him and asked what he was doing.

"I have heard that you used to sneak Prince Gong into the palace at night," he said.

"How dare you!" I nearly yelled, shocked.

"Please, quiet mistress!" he said as he tried to shush me. "Please, the empress's life is in danger."

"What are you talking about?" I asked.

"I believe the empress's life is in danger. I must see her. Tonight. No one can know. Can you get me into the palace after dark?"

"What do you mean her life is in danger? Why are you telling me this? How can I trust you?"

"I have it on good authority that tonight someone is

going to try and kill the empress dowager before the audience with the Japanese tomorrow."

"How do you know this?" I asked.

"Because *I* am the assassin," he said.

"What?" this time I nearly screamed and tried to step away, but he grabbed my arm and put his hand over my mouth.

"Please, mistress!" He dragged me further into the garden where no one would be able to see us. "Please, I need you to listen!"

I tried to fight him off, but I was an old, frail woman and he was a young military general. I could not get away. In fact, if he wanted to kill me, he could have done so easily.

"I'll remove my hand from your mouth and let you go if you promise to listen to me," he whispered harshly in my ear. I nodded and he did as he promised. He then bent his knee and kneeled before me. "I swear, mistress, I am loyal to the empress. That is why I need your help. I agreed to help Kang only to learn of his plan so I could stop it. He has assembled an army of seven thousand men just outside the city. They are to invade once she is dead so they can get rid of anyone who was loyal to her. I need to see the empress. I need to tell her what is happening. I must protect her. There could be other assassins waiting in case I fail or am caught."

"How do I know this isn't part of your plan?" I asked. "Get me to let you in the palace at night so you can finish your job?"

"I will give you proof that will implicate not just Kang, but the emperor himself. You can show it to the empress tonight. It will prove that what I say is true. And the fact that I am handing over the evidence will show that I am on her side." With that, he handed me a piece of parchment that was stamped with the imperial seal.

The paper was an imperial edict prepared by the emperor. Something like this could not be faked. "Did the emperor himself hand you this?" I asked.

"No," he said. "I have not talked to the emperor about this. Only Kang and his lackeys."

"So it is possible that the emperor is not involved."

"It is possible, but doubtful," he said. "Whoever prepared this edict has access to the imperial seals and can perfectly imitate the emperor's signature. But I believe it was the emperor. Kang still has almost direct contact with him."

"Almost?" I asked. "Who is between Kang and the emperor?"

"Imperial Concubine Pearl," he said.

I sighed. I could not believe that Pearl would make the same mistake again. "What a stupid girl. So either the emperor signed this death warrant for the empress, or Pearl did it in his name."

"Either option is not good," he said. "If Pearl has that kind of access, that kind of sway, the emperor will lose the respect of the magistrates. If he did issue the edict himself, he will lose the respect of all the people of China. He cannot kill his own mother! It is unthinkable!"

"I will give this to the empress," I said. "If she agrees that you are an ally, I will let you in the palace. Meet me at the West Gate at the hour of the rat."

"Thank you, mistress," he said. He then bowed and took his leave of me. I hid the edict in my sleeve and continued my walk.

That night, I waited until after the empress had dinner and had dismissed most of her servants to approach her. I hardly knew what to say. The relationship between my empress and Emperor Guangxu had always been difficult, but that he would try to kill her would be devastating. I knew that deep down she still hoped he would be the emperor China needed. I approached her slowly and with my head down.

"What is it, Yaqian?" she asked.

"I have to show you something, Your Majesty," I said, "in private."

She nodded and waved the rest of her attendants away. "Well," she said. "What is it?"

I reached into my sleeve and handed her the edict.

"How did you come to be in possession of an imperial edict?" she asked.

"General Yuan gave it to me as I was walking in the garden today."

As the empress opened the edict and read it, her hands began to shake and her eyes grew wide. "Do you know what this says?" she finally asked me.

"General Yuan told me his orders and about the army. Was he telling the truth?"

"It would appear so," she said. She began to weep. "My son...my son...how could you leave me to such a cruel world?"

I wrapped my arms around her. "You are not alone, Your Majesty," I said. "General Yuan said he would protect you in case there are other assassins about. We can send for Ronglu."

The empress wiped her face and sat up straight. "We must not let it be known that anything is amiss," she said. "Bring me Yuan and Lianying." I did as she ordered. The empress had Lianying discreetly bring some eunuchs and palace guards to her quarters. She and General Yuan talked long into the night. She also sent a messenger with an urgent letter for Commander Ronglu.

The next morning, everything seemed normal. The empress left her palace as planned and headed for the audience hall, but she had General Yuan by her side. When she entered the audience chamber, the emperor was clearly shocked by her presence. He rushed to kowtow to her and invited her to sit by his side. She did not betray that anything was wrong.

General Yuan was allowed to address the emperor. Everyone heard what he then said. "Your Majesty, I fear you have been given grave counsel. Many of the men who wish to advise you have been careless. If these men were to make a mistake, some might hold you responsible."

The emperor did not speak but only nodded. General Yuan took his place once again at Empress Cixi's side. Then, the Prime Minister of Japan, Ito Hirobumi, was brought forward. The Prime Minister said nothing unexpected, but he was clearly frustrated by the empress's presence. He stammered and seemed to be waiting for the emperor to say more, but he did not. The prime minister left and no agreements with Japan were reached.

After the audience was over, General Yuan and his men escorted the emperor and the empress to the Sea Palace. I do not know what was said, but later that day, the emperor issued an edict in his own hand declaring that Empress Cixi would once again be his guardian. She would assist him in ruling the empire in perpetuity. The emperor was put under house arrest and was not allowed to leave the Sea Palace. He was also separated from Pearl, who was under guard in her own quarters.

That evening, Commander Ronglu arrived and told the empress that his forces had crushed Kang's small army outside the city and had captured his fellow conspirators.

"And what of Wild Fox Kang," she asked. "Was he also taken care of?"

"Forgive me, Your Majesty," he said. "But Kang escaped. Ito gave him safe passage to Japan."

The empress ordered the execution of six men involved in the assassination attempt without a trial. People were horrified, but she did it for Guangxu.

"If the men go to trial," she told me, "everyone will find out about the emperor's attempt to have me killed. He would have to be removed from the throne by force, maybe even executed, but he has no heir. Who would rule then? We are too weak. The foreigners would invade and set up their own government. China and the Qing Dynasty would be done for. I do this for him. I do this for my country."

All the empress ever did was in the name of her country. Once again, she had managed to stage a coup and regain control of the empire with only a handful of bloodshed.

TWENTY-EIGHT

FLEEING THE FORBIDDEN CITY, 1900-1901

*T*he emperor was quite ill. He had always been a sickly person, but after his role in the plot to murder the empress was uncovered and he was imprisoned, his health got even worse. A French doctor was even brought in to examine him. I doubt the weakling could have continued running the empire on his own anyway.

Empress Cixi began ruling the empire once again. The emperor, when he was well enough, would attend audiences with her, but his presence was only for show. The screen that had separated Empress Cixi from the court was removed and she addressed petitioners directly.

Across the sea, the Wild Fox continued to plague the empress. He wrote terrible things about her, calling her a murderess, an anti-reformer, and a licentious woman who had a stable of lovers. I cannot say how many people believed the things he wrote, but it worried the empress deeply. She knew that the survival of the kingdom depended on the goodwill of the foreigners. She didn't like it, in fact, she began to resent them, but there was little she could do.

In order to court a favorable opinion of her by the foreigners, she decided to invite all the foreign women of the diplomatic corps, the wives of the foreign diplomats, to tea. It was quite exciting. While I had seen a few foreign women in my life, mostly from a sedan chair, I had never seen so many so close up.

The empress invited twelve women to tea. They brought their own interpreter and were first introduced to several court officials. Then they finally were brought to the throne room. The ladies were all a flutter with excitement. They could not stop smiling. Their dresses were so different from ours. The gowns were high-necked, but form fitting. The dresses emphasized the women's enormous breasts and round hips. Their dresses were of many colors, white, blue, green, and even black, and were covered with lace and beads. I noticed that most of them lacked any embroidery work. They also all wore fanciful hats with huge feathers that bobbed whenever they talked. And talk they did! They all chattered on like monkeys, even when someone was addressing the empress or the emperor, who the empress had specifically invited so the women could see he was not dead and report such news back to their husbands, the other women clucked on.

After each foreign woman bowed and addressed the empress, she grasped their hand and gave them a gold ring with a large pearl. She then told them – in English! – "all one family." I was quite impressed and proud of the empress. Then the women were treated to a large feast hosted by various princesses. The empress could not attend the meal because it would not be right for people to sit in the empress's presence while she was eating. After the feast, we all attended an opera performance. After the opera, the empress presented each lady with many more gifts, including some of my embroidery. The empress even stood for a photograph with some of the ladies!

Cixi fretted for days about whether or not the meeting with the foreign women had gone well, but eventually, the women and their husbands began writing about the experience in the foreign press. Never before had foreign women been allowed to see a Chinese ruler, so many people were interested in reading about the ladies' experience.

Mrs. Conger, the wife of a foreign minister, wrote in one newspaper, "We returned to the British Legation and in a happy mood grouped ourselves for a picture that would fix in thought a most unusual day – a day, in fact, of historic import." Lady MacDonald, the wife of the British minister, wrote in another paper, "all previously conceived notions of the Empress had been upset by what I had seen and heard." Lady MacDonald's husband told several court ministers that, "the Empress Dowager made a most favorable impress by her courtesy and affability." Everyone who met her majesty, like those of us who had always known her, could not help but love her.

But the goodwill did not last long. Jealous of the other European countries who grabbed land after the war with Japan, Italy stormed in and demanded land and a port of their own. Just like after the Japanese war, the Italians expected Emperor Guangxu to roll over and hand it to them. But Guangxu was no longer in charge. Empress Cixi refused. Surprisingly, Italy backed down. Cixi realized they were only a small and weak nation who didn't really want to fight, but she and the rest of the country were bolstered by this tiny victory.

Relations between local Chinese and the foreigners got more tense around the country, especially regarding the missionaries. The missionaries were all backed by their respective countries, and, thus, their countries' gunboats. They were able to act outside, and sometimes in defiance of, our laws. They would not support local beliefs or customs, which often relied on the support of the whole community. The Chinese converts to Christianity were called "foreign running dogs" for their propensity to do whatever the foreigners demanded of them. The foreigners and their foreign running dogs were always given preferences in legal disputes because of their white faces and big guns.

Even in cities like Peking, local Chinese were starting to feel like second-class citizens. They were not allowed to participate in the new horse races and foreigners, often taller and burlier than Chinese men, would pick fights with locals in the streets. Foreigners were also known for buying Chinese women as concubines, having many children with them, and then abandoning the women and children with no means of support when it was time for the men to go home to their Western wives. America, who China long considered an ally, banned Chinese from immigrating to their country.

Things then came to a head. In Shandong Province, Germany sent troops to put down riots against their missionaries. The troops burned down hundreds of homes and shot countless people dead in the street. A group called the Yihetuan – the Society of the Righteous and Harmonious Fists – fought back. The men of Shandong were known for their martial arts skills and their mystical abilities. The locals were also furious with the Germans and wanted to drive them out of Shandong. Thousands flocked to join the ranks of the Yihetuan. The Yihetuan believed that Heaven was on their side and that they would drive the foreign barbarians out with their bare fists if they had to. Foreigners called the Yihetuan the Boxers.

After the Boxers murdered a German holy man, Empress Cixi sent General Yuan to put down the rebels, even though she sympathized with them. At first, Yuan did a good job of stopping the Boxers from growing. He put to death the leaders of the gang who had killed the German. A harsh winter then blew in, burying the Boxers' wrath under a deep snow. The empress formally banned the Boxers in Shandong. She hoped that would be an end to the Boxer Rebellion.

Even though her actions were working, they were not enough for the foreigners. The same governments that ignored the murders of our people at the hands of the Germans now screamed for more Chinese blood. They wanted the Boxers to be officially banned throughout the country and for all Boxer members, not just the leaders, to be executed. Empress Cixi wanted to refuse them. She would not be told how to run her country by foreigners. But how could she refuse? The British positioned their gunboats in the harbor at the Dagu Forts and waited. Empress Cixi had defeated the Italians, but they were only bluffing. Were the British bluffing now? If they weren't, how would she fight them? General Yuan and Commander Ronglu had been working tirelessly to build up the army, but it was not enough, and we still didn't have a navy. How much the empress longed for the guidance and assistance of Prince Gong in dealing with these foreigners.

"What do you think I should do, Yaqian?" she asked me one evening.

"I have no idea, Your Majesty," I replied. "If you give into the foreigners' demands, we look weak. They may decide to attack us. They could overthrow you and put Guangxu back on the throne so they can rule through him. If you defy them, they certainly will attack and could simply destroy us. I do not envy being in your position."

"You know who would fight them," she said. "The Boxers."

"You would let the rebels run free?" I asked.

She shook her head. "No, not free, but under my direction. We are the most populous nation in the world. I have always feared that the Han would rise up and overthrow the Manchu, but what if they rose up to overthrow the foreigners? If the Chinese would all rise up, all band together, no one could stop us."

"What if you can't control them?" I asked. "What if after they are finished with the foreigners, they come for the Manchu?"

"Then let them come," she said. "If the Han can defeat the foreigners, then they will have earned the right to govern their own country."

Empress Cixi did not call General Yuan's army back, but she no longer sent them orders either. The people could sense that the army was no longer interested in fighting them, so the number of Boxers increased. They spread through the countryside like locusts. After the bad winter was followed by a spring drought, the Boxers stormed the streets of Peking, convinced that the starving time that was coming was the fault of the foreign devils. Traditionally, droughts and famines were blamed on the emperor, and were considered evidence of the loss of the Mandate of Heaven. For the Boxers to blame the foreigners and not the empress or the emperor showed just how much the people hated the foreigners. From the palace walls, we could see thousands of men and women dressed in red scarves, red shirts, and red sashes around their waists. They waved large knives in the air. The women also carried red lanterns and wore pants just like the men! The Boxers called for the deaths of all foreigners within three months.

The empress was terrified. She wanted the foreigners to leave China, not be slaughtered, especially the ladies she had entertained only a few months before and had grown very fond of. She allowed the foreigners to bring their own troops into Peking to protect the legations, but she used the Boxers to prevent too many foreign troops from entering. This play back and forth between supporting the Boxers but protecting the foreigners was a strange dance that could not last.

When the Boxers murdered a Japanese chancellor, the foreigners demanded the Boxers responsible be punished. The Boxers declared that if Imperial forces killed one Boxer, they would destroy the Forbidden City. The empress had lost control, if she ever had it. She merely ignored the demands for justice from the foreigners. "What's done is done," she said.

Muslims from the western areas of China joined with the Boxers and destroyed railways and telegraph lines. The empress lost all contact with the outside world. Some provincial viceroys tried to send messages via horse riders, but the messages were far and few between, many often lost along the way.

In Peking, the Boxers began burning foreign churches and houses. We could see the smoke of a hundred fires from inside the Forbidden City. While we received very few reports of foreigners being murdered – the Boxers still held a measure of fear of the power of their countries – the Chinese running dogs were fair game. The Boxers beat, burned, and murdered all they could. The running dogs fled to the foreign legations for help. The legations let hundreds of the Chinese converts inside and sent rescue parties out to find more, and they killed many Boxers along the way. In retaliation, the Boxers laid siege to the legations. Hundreds of foreigners and thousands of Chinese converts were trapped inside the legation walls, which nearly butted up against the south wall of the Forbidden City, separated only by a small canal. We could hear the screams of the people who were killed seeking refuge and the chanting of the Boxers outside. "Kill! Kill! Kill!" the Boxers yelled. We were living in a war zone.

The empress greatly regretted what she had done and knew it would come to a bad end. She could not fight them, but sent grandees to try to reason with the Boxers to stop their attack. It could only end in disaster for all of them, she warned, but it was too late.

The foreigners were not going to abandon their people. Eight nations who had people in the legations sailed warships into our waters and opened fire on the Dagu Fort. They destroyed the fort in a matter of hours.

The empress sat on her throne, her head bent and her face shrouded in gloom. "We were in the wrong," she said. "We did not protect the foreigners who are guests in our country. Can you blame the foreign powers for stepping in to protect their own? But what can I do? Can I simply hand over my country?"

"You could run," I said.

"I did that forty years ago," she said. "And my husband died while banished to the wilderness. We never recovered from that – I never recovered. Should I do it again?"

"It is better than dying," I said.

"Is it?" she asked. "Dying defending my country seems quite an honorable death. I could not face my ancestors if I simply handed over my country. I would rather fight to the end."

Empress Cixi declared war on all eight countries – Russia, Japan, Britain, France, Germany, America, Italy, and Austria-Hungary. The empress then gave legal status to the Boxers and commanded them to fight on. She gave them weapons and paid them with silver. But she could not control them. They burned foreign shops and looted and pillaged cities and villages alike. They ransacked people's homes. I feared for my daughter, but I had no way to contact her. Even some members of our court seemed to have lost their minds. Princes and eunuchs and guards donned red sashes and rushed out into the streets to join the Boxers. We began to fear for our lives within the Forbidden City.

One day, the Boxers dared to demand that the empress send out all members of Forbidden City to see if she was harboring any Chinese running dogs. One of the Boxer leaders claimed that if he recited an incantation over a person's head, a cross would appear above those who served the foreign god. I didn't believe the Boxer leader for a second and feared that he would kill us to demonstrate to the empress and the rest of the country just how powerful the Boxers were. I begged her not to send me out, as did several other servants, including her favorite eunuch, Li Lianying. The empress wept as she sent us out, crying that there was nothing she could do. We were all marched outside, our hearts beating hard in our chests.

The city was in ruins. Buildings were destroyed, horses and people lay dead in the streets, fires raged. A hot wind blew, bringing with it the stench of death and sulfur. We were all lined up and a tall man dressed in all the red trappings of a Boxer stood in front of the first person in the line, a very young eunuch. He said words in a language I had never heard before. His body shook and his eyes rolled back in his head. He then stopped and stared at the eunuch and declared that he was not a running dog. The eunuch thanked the Boxer leader and ran back to the Forbidden City gate. The fact that the first young man was spared did not give the rest of us hope. In fact, it might have made us more afraid. We were certain that some of us were going to die that day. Every person ahead of us who was spared only made our own death more certain. As the Boxer leader moved down the line, we all began to weep. One eunuch fainted and a girl next to me vomited. I kept my head down and cried, but stood firm. If this was my death, I would be strong, just like the empress. I only prayed that my daughter, wherever she was, would be spared such a fate.

The man stood over me, recited his incantation, and then pronounced me one of China's faithful. I nearly collapsed from relief. One of the other girls who had also been exonerated by the man ran over to help me. In the end, we were all spared. When we returned to her, Empress Cixi held us and wept. She wondered if the Boxers were actually testing her and not her servants. By agreeing to send us out, she obviously trusted them and was supporting them. She had passed their test. The rest had only been for show.

The siege against the legations lasted a month. Foreigners, innocent Chinese, and countless Boxers died. The Boxers believed they were impervious to foreign bullets, which quickly proved untrue as they were mowed down by foreign guns, yet they still threw themselves in harm's way. I will never understand the mind of a religious fanatic.

Finally, the foreign powers marched on Peking itself. Many of the viceroys, magistrates, and princes fled the Forbidden City. The maids and eunuchs poured out, many never to be seen again. The princesses and ladies in waiting were collected by their families. When the foreign armies entered Peking and were only days away from the Forbidden City, the empress finally agreed to leave. When she sent for the carriages and horses she had standing by, however, she found out that they had been stolen by people fleeing the city. When one of the eunuchs returned to the empress and told her the transports were gone, Empress Cixi stood tall, walked up the stairs of the dais, and took her place on her throne. "Then we stay," she declared. We all knew that if the empress was still in the Forbidden City when the foreign powers arrived, she would be killed. Worse, I feared she would issue herself a white scarf and do the job herself instead of allowing foreign devils to do it. I could not allow it.

I went to my room and grabbed a huge handful of coins from my savings, which was rather significant by this time, and put the coins in a bag. I found General Yuan and gave him the bag. "You must take me to find Prince Gong's daughter, Lady Hulan," I demanded.

"Madam, you know how dangerous it is outside the Forbidden City walls. Besides, the lady has probably already fled."

"I helped you save the empress's life once. You must help me now!"

General Yuan nodded. He called for his horse to be brought. He mounted his horse and then his men helped me up behind him. It had been many years since I had ridden a horse and my old legs were no longer used to it. But I knew the empress's life depended on my ability to find help, so I held tightly to General Yuan as he deftly steered his horse through the ruins of Peking to find my daughter.

When we arrived at the house where my daughter and Lady Yun lived, I feared they were gone. The house still stood, but it was dark and boarded up. General Yuan helped me down from the horse and I banged on the front gate. "Hulan! Lady Yun!" I yelled. "It's Yaqian! Open the door!" General Yuan went around the building and banged on some of the windows. Eventually, we heard a noise on the other side.

"Quiet! We don't want anyone to know we are here!" my daughter barked.

"Hulan!" I nearly cried. "I am so happy you are all right."

I heard some shuffling and boards being removed from the other side. Eventually, Hulan's servants were able to open one of the doors. I stepped in and hugged my daughter.

"Mother!" Hulan cried as she hugged me back. "What are you doing here? It is too dangerous for you to be out."

"It is dangerous everywhere," I said. "The foreign armies are here. They are going to bust down the gates of the Forbidden City. We have lost."

"Oh, Mother," she said. "What are you doing? Are you fleeing? Do you need a safe place to stay?"

"The empress cannot flee. All of her carts and horses were stolen. She has accepted the fact that she will die." My voice suddenly cracked and I held my hand to my mouth. This was the first time I had voiced my fears and I could not stop the tears from flowing. The empress had spent her life in service to the empire, but now, she would die in disgrace, murdered in her own rooms. I couldn't imagine a world without her.

Hulan wrapped her arms around me. "It is all right, Mother," she said. "What can we do? Why did you come here?"

"Do you have any horses or carts or know where we

could get some?" I asked. "Did your father leave you anything that could help us?"

"I do have some carts," she said. "And some donkeys. Not many, and they are not used to pulling the carts much anymore. I don't have much use for them. I don't know why I haven't sold them," she said.

"Heaven must have intervened!" I cried. "Even now, Prince Gong is Her Majesty's only ally." I began to weep again.

My daughter held me as Lady Yun took charge. She ordered their servants to pull out some old carts and attach the donkeys to them. It would not be a comfortable way to travel, and the poor beasts had no idea of the terrible journey ahead of them, but the empress would be able to leave the city. I could ask for no more than this.

Hulan and some of her servants went with us to guide the donkeys back to the Forbidden City. General Yuan and his men guarded our donkey carts with their lives. Indeed, just as happened forty years before, people were desperate to leave the city. Several people, regular people and some errant Boxers, tried to steal our carts. General Yuan had no time for mercy and shot anyone who got too close to us.

When we arrived at the Forbidden City, we brought our small caravan in through the west gate and lined them up in the garden. Servants, ladies, the few princesses who were left, and everyone else trapped in the Forbidden City ran out to meet us. The empress and the emperor also came out. The empress could not hide her surprise.

"Where did you find these?" she asked me.

"My...student. Hulan. Prince Gong had left them to her and her home had not been ransacked. I am only sorry this is all we could find," I explained.

The empress shook her head and did her best to hide

her tears. "No, it is more than I could have asked for. More than I deserve." She walked over to me and put her hands on my shoulders. "When I heard you had left the Forbidden City, I thought you had left me."

I looked up at her, towering over me on her pot-bottomed shoes as I bent my knees in respect. "I would never abandon you, Your Majesty."

She turned to the rest of the people and the court, who were waiting for their orders. "We only have twelve carts, and the donkeys are small. Not everyone can go, and those who can, we must only take the bare minimum of items. We cannot weigh these poor creatures down or they will not be able to take us far."

"Where will we go?" Empress Longyu asked. "Will we go to Jehol?"

My Empress visibly shuddered at the thought. "No, I will never set foot in that cursed place again. We must go to the interior. The foreigners will not want to go inland. We will go to Chang'an, the ancient capital."

With this, many people began to murmur and fret. Chang'an was nearly two thousand li from Peking through treacherous terrain. And since the empress lost contact with China outside of Peking, we had no idea what was happening in the villages and cities along the way. It would be a very dangerous journey.

The empress began assigning the few donkey carts she had to various members of the court. There was one for her, one for the emperor, one for the young empress, one for Concubine Jade, a few for the princesses who had not been able to contact their families, and the rest were for some of the grandees who had stayed by her side. She turned to me with sad eyes. I shook my head. I knew that there would be no place for a lowly *gōngnǚ* on a journey of life and death.

"The last cart is yours, Yaqian," she said.

"What?" I asked in shock.

"I am sorry that we have no room for Mistress Gong. If it were not for her generosity and willingness to share her donkey carts, we would all perish here. Please forgive me," she said to Hulan.

"There is nothing to forgive, Your Majesty," Hulan replied. "I will be safe at my home, I believe. I am so grateful that you are willing to take Mistress Yang with you."

The empress waved her hand as though it was nothing. "I will need at least one person to help me and the princesses on the journey. I cannot even undress myself without help."

"Thank you...thank you..." I finally managed to mumble.

"Which cart is mine?" a voice piped up. Everyone turned and looked at Concubine Pearl. The girl was nervously chewing her bottom lip and wringing her hands. "I can ride with my sister," she pleaded.

"Don't be ridiculous. We cannot burden one donkey with two people."

"I can walk," she said.

"A member of the royal court would not walk," she said. "Besides you wouldn't have the stamina. You would give out on the road."

"Then I am to stay here?" she asked. "You would abandon me to the foreign devils?"

"Of course not," the empress said. "I cannot have you betraying us to them, or allow them to have their way with you. Can you imagine a white devil lying with a consort of the Son of Heaven? What an insult!"

"Then what?" she asked. "What is to happen to me?"

The empress slowly stepped close to Pearl with her face

dark and her eyes narrow. "You are a disgrace, Pearl," she said. "You betrayed me, you betrayed your emperor, you have never given us an heir..."

"That is not my fault..." Pearl started to object. The empress slapped the girl across the face before she could finish.

"How dare you insult the Emperor of the Dragon Throne!" she screamed. "If there is any honor left in you, you will heed my order. Jump into that well," she said pointing across the garden, "and drown yourself. It will be the only useful thing you have ever done."

"No!" Pearl screamed. "You cannot! I cannot! I love you. I love His Majesty." She rushed to Guangxu, who stood still as a stone. "Please, my love! Save me."

Guangxu's eyes watered, but he knew he could do nothing. As the head of the inner court and the empress dowager, Empress Cixi could indeed order any member of the inner court to commit suicide to prevent dishonor from settling on the imperial family. Guangxu did not look at Pearl as she grabbed his robe and wept.

"You must stop her!" Pearl cried. "Don't let her do this!"

"Pearl!" the empress called out. "Do it now. I'll not warn you again."

Pearl stumbled out of her pot-bottomed shoes and fell at the empress's feet. "Please, have mercy!" she begged as she cried and clutched Her Majesty's robe.

"This is a mercy, Pearl," the empress said stepping back. "Take the honorable way out."

We all stood in shock. Of course, the empress could have had Pearl executed long ago for her crimes, but she had spared her to save the emperor embarrassment. But to now watch as Pearl's life slipped away was horrid. I clutched my daughter's hands, so thankful she had escaped life in the Forbidden City when she did.

"I'll not do it! I'll not die!" Pearl cried.

The empress finally sighed with exasperation and nodded to her head eunuch, Li Lianying. Lianying then motioned for a low-ranking eunuch, a very tall and strong man – qualities usually sorely lacking in eunuchs – and ordered him to carry out the empress's order. The eunuch hesitated for a moment, but only until the empress looked at him directly. Pearl stood up and tried to run, but the eunuch took only a few strides to reach her. He grabbed Pearl and tossed her over his shoulder like a sack of rice. Pearl screamed and kicked, trying to get away, but she was no match for the unusually strong eunuch. When the eunuch reached the well, he looked at the empress again. The empress nodded and the eunuch dropped Pearl from his shoulder into the well. Time seemed to stop. Her scream lasted forever as she fell. We all held our breath as we waited for her to hit the water. We finally heard a splash and then more screams and coughs as she drowned. After a couple of tortuous minutes, the garden was silent.

The empress finally broke the quiet. "Take as little with you as you can. We will leave before the hour of the goat."

*T*he road was indeed difficult. Our little donkeys lumbered along at a slow pace. Walking would have been faster, though impossible. Several eunuchs and maids who could not ride in the carts did follow us, but it was excruciating for them. Their clothes and shoes were not made for traveling.

The last time we fled the Forbidden City, we had hundreds of carts with everything we needed to survive: food, clothes, tents. This time, we had nothing. We could not burden our little donkeys, so we were only allowed to bring one small bag of items. At least Her Majesty, the princesses, and I were smart enough to wear several layers of clothing. It was August, still a warm time of year in Peking, but our trip would take months and through all kinds of weather. The second day, it began to rain. We had no way to cover ourselves, so we were quickly soaked to the bone. The maids and eunuchs who traveled with us slogged through the mud as best they could. The donkeys slowed so they would not slip. We were all miserable.

The road and the villages we came across were abandoned. The eunuchs searched several homes for provisions, but they found nothing. Many houses were burned and bodies were strewn everywhere, even those of children. The Boxers had mercilessly slaughtered everyone they suspected of being Christian converts, which sometimes meant whole villages of people were murdered. The empress wept at the carnage and destruction she saw.

"I didn't know…I didn't know…" she wept. Indeed, she had no idea the Boxers had murdered so many of her own people, but she knew they had murdered some, which should have been enough. There was little difference between the Boxers of today and the Taiping of our youth.

We finally came across an abandoned temple where we could rest, but it was so cold. The eunuchs could not find any dry wood with which to make a fire, but even if they had, they had no way to light it. Many of us had enough clothes with us that we would not freeze. Lying under several layers of wet clothes is at least warmer than not having any. The emperor, as someone used to having other people do everything for him, did not have the forethought to bring extra clothes with him. He sat in a corner and shivered for a long time before Li Lianying took pity on the boy and gave him his heavy overcoat. The boy wept in appreciation. I was only glad Lianying did not freeze to death himself. Lianying was a loyal and capable servant, someone the empress could not live without. The emperor was useless. He left the empire in ruins. He might have the blood of the Dragon, but he did not have the ability to run a nation. He tried to kill the empress! He also didn't even look at my daughter or thank her for saving his life by sharing her donkey carts. His former lover and the mother of his only son! His only child! He couldn't even look at her. As far as I was concerned, that worthless, sniveling brat could die in the wilderness just like the Xianfeng Emperor for all I cared.

Our little caravan got smaller and smaller. Each day when we woke up, more eunuchs and maids were gone. They simply could not walk with us any longer. I have no idea where they thought they would go that would be a better situation. There was no food or lodging to be found anywhere, but they abandoned us nonetheless. We had very little food stuffs with us, and it quickly ran out. We had to chew on small twigs to fight the hunger pains and force our mouths to make water for us to drink. At night, the empress wept to me as I held her in my arms.

"How could I have fallen so low?" she asked, not really wanting an answer.

I didn't know how to answer her anyway. Of course, giving authority to the Boxers was a mistake, but the foreign powers were taking advantage of us in our weakened state after our loss to Japan. But we only lost to Japan because of the emperor. It was not her fault. She had done all she could to prepare the country to succeed in her retirement. But it was not enough. She was not a man and she couldn't rule the empire in her own right. She always had to hand the reins of power over to someone else, but no one else had proven worthy. Time and again she proved that she was the only person who had the will and the know-how to govern China, but she was always dismissed. And now she was old. Eventually, she would die, then who would rule? Even if we came through this nightmare unscathed, China was slowly ambling toward disaster.

After traveling for a couple of weeks, things began to get better, bit-by-bit. The villages were slowly coming back to life so we were able to find better lodging and food. Riders from the Forbidden City began catching up with us with reports from the grandees who had stayed behind. Amazingly, the foreigners didn't burn down the Forbidden City. They even forbade their men from looting. The empress's mood lightened considerably. By the time we arrived at the palace in Chang'an four months after fleeing the Forbidden City, she arrived as regally as ever, with a full entourage, wearing a beautiful gown and headdress, and carried in a sedan chair by eight eunuchs.

Even though enemies abroad such as the Wild Fox called for the foreigners to demand the return of the emperor to the throne, and the rebel named Sun Zhong-shan said the imperial family should be removed altogether, the foreigners decided against such drastic actions. It was clear that the grandees still supported the empress, and the country needed a strong hand to help rebuild. The empress was thousands of li away in a remote place, but it quickly became apparent that she was still ruling the country. After the Boxer Rebellion, the foreigners did not feel they would have the support of the people if they tried to make any drastic changes, so they began to negotiate for the empress's return.

Almost as soon as we arrived in Chang'an, the empress began preparing for her return to Peking, so she ordered new clothes to be made for the royal family. I wanted her to arrive back in her capital as the picture of regality, one who would be counted among the greatest monarchs in the world. I started with a smooth, black silk and embroidered it myself with one hundred characters for *shou*, which means "longevity." I wanted to emphasize that the empress was now the supreme ruler and was here to stay. I stylized the characters to form circles, representing perfection, completion, and harmony. I even managed to make some of the character strokes look like the Buddha's seal, both because the empress was a devout Buddhist and because the symbol represented eternity. I embroidered each edge of the robe with a different pattern and embroidered a wide collar that swirled like the wings of a bat around her shoulders for good luck. I kept some of these threads to bring me good luck as well and placed them with the rest of my memory threads.

Over a year after our flight, my empress and the rest of her court, including myself, began the long journey back to Peking. We left Chang'an as we should have left Peking, with hundreds of carts of luggage, mounted guards, princes, princesses, grandees, and countless eunuchs. It was almost unfathomable how many items we had accumulated in only a year, but almost immediately after our arrival, trunks of gifts and tribute began pouring in from all over the country.

The procession back to Peking was beautiful. The entire route was decorated with red banners and countless people came out to cheer for the return of the court. The empress couldn't see it, of course. She was sequestered in her sedan chair because it was against the law for anyone outside the court to glimpse an imperial personage.

On the first night of the journey, the royal tents were put up and we were able to camp in comfort. That evening, while the empress and I rested by a fire, I told her about all the people who were cheering along her procession. Her eyes watered.

"You cannot imagine what that means to me," she said. "All this time, I feared that the grandees and the councilors were just telling me I had the love and support of the people because they thought that is what I wanted to hear."

"You don't need to fear any longer," I said. "The people are with you."

"I failed them so miserably," she said. "Yet, they still rely on me and need me. This will be a new start. Their trust will not be misplaced again."

All along the route, the empress made sure that baskets of food that had been sent to her were given to the people who came to watch the procession. The harvest that year had been poor, so she wanted to show the people that their faith in her as their leader and protector was not misplaced. As the baskets of food were handed out, people shouted, "Long Live the Old Buddha!" Her faith in the Buddha was well-known throughout the country, and the people began to believe she was the embodiment of love and care on

Earth. I didn't have to tell her about the people's cheers; I knew she heard them.

It took us only three months to travel back to Peking as opposed to the four months it took us to arrive in Chang'an. For the last section of our journey, we rode in a train! We boarded it in Wuhan. The Boxers had nearly destroyed the railways, but the foreigners, after they occupied Peking, rebuilt it. They also had a royal carriage built to carry her home. Riding on the train was one of the most thrilling moments of my life. I had never moved so fast before. I leaned my head out one of the windows, just for a moment, and felt the wind blow through my hair. The carriage was magnificent, all deep red wood and shantung cushions and chairs. The floor was carpeted, which felt so soft under our feet.

Finally, we arrived home. I helped the empress dress in her golden longevity robe. Then, she stepped out of the carriage and had to walk several meters to her waiting sedan chair. This may seem a small thing, but it would mean that for a moment, the empress was in full view of the people! I had expected the empress to wear a heavy veil for the occasion and had embroidered one to match her robe. As I tried to hand it to her, though, she waved it away. She stepped out of the carriage to an endless cheering crowd and waved a handkerchief at them. The happy screams from the crowd were deafening. The empress beamed and looked back at me and my, I am sure, shocked face. "I heard that Queen Victoria greeted her people this way," she said with a laugh. We had received word while in Chang'an that Queen Victoria had died. The empress wept for this woman she had never met. This was her way of paying respect to her fellow queen. I couldn't help but smile as her other ladies and I then followed her to her sedan chair. Once she was comfortably seated inside, the windows were tied shut and she was carried home.

Once we arrived at the Forbidden City, the empress, the emperor, the princes and princesses, and the empress's attendees, myself included, were taken straight to the audience hall. Before our arrival, the empress had sent orders to have the thrones rearranged. The empress's throne was centered on the dais and raised up several meters. The Dragon Throne was placed slightly in front of the empress's throne, but to her left and much lower. The empress climbed the stairs and took her rightful place on her throne. Never again would anyone question who ruled China.

TWENTY-NINE

The empress and I were no longer young. Even
though I was in good health and the empress was
still a strong force at court, no one lives forever. I began to
worry about the future of my country, not for myself, but for
my daughter and grandson. When the empress was gone,
what would their future hold? Where would they go? What
would they do?

My grandson was becoming a regular at court since his
return from America. While he was not formally recognized
as a prince, everyone knew he was Prince Gong's grandson.
He was smart and handsome and some envied how well-
educated and well-traveled he was. The more time he spent
at court, the more I began to fear that people would realize
that he was Emperor Guangxu's son, his only son, and the
heir to the Dragon Throne.

Emperor Guangxu was not well. He would take to his
bed for days, unable to even deliver his morning greeting to
his Papa Dearest. It was as if the young man was wasting
away. Worse yet, he had appointed no heir. Should the

emperor and empress suddenly die, the empire would be thrown into chaos.

The empire was changing. The Han were done with being ruled by outsiders, the Manchu. They wanted to control their own destiny. The Wild Fox, still backed by Japan, continued to call for reforms, and his writings were very popular in China. Sun Zhongshan, a Cantonese, traveled around America and Europe trying to rally international support for something called Socialism. As always, there were uprisings and skirmishes in the countryside by unhappy peasants.

The empress was aware that the tide was turning against Manchu rule. She had put into motion plans for a parliament, but it would take at least another decade to come to fruition. I doubted she would live long enough to see her last grasp at preserving the empire come to pass. Even if she did, who would be the emperor of this parliament?

The empress had been spending more time with my grandson. She gave him high-ranking appointments and encouraged the grandees to take him under their wings. I had a feeling she was grooming him to be the new heir. I couldn't let that happen. I had lived in the palace for five decades. I had seen the deaths of two emperors and would most likely see the death of another one soon. I had seen unhappiness, torture, and misery descend on the lives of all who came within the walls of the Forbidden City. I couldn't let such a future befall my grandson.

I took a sedan chair to visit my daughter and her son in the city.

"Mother, have you finally lost your mind?" my daughter asked. "We have a good life here. My shop is prosperous and Arsalan is doing very well at court."

"Which is precisely why you and he must leave," I said. "I fear the empress will name him as her heir."

"Which is what she should do," my daughter snapped. "He *is* the emperor's heir."

I glanced at my grandson who shifted uncomfortably at this unabashed declaration by his mother.

"He is the emperor's son," I said. "Not his heir. Chinese emperors do not have a clear line of succession as they do in the West. Guangxu could name anyone he wants as heir."

"He is a Dragon Prince," she said. "And he should be acknowledged as such."

"Should he?" I asked. "If he was a prince, he would not be able to live here with you. He would not have studied in America or have learned English. He would be married and have a dozen concubines. He would be stuck in the past. He wouldn't be the smart, modern man who sits here now."

"You denied him his birthright," my daughter yelled. "As you did me!"

I sighed and leaned back in my seat. I wasn't going to get into a yelling match with her. Hulan was always a better tiger than I was.

"Arsalan," I said, addressing the boy, "you have spent much time in the palace. What do you think? Would you want to be as those princes and grandees? Do you want to be made the heir?"

"I have thought about it," he said. "I have many ideas I think would help China in the disaster that is to come."

"There," Hulan said. "You see? He could be the emperor who changes China for the better."

"No, Mother," Arsalan said, raising a hand to stop her from speaking. "I do have many great ideas, but Grandmother Yang is right. The court is still stuck in the past. I don't think that change in China will come from the throne.

I think change will only come from the people, the common man."

"You are like those revolutionaries!" Hulan shrieked. "Like that rebel Sun and the Wild Fox! Crazy men who want to overthrow China and kill the empress!"

"Mother, calm yourself," he said. "I support the empress and her reforms. But I think she will die before they can result in any real change and that Emperor Guangxu will rescind them. He will try to take us back to feudal days, but the people won't stand for it. There will be a revolution, Mother. It is only a matter of time. The only person holding the empire together is the empress."

"Exactly my point," I said. "This is why you must leave. War is coming, and I don't want you caught up in it. What if the Throne is defeated and the people kill the emperor? Like the French? Or like the British have done. When the people revolt, the old leaders die. Sometimes their wives and children too. If they even suspect that Arsalan is connected to the Old Blood, he could end up on the scaffold!"

"Oh, Mother," Hulan sighed, exasperated. "You are exaggerating. You are getting paranoid in your old age."

"I don't know," Arsalan said. "I have learned a lot about the inner workings of the court and the people in charge in recent months. I don't know if Grandmother Yang's fears about me being murdered are grounded, but revolution is coming. China will not be safe after the empress dies. And I wonder if, like Sun Zhongshan and the Wild Fox, I could do more good for the country by being on the outside."

"You would leave China?" my daughter asked. "You would leave your country, your homeland, in her time of need?"

"The thought had crossed my mind."

"I cannot believe what I am hearing," my daughter said.

"I would want you to go with me," he said. "Both of you. I wouldn't leave you behind to an uncertain fate."

I didn't respond to that. I wanted to encourage him to leave and didn't want him to change his mind if he knew I wouldn't be going with him. As much as I wanted him and my daughter to flee, I couldn't abandon the empress.

"Could you leave?" I asked. "Do you have a way out?"

"I'm not sure," he said. "That is why I had not considered it too seriously. I went to school in America, all my contacts are there. But because of the Chinese Exclusion Act, I can't really go there on my own. I was only able to go as a student because anti-Chinese sentiment wasn't as bad back then and we had to agree to leave after our schooling was done. I can't simply show up on a boat now and expect to be allowed in."

"Ridiculous!" I said. "China and America have always been allies. They have always been the most reasonable of the foreigners."

"The American government, like the Chinese government, is not always a reflection of its people. In the past, the American government has welcomed ties with China, but over the decades the people have fought such cooperation."

"Idiots," I mumbled. "Where else could you go? What about England?"

"I can't believe I am actually hearing you two plotting our escape from China," Hulan grumbled. Arsalan and I both ignored her.

"Legally, England is open to us," he said. "But it would be a very difficult society to navigate without the right connections, the right introductions. We wouldn't be able to find a place to live or even a hotel to stay in. And you and

Mother would need a lot of help in day to day life since you don't speak the language."

"But you don't think you have this kind of connection?" I asked.

Arsalan shook his head. "I have sent inquiries to a few people I know, but I do not feel confident about my prospects."

I sat back in the chair and thought for a moment. I didn't know any British people either. I had spent so much of my life sequestered in the Forbidden City. Even the few ladies the empress had been able to admit, I did not speak to since I didn't speak English.

But then I remembered the one English man I did speak to many years ago in the dungeon under the Forbidden City. Harry Parkes. Then I remembered the slip of paper my prince had given me on his deathbed, the name of Harry Parkes' daughter! I began to weep at the thought of how, even now, even so long after his death, my prince was caring for me and our descendants.

Arsalan rushed over and put a hand on my shoulder. "Please, do not fret, Grandmother," he said. "We will find a way."

"No," I said, brushing his hand away. "I am not fretting. I think I know a way to get you out of China."

I went back to the palace and retrieved the name and address of the woman from my collection of memories. When we arrived at the address in the British Legation, I was very nervous. My legs didn't want to work as my grandson helped me from the sedan chair.

He knocked on the door and a tall white man in a black suit opened it. He didn't seem to want to admit us, but after my grandson said some things in English, he allowed us to enter.

I had spent over fifty years living in a palace, but I was still awed by the beauty of this foreign-style home. A golden and crystal chandelier dangled over our heads. A large, gilded mirror stood on either side of the entryway. The walls and floors were made of a polished red wood, but the floors were covered with ornate rugs from the Middle East. A staircase ahead of us twisted around to go to a second floor. A second floor! The whole of the Forbidden City, except for the Hall of Supreme Harmony, where I had never been, was all on the same level. The tall man led us into a side room and motioned for us to sit on plush, cushioned chairs that were nothing like the carved wood Chinese furniture I was familiar with. Every wall of the room was covered with art in golden frames. Some were portraits, some were Western oil paintings, some were Chinese ink and wash paintings. There were little knickknacks on every surface, small boxes and porcelain figures. On one little table, in a round frame I found a piece of my double-sided embroidery. The frame had beveled glass on each side and would spin so that you could see a tiger on one side and a peacock on the other. Even to me, the piece and the presentation were exquisite.

As I was examining the piece, a white woman entered

the room and looked very surprised to see us. She said something in English and my grandson began talking to her. After a moment, her shock melted away and she rushed over and took my hand with tears in her eyes. She began jabbering in English, but then my grandson began to translate.

"I am so happy to finally meet you," she said.

"You know of me?" I asked, my grandson translating what I said.

"Of course!" she exclaimed. "My father never tired of telling the story of the beautiful Chinese girl with bound feet that snuck into the dungeon of the Forbidden City and saved his life. You are a legend in my family."

My head dropped and tears filled my eyes. I waved her away. "It was nothing," I said.

"Nothing?" she asked in shock as she led me over to a couch to sit down with her. She never let go of my hands. "My dear Yaqian. May I call you Yaqian? My father would have died if not for you. So many of his men did die. My father wanted so much to see you again, to thank you, but Prince Gong always said it couldn't be done. The prince said that if your involvement had been revealed, you would have been discovered as a traitor, so he had to keep you secreted away. But my father never forgot you. He told everyone about you. If it wasn't for you, I never would have been born! My whole family owes you a great debt."

"I don't know how to reply," I said, so my grandson took over. He told her of his desire to leave China for England but that he lacked connections.

"You are very lucky we happened to be in residence," Mrs. Keswick replied. "Most of my husband's business is in Hong Kong and Shanghai, so we were thinking of closing the house here permanently. You are right, China is changing. Everyone can feel it. We are leaving for England in a few days. We will stay there for at least the season. We would be happy to take you all with us and make the necessary introductions. I could even help Hulan open a shop. All of the women here simply love her embroidery work. I am sure it would fetch even higher prices in England."

"That is all good news," I said. "But you won't need to make room for me. I'm staying. I just needed to make sure my daughter and grandson would be taken care of."

"Mother, no," Hulan gasped.

"I have already made up my mind," I said. "I cannot leave the empress. I am too old to start over in a new place. I will die here, no matter what becomes of my country."

"Are you sure, Yaqian?" Mrs. Keswick asked. "We would be more than happy to take you with us. I promise, you will not be a burden."

"You are too kind," I said. "Far kinder than I expected. But I have already made my choice. As long as Hulan and Arsalan are safe, I will be content here."

For the next few days, as they prepared for their journey, Arsalan and Hulan did all they could to convince me to go with them. I began to fear they would take me by force. But in the end, they honored my wishes. I collected everything I had of value, all of my cash, my jewelry, my embroidery work, some of my clothes, everything, and gave it to Hulan. I was certain she and Arsalan would be prosperous in their new lives, but I wanted them to have the best start possible. The only things I kept were a few robes, my embroidered slippers, and my memories. I journeyed with them to the port and watched as they climbed the plank of the huge ship. Mrs. Keswick and her husband – a huge, loud, red, Scottish man who was frightening at first but was one of the nicest men I had ever met – wished me good-bye and asked me one last time to go with them. Of course, I declined, but I did weep as they left. They all stood on the railing and waved to me as the ship pulled away. I held a red handkerchief in my hand and I waved it until the ship sailed out of sight.

THIRTY
THE FORBIDDEN CITY, 1908

*T*he empress had been ill for some time, but I had not been allowed to see her. Her grandees, her ladies, the princesses and princes, and all manner of distant relatives were taken before her one by one to express their love and devotion to her in hopes of receiving her blessing or a gift. As a court servant, even of a high rank, I would have to wait until she summoned me. I was beginning to think she wouldn't, but, finally, the empress sent for me.

Her room was dark, with all the curtains drawn and doors shut, lit only by a few candles and braziers. The room was smoky with incense and hummed with the prayers of a few monks standing nearby. Several eunuchs, including Li Lianying, stood near her, ready at a moment's notice to get their empress anything she might need. One of her grandees, Zaifeng, a younger brother of Emperor Guangxu, was sitting by her bed. When I entered, Lianying leaned over and whispered to the empress that I had arrived. I walked halfway across the room and then kowtowed, even though she couldn't see me. When I raised my head, Zaifeng was motioning for me to approach. When I reached the foot of her bed, Cixi waved her hand, dismissing the servants and Zaifeng. Everyone, even the monks, left. This seemed quite unusual to me since should the empress die, everyone would want to know her last words and decrees, and who would believe the words of a servant?

After they had all left, Empress Cixi motioned for me to sit by the bed. I did so, and then I took her hand in mine.

"Look at us," she said. "Two old women."

"You are ageless, Your Majesty," I said. "You look the same as you did the first time I saw you all those many years ago."

"You lie," she said. "But I appreciate it. I hope even as the last breath leaves my body, my grandees will still tell me that I am living. Maybe the transition from this life to the next will be so seamless I won't even notice it."

I wasn't sure how to respond, so I just stroked her hand. I believed that with a will of iron such as hers, everything, even her death, would happen just the way she decreed it would.

"I called you here for a reason," she said. "I need you to do something for me."

"Anything, Your Majesty," I said, leaning closer.

"There is a vial on my dressing table," she said, glancing that way. "Small, blue, filled with white powder. I need you to make sure the emperor drinks it."

"What?" I asked. "Majesty, you cannot..."

"I can, and you will," she said. "You must do this for me."

"There must be someone else who is better suited to the task," I said. "Lianying?"

"Lianying has too much compassion for the boy, too much sympathy. He could never do it."

"I can't believe you are asking this of me," I said. "If I am caught…"

"Good thing I already outlawed the Death by a Thousand Cuts," she said before letting out a hacking laugh.

"But why?" I asked. "He is your heir."

"Some heir," she scoffed. "He already tried to kill me at least once. He would have done it a hundred times by now if I hadn't guarded him so closely."

"But he is the emperor. He is supposed to rule when you are gone. What harm can he do you after you are gone?"

"Plenty!" she said. "You know what damage that Wild Fox already did to my reputation, in China and abroad. What vile things will Guangxu say when my body is cold? And what about the empire? The last time he took over, he ruined us. He stopped all my reforms, the railroad, the currency reform, stopped sending students abroad. He took us into war with Japan and bankrupted us. I handed him a country made of gold and he gave it back as mud. When I am gone, he will do it again. He will stop the changes. He will call the students back or abandon them. He will war with the foreigners. He will end the plans to institute the parliament. He will be the end of not just the Manchu Dynasty, but of China."

The empress began to wheeze and cough. I patted her back and rubbed her arm. "Shh," I said. "Calm yourself, Your Majesty. Do not worry yourself so. Everything will be fine."

She leaned back on her pillow and took long, low breaths. "It will only be fine if that boy is gone," she said.

"But, he is your son, your heir," I said. "Who will take his place if you are gone?"

"I don't suppose your grandson would be willing to take

up the mantle?" she asked with a twinkle of mischief in her eye.

"I don't know what you mean," I said, as stupidly as ever.

"Don't lie to me on my deathbed, Yaqian."

"How did you know?" I asked.

"I've always known," she said. "I have spies everywhere."

I glanced around the room, wondering just who was watching us now. "What did I ever do to make you spy on me?" I asked.

"I was right to spy on you! You were keeping secrets from me!"

"I was right to keep secrets from you! You were spying on me!"

"So here we are," she said. "Give me the boy."

"Why? He is a bastard. A nothing."

"He is your grandson. He is Prince Gong's grandson. He is the son of an emperor."

"Not officially. Prince Gong has other sons and grandsons who would all be better..."

"I don't know their mothers. I don't trust them. They are conniving and scheming and who knows where they came from. Vapid, brainless girls. But the grandson of you and the prince, the two people who I trust more than anything in the world. He went to school in America. He is smart and modern. There is no one better to follow in my footsteps."

My heart broke for her. Maybe I shouldn't have sent Hulan and Arsalan away. On her deathbed, the only thing she cared about was her empire, her dynasty, and making sure they endured. But I could not give her this comfort. I had already sent the boy away and there was nothing else I could do.

"It matters not," I said. "The boy and his mother are gone. They took a steamer to England yesterday."

"You fear for the future of my kingdom as well. You believe it will fall without me at the helm."

"I do not know that it will fall, Your Majesty. I do not know what will happen. But I do know change is coming. Maybe it will be all good changes, but in case it is not, I had to make sure my daughter and grandson would be safe."

"And what of you?" she asked. "They left you here to face an uncertain future alone?"

"I am not alone," I said. "I am here with you."

"Then do this for me," she said. "You secreted my heir away, the least you can do is end that wretched Guangxu before it is too late and he ruins what little empire I have left."

I walked over to the dressing table and picked up the blue vial. I opened it and held it to my nose. The white powder inside was odorless, so I assumed it was also tasteless.

"How should I give it to him?" I asked.

"Take that pot of tea over there, the chrysanthemum. Take it to him as a gift from me. Mix the powder in. It will make him very sick, but it won't work immediately. Hopefully you will be gone long before he dies and they won't connect you to it."

"They won't let me in to see him," I said.

"There is a passage, a hidden one. I'll explain it to you. I'll call all the guards and eunuchs to me. You should be able to slip in and out easily."

"You never said who you would appoint as heir," I said.

"Puyi," she replied. The three-year-old son of Zaifeng.

*T*he hidden entrance to the emperor's Sea Palace was exactly where Empress Cixi had said it was. Behind a row of hedges in a secluded corner, the secret passage led to a long corridor far enough from the emperor's rooms that not many people would pass by. Did the emperor have any idea this was here? Is this how she had always known what he was doing? How many times had the empress sent one of her eunuchs or ladies here to spy on the emperor?

The Sea Palace felt almost completely deserted. As I left the empress, she had gone into a fit, crying and wailing, so every available servant, every courtier, every grandee ran to her side. Even though the emperor was also sick, she took precedent. As I entered the emperor's chambers, he was in his bed all alone, his short, shallow breaths the only sound.

I approached quietly and cautiously, so as not to disturb him. As I stood by his side and looked at him through the gauze mosquito netting, he already looked dead – pale, waxy, tired even though he was asleep.

He must have sensed my presence because he opened his eyes and looked directly at me. "Is she dead?" he whispered. "Have you come to inform me of her death?"

"No," I said, kneeling down and pulling the gauze curtains back. "Her health is failing, but she has not left us yet."

"Then why are you here?" he asked.

I held up the teapot. "She bade me bring you some of

her prized chrysanthemum tea as a gift. Quite possibly her last gift."

He coughed as he tried to laugh. "Afraid of the afterlife is she? Trying to make amends? Wanting forgiveness? Well, that old bitch shall have none of it from me." He coughed harder and doubled over in pain. I set the teapot aside and helped him sit up against his many pillows.

"Please, Your Majesty," I said. "Do not strain yourself. You are quite unwell."

"I'll pull through," he said. "I am stronger than I look. I will pull through."

He leaned back on his pillows, closed his eyes, and took a few deep, calming breaths. I thought for a moment he might go back to sleep. Perhaps it was for the best. If he was asleep, I wouldn't be able to do what the empress had commanded. Who knew how much time I had left before his eunuchs returned and either I slipped out or they threw me out. I didn't think I could do it. I was grasping for any excuse to free me from my task. I sat silently, not disturbing him as he started to drift off.

But then, he roused himself, opened his eyes, and spoke clearly, as if he was suddenly able to will himself back to good health.

"You will tell me, won't you?" he asked. "As soon as she is dead, you must tell me. I will be the true emperor again in that moment and I mustn't waste any time."

I nodded. "Yes, Your Majesty. I will inform you immediately of any change."

"Good," he said with a nod. "There is much work to do. So much damage to undo."

"Damage?" I asked.

"Yes. I suppose a servant would have no knowledge of the greater workings of an empire. You, someone who has lived her whole life in the safety and comfort of a palace, know nothing of the lives of the common people or what it takes to run a government."

I didn't respond. Of course, a large part of me wanted to tell him of my childhood, my years of tending fields. How the life of a servant was hard work. How the empress had unburdened her frustrations as regent to me many times, so I had a very good idea of what difficulties she had faced and how the country was once again peaceful and prosperous in preparation for a new heir. But I didn't. He wasn't interested in what I – a servant, a woman – knew about politics or thought about the future. He only wanted someone who would listen to him; he wouldn't listen back.

"All of these reforms she has put into place must be stopped. A parliament! Can you believe it? Give power to the people? Commoners? What can they know? If the people can govern themselves, what is the purpose of a Dragon Throne? She has sown the seeds of the end of our rule."

"England has a parliament and a king," I could not hold back from saying.

"Bah! England!" he nearly shouted. "That is the other thing. We must drive these foreign devils from our shores! They cannot be allowed to govern us, to steal our lands, to enslave our people. They are draining us dry. I'll ring out the alarm and have all of them slaughtered at once, the legations burned to the ground. China will be Chinese once more."

I wanted to tell him he wouldn't win. As much as Empress Cixi had done to build up the military, China still had no navy. And the foreigners here were a fraction of their numbers abroad. If we slaughtered their people, they would send in troops in droves. They would overthrow the emperor and set up their own government. Empress Cixi had made mistakes, but she never lost the throne. Even in exile, she was always the empress and the foreigners made sure she was reinstated because she had the love and devotion of both the people and the nobles. This boy-emperor had neither.

Empress Cixi was right. If she died and Guangxu was the man on the throne, that would be the end of the Manchu Dynasty. Either the people would overthrow his repressive, authoritarian regime or the foreigners would depose him in favor of a more Western-friendly appointment.

But would Puyi be any better? Like the two emperors before him, Puyi was a babe and could not rule on his own. Why would she put another child on the throne? Without her there to rule in his stead, who would take the lead? It appeared that she had put great trust in Zaifeng.

Zaifeng was Guangxu's brother, but the two were nothing alike. I suspected that in Guangxu and Zaifeng, Cixi was reminded of her husband, Xianfeng, and his brother, Prince Gong. Had Empress Cixi secretly wished that their father, the Daoguang Emperor, had appointed Prince Gong as his heir instead of Xianfeng? Xiangfeng, like his father, hated the foreigners and spent his life fighting them. Prince Gong saw value in the foreigners' ways and strived to learn from them. How different all our lives would have been if Prince Gong had been emperor. I began to understand that in appointing Zaifeng as regent, Empress Cixi was attempting to right the wrongs of the past. Zaifeng was the Prince Gong of a new generation.

While thinking all this, the emperor had continued his rant about all the wrongs of his Papa Dearest he would right as soon as she was dead. He had begun to work himself up into a frenzy and again began to cough, this time violently. I picked up my teapot and a cup from the side of the table and poured the tea. I helped him lean back and drink the poisoned draught. Then I poured him another cup and helped him drink that one as well. I didn't know how much of the tea it would take to work, but I didn't want to leave the job undone. I poured him a third cup.

"Enough, enough," he said, trying to push my hand away.

"No, Your Majesty," I said. "You must drink. You are ill and must be well again."

He drank the tea but then threw the cup against a wall, smashing it into countless pieces instead of giving it back to me. He looked at me with something like anger in his eyes. "Crone," he said, "return to me when she is dead."

I nodded, picked up my teapot, and headed back down the corridor to my secret exit.

The emperor died several hours later. Only his wife, Empress Longyu, was with him when he died, so there were no doctors there to help him, no grandees to listen to his last words or to hear his final wishes. All of the palace's residents and important visitors were attending to the empress or were waiting outside of her palace for any news.

Did he tell Empress Longyu I had been there?

I was not permitted to see Empress Cixi again. I didn't get to say goodbye or tell her what I had done. I do not know who told her that the emperor was dead, but she certainly knew because one of her final decrees was to appoint Puyi as her successor and Zaifeng as his regent. She also appointed Empress Longyu as the new dowager empress and said she would be the person to make the final decision in a time of crisis.

Even though the title of dowager empress belonged to Longyu by right, no one expected the role to carry any weight or authority with it. Neither Empress Cixi nor the emperor had shown Longyu much care or gave a grain of rice for her thoughts. Longyu was like a willow, always swaying and easily bent. I do not believe her shoulders even knew how to stand up straight. Yet she was now the most powerful person in the empire until Puyi came of age. Even though Zaifeng would be the regent and make all of the decisions for the country in day to day life, in a crisis, all decisions would be made by Longyu. And it would only be a matter of time before a crisis would come. No one could understand why my empress would put such a burden on such a weak woman as her last act. The empress must not have been in her right mind at the end.

*M*y empress died during the afternoon the day after Guangxu passed. While the emperor had died nearly alone, the empress died surrounded by her eunuchs, her ladies, and countless magistrates and grandees. While no one, save his wife, wept for the emperor, the wailing and lamentations for the empress started in her chambers, resonated throughout the Forbidden City, and eventually engulfed the country.

I was alone in my chambers when it happened. I was sitting by the window working on her funeral banner, a six-foot long piece of embroidered silk that would be placed on her inner coffin. Her death was the end of an era, but I knew she would be happy as she met her ancestors. She had done her best by them and held their kingdom together. Her funeral banner, which would tell the story of her life and lead her to Heaven, had to be magnificent.

Unfortunately, even after living among Manchus for so long, my understanding of the afterlife was very Chinese. I blended what I knew about Heaven and life and death with what I knew the empress believed and told the story as best I could.

I started with bright yellow silk, as befitting an empress of China. At the top of the banner, I wove pink chrysanthemums, her favorite flowers, and orchids, the first name she was given upon entering the palace. These were to represent her birth and the beginning of her life as a consort to the emperor. Magpies, lovely little birds that can come together and create a bridge to Heaven, fluttered around the flowers.

Below that, I embroidered two five-clawed dragons, one for her husband and one for her son. On their left, I embroidered a crescent moon, and on their right, a red sun. These symbolized the heavenly realm above that of humans, since the emperors are the Sons of Heaven. I dotted golden fish swimming around the dragon on the left, the dragon representing her husband.

Then, I embroidered the likeness of the empress herself centered on a dais surrounded by her ladies, her eunuchs An Dehai and Li Lianying, and her most important grandee, Prince Gong. In her left hand, I put a small scepter, similar to ones I had seen in paintings of Queen Victoria. I knew the empress would like that. One of her ladies held a green parasol over her head.

Below that, I embroidered the empress meeting with the Lords of Heaven. She is bowing to them, but not kneeling, and they happily welcome her. Lovely bats and phoenixes fly around her, demonstrating that she is not sad or suffering, but is enjoying all the comforts of the afterlife.

At the very bottom is her coffin, surrounded by those she left behind to mourn her. Plates of food, cups of wine, and a treasure vase are there. Incense is burning, even smoke is wafting, and all are kneeling before the coffin. I am there as well.

When I was finished with the funeral banner, something was missing. Laid out before me, it was beautiful, the empress would be pleased, but I remembered what Lady Tang had told me long ago about my embroidery lacking soul. She was right. The funerary banner for my empress, perhaps my last great work, should have every ounce of myself in it.

I went to my dressing table and pulled open the bottom drawer. There, in a small box, were my threads of memories. When I kept my first piece of silk thread all those years ago, I had no idea why. What use to me was one piece of thread? I now realized that each thread when placed together with all the others represented my whole life. From the first shoe I had embroidered to my empress's funeral banner, my life was one long silk thread. I poured out the contents of the box and began to weave the threads of silk into the funerary banner.

The blue thread from the first shoe I embroidered I weaved into the clouds at the top of the banner. A piece of orange thread from the tiger shoes I had embroidered for her son I weaved into a magpie flying to heaven. A piece of gold thread I had used to make Prince Gong's marvelous dragon robe I weaved into the robe the prince was wearing on the funeral banner. The last strand of her son's hair that I had used to embroider children on a piece of silk as a memorial for the young emperor I used to outline the dragon that represented her son.

On and on, my memories, my life, became one with Empress Cixi. My soul became eternally entwined with the embroidered funeral banner that would forever blanket My Empress.

THANK YOU

I hope you enjoyed *Threads of Silk*. Subscribe to my mailing list so you never miss a new release.

http://amandarobertswrites.com/subscribe-threads-of-silk/

AUTHOR'S NOTE

There was much debate and discussion about whether I should use the Wade-Giles Romanization of Chinese words in this book, which was more popular during the time period the book is set, or modern Pinyin. I decided to use Pinyin for most names and words since it is the system modern readers are familiar with. Chinese place names, though, are accurate for time period. Peking and Chang'an, for example, were the names Westerners and Chinese would have used at that time; the names Beijing and Xi'an were not adopted until long after the end of the Qing Dynasty.

THE MAN IN THE DRAGON MASK

https://books2read.com/dragonmask

One Face

Two Men

And A Secret That Could Destroy An Empire

At the dawn of the Ming Dynasty, the emperor will do anything to ensure the future of his empire. Building the Forbidden City in fulfillment of his father's dreams is only the beginning.

But few people share the emperor's vision.

When a consort's betrayal has devastating consequences that rock the imperial court, the emperor discovers that the fight for the dragon throne has only begun.

ABOUT THE AUTHOR

 Amanda Roberts is a USA Today best-selling author who has been living in China since 2010. She has an MA in English from the University of Central Missouri and has been published in magazines, newspapers, and anthologies around the world. Amanda can be found all over the Internet, but her home is AmandaRobertsWrites.com.

- facebook.com/AmandaRobertsWrites
- instagram.com/amandarobertswrites
- bookbub.com/authors/amanda-roberts-2bfe99dd-ea16-4614-a696-84116326dcd1
- goodreads.com/Amanda_Roberts

ABOUT THE PUBLISHER

RED EMPRESS PUBLISHING

Visit Our Website To See All Of Our Diverse Books
http://www.redempresspublishing.com

Quality trade paperbacks, downloads, audio books, and books
in foreign languages in genres such as historical, romance,
mystery, and fantasy.

Made in the USA
Coppell, TX
17 March 2023

14389555R00236